Saving You

ALEX TAYLOR

Saving You

Destined Love Book 2

Alex Taylor

Character art by Paige Moreland

Cover Design by Kim at KBG Designs

Editing by Editing by Andrea

Print ISBN: 978-1-0688632-2-6

Ebook ISBN: 978-1-0688632-3-3

To the people who felt unworthy,
and those who stepped up and showed them their worth

Author's Note

Please note that some of the subject matter in this book may be
triggering for some people.
If any of the following subjects cross a line for you, please do not
continue.
Your mental health matters.

Domestic Abuse (not between the MCs)
Discussions of PTSD & on page nightmares
On page gun violence
On page death (through a flashback)
Mentions of feelings of inadequacies
Mentions of parental neglect (not by the MCs)
Mentions of car accident & drunk driving
Discussions of sexual assault (not experienced by either MC)
Explicit sex scenes

Looking for a Dicktionary? Check out the back of the book

Playlist

We Are Never Ever Getting Back Together
(Taylor's Version)
Taylor Swift

I Guess I'm In Love
Clinton Kane

Unconditionally
Katy Perry

New Years Day
Taylor Swift

The Good Ones
Gabby Barrett

Moral of the Story
Ashe

Labyrinth
Taylor Swift

Beautiful Things
Benson Boone

Say You Won't Let Go
James Arthur

Love Someone
Lukas Graham

Little Bit Better
Caleb Hearn, ROSIE

Late Night Talking
Harry Styles

Spin You Around
Morgan Wallen

Earned It
The Weekend

You Are In Love (Taylor's Version)
Taylor Swift

Timeless (Taylor's Version) (From the Vault)
Taylor Swift

Crazier
Taylor Swift

Date Night (feat. Morgan Evans)
Kita Alexander, Morgan Evans

Thank God
Kane Brown, Katelyn Brown

Beautiful Crazy
Luke Combs

Show You Off Tonight
Lee Brice

Think I'm In Love With You
Chris Stapleton

Die For You
The Weekend

One Call Away
Charlie Puth

Wherever You Will Go
The Calling

CHAPTER 1

Caleb

Fuck!

My radio continues to squawk as dispatch relays more information about the domestic violence call I'm being routed to. These are my least favourite calls. Not that any are really my favourite.

My knuckles turn white as my grip on the steering wheel tightens. I wind my way through the streets of Vancouver's west side, lights flashing and siren blaring. Dispatch reports that a child made a call saying her daddy is hitting her mommy. Anger radiates through me. Hitting a woman makes you the lowest of low, but to do it in front of children, especially your own, makes it so much worse.

I've barely thrown my car into park before I jump out and rush up the front steps. With one hand on top of my gun, I bang on the door hard enough I feel the vibration up my arm.

"Vancouver Police," I yell.

Raised voices on the other side of the door come through unintelligibly. No one answers.

Again, I bang my fist. "Vancouver Police, answer the door."

The raised voices quiet, and heavy footsteps make their way to the front door. The door is thrown open forcefully, and an angry-looking man stands on the other side.

He's got nothing on my six-foot-three frame, but he puffs out his chest, making himself appear as big as possible before saying, "Can I help you, officer?"

"Good evening, my name is Officer Sutton. We got a call about some yelling at this location. Can you please step outside with me?"

The guy looks me up and down, assessing me, before he nods, stepping outside and closing the door. I lead him into the front yard.

"What's your name?" I ask, grabbing my notepad out of my belt.

"Derek," he says.

I look up from my writing and stare at him. "Got a last name, Derek?"

"Porter."

"Okay, can you tell me what's going on?"

"My ex-wife and I just got into a little disagreement. Everything's okay."

The sirens of my backup are getting closer, and the sound causes Derek to look over his shoulder. He stiffens slightly. It's small enough that if you aren't trained, you may not notice it.

"Man, is this all really necessary? It was just a small argument between me and my ex. Everything's all good," Derek pushes.

"Well, I have to check on all the occupants of the house. You'll need to stay here with Officer Collins and Officer Macky while I go inside." I step around him as Collins makes it to my side.

I cautiously swing open the front door, calling, "This is Officer Sutton of the Vancouver Police Department. I'm coming in."

Silence greets me on the other side. I methodically make my way through the rooms on the first floor. Once they're all cleared, I slowly make my way up the staircase, taking in the family photos that line the wall. The photos all seem to be of a stunning blonde and a little girl who has the same blonde hair and freckles. I assume it must be mother and daughter and they're the ones that reside in the house.

When I get to the top of the stairs, I still, and my body goes tight as the sound of muffled crying reaches my ears. I deliberately make my way down the hall, following the crying. As I do, I check the rooms to ensure they're empty. I stop when I'm at the last door on my right. As soon as I start to open the door, I hear a scream—the scream of a child.

When the door is fully open, my heart is ripped from my chest. The blonde woman, from the photos, sits on the floor in the corner, holding her daughter to her chest as she rocks and soothes her. The woman's face is covered in red spots I know will be severely bruised by tomorrow. She has a split lip and a cut above her left eye. She sits there stoically, not a single tear running down her face as she holds her daughter's small frame like her life depends on it. She continues to coo to her, telling her, "Mommy's okay." The little girl can't be any older than five.

The girl spots me and wipes at her tears as she slowly takes me in.

I click my radio and say into it, "I've got the mom and daughter in the daughter's room on the second floor. Last door on the right. Hold the father outside."

Collins acknowledges my instructions, and I turn down the volume of the radio and crouch, wanting to get closer to their level.

"My name's Officer Sutton, you guys are safe now."

"Thank you," the mom says.

"You must be the brave little girl who called 911?"

Her blonde hair bobs as she nods.

"Do you think that you can come with me so we can have some people look at your mommy and make sure she's okay?"

The little girl nods and gets up from her mother's lap. I make my way over to where they are and offer my hand to the mother. She doesn't take it, choosing to get up on her own. The two of them hold hands as I lead them towards the front door.

Outside, the father has been put in the back of a cruiser, and an ambulance is sitting on the curb. I lead them over to the back of the rig, and the paramedics get to work right away.

I go to step away to check in with Collins when a little hand wraps around mine. Looking down, I see the girl looking at me, tears still in her eyes. It guts me to see her like this. I duck down and ask her, "What's your name?"

"Charlotte." Her voice is soft and tentative.

"My name is Caleb. Would you like to sit with me while these people help your mommy?"

Her nod is small.

I lead us to the sidewalk, taking a seat, and she sits beside me. I pull my phone out and open a video of cats jumping when they see a cucumber I had come across earlier.

"Do you want to see a funny video, Charlotte?"

She looks up at me, her face so innocent and sweet, and nods.

I spin my phone, allowing the video to take up the entire screen, and hold it for her. A small smile spreads across her face when it starts, and by the end, she is laughing this beautiful child's laugh. I relax slightly at the sound of it, knowing this is providing her with some slight relief after she has just experienced something no one should ever have to, let alone someone her age.

A shadow looms over us just as the video finishes. Looking up, I'm met with the most beautiful set of blue eyes I've ever seen. My breath catches in my lungs. Now, in the light, I take in all of her features, her full lips and long lashes, the curves of her hips, and her full chest. There's no missing her beauty, even if you wanted to. I shake my head and clear my throat. I need to be in work mode, not lusting over a victim, I chastise myself.

She looks down at me. "Thank you for staying with my daughter, Officer Sutton."

"Of course. I do need to get a statement from both of you before we leave. Would you like to go inside for that?"

She nods and I get up, offering my hand to Charlotte. I try to let go so she can hold her mom's, but she doesn't let go, so I hold on. We make our way into the house, and Charlotte's mom leads us into the kitchen. Charlotte takes a seat in front of a drawing she must have been working on earlier.

"Would you like something to drink?"

"Water is fine, thank you." I take a seat at the table.

Handing me a glass of water, she sits across from me with a cup of tea settled between her hands.

I pull my notepad out again and open it to the same page as before. "Can I get your name?"

"Bailey Emerson."

"Okay. Do you mind if I call you Bailey?"

"Sure."

"Can you please tell me what happened today?"

She looks over at Charlotte and then back at me, nodding. "Derek was over for his visitation with Charlie. They were in the kitchen. I was in the living room cleaning when he came out. He wanted to talk about getting back together. I told him he was here to spend time with Charlie and it wasn't an appropriate time to have that conversation. He kept pushing and when I continued to refuse, he slapped me across the face."

Her hand absently moves to her face, brushing over a pink spot. She notices, and her hand instantly drops back into her lap.

"When I backed away, he gripped the top of my arm and said, 'You're mine Bailey, you'll do what I say.' I tried to pull out of his grasp, and he slapped me again. I heard Charlie scream and run upstairs. He yelled in my face for a couple of minutes before he hit me again, but that time I was able to get out of his grip. I was running upstairs when I heard someone knocking on the front door."

I'm so fucking happy I was only two blocks away when the call came over the radio. I don't want to know what would have happened if it had taken me longer to make it here. "Bailey, I need to ask Charlotte some questions. Do you mind if I do that right now?"

"No, of course not."

I twist my chair and face the beautiful little girl who is drawing silently beside me. "Charlotte, can you tell me why you called 911?"

"Daddy was yelling at Mommy. She said 'ow' and Daddy kept yelling. He hit her. Mommy says we aren't supposed to hit, we are supposed to use our words. Mommy was hurt. She needed help."

"That was very good, Charlotte. You were very brave and smart to do that." I look back at Bailey and give her a soft smile. "You have an amazing little girl here."

She smiles back at me. Reaching out, she runs a hand over her daughter's hair. "Yeah, I do."

I pull one of my cards out of the breast pocket of my vest and hand it to Bailey. "This is my card. I want you to call me if you have any more issues. He's going to be booked today, so he shouldn't be a problem." I turn to Charlotte again. "Charlotte, you did so well helping your mommy. It was nice to meet you."

I slip out of my seat and stand. "Have a nice evening."

Before I can turn for the front door, Charlotte is off her chair with her arms wrapped around my legs.

"Thank you for helping Mommy, Caleb."

I look down at her and run my hand over the top of her hair. "You're welcome, Charlotte."

She unwraps her arms from around my legs, and I make my way to my cruiser and head to the station. The entire drive back, I have a niggling feeling in my gut like I left something back inside that house.

CHAPTER 2

Bailey

I watch as Officer Sutton walks out the front door and Charlotte gets back in her chair. She continues to draw quietly as I sit, my mind trying to process the day's events. I shake my head before I can think too much about it. I need to be strong for Charlie. I look at the clock on the stove and realize it's past dinnertime.

"Baby Girl, do you want mac and cheese for dinner?"

She looks up at me with a hopeful expression. "With hotdogs?"

"Yeah, with hotdogs."

She nods enthusiastically.

I get up and make dinner. Luckily, I'm right-handed because my left is so sore, I'm not sure I'd be able to cook with it. When our food is done, I plate it and Charlie and I sit at the table to eat. When we finish, I take her upstairs for a bath, filling it with bubbles and her favourite toys. I stay in the washroom with her, knowing that as soon as I'm alone, the stony facade I've put up will crumble into a million pieces around me and I won't be able to stand.

The feeling of my little girl curled into my side as I read her a bedtime story places a tiny patch on my very broken heart. Once she's fallen asleep, I sneak out of her room and into my en-suite washroom.

I evaluate myself in the mirror. White Steri-Strips over my left eye and my split lip jump out at me, and I grimace, causing me to wince in pain. The marks on my face are tender, the redness is going down and the bruising colour is starting to appear.

I steel myself as I slowly remove my clothes, tossing them in my laundry hamper. I feel so ashamed for letting this happen. Not only did I put myself in this situation, but Charlie witnessed it. Turning on the shower, I wait for the water to warm before I step under.

The water immediately melts my walls, and I slump to the base of the shower as chest-heaving sobs escape me. My head rolls back and to the side. As the water washes over me, I watch it go down the drain along with what little strength I had left for the day. I sit under the water for what feels like forever.

When my sobs finally subside, I force myself to stand and wash my hair and body. I move gently over my sore spots, not wanting to aggravate them. Turning off the water, I change into my ugly comfy jammies and climb under the covers. I fall asleep hoping today was all a dream.

Owww, that's the only thought that goes through my mind as I wake up. My head is pounding, my left eye is partially swollen, my mouth is dry, my upper lip hurts, and my left arm throbs where it was grabbed yesterday. I lie in bed, taking deep breaths. After a minute, I push myself to get up and slowly head to Charlie's room. I peek my head in and see she's still asleep. When I get to the kitchen, I make coffee before grabbing my phone and pulling up my best friend's number.

"Hey, hun. How are you?" Lily answers.

"Okay, you?"

"I'm good. What's up?"

"Can you do me a huge favour? Can you take Charlie for the weekend?"

"Of course, hun. What happened?"

"I'll tell you when you get here."

"Okay, I'll be there in twenty."

"Thanks, Lil, love you."

"Love you too. See you soon."

I hang up and pour myself a cup of much-needed caffeine. I

want to spend the weekend with my girl, but I don't want her to see me like this. Hopefully, after a couple of days, it will all look better. Taking my coffee into the living room, I settle on the couch and turn on one of my shows.

Twenty minutes later, the front door opens and Lily walks in. She stops at the entrance to the living room. I hear her sharp intake of breath all the way across the room, and it breaks me. A sob leaves me, and Lily is beside me in an instant, holding me and softly brushing her hand through my hair. I lean into her, absorbing her strength.

After I catch my breath, I tell Lily about what happened with Derek. I can't look her in the face as I recount the story. I fidget with my fingers in my lap. When I finish, she pulls me into her again and I rest my head on her shoulder.

"You know this isn't your fault, right?" Lily's words turn my stomach. How can she say that? I'm the one who brought Derek into my life and, in turn, Charlie's. I'm the one who didn't just listen to him yesterday and talk to him like he wanted. If I had given in, maybe it would have turned out differently.

"Bailey, get out of your head. This was not your fault. You can't blame yourself for the actions of someone else."

I nod, but her words don't fully seep in.

"Aunt Lily!" Charlie yells from the top of the stairs. She rushes down and throws herself onto Lily's lap, wrapping her arms around her neck.

"Hi, sweet pea. What do you think about spending the weekend with Aunt Lily? We can go get pancakes for breakfast!"

"Yay!" Charlie screams.

"Why don't you go get dressed and pack a bag and then we can head out?" That's all it takes for Charlie to scramble off Lily's lap and run right back upstairs.

"Thanks, Lil," I say.

"Anytime, you know that, hun." She leans down and places a quick kiss on my forehead before she joins Charlie.

As I'm plating my breakfast, I hear them come down the stairs, and the next thing I know, Charlie is wrapping herself around my legs. I remove myself from her grip and crouch to her height, wrapping her in my arms.

"I love you, Baby Girl," I whisper in her ear before releasing her.

"Are you okay, Mommy?"

"Of course, Baby Girl. Now go have fun with Aunt Lily. Be good for her." With a quick kiss on her cheek, I send her off.

I spend my weekend doing a lot of nothing. I relax in the bath and on the couch, reading or watching TV. By Sunday evening, my face isn't as swollen and my cuts don't look as bad. The bruises can be covered with makeup, so I decide to still go to work tomorrow. Lily has agreed to keep Charlie for the night and drop her off at school in the morning on her way to work.

Monday morning, I gently apply makeup to my face, covering my bruises as much as possible. Thankfully, I make it through my workday without anyone asking questions. I'm so happy to pick up my Baby Girl. When she sees me outside her school, she runs to me, wrapping her arms tightly around my neck, and I chuckle. She's stronger than you'd think.

"I missed you, Mommy!"

"I missed you, too, Baby Girl."

I give her a quick squeeze before pulling back and placing a kiss on her forehead. I get her settled in the car and we make our way home. My girl brightens my day. She's sitting in the back of the car singing along to the music, just enjoying life. After we make our way inside, I get her settled at the kitchen table doing her homework and fix her a snack.

I'm folding laundry on the couch when she comes and sits beside me.

"What's up, Baby Girl?"

"Mommy, can we bring Caleb cookies? Today at school we talked about Thanksgiving and what we're thankful for. I want to say thank you to Caleb."

Something catches in my throat. My sweet girl has spent her day wanting to thank the man who came and saved us from her father. I remember the feeling of safety that washed over me looking into his steel-grey eyes. His large frame towered over my five-foot-three one, but I didn't feel a need to cower. His blond hair was cut short on the sides but had length on top. I wanted to run my fingers through it and feel how soft it is.

I shake my head. I'm not in my right mind. He saved us from a scary experience, and I'm projecting feelings onto him because of it.

"Yeah, Baby Girl, we can take him cookies."

She's so happy she jumps straight off the couch and does a little happy dance.

"What flavour should we make him, Mommy? Chocolate chip? Maybe M&M, I think he'd like M&M. We should make him both!"

I smile as she rambles about cookie flavours.

We do our grocery shopping on Thursday and spend Saturday baking. Charlie is so excited to help. She stands on a chair in front of the counter, biting the side of her lips while she carefully measures the ingredients. I hold back a small laugh because she's so adorable.

Watching her like this, so happy doing something as simple as baking cookies with me, fills me with joy. While the cookies are in the oven, she draws him a card. It's late by the time both types of cookies are done.

Putting her to bed, she talks excitedly about going to the station and seeing Caleb. I smile at her, happy she's okay after last Friday's events and that she's happy and excited about something. I toss and turn in bed, memories of that day replaying in my mind.

Lily comes over on Sunday for Thanksgiving dinner.

As I make breakfast for Charlie and me Monday morning, she comes running down the stairs so fast I fear she'll trip and fall.

"Mommy, is it time to go? Can we take the cookies to Caleb?" I can feel the excitement radiating off my little girl.

"Not yet, Baby Girl. We're going to eat breakfast and then we're going to play outside for a bit. I thought we could go to Sammy's for lunch and could stop by the station on our way. How does that sound?"

"Yay!"

We eat quickly before we head upstairs to get dressed. Going into my closet, I find a T-shirt and cardigan to cover the bruises on my arm, a pair of jeans, and black knee-high boots. It's October now, and the cool Canadian weather is starting to bite.

Downstairs, I find Charlie waiting for me by the front door. I put her jacket on her, making sure it's zipped up. I offer her gloves and a toque, but she says no to the gloves, so I tuck them into my purse for later. I grab my jacket, and we head out and towards the park. Charlie makes friends with the other kids quickly and is running all over. I find a bench to the side where I can watch her while I read my book on my phone.

When the other kids are called by their parents, Charlie runs up to me with a huge smile.

"Is it time to go see Caleb, Mommy?"

"Yeah, Baby Girl. We'll head home and drive to the station."

She jumps up and cheers before grabbing my hand and trying to pull me off the bench. I let out a small laugh as I get up, and we walk hand-in-hand back to the house.

The entire car ride, she is full of energy, shimmying in her booster seat as she tells me just how excited she is to see him again.

My stomach tightens as I pull into the parking lot of the station. The last time I saw this man was my lowest moment. I wasn't able to protect my daughter. She was the one who had to call 911.

What must he think of me for putting my daughter in that situation? He must think I'm a horrible mother, and I can't blame him because I can agree. Charlie never should have been in a situation to witness that. Derek never should have done it, but I know him. I should have handled the situation better, knowing she was in the house with us.

Charlie's voice pulls me out of my nervous mind.

"Mommy, I want to go inside."

Opening my door, I move to the back of the car, unbuckle her, and grab the container of cookies from the backseat.

"Can I hold the cookies? I want to give them to Caleb."

I smile down at her. "Of course."

Handing her the cookies, she holds the container with two hands like it's the most precious treasure in the world. I pull open the door to the station and head to the front counter, where I'm greeted by a woman who appears to be in her early thirties.

"Good afternoon, what can I do for you?"

"I want to see Caleb," Charlie calls from beside me.

I run a hand over her hair and smile down at her before returning my gaze to the officer. "Good afternoon, we're here to see

Officer Sutton. My daughter wanted to drop something off for him."

"Oh, well, I'm sorry, but he's out right now."

As she says it, the breath leaves my lungs as Officer Sutton walks through a door at the back of the room. His blond hair looks like he's been running his hand through it and his shirt strains against his muscles as he walks. Like he senses me looking at him, his gaze snaps to me.

"Caleb," Charlie calls, causing us to break eye contact.

He looks down at her, and a smile tips his lips. I'm not sure how someone his size manages to move as gracefully as he does when he comes to stand in front of us. He immediately crouches to Charlie's height.

"Hi, Charlotte. How are you?"

"I'm good. I brought you cookies and a card," she says as she thrusts the container out towards him.

He chuckles as he looks at it. "You did, did you? That was very nice, thank you."

"They're my favourite flavours, too. Chocolate chip and M&M."

His eyes widen playfully. "You made me two kinds of cookies? You know, chocolate chip cookies are my favourite."

Charlie's eyes go wide too. "They are? We have the same favourite cookie."

"We do. This is my favourite thing this week. Thank you, Charlotte."

He stands and smiles. "Hi. Thank you for the cookies." This time, his words are directed at me, and a blush fills my cheeks.

"You're welcome. Charlie came home from school the other day talking about Thanksgiving and said she wanted to do something to say thank you to you."

"That was thoughtful."

"Caleb, we are going to Sammy's. Do you want to come too? They have really good chicken strips and chocolate milkshakes."

I run my hand over her hair. "Oh, honey, I'm sure that Officer Sutton is busy. We should let him get back to work."

"Okay."

Disappointment fills her voice, and Caleb obviously notices, too, because he says, "Actually, I'm just getting off shift now. If you can give me five minutes, I'll go change and we can head over there."

"Yay!" Charlie exclaims as she does her happy dance right there in the middle of the reception area of the station. Caleb chuckles at her antics before looking at me and mouthing, *Is it okay?* I nod. A small smile tips his lips before he turns and makes his way to get changed.

CHAPTER 3

Caleb

After the day I had, I planned on going home, making myself some food, taking my black lab Finn for a quick walk, showering, and heading straight to bed. Not only did I work the evening shift, but I had an overdose call today and the girl didn't make it.

Even after serving overseas, losing someone never gets easier. I've learned my ways to process it, and that usually means spending time by myself, but there was no way I could live with the disappointment on Charlotte's face when Bailey said I couldn't go to Sammy's with them. So a change of plans it is. I'll go to lunch with them and then head home.

When I join them again, Charlotte runs up to me and grabs my hand like it's the most natural thing in the world. Bailey watches us with a beautiful smile. I open the door for them, and we walk through the parking lot. When we don't stop, Bailey asks, "It's okay if I leave my car in the parking lot, right?"

"Yeah, you're all good."

Charlotte spends the entire walk telling me about her week at school and the new friends she made at the park today. She is so full of life and energy, something I'm not used to. When we get to the diner, we make our way to a booth. Bailey slides in on one side all the way to the window, and I sit across from her.

"I want to sit with Caleb," Charlie says as she slides in beside me.

Her little legs can't reach the ground as she sits. She rubs her hands together excitedly as the waitress comes over to get our order.

"You have to get a chocolate milkshake, Caleb. It's the best!" Charlie says.

I order one, and a giant smile spreads across her face. Charlie continues the conversation, requiring no prompting from her mother or me. When the waitress comes back with our drinks, Charlie insists I order the chicken strips just like her, so I do.

As our food is delivered, another person slides into the booth beside Bailey and steals a fry off my plate before plopping it into their mouth. Bailey stiffens. Not like she's scared, but like she's unsure of this new person.

"Hey, Caleb," Olivia says once she's finished the fry.

She has a big, shit-eating grin on her face as she takes in me sitting with Bailey and Charlotte. Olivia is one of my best friends' sister and another's wife. I've gotten to know her well over the years. This past summer, we all spent more time together because Liv started coming to our hockey games, and we even did a big group camping trip.

"Hey, Liv. What's up?"

"Oh, nothing much. Who are your friends?"

"Olivia, this is Bailey and this is Charlotte. Bailey and Charlotte, this is Olivia."

A soft hello comes from Bailey, and Charlotte waives at Olivia.

Olivia smiles at Charlie. "Charlotte is such a beautiful name, and it fits such a pretty girl."

Charlotte blushes as she says thank you, and Josh walks up. "Is my wife bothering you, man?" he asks jovially, reaching out and giving my hand a quick shake.

Bailey's body relaxes at Josh's words. Was she worried that Liv was my girlfriend or here to make a move? A sense of happiness rises in me at her potential jealousy, yet I have no right. I push that feeling down and away. The last thing I need is to be lusting after a victim I helped. Not that I would ever use that word to describe Bailey. She's a survivor. Anyone who goes through what she has and comes out the other end of it is a survivor.

"No, just stealing my fries," I say as Olivia reaches over and steals another.

"The baby wanted another fry," she says with a smile as she rubs her belly.

Josh smiles at her with a look so full of love and devotion. He's looked at her like that for years and never made a move. I was happy when he told us a few months ago they were together and he was going to propose. Although he didn't really tell us so much as he was checked on the ice during one of our games and Liv's protective side came out.

She rushed onto the ice to check on him, calling him "babe," before punching the guy who checked him in the face. Josh had to pull her away from him. It kind of outed their relationship. The following weekend, we found out they were expecting. They got married last Saturday in a small backyard wedding and they've never looked happier.

Charlie's interest is peeked by Liv's comment. "You're having a baby?"

"Yup, our little baby will be here in April." She continues rubbing her belly.

"That's so cool," Charlie says wistfully.

A noise chimes as Josh pulls his phone out. He pockets it and informs us they need to go.

"Still good for Saturday?" he asks.

"Yup, I should be home by five."

Olivia immediately reaches out and grips Bailey's arm. "Oh, you should join me and my friends for our girls' night on Saturday. We are doing movies in pyjamas at our place with all of our favourite junk food. You and Charlotte should both come."

"Oh, I don't know..." Bailey starts.

"Can we, Mommy, please? Pretty please, Mommy. It will be so much fun!" Charlie pleads.

Bailey seems to resign herself and nods her acceptance as Olivia slides out of the bench.

"Yay, I can't wait." She pulls out her phone and hands it to Bailey, who adds her number before Liv and Josh leave.

"What in the world just happened?" Bailey asks under her breath.

"You have a girls' night planned with Olivia and her friends, I guess," I say.

Her head shoots up, and she looks me straight in the eye. "But why? She doesn't even know me. Why is she just inviting me and my daughter over to her place for a girls' night?"

I shrug. "I don't know. I do know Olivia is good people and her friends are too. They will do anything for each other. You guys will be safe if you want to go."

Her gaze flicks over to Charlie. "Yeah, I told Charlie we would. I'm still not sure why she invited us."

I know Olivia is someone who likes to be there for and support other people, but I'm not entirely sure what caused her to invite Bailey and Charlotte.

Charlotte continues to carry the conversation as we finish eating. Once we finish, I ask for the bill and Bailey tries to fight me on paying for their meals, but I wave her off. Charlie slides out of the booth, and I follow. When I'm out, she reaches for my hand and looks behind her to make sure Bailey is following us.

Having this little girl feel so comfortable with me that she wants to hold my hand as we walk back to the station has my chest tightening, and I use my free hand to rub it.

The air is crisp outside, and Charlie's little hand feels cold in mine. I look to Bailey and ask, "Does she have any gloves?"

Bailey reaches inside her purse and hands me a pair. I manoeuvre us off to the side of the sidewalk and crouch in front of Charlie.

"Your hands are getting really cold. Why don't we put these on?" I ask, opening the first glove so she can slide her hand inside. She nods and puts the first one on and I help her with the second. I pull her zipper higher and make sure she's fully bundled.

Looking up, my eyes catch on Bailey's. A soft smile pulls at her lips as she watches us, and I smile back. Standing, I take hold of Charlie's hand again, and we finish our walk back to the station. When Bailey moves to help Charlie into the car, Charlie backs away and asks me to do it.

Before Bailey can say anything, I step up and say, "Sure, Little Bear."

I help her into the car and buckle her seatbelt before opening the door for Bailey.

"Thanks for indulging her today," she says.

"Of course. I had fun. Thanks for the cookies."

"Anytime. Well, I guess we should be going. It was nice to see you again, Officer Sutton."

"Caleb, please. It was nice to see you, too, Bailey."

A blush tinges her cheeks, and I stifle a groan as I wonder if the beautiful pink blush spreads down her chest. I step back, and she climbs into her car as she says goodbye. I watch as the two of them drive away. I quickly run into the station, grabbing my cookies from my locker before heading home for a much-needed shower and sleep.

I wake from my sleep drenched in sweat, my chest heaving. I look at the clock beside my bed and see it's 3:23 a.m. Knowing I won't be able to fall asleep again anytime soon, I hop in the shower before moving to the living room, where I settle in with a book. I wake up later in the morning on my couch with my book lying on the floor.

I spend the week doing things around my place, hanging with Finn, and working. On Saturday morning, I head to my mom's place. Mom insists on a family meal at least once a month; this month it's Saturday brunch.

Arriving at her place, I notice my brother, Max, is already there with his wife, Sarah. I walk into the kitchen, giving Mom a kiss on her cheek before joining Max and Sarah at the kitchen table.

My dad died during his tour of duty when I was young. He's the reason I joined the service. My joining scared the shit out of Mom, but she understood I needed to do it, that it gave me a connection to Dad I desperately needed at the time. Max decided to attend a local school to become an architect. He and his wife live a comfortable life and are now expecting their first child; Mom couldn't be happier, but now she's pressuring me to find a woman and settle down.

I help Mom set the table, and then we all settle in to eat. Mom's chocolate chip pancakes are my favourite. They've barely hit my plate before I begin scarfing them down. Max just chuckles, and I toss a balled-up napkin at him.

He retaliates by asking, "So, Caleb, you dating anyone?"

I scowl at him as Mom takes the bait. "Oh, Caleb, it's time you settle down with someone, build a life, start a family."

I groan. "Mom, we've talked about this. I don't plan on settling down. I've got too much baggage."

She reaches out and pats my hand. "Honey, no one ever has too much baggage to settle down. You find someone to help you carry the load."

"I don't want someone to have to help carry the load."

Mom gives me a sad look before she continues eating and asking Sarah about the baby.

After brunch, I head home and get set up for poker night with guys. At 5:30 p.m., Grayson shows up with a couple of six-packs of beers, and fifteen minutes later, Josh and Matt come strolling in. We all gather around my dining table with a beer and snacks and settle in.

As I shuffle the deck for our second hand, Josh asks, "So what's going on with Bailey and Charlotte?"

"Nothing," I say and deal.

"Who are Bailey and Charlotte? You having two girls at once?" Grayson asks.

Josh coughs on his beer. "Man, Charlotte is a kid."

The look on Grayson's face as he puts his hands up in a defensive gesture has me wishing I'd taken a photo.

"How was I supposed to know? What are you doing with a woman and her kid?"

"I responded to a call at their place. Charlotte was talking about Thanksgiving at school and wanted to do something for someone to say thank you. She asked her mom if they could make me cookies, and they delivered them to the station. Charlotte asked if I could go to lunch with them. When Bailey said I was probably busy, I couldn't take the look of disappointment on Charlie's face, so I joined them." I don't think I've ever eaten as many cookies as I have over the last five days; there's not a single one left.

"Who knew you were such a softie?" Matt chuckles.

"Oh, you're telling me that when your niece or nephew is born, you won't be soft for them? There is something about disappointing a kid that's just too hard to do," I say.

"I just don't think I've ever seen you interact with a kid before."

I shrug because Matt's right. I don't interact with kids much. None of my friends or family have kids yet, so I'm not often in the position to do so. Before my last tour, I would have told you I wanted to be a father, that I wanted a wife and a house full of kids running around. I still love kids and I can't wait to be an uncle. I just don't see kids of my own in my future.

"Well, Olivia is super excited to get to know Bailey and Charlotte. She hasn't been able to stop talking about them. She texted Bailey as soon as we got home Monday," Josh says, pulling me from my thoughts. "All she's been able to talk about this week is them and the doctor's appointment we had."

"How did it go? Did you guys find out the sex?" Matt asks.

He's extremely excited to be an uncle. When it came out that Olivia and Josh were seeing each other, Matt was completely supportive. We found out at their wedding he kind of orchestrated the whole thing.

When Liv caught her ex cheating on her right after they had signed a new lease and she had given up her apartment, she needed a place to stay. Matt was the one to put the bug in Josh's ear that she needed help. The forced proximity had him confessing his feelings for her while he helped her complete some summer checklist he assures us all no one will ever see. So now Matt's best friend is legally his brother and giving him a niece or nephew.

"No, we decided to keep the sex a surprise. We won't know until they're born. Olivia has begun decorating the nursery with gender-neutral colours. We've started getting the furniture and setting it up. She's started nesting earlier than I thought she would, but it makes her happy."

The look of utter love on Josh's face as he talks about his wife and unborn child causes a pang of longing stab to through me. I take a sip of my beer, trying to wash the feeling down.

We spend the rest of the night playing poker and talking about our game tomorrow and the current hockey season. When we decide to call it a night, the guys help clean up and then head home. I head to bed and once again I wake up in the middle of the night out of breath and drenched in sweat.

CHAPTER 4

Bailey

We arrive at Olivia's place at exactly 6 p.m. Charlie is grinning ear to ear in her unicorn onesie pyjamas, holding her favourite stuffed cow, Vanilla. The muscles in my arms strain as I hold the bags I brought with us. I wasn't sure what to bring to a practical stranger's house for girls' night, so I brought juice boxes and snacks for Charlie, wine and sparkling non-alcoholic cider for the adults, homemade cookies, candy, and chips. It was like I was a kid in the grocery store.

A smiling Olivia opens the door and immediately wraps her arms around me. "I'm so glad you guys came."

"Thank you for having us." I force a smile, feeling unsure about all of this.

She ushers us in, helping take a couple of the lighter bags from me. Olivia looks amazing. She has the pregnant woman glow and her curves are stunning. Her auburn hair is pulled back in a ponytail that swings as she walks. We follow her into the living room where three more gorgeous women sit.

A brunette a few inches taller than me jumps off the couch and hurries towards us. "You must be Bailey and Charlotte. Liv has been so excited for you guys to come. I'm Zoey, that's Hannah, and that's Eliza," she says, pointing at a stunning, model-like blonde and a classically beautiful woman with black hair. Eliza looks like someone who doesn't realize just how beautiful she is.

I give a little wave. "Hi, it's nice to meet you. Thanks for having us."

"Of course, come have a seat. We were just chatting," Hannah says.

I put our bags down beside the couch and usher Charlie over to one side of the large sectional couch that sits in the middle of the expansive living room. We take a seat, unsure of all the new people.

"Charlie, I have some craft stuff if you'd like," Olivia says as she hands me a glass of sparkling cider she must have opened. Charlie perks up.

"Really?"

"Yup, I have tons of extra stuff from our fall crafts at school."

"You go to school?" Charlie asks.

"I teach sixth grade." Olivia and Charlie chatter as they get some crafts set up at the dining room table.

"So, how did you meet Caleb?" Hannah asks.

I shift uncomfortably. "Officer Sutton responded to a call at our house. He helped us out. Charlie wanted to do something nice for him for Thanksgiving, so we dropped cookies off at the station. My persuasive daughter then convinced him to join us for lunch. That's when we ran into Olivia and Josh."

"Caleb's a good man," Zoey says. "I've gotten to know him a lot more since Liv and Josh started dating. We all know, if we ever need anything, we can call him and he'll be there."

I nod, taking in her words. These girls have no connections to Caleb, other than being his friend's wife's friends, and they all know he'd be there for them if they needed it.

I wonder what it's like to have someone like that in your life. Lily has been the only constant in our lives. My parents passed in a car accident with a drunk driver when I was twenty. Charlie was only six months old. Derek and I split a year and a half ago, although he wasn't around much before the split. He only started coming back around when the divorce was finalized, and it's irregular visits. Neither Charlie nor I can rely on him.

A hand gently grasps my arm. "You okay?" Eliza asks.

I smile softly. "Yeah, I guess my mind just wandered."

She assesses me with her gaze like she can see more than I want her to. Giving my head a little shake, I look back at the girls. "So, how do you all know each other?"

"Liv and I grew up together. We met Han and Liz while we were at UBC," Zoey says.

"I think that was the only positive thing to come from that house party," Hannah remarks.

Olivia comes back into the room and settles beside me.

"So, what did I miss?" she asks as she rubs her belly.

"Bailey just told us how she met Caleb, or as she calls him, Officer Sutton," Hannah says, making me blush.

Calling him Caleb feels too familiar. He's just the officer that responded to our 911 call. I don't want them to think this is more than it is. I don't want to confuse myself into thinking it's more than it is.

"He showed up at our place after a 911 call. That's it. It's nothing more," I say.

The girls stare at me, assessing me and my response.

It's Olivia who breaks the silence. "So, what are we doing tonight? Taylor Swift dance party or movie night?"

"Taylor Swift!" Charlie calls from the dining room.

The girls laugh, and Olivia plays "Shake It Off" through the speaker system. Charlie runs into the living room, her crafts forgotten, and dances with us. My entire body relaxes as we dance and laugh, not caring about making fools of ourselves. We dance for what seems like an hour. At the end of our little dance party, Charlie curls up on the couch with a blanket and cuddles Vanilla. We settle in with snacks and *How to Lose a Guy in 10 Days*.

As the credits begin to roll, Josh comes in the front door. He walks over and kisses his wife and rubs his hand over her belly. I smile, remembering what it's like to share that experience with someone. I enjoyed being pregnant with Charlotte and wish I could do it again, but that would require me to ever trust a man enough to give him the shattered pieces of my heart and soul.

Derek didn't just physically hurt me. The change in him from my loving husband to a man who took out his anger and frustration with his fists broke my heart. I thought I knew him. I thought I had found the man I would spend the rest of my life with. The man who would be by my side to raise our daughter. I guess I didn't really know him.

"Do you guys want to spend the night? We have a few spare rooms. You can stay in one. I'm making breakfast in the morning. The girls are all crashing," Josh says.

Looking over at a sleeping Charlie, I don't want to disturb her by taking her down to the car and then having to get her inside and up to her bedroom.

"That would be great, thank you."

He nods. "I'll help you move her."

In seconds, he has his arms under her legs and back and is carrying her down the hallway. He walks into a room with a queen-sized bed in the centre. A black comforter is spread over the bed with pillows to match. I rush in front of him, pulling back a section of the covers so he can place her in the bed. I thank him and follow him back out to the living room. Saying good night to the girls, I grab the bag of stuff I brought for Charlie and head back into the bedroom. Settling into bed, I realize that tonight was one of the best nights I've had in a long time.

When I wake up in the morning, it's to an empty bed. I jump out of bed, not sure what Charlie would have gotten into while I was asleep. Walking into the living room, I find her in the kitchen wearing an apron, helping Josh cook breakfast. They both smile as they work together. I look to the dining room and see Liv and Zoey at the table. Liv has a dreamy look as she watches her husband cook with my daughter.

"Morning, Bailey," Zoey calls when she sees me.

"Morning." I grab a seat beside her, and Charlie slowly makes her way to me with a coffee mug in her hand.

"Good morning, Mommy. I made you coffee," she says with a proud smile.

"Thank you, Baby Girl." I kiss her forehead before she rushes back to Josh. Making eye contact with him, I mouth *thank you*, and he smiles.

"Oh, I love Josh's breakfast," Hannah says as she and Liz join us.

"Did they tell you the story about our first breakfast here after a girls' night?"

"No."

"So this was when Josh and Liv were totally in denial that they both liked each other. Josh offered Liv the spare room when she needed a place to crash. He let her host girls' night one Saturday when he had poker. We woke up the next morning and Josh basically told us we had to stay for breakfast. He made all of Liv's favourites. We then mentioned Liv's summer checklist."

A blush spreads across Liv's cheeks as she hides her face in her orange juice.

"Best decision I ever made," Josh says as he kisses the top of her head and places a plate of bacon on the table. "Han, can you wait until the table is fully set before you get into the bacon please." He grins, and Hannah just sticks her tongue out at him before he returns to the kitchen.

Charlie carries a plate of toast, while Josh carries whipped cream and syrup between his arm and body, a plate of French toast in one hand and eggs in the other. They place everything on the table and it looks delicious.

"Josh, may I have some orange juice?" Charlie asks from her spot beside me.

"Of course."

He heads into the kitchen, returning with a glass of orange juice. She says thank you before taking a big sip, licking her lips with a *mmmmmmhhhhh*.

I put some food on her plate and load up mine.

Olivia rubs her hands together in excitement. "I'm so glad I can eat eggs again," she says.

"Pregnancy aversions?" I ask.

"Yeah, the egg aversion was horrible. I would sometimes crave the taste, but the smell was off-putting. I craved pickles too. It was actually how we figured out I was pregnant." She laughs.

Josh reaches across the table, taking his wife's hand and rubbing his thumb over the back of it with a soft smile.

"What time's the game tonight?" Zoey asks.

"Today's an early one. We start at four," Josh says.

"Game?" I ask.

"Josh and the guys play rec hockey. You and Charlie should totally come today. It will be fun. We can get hot chocolate, too," Olivia says.

"I've never watched hockey," Charlie says.

"Well, all the more reason you should come," Hannah says with a mischievous smile. She shares a look with the girls, and I'm not sure if I should be worried.

"Can we go, Mommy? I wanna watch hockey and sit with Liv."

All eyes are on me, and I know no matter what I say, these women and my daughter will wear me down.

"Okay, Baby Girl, we can go. But you have to eat all your breakfast and get ready for school tomorrow. You won't have time after the game."

"Yay!"

Conversation with everyone is easy. I learn that Zoey's in law school, Hannah's a nurse at Vancouver Memorial, Eliza's an accountant, and Josh is the CEO of Lincoln Enterprises.

I help clean up the dishes before gathering Charlie and our stuff. Olivia texts me the address of the rink, and I promise we'll meet them there. With hugs goodbye, Charlie and I head home. I make sure Charlie's homework is done and her clothes are set out for school tomorrow. I get her a bag packed for the game, and we walk out the front door. I hope it's a smooth and uneventful evening.

CHAPTER 5

Caleb

Walking into the lobby of the rink, I see Matt, Josh, Grayson, Olivia, Zoey, Hannah, and Eliza standing in a group. I join them, stopping between Grayson and Matt and tipping my chin in acknowledgement. Olivia is telling everyone about the registry she got set up after hassling from her friends and family. As I'm about to ask her to text me the link, someone calls my name. I turn around just in time to see a little blonde-haired bundle run straight for me. I drop my bag to the floor as she wraps her arms around my legs and smile down at her.

"Hey, Little Bear, what are you doing here?"

"I want to watch hockey with Liv." She gives me a big toothy grin, and I think I melt a little inside.

"Oh yeah? I hear Liv is a lot of fun to watch hockey with. You've got a good buddy there."

"Really?"

"Really."

I look up, my breath catching when my gaze meets Bailey's. My eyes trail her body as I take her in. Dark-blue skinny jeans hug her every curve in a way that has me wanting to smack her ass to see if it jiggles in them. A green T-shirt is pulled snugly against her chest, leaving nothing to the imagination. Her blonde hair is pulled into a ponytail that has thoughts of wrapping it around my hand as I fuck her from behind filling my mind. I hold back a groan.

Bailey is not someone I should be lusting over, but she's the only woman to ever cause this visceral reaction in me.

"Hey, Bailey."

She smiles at me. "Officer Sutton."

"Bailey, please, call me Caleb."

She clears her throat and nods. "Charlie, why don't we go and find some hot chocolate before the game," she says.

"But, Mommy, I want to go with Caleb."

I run a hand over her hair. "I can take her and show her the ice and the gear if you want to grab some hot chocolate. I've got time before I need to be ready."

"Oh, I wouldn't want to impose—" she starts, but I cut her off.

"It's not a problem. Little Bear, you're with me."

Charlie jumps and cheers. As I reach down to grab my bag, I'm reminded we aren't the only ones here as my eyes meet Grayson's and his shit-eating grin.

I throw my bag over my shoulder and introduce Bailey and Charlotte to the guys. "Bailey and Charlotte, these are my friends, Grayson and Matt. Matt's Liv's brother." I point to each as I introduce them. "Guys, this is Bailey and Charlotte."

They give a tip of their chins and say, "Hi."

Charlie puts her hand in mine, and I smile down at her. "You ready to go check out the ice?"

She nods her head so fast, I'm not sure how she doesn't get sick.

I crouch and make sure her jacket is zipped and her toque is secure. "It's cold in there. Do you have gloves if you need them?"

She shows me her gloves, and I lead her through the sliding doors and into the cold area of the rink.

There are four rinks inside this building, each in a corner. We walk up the centre hallway towards the one we're using today. I peek my head into the dressing room and see everyone's dressed.

"Little girl coming through," I call as I push the door open and lead Charlotte inside to show her where I get ready.

I place my bag on the floor and unzip it. Pulling out my skates, I show them to her. "These are my skates. I keep a cover on the blades because they're very sharp. If you're not careful, you can really hurt yourself."

She watches with rapt attention as I continue.

"This part comes up high over your ankle to protect you from pucks and sticks. It also makes it so you can't hurt your ankle as easily." I reach into my bag and grab a roll of stick tape. "I use this to tape my stick. The tape protects the blade and allows me to hold on to the top."

She examines the blade and the grip I've made.

"Do you want to help me re-tape my stick?"

She excitedly says "yes." I position her between my legs so she can help, and she pulls the existing tape off the blade and then helps place a piece along the bottom of it. I show her how I wrap it around the blade, heel to toe, leaving no open space. After a couple of wraps, I let her take over, and she does a surprisingly good job. She does this adorable thing where she sticks her tongue out and bites it as she concentrates.

"That's so good. Maybe I should always have you tape my stick," I say, and she grins at me, so proud of herself.

Josh, Matt, and Grayson walk into the dressing room, and I figure it's time to get Charlotte out of here so the guys can change.

"Okay, time to go find your mom."

"Okay. Caleb, next time can I tape your stick pink?" she asks.

I grin. This adorable little girl has only known me for two weeks and in that time, she has made me cookies, asked me to join her for lunch, asked to spend time with me before my game, and now wants to tape my stick in the future. Not only does she want to tape it, she wants to pick a colour. I'm not sure I could say no to the request even if I wanted to.

"Yeah, Little Bear, you can tape it pink next time."

Leaning my stick against the bench, I get up and lead Charlie towards the bleachers where I know Liv and the girls will be. I lift her onto the second level of the bleachers beside her mom.

"Remember, we'll be wearing red," I say before turning and heading back to the dressing rooms.

I push open the door and take a seat with my stuff.

Before I even have my shirt off, Grayson asks, "So, you're sleeping with the mom?"

I look up and shoot him a glare. "No, I'm not sleeping with Bailey."

"Well, she sure seems to blush a lot around you," he says.

"You're seeing shit." I continue to change into my gear.

"You should go for it," Grayson adds after some time.

"The last thing Bailey or Charlotte needs is my baggage. Even if I were interested, I wouldn't force that on them. They have enough of their own shit to deal with."

Grayson drops his voice low so only I can hear him. "You still having the nightmares?"

He's the only person I've told. I haven't even told my family about them or waking up drenched in sweat. When I got back from my last tour, Grayson noticed a change in me. Being a doctor, he figured it was PTSD, and he's probably right. I told him about my nightmares and waking up each night but haven't been able to muster the ability to go see someone for it.

I give him a slight nod as I continue to lace up my skates.

"You know if you need to talk, I'll listen, and if you need an outside person, I'd be happy to recommend someone."

My entire body is now rigid. I don't like talking about this. I don't want to talk about my nightmares, what happened during my tours, or why I chose not to re-enlist at the end of my last one. I slap my hands against my thighs before pushing to standing. "Yeah, I'm all good, man, thanks." We both know that's not the truth, but he doesn't press further.

I grab my sticks and head out to the bench. Stepping onto the ice, I push away from the boards and let my feet glide me over the ice. The movements are like second nature. The more I move around the ice, the more my body relaxes.

As I round the ice near the bleachers, Charlie excitedly yells, "Go, Caleb!"

She does a little happy dance when I wave at her, and I can't hold back my grin. I don't think I've smiled this much in such a short time in years. After hitting a few pucks into the net, we gather all the pucks and I skate to centre ice for the face-off.

Josh takes his spot at centre, I'm to his right, and Matt's behind me. The puck drops, and Josh wins the face-off, sending the puck back to Matt. He passes it to me, and as soon as I feel the puck connect with my stick, I'm skating towards the other team's goal. I pass the puck to Josh just as I'm slammed into the boards. I keep my footing and make my way across the ice, positioning myself to receive the puck from Sam. He fakes a shot on goal and sends it to me. Pulling my stick back, I wait until the puck is almost to me. My stick comes down and sends a slapshot straight at the goal. The goalie catches the puck, forcing a stoppage and a new face-off to his right.

The other team wins the face-off. They move to send the puck across the ice, but Nick, one of our players, gets his stick on it, sending it over the boards into the other team's bench.

A new face-off has Josh winning it, sending it my way, and I wind up for another slapshot. This one makes it in just over the goalie's right pad.

Arms thrown in the air, I skate past our bench, bumping fists with the guys before getting off the ice and joining them. Sitting, I feel a tug on the sleeve of my jersey. I turn, and Charlie's standing there with her fist out.

I bump my fist with hers before saying, "Little Bear, I need you to either get down so you're lower than the top of this"—I point to the top of the boards—"or stay behind the glass. I don't want you to get hurt, okay?"

With a sad look, she nods, and I hold my hand out for another fist bump. That earns me a smile before she bumps my fist and goes back to join her mom and the girls, who are looking at me with soft smiles.

The rest of the game moves fairly quickly, and we win in a close game, 3-2. When I get up to go to the dressing room, Charlie collides with me while calling, "You won, Caleb, you won!"

"We did," I say, crouching down. "Do you wanna go on the ice before they take the Zamboni out?"

She nods vigorously, so I take her hand and lead her to the ice.

"You have to go slowly, or you'll fall," I say, holding onto her hand and slowly gliding backwards. After a couple of steps, she slips, but I catch her before she hits the ice. I pick her up, and she wraps her legs around my waist and her arms around my neck. My chest tightens as I hold her close to me. The smell of her strawberry shampoo fills my nose as her blonde hair tickles my cheek.

"You want to go for a spin?" I ask.

She nods, and I skate along the boards, slowly picking up speed. She giggles and squeals the faster I go. The smile that's spread across her face lights up all her features, and I'm speechless. Seeing this little girl this happy and carefree because of something so simple I've done. If I were to go today, at least I've done something good in this life.

After we finish a lap, I exit at the same place we entered. I put her down, and she hugs me tightly.

"Thank you, Caleb," she whispers, and I melt. I never thought I'd be this soft for a kid, but she's got me and it's only been two weeks.

"You're welcome," I croak.

I look up and see Bailey leaning against the wall, watching us. I can't read her expression, but it looks like it's something between pain and longing. I want to pull her into my arms and tell her everything will be alright.

"I've got to shower and change. You guys sticking around or heading home?" I ask Bailey.

Bailey pulls out her phone, checking the time. "We've got to get home. This one has to get to bed for school tomorrow. Thank you for taking her on the ice."

"Anytime. It was nice seeing you. Have a good night." I look down at Charlie and run my hand over her head. "Good night."

"Good night."

She waves at me as I move to the dressing room, walking backwards for as long as I can so I can continue to watch them. I push the door open and see half the guys have already finished their showers and the other half are lounging around drinking. Josh walks out of the shower as I take a seat.

"She's cute," he comments as he takes a seat a couple of spots down from me.

I smile to myself. "Yeah, she is."

"Are you going to stick around? Seems like she's getting attached." Josh's question has me stiffening. I can't let Charlie get attached. I'm not her dad, and her getting attached to me can only lead to disappointment.

"It's nothing. Olivia is the one who invited them. I haven't seen either of them since lunch on Monday."

I feel Josh's assessing stare. It makes me uneasy, especially since he's not usually this analytical. He's observant, but I don't usually get peppered with questions.

"I don't know man, just make sure she doesn't get too attached if you don't plan on sticking around. The way she's clung to you so quickly makes me think she lacks a male figure in her life."

That hits hard. I know what it's like to grow up without a father, and I know Charlie's father is not the best or most reliable person. I just nod and get undressed, calling "bye" to him as he leaves to find his wife. I'm the last person out of the shower and I take my time getting dressed, allowing Josh's warning to really sink in.

I have to keep my distance from Bailey and Charlie if I'm not certain I can commit to being a constant in their lives.

CHAPTER 6

Bailey

The entire drive home, Charlie talks about how cool it was to watch the game and how much fun she had skating with Caleb. The absolute joy in her voice has me grinning.

Charlie has never been a sad or unhappy kid, but I can't remember ever hearing her this happy. It makes me happy to hear her like this, but it also has me questioning where I've failed as her mother. Why is she not this happy at home?

I know not having her dad around isn't easy on her. Derek didn't come around a lot during the separation, so Charlie didn't see her dad often. By the time the divorce was finalized, she was beginning to adjust to our new normal. He's been making an effort to be around more, saying he wants to use his court-mandated visitation. But rather than spending time with Charlie, he's been using this time to try to win me back. He still doesn't understand there is no way we're getting back together.

By the time we get home, Charlie is exhausted. After a quick shower, she gets ready for bed. I don't even make it through half a book before she's fast asleep.

Sneaking out of her bedroom, I quietly close her door and move to my bedroom, where I shower and climb into bed. The cool sheets feel smooth against my skin.

My mind wanders back to the game and watching Caleb skate along the ice. Watching him with Charlie, his pure strength when he hit other players into the boards, the power of his legs as he pushed himself to fly across the ice.

My hand slides down my body, slowly over my stomach, to the tops of my thighs. I slowly run a finger through my folds, feeling just how wet I am picturing him from tonight. I flick my finger over my clit, and a jolt moves through my body, forcing a groan up my throat. I have to bite my bottom lip. I continue to slowly work myself, building my release until I'm wound so tight my toes are curled and my body arches off the bed.

Images of what I think he looks like under all that hockey gear have me exploding. I turn my face into my pillow, muffling the moan that tears through me as I come. I work to catch my breath after having the best orgasm I've ever had.

That is so fucking sad.

I was married for four years, and with Derek for six, and I just had the best orgasm I've ever had while fantasizing about a man who probably never wants to get involved with me and my baggage.

Letting out a deep sigh, I get up and head into my washroom, cleaning myself up before climbing back into bed. I toss and turn until sleep finally takes me.

My alarm wakes me up at 7 a.m., and I quickly turn off the annoying thing and toss my blankets to the side. The cool air hits me, helping wake me up. Climbing out of bed, I grab my robe and go wake up Charlie, making sure she gets out of bed before I head downstairs to cook breakfast. I scramble eggs, fry bacon, and get toast ready, calling for Charlie when I'm about to plate the food.

She moves slowly into the kitchen and slides into her chair, rubbing her eyes. Running my hand over her hair, I place a kiss on the top of her head as I give her a plate. She's quiet as she eats, and I don't push her to talk. Like me, she's never really been a morning person, but she doesn't give me issues about getting up for school, so I let her go about her morning how she wants to.

When we've finished eating, we brush our teeth before heading out the door and I drive her to school. As she jumps out of the car, she calls out, "Bye, love you," and joins her friends on the playground. In desperate need of coffee, I go to a drive-through and get a pumpkin spice latte before heading to work.

I'm an office manager for a medical practice in the city. Five doctors work out of the office as well as other locations. It's my job to make sure everything runs smoothly and coordinate the doctors' schedules.

I'm running the reception desk to cover for someone who called out sick today when the front door opens. I plaster on my usual customer service smile when I look up. My eyes widen as I come face-to-face with Caleb.

I thoroughly take him in. His black Vancouver Police Department shirt stretches, showing just how muscular he is, and his jeans are so tight across his thighs I'm surprised the seams haven't ripped. They lead down to black boots so large, I wonder if it's true that shoe size can be an indicator of the size of a man's dick. I swallow harshly, ripping my gaze back up to his.

Fuck. He just caught me practically drooling over him.

With my smile back in place, I say, "Good morning. How can I help you?"

He smirks. "Good morning, Bailey. I have an appointment with Dr. Markstrom."

I quickly begin typing in the computer and see he's here for an annual department-mandated physical. As he leans on the counter, I watch the veins that bulge in his arms and swallow.

"How did Charlie get to sleep last night?" he asks. Him asking about her has my heart skipping a beat.

I clear my throat. "She slept well. As soon as I put her to bed, she was out. She was wiped."

The smile that spreads across his face is soft, as though it genuinely makes him happy that my daughter slept well. My mind rushes back to me in bed last night, getting off to thoughts of him. I squeeze my thighs together as I reach for an intake form, grab a pen, and hand them to him.

"Can you please fill these out and return them to me." My voice comes out more breathy than I'd like. I clear my throat before finishing. "Dr. Markstrom should be ready for you shortly."

He nods, taking the forms and settling into a chair in the waiting room. As soon as he's seated, I shoot out of my chair and move into the backroom where I fill my water bottle with cold water. I chug half the bottle before my body returns to normal.

Of course, the man I lay in bed thinking about last night while I made myself come is a patient at this clinic. It's like the universe decided to add one more reason this man is forbidden fruit. He responded to a 911 call at my house, I have a lot of baggage, the man looks like a fucking god while I have a mom body, and he's a fucking patient.

I thump my forehead against the wall, taking a deep breath before heading back to the reception desk.

Caleb is leaning against the desk when I get back. He smiles as he hands me the documents. I take them with a smile and review his answers while I add them into the system. I look at his date of birth, September 18, and note the year is three before mine, I just turned twenty-six so he turned twenty-nine last month.

His emergency contact is his mom, and I noticed during our first few interactions that he doesn't wear a ring, so he's probably unmarried and not in a long-term relationship. No family history of heart disease or cancer, and he has no concerns he wants to bring up with the doctor.

I mentally slap myself for looking more thoroughly at his form than I do other patients'. The only thing that doesn't have me feeling like complete shit is Caleb seemed to have no issues with me seeing this information.

Dr. Markstrom comes out and calls Caleb's name. Caleb smiles at me as he follows him. When they're both out of sight, I shoot a text to Lily.

BAILEY

I'm going to hell.

LILY

Why? What happened?

BAILEY

You remember Officer Sutton? Well, he's a patient here and I may have taken a special interest in his intake form after he filled it out.

LILY

If you haven't divulged anything and haven't crossed any lines, you're good. Don't stress, hun.

BAILEY

I may have crossed a line...

> I may have used fantasies of him to get off last night. 😏😘

LILY

> Oh, really? You go girl!

> You haven't crossed any lines. You're okay. I'm here to talk if you need to.

Putting my phone away, I lean my head back on the chair, closing my eyes and taking a deep breath. Lily is right. As of right now, I haven't crossed any lines. I just have to keep it that way.

Caleb and Dr. Markstrom come out a while later. They shake hands before Caleb grins and waves as he leaves the office.

I'm in a rut the rest of the day, my mind constantly wandering back to Officer Caleb Sutton. After I get Charlie to bed that night, I send Lily another text.

BAILEY

> If I can get a sitter for Saturday, you and me, a bar, and lots of booze.

LILY

> Down. Let me know.

I text my regular babysitter asking if she can work on Saturday and when she confirms, Lily and I make plans to meet at one of our favourite bars in the city.

On Saturday night, I pull out my trusty little black dress and do a light makeup look before heading downstairs. Charlie is curled up on the couch with Vanilla and her babysitter, Taylor. They have *Paw Patrol* on the TV and a bowl of popcorn between them. I kiss Charlie on the head and tell her to be good for Taylor before I head outside to meet my Uber.

The cold air bites, and I tighten my jacket around me, but it doesn't protect my legs. I hustle to the car, climbing in the back and rubbing my legs, trying to combat the cold. It's a short drive to the bar, and when we get there, I hop out of the car and rush into the warm building.

When I walk in, I spot Lily sitting at the bar. I raise a hand, catching her attention as I make my way through the throng of people. She passes me a strawberry margarita when I get to her. Grabbing it, I take a large sip.

"I really need to get laid," I say as soon as my glass hits the bar top. Sliding onto a stool, I face her. "And I don't mean just any kind of sex. I mean toe curling, back arching, forget my name, can't walk the next day sex. I've never had that sex before. God, this dry spell is killing me," I groan and lay my head on the bar.

"I volunteer," a voice says behind me.

I turn and look at the man who was obviously eavesdropping and take him in. He's probably twenty-one or twenty-two and has that stereotypical frat boy-fuckboy look.

"Oh, honey, you're a baby. One, I doubt you could handle me, and two, you're a little young. You might want to try someone your own age."

I turn back to Lily and take another huge sip of my drink. "New criteria: must be at least my age, and he has to look like he knows what the fuck he's doing."

I raise a hand to the bartender and point to my drink. She nods, and I suck down the last of it. Lily listens to me ramble as my new drink is placed in front of me. "Did I tell you I had the best orgasm of my life while thinking about Caleb? I was with Derek for six years and I'd never come like that. I don't even want to imagine what it would be like if he actually did touch me."

"Oh, tell me more, Bailey," a familiar female voice says.

I choke on my drink and pat my chest as heat climbs up my neck and spreads across my chest. Once I've got the cough under control, I turn on my stool and come face-to-face with Hannah, Zoey, Olivia, and Liz, who are all grinning at me. I offer them a weak smile and wave.

"Hi," I croak, and Lily elbows me. "Lily, this is Hannah, Zoey, Olivia, and Liz."

They all wave at Lily as I introduce them.

"So, we were just grabbing a table. Why don't you join us and fill us in," Hannah says as she grabs my hand and pulls me off my stool.

Lily grabs our drinks and follows as Hannah drags me. Hannah stops at a corner booth that wraps around a large table. She ushers me in like her intention is to prevent me from running. I slide in, trying to adjust my dress that keeps trying to ride dangerously high up my thighs.

Lily puts my drink in front of me, and I finish it. Holding up the empty glass I say, "I'm going to need another, or better yet, why don't you bring a pitcher over."

The girls all grin, and Lily and Liz make their way back to the bar.

I smile at Liv. "So, you must be the designated driver tonight?"

"Nope," she says, popping the p. "Josh agreed to pick us up. He and the guys are doing poker tonight." She runs a hand over her belly. "I'm not drinking tonight, but he didn't want me to lug the girls by myself later." She smiles softly as she talks about her husband. It sounds like he takes care of her completely. I wish I had that, but right now, I'd settle for some good orgasms.

Lily and Liz return with a tray full of drinks and a pitcher of margaritas. Lily, being the angel she is, immediately fills my glass right to the top. I take another large sip, preparing for the questions that are going to come now that everyone is back at the table.

Hannah adjusts herself so she's facing me. "Okay, spill. What's going on with you and Caleb?"

"Nothing, absolutely nothing," I say.

She arches a brow.

"Seriously, nothing. If he wasn't forbidden fruit before, after Monday, he one hundred percent is." I groan as I lean my back against the booth.

"Okay, why is he forbidden fruit? And what happened Monday?" Liv asks.

"Well, let's see. First, he responded to a 911 call at my house after my abusive ex-husband showed up, grabbed me, and scared the shit out of my daughter enough that she called 911 on her dad. Second" —I tick off the numbers with my fingers—"I've got baggage between my ex and a lack of support, besides Lily, and a kid. Third, he looks like a Greek fucking god, and I've got a mom bod. And lastly, the fucking icing on the cake: He's a patient at my work. He walked into the office on Monday for a doctor's appointment. All of that equals forbidden fruit," I finish explaining, looking around the table full of assessing looks.

Hannah breaks the silence. "Babe, to be honest, the only one I see as an issue is that he's a patient at your job, but he could always go and find another doctor. So there's the solution to your only real problem."

"What about the fact he responded to the 911 call, I have baggage, and the man is so far out of my league it's not even funny."

Hannah throws her head back and laughs. She fucking laughs. I scowl at her, but it only causes her to laugh harder.

"Babe, firstly, Caleb would never hold that call against you. Secondly, we all have baggage, and I can guarantee you that man has baggage most of us don't even know about. And lastly, you're hot as fuck. So stop saying he's out of your league. He is totally in it."

I hide my face in my drink and take another sip. No one other than Lily has built me up in a long time, and I've known her for years. Now I have a practical stranger sitting here, taking apart every negative thing I've just voiced. My body is warm, and I'm not sure if it's the alcohol or the affection I have for this woman.

"She's right you know," Liv says. "I'll let you in on something. Before Josh, I had some major self-image issues. My ex cheated on me all while telling me how I needed to improve my body. I really struggled with it. It took the support of these girls and a lot of affirmations from Josh to make me believe I was worthy." A blush stains her cheeks as she talks about affirmation from Josh. "These girls wouldn't lie to me and they won't lie to you either. If it wasn't for them, I don't think I'd be able to have the happy, healthy, and loving relationship I have with Josh."

The girls each put a hand in the middle of the table and they all grab on and squeeze. I feel all their eyes on me as I stare at their hands. Lily adds hers and nudges me. I add mine, using my free hand to wipe the moisture from the corner of my eyes.

"You girls are the best," I choke out.

We separate, and I finish my drink before pouring another and chugging it. "Okay, enough touchy-feely shit. Who's going to dance with me?"

Zoey and Hannah slide out of the booth, and the three of us make our way to the edge of the dance floor.

My arms go above my head as I move my hips to the music. The alcohol hits, and my body temperature rises. I lose all worry about how I move in front of all these people. Hands grip my hips, and a body press against my back. I move my hips with theirs, tossing my head back with my eyes closed. The grip on my hips tightens as warm air dances over my neck.

"Why don't you and this sexy ass of yours go into the washroom with me for a good fuck."

I jolt at the words. "Let go of me. I'm not interested," I say.

I go to move out of his hold, but his grip doesn't relent. He pulls me backwards so I can feel his erection pressing into my ass.

"Oh, you know you'll like it. You're practically asking for it the way you're shaking your ass in this dress."

Just as I'm about to whirl around on this douchebag, his body is suddenly ripped away from me. I turn around quickly, reaching out and grabbing the nearest thing to settle myself. I realize it's an arm.

"She said she wasn't fucking interested. Take the hint and get lost," the man who pulled away the creep growls.

The guy that was pressed against me has his arm pulled behind his back as my saviour towers over him. My head tips back as my eyes trail up my saviour's body. My eyes take in the defined muscles and the way the material of his jeans hugs his large thighs and his shirt stretches across his chest. I inhale a familiar scent of bergamot and something slightly sweet, and my gaze is met by panty melting, steel-grey eyes.

Caleb smirks. "Panty melting?"

I inhale sharply. "Fuck, did I say that out loud?"

I know I've had a lot to drink if I've lost my filter. I quickly turn, throwing my arms out to steady myself, and make my way back to the table. When I get there I reach a hand out to Lily, making a grabbing motion, and she hands me my drink.

"No filter Bailey is here," I say, and she throws her head back and lets out a loud laugh.

"What did you say?"

"Panty melting," Caleb responds from behind me.

I point a thumb over my shoulder at him. "That. I said that." I take another large drink.

Lily's eyes go wide and bounce between Caleb and me before a smile spreads across her face like she's just solved the problem of world hunger.

"You must be Officer Caleb Sutton," Lily says, and I scowl. Of course she had to say it like that. Now he's going to know I've talked about him.

He reaches a hand out to her, and they shake. "I am. And you are?"

"Oh, I'm Bailey's best friend, Lily. Just know if you ever need a babysitter, I'm the one to call."

I bang my head against the table and groan. How drunk is Lily? Is this some kind of nightmare? It has to be, because why else would my best friend be basically throwing me at a guy she's never met?

A hand goes between my head and the table. Heat envelops me from behind as Caleb wraps around my back.

"Bailey, baby, let's not do that," he whispers in my ear.

"You just had a quicky in the washroom didn't you?" Hannah's voice cuts through the noise around us, and my head snaps up.

I grip Caleb's arm as my head spins. I just now notice Olivia isn't at the table and she and Josh are making their way to us. Olivia slaps Hannah's arm and shushes her.

"Why the fuck do you have to be so loud?" she whisper-hisses.

"Well, at least you're getting some good sex. You could be like our girl Bailey over here," Hannah hikes a thumb at me.

I groan and let my head fall to the table again. Why? Why did she have to say that in front of Caleb of all people? Caleb groans, and my body heats, a blush spreading across my entire body.

"Liv is the only one getting anything decent," Zoey says, and all the girls nod.

That at least makes me feel better. I go to stand, but I stumble. My legs feel like jelly and my head won't stop spinning. The next thing I know, arms are being wrapped around me under my ass and I'm being tossed over a shoulder.

"Apple ass," I yell when I come face-to-face with a perfect tight ass that looks so biteable. I can feel my body shake as Caleb laughs.

"I'm going to take her home. Lily, you want a ride?"

She must nod because I hear her gather her things and a chorus of byes called as Caleb walks out of the bar. I groan as he places me in the front seat and does my seatbelt for me. I pass out on the ride home, and the next thing I know, I'm being carried up the stairs in my house and placed in my bed.

Bailey

I wake to the smell of bacon, my head pounding, and cottonmouth. Rolling out of bed, I go downstairs where I catch sight of Charlie sitting at the kitchen table drawing and Lily cooking breakfast. I kiss the top of Charlie's head and tell her good morning before going to the coffeepot and pouring myself a generous cup. Turning to Lily, I smile.

She raises an eyebrow and asks, "How you feeling this morning?"

Taking a quick look over my shoulder and seeing Charlie isn't paying us any attention, I look back at Lily and whisper, "Better than I deserve. I really made a fool of myself, didn't I?"

Lily stirs the pan. "I wouldn't say fool, but yeah, unfiltered Bailey came out last night."

I grimace. "I can't remember. How did we get home?"

She grins. "Caleb brought us back here. He carried you out of the club, inside, and put you to bed."

I drop my head back and groan. A flush of embarrassment climbs up my neck and cheeks. I can't believe I let that man see me like that, or that he had to carry me and bring me home. Thank God the plan for last night was for Taylor to crash in Charlie's room. Taylor tends to prefer earlier nights, so I got an air mattress so she could crash here on the nights she doesn't want to go home late. I also paid her before I left last night.

My phone buzzes on the counter.

OLIVIA

Hey! Just thought I'd check in after last night. How
are you feeling?

BAILEY

Hey, thanks for checking in. I'm doing good, all
things considered. How are the girls?

OLIVIA

They're good. They weren't quite as wasted as you
were 😖

BAILEY

I've been told. 🙈

OLIVIA

The girls and I all enjoyed hanging out with you
and Lily last night. Let us know when you're down
for another girls' night!

Lily watches as I put my phone down and arches a brow.

"Olivia," I say. "She was just checking in to see how I was feeling. She said to let her know when we're ready for another girls' night."

Lily smiles. She finishes cooking breakfast and the three of us sit at the table enjoying our food while Charlie tells us about her night with Taylor. Lily spends the day with us watching movies until it's time to get Charlie to bed.

The next morning when I walk into work, I get started on the stack of patient files that require phone calls. Caleb's file is on top. Dr. Markstrom's note asks me to call and schedule a phone appointment for him to relay the results of his physical. I close my eyes and take a deep breath, pushing aside lingering embarrassment, before dialling his number.

He answers after three rings. "Sutton."

Clearing my throat, I say, "Good morning, Officer Sutton, this is Bailey calling from Dr. Markstrom's office."

I hear his smile through the phone as he says, "Good morning, Bailey. How are you?"

"I'm good. You?"

"I'm doing well. You were okay yesterday morning?"

I close my eyes and lean back in my chair. I want to keep this conversation as professional as possible. "Yes, thank you. I'm calling because Dr. Markstrom would like to set up a phone appointment with you to go over the results of your physical. Does tomorrow morning at 10 a.m. work for you?"

He pauses before clearing his throat. "Yes, that works. Thank you, Bailey."

"You're welcome. Have a good day, Officer Sutton."

"You too."

I hold the phone to my ear even after the click and the dial tone kicks in. Disappointment runs through me. I don't understand it. I was the one who wanted to keep the conversation professional, so why am I disappointed he hung up?

I spend the rest of my shift trying to understand this feeling. It's put me in a mood I don't notice until I pick Charlie up.

"Are you okay, Mommy?"

I look in the rearview mirror at her and smile. "Of course, Baby Girl. Why do you ask?"

"You haven't asked me a hundred questions about school. You always ask me lots of questions." Darn, my daughter is observant.

"I'm sorry. Why don't you tell me all about your day? What was your favourite thing?"

She tells me about a new friend she made at recess and the book they read about bears. When we get home, I help Charlie with her homework and make us dinner. When I'm lying in bed that night, a text comes in from Olivia.

OLIVIA

> Doing a girls' day on Saturday. Brunch and mani-pedis. Bring Lily and Charlie. Can't wait to see you!

I grin at my phone. This girl is relentless, trying to pull me into her fold of friends. I send her a thumbs-up emoji and forward the message to Lily, who confirms she's in.

Saturday, we all meet at Sammy's at 11 a.m. Charlie's so excited for a girls' day. The chime of the door rings in my ears as I look around the diner for the girls. Olivia spots me first, her arm waving excitedly above her head as she tries to gain my attention. Charlie runs over to the table, her blonde hair flying behind her. I follow and smile at the girls as Charlie slides in beside Olivia and I slide in beside Hannah. Olivia has a kid's placemat with crayons set up and is colouring when Hannah leans into my side and whispers, "So... did anything happen with Caleb last weekend?"

I look around, wishing I had a glass of water to drink to put off answering her question.

"No, he just brought Lily and me back to my place."

She assesses me. I'm relieved when the waitress comes to take our order. I order a hot chocolate with whipped cream for Charlie and a coffee for myself. Lily shows up when our drinks are delivered, and we all chat.

It's amazing how these women have embraced the three of us. Especially Charlie. After she was born, I lost a lot of my friends. They didn't understand that I now needed to schedule my life around having a child. They tried at first, but after a few months, the texts and calls stopped, and I was left with Derek, Lily, and Charlie. Now, all I have is Charlie and Lily, and I'm perfectly happy with that.

I'm pulled out of my thoughts when Lily nudges me.

"Mommy, can we go?" Charlie asks.

I look to Lily, but it's Olivia who chimes in. "After our mani-pedi, we are all going to the guys' game. I asked if you guys wanted to join us?"

I look at Charlie and see the hope written all over her face, but I don't know if I can handle seeing Caleb again—especially so soon after I made a complete fool of myself in front of him.

Lily doesn't skip a beat answering for us. "Of course, we'd love to go. I heard all about the last game. I want to see this."

Lily grins at me, and I glare in return, but it melts away when I hear the excited cheer that comes from my daughter. How can I deny her something that makes her so happy and doesn't cost me anything but time, and maybe a little bit of my sanity?

Olivia and Zoey insist on being with Charlie while she gets her nails done, so that leaves me with Lily, Hannah, and Liz as we get our pedicures. I take a seat, and Lily grabs the one to my left, Hannah to my right, and Liz to her right.

As soon as we're settled, Hannah starts in on the questions. "So, are you going to make a move on Caleb?"

My eyes widen in shock. "No, of course not. Why would you ask?"

"Because you obviously have some sort of feelings for him. You should take the jump. It's the twenty-first century, women can make the first move."

I quirk a brow. "Have we completely forgotten everything we talked about on Saturday? What about the fact that I completely embarrassed myself in front of the man and he had to carry me out of the bar? I have no desire to put myself in that situation."

Hannah stares me down, but it's Liz who says something. "Girl, he went feral when he saw that man touching you after you told him you weren't interested. He was already tense just seeing you dancing with the guy. I don't think your attraction is a one-way street. If you're interested in him, maybe Hannah's right and you should make a move."

My mind drifts back to the night in the bar and the way Caleb growled at the guy. I shake my head because the last thing I need is to convince myself something could happen between us.

"Mommy, look at my new nails," Charlie calls as she runs up to me.

"They're beautiful, Baby Girl. Are you going to get pink on your toes, too?"

"Yeah, and Aunty Liv got the same colour as me, too. We match!"

My throat tightens at Charlie calling Olivia aunty. She hasn't had a lot of people in her life that have been there for her. The fact she's connected with Olivia this quickly and feels so comfortable fills me with a mixture of happiness and worry.

Will she lose Olivia the same way I lost all the people I thought were my friends until I had Charlie? The last thing I want is for Charlie to lose people. I smile at her and look up, my gaze catching Olivia who smiles brightly at us. I'm going to have to hope for the best. Hope that these people will stick around and I'm building a new support system.

"I'm going to go back with Aunty Liv," Charlie says as she runs back across the salon.

I look at Lily and her soft smile as she watches Liv and Charlie together. I take a deep breath, trying to gather myself.

"You okay?" Lily asks.

I close my eyes and nod as she grabs my hand and squeezes. She was there for the aftermath with my old friends when I got pregnant. She knows I've been worried about not having a support system and group of role models for Charlie.

When we finish with our nails, we make our way to our cars and agree to meet at the entrance of the rink. Charlie is bouncing with energy when I pull into the parking lot. I've barely parked the car and turned it off before her seatbelt is undone and she's trying to make her way out of the car.

"Whoa, Baby Girl, you've got to wait for Mommy and Aunt Lily," I call.

"Sorry," she says meekly as she waits for help to get out. "I just really want to go see Aunty Liv."

I hold her hand as we make our way across the parking lot. As soon as we are on the sidewalk and she spots Liv, she's running towards her.

As we walk inside, I hear a collection of male voices. One stands out to me. It's one that's been a part of my nighttime fantasies.

Caleb.

Charlie runs to him, seemingly forgetting everyone else.

"Caleb," she calls.

He stops his conversation, smiling at her and crouching as she runs at him. "Look at my nails." She thrusts her hands at him, and he takes them in his. The size difference is almost comical.

"They're gorgeous, Little Bear."

She smiles like he's given her the world's best compliment, and I melt a little. Somehow, meeting this man has brought all these people who have embraced both Charlie and me and make her smile into our lives.

"Aunty Liv got matching nails too."

Caleb arches a brow. "Did she? Now, isn't that special?"

She nods vigorously. "Caleb, can you take me on the ice again? Please? It was so much fun last time."

"If it's okay with your mom, yeah, we can go on the ice again."

Charlie looks at me and does her little pouty face she only pulls out when she really wants something. Caleb stands up and makes his way to my side.

"Yeah, you can go on the ice." I look to Caleb. "Thanks, Officer Sutton."

Caleb leans in close, his warm breath skates over my ear and goose bumps erupt across my skin. "If you don't stop calling me Officer Sutton, I might have to take you over my knee to teach you a lesson," he whispers.

A shiver runs through me and I know the moment he notices it because I feel and hear his sharp intake of breath.

"Do you like that idea, Bailey? Do you like the idea of me bending you over and spanking you?"

I nod almost imperceptibly. He groans, and I squeeze my thighs together, trying to quench the growing ache between my legs.

"Woman, you're testing my limits," he says before taking two steps back, creating distance between us and calling to Charlie, "Let's go, Little Bear."

He's been using this nickname with her and I'm not sure where he's got it from, but every time it draws me into him more. He shows my daughter an affection I wish her own father would.

The two of them walk towards the rinks hand-in-hand, Charlie rambling on to him as he nods.

"He's a good one," a voice says beside me.

I turn and am met with deep blue eyes, the same shade as the Pacific. I know he's one of Caleb's friends, but I'm not entirely sure who he is.

He seems to recognize this and says, "I'm Grayson. I've been friends with Caleb for years, since before he did his first deployment."

My eyes widen.

"He didn't tell you he served, did he?"

I shake my head.

"I don't know everything he went through over there. I've never really asked, and he doesn't like to talk about it." He sighs at the ground before looking at me again. "He's been different since he's been back, but I've never seen him smile as much as he has with your daughter. I just wanted you to know, he's a good one. You can trust him."

I nod and watch Grayson walk towards the rink with Josh and Liv's brother as I stand here and try to process everything he just dropped on me. That along with the dirty whispering Caleb did before he walked away has my mind all over the place.

Olivia links her arm with mine, and we make our way to the bleachers. The girls talk as we wait for the start of the game, but I tune them out for the most part as everything tumbles in my mind.

When Charlie comes back from hanging out with Caleb, she practically ignores me, opting to hang out with the girls. I sit back, watching Charlie with them and the game. Every time Caleb is on the ice, Charlie is up and cheering for him. The girls all watch her with smiles, and she even gets smiles from some of the guys. The game moves quickly, and Caleb scores the game-winning goal. I watch as he skates and bends over picking up the puck and bringing it back to the bench to hand it to Charlie.

Excitement radiates off her before she even makes her way to me. She talks a mile a minute as she replays watching Caleb score and how she's so happy he gave her the puck. The guys all come off the ice, and Josh is immediately at Olivia's side, kissing her as she smiles at him.

"Burgers and fries upstairs?" she asks, and he nods. She looks around him at the other guys. "You guys joining us for dinner?" They all agree, and she says, "Text me your orders and I'll take care of it."

Charlie tugs on the sleeve of my jacket, and I look down at her. "Mommy, can we have dinner with Aunty Liv?"

Olivia joins in. "Yeah, Mommy, can you have dinner with Aunty Liv?"

Liv's brother throws his head back and laughs. "Are you going to indulge your child's every whim the way you seem to do with Charlotte here?"

A grin spreads across her face and a mischievous glint fills her eyes. "Nope, but it's my right as an aunty to spoil and indulge. Just wait until you have kids. I will be the favourite aunt."

"Not happening anytime soon, little sis, but does that mean I have free reign to spoil your kid?"

She chuckles. "I think Josh will have you beat. I'm going to end up being bad cop all the time. He's already filled the nursery with stuffed animals, blankets, toys, and books." She runs her hand over her belly. "This child will want for nothing, especially with Josh as their dad."

The affection in her voice has tears pricking at the corner of my eyes. I want that for Charlie. I want her to know the unwavering love and affection of a father.

I turn my head and pretend to cough as I discreetly wipe at my eyes. I feel heat at my back as a hand grips my hip, giving it a squeeze. I look up and meet Caleb's concern-filled eyes. It's like he can see a part of me I don't show anyone else.

He breaks eye contact and looks at Charlie, but his hand remains on my hip. "I hear they have a great grilled cheese sandwich," he says.

Charlie starts bouncing on her toes, gripping her hands together and placing them below her chin. "Please, Mommy?"

"Yeah, we can stay for dinner."

Charlie wraps her arms around my legs and looks up at me. "Thank you."

I smile and run a hand over her soft blonde hair. It may seem like she's been asking me for a lot lately, and I've been giving in, but all she's asked for has been to spend time with these people who have completely embraced her. I can't take that away from her.

"Why don't you order me one too," he says. I feel Caleb's breath against my ear as he leans down and whispers, "I'll see you up there."

He squeezes my hip again before walking towards the dressing room. Goose bumps scatter across my arm and neck, and my cheeks are flushed. The moment he steps away, I immediately miss his warmth and wrap my arms around myself, attempting to fight the cold.

Hannah grins at me from behind the other girls, and I stick my tongue out at her. It's childish, but I don't know what else to do. Maybe she's right and my feelings and thoughts aren't one-sided.

Caleb

I walk into the dressing room and make my way to my bag. Taking a seat, I put my helmet on the bench and drop my head into my hands, running my hands through my hair.

I'm failing. I told myself I would create distance between myself and Bailey and Charlie. I've gone twenty-nine years without meeting this woman, and now I've seen her several times over the last few weeks. And every time I do, I'm completely enraptured by her.

She's trying to hide her pain from everyone around her, but I see it, and all I want to do is take that pain away.

"You're fucked," Grayson says.

I turn and glower at him. I know this, I really don't need the fucker pointing it out; and what does he do? He fucking laughs at me while he slaps his knee. He's enjoying this way too much. So, I decide to get a reaction of my own from him. It's not my usual tactic, but I'm all turned around right now. This isn't me. I don't get hung up on a woman.

"So, you've been seeing a lot of Hannah with her being at all these games."

That sobers him up really quick, and I smirk. I see the wheels turning in his head as he decides how to get me back. I can tell the exact moment he figures it out.

"Who thinks Caleb will marry Bailey," he calls to the entire dressing room.

His question has the loud voices quieting and everyone looking our way. More than half the hands in the dressing room go up. What the hell? What in the world would make them all jump to that crazy conclusion? How do all of them know who Bailey fucking is?

"I'm not even dating the woman. How did you manage to jump to us getting married?"

"Man, you've smiled more in the last few weeks than I've seen you smile all year. There is something there. Plus, I saw the hip grab and I heard all about your defending her at the bar last weekend. Just call it as I see it."

"Grayson knows your private ass the best. If he says you'll marry her, I believe it," Luke calls from the other side of the room, and a few guys nod.

"Have you ever had a girlfriend?" Matt asks.

"Yeah," I say. My last relationship ended within five months of returning from active duty. The nightmares and occasional mood swings or zoning out were just too much for her. She just packed her stuff one day and left. After Gina, I decided no more relationships.

"When?" Matt's being annoyingly persistent.

"It's been a while." Five years.

"That's all you're going to say?"

"There isn't much more to say about it. I've dated, but the last one didn't end great. I decided not to date anymore."

Matt and Josh watch me as though they're looking for more between my words. I consider them both two of my closest friends, but I haven't been able to open up to them about everything.

They drop the conversation, and we shower and change before heading upstairs. Making our way into the restaurant, we find the girls at a long table in the centre of the room. We walk over to them, and Josh heads straight towards Liv. They always find each other when they're in the same room. It's as though they're two magnets drawn to each other. It looks like they purposely left the seat beside Liv open for Josh.

As soon as Josh makes it to the table, Charlie turns in her chair and spots me. She jumps out of her seat and runs to me, grabbing my hand.

"You're beside me, Caleb."

She pulls me along, and I follow with a smile. As soon as we're seated, she looks at her mom. "I get to sit between Aunty Liv and Caleb," she says excitedly.

"Yes, you do, Baby Girl." Bailey looks at her with overflowing affection and love; but there's something else, something sad.

"Don't tell me Aunty Liv has replaced me as your favourite," Lily says.

Charlie looks directly at Lily and shakes her head. "No, Caleb's my favourite." She then turns back to the colouring sheet in front of her. I'm left speechless, and people are looking at me curiously.

"Thank you," I say.

"You're welcome," she says, not looking up.

Our server, along with the help of her coworkers, delivers our food as well as a few pitchers of water. With her food in front of her, Charlie does a little happy dance in her seat. I take a bite of my grilled cheese and let out a groan. Turning to Charlie I say, "This is really good."

She nods as she takes a bite, gooey cheese strung between her sandwich and mouth. Matt and Zoey seem deep in conversation, while everyone else talks around them.

When Charlie finishes eating, she returns to her drawing, but after a few minutes, she looks at me and asks, "Can I sit in your lap?"

My eyes immediately find Bailey's, and I mouth, *Can she?*

She nods. I reach over to Charlie, positioning my hands in her armpits and pulling her onto my lap. When she's settled, I bring her paper and crayons with so they are in front of me.

"Do you want to play tic-tac-toe with me?" I ask.

She nods, and I draw the board, allowing her to make the first move. We play a couple of rounds before she adjusts herself in my lap, leaning into me like she's going to fall asleep. I wrap my arm around her, making sure she's secure. I take a deep breath and inhale the smell of her strawberry shampoo. The smell winds around me, and I feel myself getting tired. My head moves as I track the conversations around the table. Olivia catches my attention when she slides into Charlie's chair.

"You're good with her," she says as she reaches forward and tucks a piece of hair behind Charlie's ear.

"She makes it easy," I say with a soft smile.

"Don't write yourself off like that, Caleb. Not everyone is as good with kids as you are with her. She can read it too. She's taken with you, and I have a feeling she's a good judge of character. If she didn't feel safe and comfortable with you, she wouldn't be asleep in your lap right now."

I meet Liv's eyes and see the truth in them. Being a teacher and dealing with kids daily, I trust her judgment. Something squeezes my heart. It's not something to take lightly, having a little girl as sweet as Charlie feel safe with you. Especially when she's seen what she has.

"Thanks, Liv."

She nods and moves back to her seat beside Josh.

Bailey looks over at me, shock filling her face. I don't think she's looked over here since Charlie's fallen asleep. She comes to my side, saying, "I should get her home." She moves to grab Charlie, but I hold up my hand and say, "I've got her. Just let me get the bill and I'll carry her to your car."

"I don't want to put you out. I can take her."

"It's no problem, Bailey. I'll take her."

She appears to resign herself and waives over the server. I ask for the check for the three of us. When the server returns, I take it before Bailey can and ask for the machine. Bailey opens her mouth like she's going to argue, but the look I give her tells her not to. When I finish paying, I run a hand over Charlie's back.

"Little Bear, it's time to go home."

She nuzzles deeper into my chest.

"Little Bear, can you wrap your arms around my neck?"

Her eyes open slightly, and I get a view of the beautiful blue that matches her mother's. She wraps her arms around my neck, and I stand. I make my way over to the guys giving them each a handshake before adjusting Charlie and grabbing my hockey bag. Bailey takes my sticks, and we make our way to her car.

"Thank you for carrying her."

I face her and smile. "It's no problem, Bailey. If I didn't want to, I wouldn't. I'm not really known for doing things I don't want to."

Her eyes bounce around my face, and she seems to read my sincerity, a small smile spreading across her face. When we get to her car, she unlocks it and I get Charlie settled in the back.

Bailey fiddles with her phone, and I grab it, swiping up and turning it to read her face, unlocking it. Opening her contacts, I add myself then give her it back.

"Text me when you get home," I say, opening the driver's door for her.

"Yeah. Thank you for everything today. I guess, I should also apologize and thank you for Saturday," she says, a blush spreading across her cheeks and down her neck. Her eyes dart everywhere but my face.

I grip her chin, forcing her to look at me as I say, "Bailey, there is nothing to apologize for. If you ever need anything, please call me."

She nods, her eyes remaining on mine. Her eyes are the shade of the sky on a bright summer day, and I could stare into them for the rest of my life. I clear my throat and take a step back, dropping my hand.

"Please remember to text me when you get home. I want to make sure you're safe."

"I will. Thank you," she says as she climbs into her car and drives away.

My eyes track her car until I can no longer see her taillights, and only then do I make my way to my car and head home. During my walk with Finn and when we get back home, I constantly check my phone, waiting for it to ding with a text notification. After twenty minutes of checking it every minute, it dings.

BAILEY

Home safe and sound. Charlie is curled up in bed with Vanilla. She's definitely out for the night. Thank you for tonight.

CALEB

Anytime. Sleep well, Bailey.

BAILEY

You too.

I plug my phone in beside my bed and climb in. My mind goes over the events of today, how much I enjoyed having Charlie there, cheering for me. How something as small as giving her the puck from the game-winning goal made her shine with happiness.

Mom's pressuring me to settle down starts to go through my head. I remember how I felt when Liv said Charlie would only have fallen asleep in my lap if she felt safe. That is probably the most satisfying feeling I've ever experienced. Knowing that Charlie, who has seen her father get violent with her mom and would have every right not to feel safe around men, feels safe with me.

I'm drawn to Bailey. I want to know everything that's going on in her head. Why does she have a mixture of sadness in her eyes when she looks at Charlie, but especially when she looks at Charlie and me together? Questions bounce around my head as I try to fall asleep, but when I do finally crash, I dream of Bailey and Charlie and it's the first night in forever I don't wake up from a nightmare.

I spend Sunday with Finn around the house doing chores, at the dog park, and watching a couple of hockey games on TV. Monday morning, I make my way to work and when I get there, my staff sergeant calls me into his office.

"Sutton, I need you to help the group of doctors and nurses coming in today offering flu shots. They'll be setting up in conference room A."

I nod. As always, Staff Sergeant Bell is straight to the point. "Is there anything specific you need done?"

"Just make sure they have everything they need. They need a liaison while in the station."

"Sounds good." I pat my thighs before pushing out of my seat and heading to the reception desk. I tell the officer managing walk-ins to let me know when the people doing the flu shots are here and return to my desk to follow up on some of the recent reports.

Half an hour later, my desk phone rings. I answer and am told they're here, so I make my way to reception. I stop short when I see blonde hair pulled back into a high ponytail, a light-blue blouse, and a black pencil skirt that hugs hips and an ass I'd recognize anywhere.

Bailey.

I walk up behind her and lean over her shoulder until my lips are right beside her ear.

"Hello, Bailey," I whisper, and she jumps, clutching her chest as she spins and stares at me. I throw my head back and let out a laugh, one I feel in my stomach and chest. Her hand reaches out as she play-fully slaps my arm.

"What the hell, Caleb? You almost gave me a heart attack."

"I'm sorry, Bails, I couldn't help myself."

She rolls her eyes.

"You here to do the flu shots?"

"Yeah, I'm managing the intake while the nurses and a doctor do the shots."

"Okay, well I'm your liaison for the day. If you guys want to gather your stuff, I'll take you back to get set up."

She nods and turns to the group of people standing in a circle behind her. They pick up the bags at their feet and follow me through the main door after we're buzzed in, and we head to the conference room.

"You can rearrange the room however is best for you. I'll be staying in here with you guys today. If any of you need to leave the room, you'll need to be escorted. Let me know if you need anything and I'll get it for you."

Everyone nods, and I grab a chair and take it to the corner. When they begin to move tables, I step in, having them tell me where they want them. I bring in another officer, and we get the tables into the proper spots. I take my spot in the corner and watch as they finish setting up. I can't take my eyes off Bailey the entire day. I watch as the guys who come in for their shots smile and flirt with her and how she smiles back.

I clench my fists trying to fight this feeling rising inside of me. I want to go over there and stake a claim to her, tell all of these guys to fuck off, she's mine—but I can't. I don't have that right, and I'm not going to overstep with Bailey.

I watch as Officer Cain sets up camp in front of the table Bailey's using. He's a player. We've all heard about his escapades either directly from him or through the rumour mill, and I don't like watching him flirt with Bailey. He leans over the table and moves like he might reach forward and brush the stray strand of hair that's fallen from her ponytail behind her ear.

That's it. I push out of my chair and stalk directly towards them. "Cain, either get back to work or get your shot. This is not a time to be flirting."

He shoots me a cocky grin. "I'm just killing time until they're ready for me, Sutton."

I place a hand on Bailey's back and feel her lean into my touch slightly.

"Why don't you go take a seat in one of those chairs over there, Cain. I'm sure Bailey can call you when she's ready."

He stares at the placement of my hand before making eye contact with me again.

"Whatever you say, Sutton."

He has this look like he now knows this major secret no one else does, and I don't like it. I watch as he moves towards the empty chairs and takes a seat.

I lean over Bailey and whisper, "I'm not sure I enjoy sharing your smiles with all these fuckers, Bailey. You're going to make me do something we're both going to regret."

She swallows audibly before her head turns towards me. She licks her lips, and my eyes track the movement. I hold back a groan as I think about other places her tongue could be and just how good it would feel.

"I'm not sure we'd both regret it," she whispers, and God if that doesn't almost have me breaking my resolve.

"What am I going to do with you, woman?" I say before standing straight and making my way back to my chair.

For the rest of the shift, I watch Bailey. Her smiles are very professional with all the guys, and she looks over at me every once in a while, a blush spreading across her cheeks every time.

When they begin packing up, I walk over to Bailey. "I have your cookie container in my locker, why don't you come and get it."

She looks over her shoulder at her co-workers before she nods and places the batch of documents in her file. I pull another officer in to watch over everyone else then we make our way to the locker room.

CHAPTER 9

Bailey

The heat of Caleb's hand radiates over the small of my back as he guides me towards his locker. My skin has felt like it's on fire ever since Caleb scared me in the lobby. Watching him move the tables for us didn't help. I almost drooled as his muscles moved under his shirt. I had to squeeze my thighs together to try to quench the ache building between my legs. I didn't think I could be more turned on by him today. That was until he was behind me basically telling Officer Cain to fuck off. I can still feel his breath skate across my ear as he whispered that he didn't like sharing my smiles with these guys.

For the rest of the shift, I kept stealing looks at him and making sure my interactions with the other officers were entirely professional. None of those men piqued my interest, anyway. No one seems to do that besides Caleb.

He pushes open the door to the locker room, holding it open for me. I follow behind him as he walks to the end of the aisleway and takes a left, stopping three lockers down on the right. He spins the lock and opens the door, reaching to the top shelf and pulling down the container that Charlie and I delivered the cookies in.

A picture attached to the inside of the door catches my eye. I take a step closer and realize the photo is of Caleb and Charlie from the day he took her on the ice. He's still in his hockey gear, and

Charlie is wrapped around him. They both look so carefree with their heads tipped back, laughing. Charlie's face is full of pure joy.

In the short time I've known him, I don't think I've ever seen Caleb as relaxed as he looks in this picture. He usually looks wound up, like he's just waiting for something to happen. Here, he looks completely in the moment.

I turn and face him. The same smile from the photo is spread across his face as pink tinges the tips of his ears and cheeks. This small thing means so much. This photo in Caleb's locker has me saying fuck it.

I reach up, wrapping my hands around the back of his head and pulling it down to mine as I go on my tiptoes and kiss him. He's rigid for a second before his body relaxes into me. His hand goes into my hair, gripping it tightly and angling my head how he wants as he devours my mouth. He kisses me with urgency, like if he slows or stops, it will all end, and I kiss him back the same way. I moan into his mouth as his grip tightens in my hair.

He groans, breaking the kiss and trailing his lips across my jaw and down my neck, finding a sensitive spot where my shoulder and neck meet. His hand leaves my hair, and both of his hands find the backs of my thighs, lifting me. I wrap my legs around his hips, and he walks us into the lockers. His lips move back up my neck as he nips and licks his way along it. When his lips meet mine again, the kiss is less urgent. We explore each other's mouths slowly, savouring the taste of each other.

He rolls his hips into my centre, and I feel how hard he is. I throw my head back as I moan, and he rolls his hips again.

"Fuck, Bailey. You're unravelling all my control," he groans into my neck.

The sound of the door opening echoes in the room, and Caleb quickly sets me down. I pull the hair tie from my hair and adjust my skirt back down my legs. Looking around, I don't see anyone. Hopefully, they're down the first aisle of lockers. I see an open door that looks like it leads to a washroom and duck into it. I take myself in as I look in the mirror. My cheeks are flushed, my shirt is a little askew, and you can tell someone had their hands in my hair.

"You look good like that."

I turn to face Caleb, and my face heats as his eyes take me. "Like what?"

"With your cheeks flushed and your hair thoroughly mussed." He grins.

I spin and fix my hair, pulling it back into a ponytail. He comes up behind me, his presence making my skin tingle and heat like it does every time he's near me.

"I want to see you like that again," he whispers in my ear, causing my blush to deepen. I've never been as pink as I am right now in my entire life. By the time we walk out of this room, I'm going to be as red as a tomato.

"Play your cards right and you just might get to, but not here," I say.

He grins before taking a step back and gesturing for me to leave the washroom first. I stop at his locker and grab the container off the bench, and we make our way back to the conference room. I feel the stares of people as we make our way through the office. I touch my lips, still able to feel Caleb's on mine. I can still taste him. Can everyone in here tell Caleb just gave me the best kiss of my life? I look at Caleb over my shoulder. He just grins, and I shake my head.

When we get back to the conference room, Caleb dismisses the other officer. We grab our stuff, and Caleb escorts us to the reception area. I'm almost to the front door when Caleb calls, "Bails."

I turn and face him, smiling at the nickname. "Yeah?"

"You and Charlie free Friday night?"

"I think so. Why?"

"I wanna take Charlie skating. I told her I'd teach her."

My grin widens. Caleb made a promise to Charlie and is following through with it.

"Sounds perfect. I'll tell her. What time?"

"I'll pick you guys up at six. We can get dinner after."

"It's a date," I say, and my eyes instantly widen. He just offered to teach my daughter to skate. He didn't ask me out.

I'm about to backtrack, but he grins and says, "It is."

I duck my head before turning and following my coworkers out the front door. I head back to the office to lock up the files from today before picking up Charlie from school. Just as I unlock the front door and send Charlie into the kitchen to start her homework, my phone buzzes.

CALEB

You make it home ok?

I smile down at my phone.

BAILEY

Yeah, Charlie and I just walked in. You home?

CALEB

No, still have a couple hours on my shift.

BAILEY

What time you off?

CALEB

7 p.m.

BAILEY

Stay safe.

CALEB

Always.

I look up at Charlie working at the kitchen table and decide maybe we should make Caleb dinner. If I'm going to go with the fuck it mentality, I might as well go all in. I walk over to the table and sit across from her.

"So Baby Girl, what do you think about making Caleb dinner tonight? He won't be off work until later."

She jumps in her seat and smiles widely at me. "Yes, Mommy, can we? Can we make tacos? I think he'd really like them."

"Let's see if we have all the ingredients," I say before checking the kitchen.

"Looks like we have everything. Let's get your homework done and then we'll start cooking and call Caleb and see if he wants to join us."

Charlie returns to her homework, and I pull the ground beef out of the freezer and unload the dishwasher. When we finish our tasks, she helps me cook dinner. I put the ground beef in a saucepan and season it while Charlie pulls a couple of leaves off the head of lettuce.

She stands on her stool in front of the counter with me behind her as she helps me cut the lettuce. I've been working on kitchen safety with her. She knows how to properly hold a knife and use it, although I never let her use one unsupervised and I've always guided the knife so far. She's enjoyed learning how to cook and being helpful.

At 7 p.m., I grab my phone and pull up Caleb's number. I hold my breath as I listen to it ring. After three rings, I hear a click on the other end and Caleb's voice.

"Hey, Bails."

I squeeze my thighs together, the sound of his voice and the way he says that nickname makes me needy.

"Hey," I breathe out. There's silence on both ends of the phone. I clear my throat. "So, Charlie and I were wondering if you'd like to join us for dinner. Charlie picked a meal she's sure you'll like." I chuckle.

"She did, did she? Well, how can I say no to that? What should I bring?"

"Just yourself."

"I'll be there in thirty minutes."

More silence lingers on the line as I smile like a fool. "See you then," I say.

"See you then."

I hang up and look at Charlie. "He's on his way. Why don't we make sure all your toys are cleaned up in the living room?"

She runs straight in there, and I hear the sound of her toys as she puts them in the bins. I grin to myself as I stir the ground beef, turning it down so it doesn't burn, and put the taco shells in the oven. I set the table and clean up the mess we made in the kitchen. As I hit the start button on the dishwasher, there's a knock at the front door. I'm suddenly full of nervous energy. I make my way into the living room, and Charlie is jumping up and down on her toes in the entryway. Her grin is so large I can see all her teeth.

I walk to the door, check the peephole, and see Caleb on the other side. When I pull it open, the breath leaves my lungs. Caleb is grinning at me, his smile so large and real there are lines around his eyes. His shirt is pulled tight across his chest and his jeans are sculpted to his body. I remember the feeling of my legs wrapped around his waist as he held me against the lockers earlier today. Heat fills my cheeks.

"Caleb," Charlie calls, and he crouches so she can wrap her arms around his neck as she hugs him.

"Hi, Little Bear."

She pulls back, and he stands.

"Hey, Bails." He holds up a shopping bag I hadn't noticed. "I brought dessert."

I step back and allow him room to come inside. Charlie grabs his hand and drags him to the kitchen. I follow behind them, take the shopping bag from Caleb, and stow the ice cream in the freezer.

"Mommy and I made tacos. You'll really like them," Charlie says excitedly.

Caleb smiles at her, and it melts me a little. This man looks at my daughter with such affection, so much so that he has a photo of the two of them in his locker.

"I do love tacos. It looks like you've got all the best stuff for them too."

We take our seats, Charlie insisting on sitting beside Caleb.

"Caleb, can you help me make my taco?" she asks, and he reaches over, grabs a shell, and makes it in the exact order she says the ingredients. He watches as she takes a large bite of her taco, stuff falling out of it and all over her plate. She smiles at both of us as she continues to eat.

"So, did your mom tell you we're going skating on Friday?" he asks.

Charlie's eyes widen comically. "We are?"

"Yup, I'm going to teach you how to skate. Then we can go and have dinner."

Charlie does a little dance in her seat, causing more of her taco to fall apart. I take in how happy she is. Before these last few weeks, I can't remember the last time she was this happy and carefree. She wasn't closed off after Derek left, but she felt the changes in the house. And I know that although she's seen the hurt he's caused me, she misses her dad. That male role model in her life. It's been difficult knowing I can't be everything for her; I've tried my hardest to make sure she knows she's loved and safe with me, but one person can't fully take on the role of two.

Charlie talks about how excited she is to go skating and what she's going to wear.

"Mommy, can you skate?"

Her question pulls me from my thoughts, and I shake my head quickly as I come back to the present.

"I haven't tried in a long time," I say, not wanting to admit I look like an elephant trying to walk on ice when I get out there. I was hoping to stand on the sidelines and watch Caleb teach Charlie.

Caleb arches a brow. "Bails, are you saying you can't skate?" Humour fills his voice.

"Not exactly. I can push myself along the boards. That's about it."

He grins. "Guess I'm teaching both you girls."

Caleb tells us about how his dad taught him to skate when he was a kid and how much he loved it and how that lead to him playing hockey. Charlie and I are both on the edges of our seats, listening to everything he says, but for different reasons. This is now something she can have in common with Caleb, a male role model teaching them to skate. But for me, it's that I want to know everything about this man. I want to know what makes him tick, what makes him sad, angry, and happy. What are his favourite things in life? What's his favourite colour? His favourite season? I can't remember the last time I wanted to know everything about a person, the way I do with him, and it scares the crap out of me.

When we finish our tacos, Caleb helps clear the dishes while I get the ice cream and dish us each a bowl.

"Mint chocolate chip is my favourite. Thought I'd share it with you ladies tonight," he says as we settle back at the table. I mentally add it to the list of things I now know about him.

His father taught him to skate.

His favourite flavour of ice cream is mint chocolate chip.

He served overseas but doesn't readily share that with people.

His friends all say he's a good one.

My list may not be large, but I hope to continue adding to it.

As soon as Charlie finishes her ice cream, I tell her to say her good nights and head upstairs to get ready for bed. She hugs Caleb before slowly making her way upstairs. I take our bowls to the sink, soaking them before looking at Caleb.

"I've got to make sure she's brushed her teeth and changed into her jammies," I say, and he smiles and nods. Not a big smile, but a soft intimate one that has me wanting to climb right into his lap. I close my eyes and take a breath, shaking that thought from my mind before smiling back at him and going to find Charlie. She's in her room changing into her pyjamas when I walk in.

"You brush your teeth?" I ask, and she nods. "Let me smell."

She opens her mouth wide and breathes right in my face, and the smell of mint from her toothpaste fills my nose.

"Good. Now let's climb into bed and read you a bedtime story."

"Can Caleb read me a story?" she asks as she rubs her eyes.

"Let me go ask him."

Walking into the kitchen, I find Caleb unloading my dishwasher. "You don't have to do that," I say.

He continues, despite my interruption. "I don't mind. Charlie in bed?"

"She was actually asking if you'd read her a bedtime story."

He puts a plate away and turns to me. "Of course, anything for her."

I lead him upstairs and into Charlie's room. As soon as she sees him, she scoots to the inside edge of her bed and pats the spot beside her.

"Caleb, you're going to read me a story?"

"Yeah. What story are we reading tonight?"

"*Llama, Llama, Red Pajama!*"

He chuckles, grabs the book from the bookshelf beside her bed, and climbs on top of the covers beside her. She snuggles into his side, and I watch the entire interaction from the doorway. He's so good with her. He gets right into the story, and she falls asleep before the book is over, but he reads it until the end.

When he's done, he stares down at her, and I wish I could read the emotions that cross his face as he stays there and watches Charlie. After a few minutes of silence, he slides out and makes sure she's covered and has Vanilla tucked right beside her before he meets me at the door. I step out, closing it softly before he follows me down the stairs into the living room.

Caleb

When we reach the last stair, all I want to do is grab Bailey, push her up against the wall, and take her mouth. I want to trail my lips down the soft skin of her jaw and neck. I want to taste her. I want to hear her moan my name, but I hold myself back and follow her into the kitchen where I resume putting away the dishes.

"You really don't have to do that, Caleb," she says, and I turn to face her.

"Bails, you and Charlie cooked me dinner. I don't mind helping with the clean-up, including putting dishes away. Why don't you grab a glass of wine and you can keep me company?"

She stares at me for several seconds, her beautifully bright blue eyes bouncing between mine. She nods and turns to the cabinet, pulling down two glasses. She pops the cork off the bottle of wine on the counter and pours two glasses, pushing one my way. I grab the stem and tap my glass with hers before taking a sip.

She sits at the island and spins her wine glass between her fingers. She seems unsure. I rest my forearms on the kitchen counter, leaning on them, my wine glass between my hands.

"You seem nervous," I say, and her eyes widen slightly, just enough that I notice, and she licks her lips. I swallow as my eyes track the movement.

"I haven't dated anyone in a long time."

Her back straightens like she's on full alert.

"Not that this is a date, not that we're dating. I didn't mean it like that. It's not like you want to date me because look at me and my baggage and then look at you and your hotness. Someone like you would never go for someone like me. Plus, you're a patient at my job. Please ignore me." She sighs. "Yes, I'm nervous."

I grin at her and her little rant. "Bails, calm down. Look at me."

When her eyes meet mine, I stare into them for a few seconds before I continue.

"Let's unpack all that. First, I already switched doctor's offices. Second, I am looking at you, and I love everything I see. Don't ever think I'm out of your league when, clearly, it's the other way around. You're beautiful and sexy. You're also smart and caring, and I want to know more about you so I can add to that list of great things about you. Third, we all have baggage. Yours won't scare me away. Mine is more likely to scare you away. Fourth, I appreciate the comment on my hotness."

I smirk as I move around the kitchen island, stopping beside her barstool. She turns to face me. I grip her chin between my thumb and forefinger, lean in close, and whisper, "And lastly, do you want this to be a date?"

Her mouth parts, the air that escapes dusting over my lips. My question hovers in the air between us. She closes her eyes and takes a deep breath before opening them again and meeting my gaze. She nods, and I smile.

"Good, because I do too," I whisper over her lips before kissing her.

I take my time brushing my lips over hers, relishing in the soft feeling of them. I deepen the kiss, and her arms wrap around my neck. The hand on her chin moves to wrap around the front of her neck while the other grips her hip and squeezes. She moans, and I lick the seam of her mouth, seeking permission. She responds by opening, and our tongues meet, fighting for control. My grip on her neck tightens slightly. She surrenders control to me, and I groan in response.

She spreads her legs, giving me space. I take full advantage and step between them, wanting as little distance between us as possible.

Breaking the kiss, my lips trail along her jawline as I lick and nip my way to her neck. I wedge my hands under her thighs and lift her onto the kitchen counter. She throws her head back as I position her just how I want. My erection presses into the zipper of my jeans. I bite her neck before licking it to soothe the pain. Her legs wrap around my hips and pull me in closer, and I instinctively roll my hips into her centre.

Her legs tighten around me, and my brain re-enters my body. I don't want just a hook-up with Bailey. If we're going to do this, I'm going to do it right. I drop my forehead to her shoulder and groan before grabbing her legs and unwrapping them from around me. My gaze lifts to hers, and embarrassment fills her expression. I know I need to put an immediate stop to it.

My hand moves to the back of her head, and I grab a handful of her hair. "Bailey, I want you, but I want to do this right. So I'm going to stop us before we go too far, and then I'm going to see you and Charlie for our date on Friday. Okay?"

The embarrassment fades, and a softness takes over her expression, one that looks almost grateful. She nods, and I take a step back, helping her off the counter.

"I should probably head home," I say, moving towards the living room, and she follows me. Opening the door, I step onto the front step before turning back to her. "Thank you for tonight, Bails."

She smiles at me. "Of course."

I kiss her softly, our lips barely touching, just enough that I can taste her and feel the bolt of electricity that goes through me.

"Lock up behind me," I say before jogging down the steps to my truck.

She watches me from the doorway. I turn the truck on but don't drive away until she closes the door. Pulling away from the curb, I make the drive home with a grin on my face the entire way.

The rest of the week drags on. I power through my shifts at work and manage to make it through our game this week, despite us losing. Finn keeps me occupied at home. Bailey and I text about random things throughout the week, and she tells me just how excited Charlie is to learn to skate. I'm excited to teach her. I remember my dad teaching me as a kid. Some of my favourite memories with him are out on the ice, and I'm glad I get to share that experience with Charlie.

Arriving at their place Friday night, I stop and take a deep breath. This is the first actual date I've been on in a while, and it's a lot. Not only am I taking Bailey out, but Charlie as well. They're a package deal and I wouldn't have it any other way, but this is huge and I don't want to fuck it up.

I'm still not sure how everything is going to go. This date doesn't mean that all of my issues are magically gone. I'm just deciding to try and move past them and give this a shot with Bailey.

After a minute, I hop out of my truck, make my way to the front door, and knock. Charlie's excited voice travels through the door and has me smiling already. Bailey opens the door, and my smile grows. She has her hair partly pulled back, and the bottom is in loose curls. She has a natural makeup look that makes her eyes pop, and her lips are painted a soft pink I want to kiss off her.

Charlie, calling my name, pulls me out of my trance of staring at Bailey.

"Hey, Little Bear. Are you excited to go skating tonight?"

She bounces on her toes as she grins. "Yes, it's going to be the bestest!"

I pass the bouquet of pink carnations in my hand to her. "These are for you," I say before passing the bouquet of red roses with baby's breath to Bailey. "And these are for you."

Both of them smile at their flowers. Bailey looks at hers, then Charlie's, then back to hers before she looks at me again. There's a small tear in the corner of her eye. I step forward and use my thumb to brush it away.

"What's wrong, Bails?"

She takes a deep breath and closes her eyes. When she opens them again, the glassiness is gone. "Nothing. These are beautiful, thank you."

I search her eyes for more and find nothing. She has her barrier up.

"You're welcome."

She holds the door open further, allowing me to step inside and follow them into the kitchen. Bailey pulls out two vases and fills them with water before helping Charlie get her flowers ready and then her own.

"Mommy, can I have these in my room?"

"Of course, Baby Girl, but let Mommy carry them upstairs. We don't want to spill them."

"Caleb can help me." She looks up at me with wide, hopeful eyes.

"Yeah, let's take them right now," I say, reaching out and taking the vase before following Charlie as she runs upstairs.

"I want them right beside my bed," she says as she taps her nightstand.

I put them down, positioning them far enough away from the edge that they shouldn't fall. Charlie wraps her arms around my leg and squeezes tight.

"Thank you, Caleb. I've never got flowers." Her voice is tinged with sadness.

I reach down, unhooking her arms from me before crouching in front of her and pulling her into a proper hug. "You're welcome."

She holds me tight for a few moments before she steps back. "Skating," is all she says, and I smile.

"Yeah, skating. You ready?"

She nods and runs out of the room. Bailey is standing at the base of the stairs, smiling at us. We grab our coats and make our way out the front door. Bailey reaches into her purse and pulls out her car keys.

"Do you want to take my car, or should I just grab her booster seat out?'

"We're all good in my truck."

Unlocking it, I open the back door and help Charlie in. I buckle Charlie in, making sure everything is secure, and turn around. Bailey's staring at me, mouth agape. I chuckle and walk up to her, placing two fingers under her chin and help her close it.

"Bails, you good?"

"You got her a booster seat?" Her voice is full of vulnerability.

"Yeah, I did. If I want to take you girls out, I need to make sure I have the proper things. I need to know you two are safe, so I grabbed the best-rated one and installed it. Now, no matter what, I know Charlie can ride safely in my truck."

Tears gather in the corners of her eyes. I cradle her face and wipe them away gently with my thumbs.

"Bails, what's with the tears today?"

She closes her eyes and takes a deep breath as if trying to gather herself. When she opens them, I fall into their bright-blue depths. They shine with her held back tears, and I want nothing more than to take any and all pain away from this woman.

"Nothing, it's just a lot to take in. Thank you, Caleb."

We stand there for a beat before I lean forward and place a soft kiss on her forehead. Her skin is soft against my lips, and her sweet scent fills my nose. I'll never be able to smell the mix of vanilla and jasmine and not think of this woman in front of me for the rest of my life.

Taking a step back, I open the passenger door, offering Bailey my hand as she gets in. When she's seated, I grab the seat belt and secure it for her before jogging around the front of the truck and sliding in. I start the truck and ask, "Everyone ready to go?"

Charlie excitedly says, "Yeah," while Bailey nods.

The radio plays softly in the background as we play a game of Eye Spy on the way to the rink. When we get there, I grab my skates out of the back, and Charlie insists on holding both Bailey and my hands. Inside, I pay for both Bailey and Charlie's rentals, insisting they both wear hockey skates instead of figure skates.

Bailey hangs around the boards while I help Charlie onto the ice. I hold her hands as I skate backwards and she gets her footing. She starts off slowly, figuring out how the blades feel as they glide and how hard she needs to push off.

I catch her a few times as she falls, but she begins to pick it up. After a couple of laps, I'm able to let go and just watch her as she slowly skates towards me. Her smile is contagious as she holds her arms to her side and slowly pushes forward. When we get back to Bailey, I attempt to show her how to stop, but it's not as easy for her. She slips a little, and I catch her, righting her on the ice.

"Did you see me, Mommy? I did one whole time all by myself!" Charlie exclaims.

"Yeah, Baby Girl, you did great!"

"Now it's your turn, Mommy."

"Come on, Bails, time for a spin," I say, reaching out my hand.

She takes it hesitantly, and I begin to move backwards as she lets me drag her along. Charlie works to follow us, and I make sure to keep a slow pace so I don't lose her.

I stop us and reposition myself behind Bailey, placing my hands on her hips and leaning in, my mouth beside her ear. "Just push off with your right foot, nice and easy."

She pushes off slightly, and I glide behind her.

"Mommy, you're doing it," Charlie says from beside me.

I smile down at her, watching and making sure she's doing okay. After we do a lap around the ice, we come to a stop, and Charlie asks, "Caleb, can you go around as fast as you can?"

"You want me to go as fast as I can?"

"Yeah, like superfast."

"Okay."

I turn, moving a little bit away from the boards so I can miss all the people using them as support, and I start. The air moves through my hair as I go on a straight breakaway up the ice. I lean into the turn at the end as I barely go over the goal line. My legs move faster as I hit the straightaway again.

I grin. It's been a while since I skated for fun, without it being for a game. I lean into the next turn and when I hit the straightaway, I head straight for Charlie. As I get close, I grab her, picking her up while still skating, and continue in my loop. She giggles as I lean into the turn, bringing her with me. She holds on tight, and I hold her back just as tightly. When we get back to Bailey, I stop quickly, sending ice shaving all over her legs. Both girls burst into laughter, and I follow suit.

I can't remember the last time I had this much fun and laughed like this. We continue to skate around for another half an hour before Charlie says she's hungry. We return their skates and head back out to the truck. I drive us to a little hole-in-the-wall Italian restaurant I want to share with them.

I've never brought anyone here. It's a place I came to after my first tour with a buddy I served with. We frequented it during our leave, and when he didn't make it home, I couldn't bring myself to share it with anyone else. But now, now, I want to share it with Bailey and Charlie. I may not be able to completely open up to them yet, but this is a first step. Sharing this isn't going to be easy.

I find parking in front of the restaurant and jog around the truck, opening Bailey's door and helping her out before I go to the back and grab Charlie. Opening the front door of the restaurant, the smell of spices and pasta hits me.

The terracotta-orange walls and the pictures bring me back to the late nights here with Tyler. I remember sitting at a corner table laughing for hours as he did some impression or told me stories from his childhood.

The memory is ripped away as the sounds of his screams invade my senses. I stiffen and start turning my head rapidly, looking for him. Looking for my friend as he cries out in pain. The smell of sand replaces the smell of food, and my nose scrunches. I hate that smell.

My skin radiates with heat, and I feel a soft hand on my arm. I want to flinch, to pull away or shove it away, but I force myself to remain still. It gently squeezes my arm, and then I hear my name. My head snaps in the direction of the sound, and the sounds of the past begin to fade as I slowly come back to the present.

Bailey's eyes captivate and hold me in place. She doesn't say anything else. Her nose flares as she takes a deep breath, her eyes encouraging me to do the same. I mimic her, inhaling deeply and allowing the air to fill my burning lungs. I hold it with her, releasing it as I feel her warm breath dance over my skin.

We do this two more times; me following her lead as we breathe together. Her face is full of worry, and I do my best to offer her a reassuring smile.

The bustling restaurant and smell of the food replace the screams and sand. My skin feels cool again, except for the spot where Bailey's hand is squeezing my arm.

"Is Caleb okay?" A note of fear fills Charlie's voice as she asks the question.

I look down at her and see it in her eyes too. I crouch in front of her, taking her hands in mine.

"Yeah, Little Bear, I'm okay. I haven't been to this place in a really long time. I've only come here with one other person. I was just remembering them."

Charlie nods, and I look at Bailey. I can tell she knows they weren't all good memories I was experiencing. *I'm okay,* I mouth to her, and she nods slightly. I plaster a smile on my face and approach the hostess stand to give them my name, and they lead us to a table in the corner.

CHAPTER 11

Bailey

Caleb's entire demeanour changed the second we walked into the restaurant. It was like he completely disassociated. His head jolted as he looked around. His eyes were wide and alert, and at one point, his nose scrunched, almost in disgust. Not wanting to startle him, I placed a hand on his arm and softly squeezed as I whispered his name. When his eyes found mine, I knew what he was experiencing at that moment wasn't pleasant. There was pain written all over his face, but mainly in his eyes. His steel-grey eyes were darker than I'd ever seen them, and his pupils were as wide as saucers.

Using my eyes, I encouraged him to breathe with me, and he did. I'm sure the smile he offered me after was meant to be encouraging, but it didn't fool me. Whatever he had gone through in those minutes had been difficult for him.

Seeing him reassure Charlie was a whole other thing. He told her the truth without telling her too much. So many people hide things from kids, but they're smart and observant. They notice things most people don't, and I know Charlie could tell Caleb wasn't acting like he usually does. She seemed satisfied with his answer, and she took his hand as the hostess led us to our table.

I read over the menu as Caleb helps Charlie decide what to get. Caleb and I sit in rapt attention as Charlie tells us her favourite things about skating tonight and how she wants to do it again.

I can tell Caleb isn't as relaxed as he was before we stepped into the restaurant. His shoulders are pulled back and tension radiates off him. He smiles at Charlie as she talks. I know his smile is real because of the wrinkles around his eyes, but it doesn't have its usual brightness.

Reaching across the table, I grab his hand and squeeze it. His head turns, and he meets my gaze. His eyes dart between where I'm holding his hand and my eyes. After a few seconds, I watch his body relax slightly and I smile as he squeezes my hand back.

Our hands stay intwined as we talk until our food is delivered. Caleb is reluctant as he pulls his hand away from mine for the server to put our food down. Caleb helps Charlie with everything she needs. I'm so used to having to help her with her food whenever we go out to eat that it's weird to sit here and be able to just eat my food. We talk and laugh with each other, and it's beginning to feel like the most natural thing in the world. The three of us are so comfortable with each other, as if this isn't new.

After we finish our pasta, Caleb and Charlie decide to share a dessert. They order a brownie covered in vanilla ice cream, chocolate, and caramel drizzle. Caleb pays the bill, and we gather our jackets and scarves and head to his truck. I stand back and watch as he helps Charlie get settled into the booster seat he bought. I'm still in shock and awe at the fact this man went out and bought it. Not only did he buy a booster seat for her, but he did the research and found the best-rated one.

When Derek and I had Charlie, I was the one who pushed for us to get everything ready to bring her into this world. I did the research and the budgeting. I made a list of everything we needed and put together a registry. Seeing someone else value my daughter enough that they went through the trouble her father wouldn't has me wanting to melt into a puddle. But I can't. I have to remember that Derek was sweet in the beginning too. It was after we got married that things changed. Then, the yelling started. The blaming me for everything that went wrong started. And after Charlie was born, the physical violence started.

First, it was just grabbing my arms tightly while yelling in my face because he was mad she was crying and I hadn't stopped it. Then it escalated to him hitting me because the house wasn't clean, Charlie was crying, and, in his words, all he wanted was some goddamn peace and quiet and a clean fucking house.

For years, I blamed myself. For years, I covered the bruises and didn't say anything, pushing through, thinking things would get better and my relationship would go back to the way it was before because I loved him. That was until he threw me down the stairs one day because Charlie had drawn on the walls in the upstairs hallway. That was my breaking point. Charlie had seen the whole thing. She was young enough that I'm not sure if she remembers it, but I couldn't risk it happening again.

I went to the hospital with four broken ribs, cuts all over my face, a split lip, and a bruised tailbone. That night after the visit to the hospital, I took Charlie to Lily's and filed for divorce the next morning. There was no going back for me.

I got the house when the divorce went through as I had inherited it from my parents when they passed, so Derek had to find somewhere else to go. He spent the next few months love-bombing me, trying to get me to change my mind. He apologized for throwing me down the stairs, saying it would never happen again. He started telling me about all the amazing things he would do for me if only I'd take him back. But I held strong. I knew I couldn't put Charlie in that situation again.

I was granted full custody, but Derek was granted supervised visits with Charlie. As he had not previously shown any violent tendencies with her, I couldn't keep her away from him. So that meant every other weekend, I was forced to see him. Forced to face the man who had hurt me, both physically and emotionally.

He used his visits to try to win me back, but I kept forcing his attention back to Charlie. Having him arrested is likely the only reason I haven't heard from him recently, and I thank God for that.

Caleb opens my door and helps me up before leaning across and doing my seat belt for me.

"Got to make sure you're both safe," he says with a smile before retreating to the driver's side.

We drive in silence as music plays through the stereo. When he gets to my place, he pulls up to the curb and opens my door, helping me down before moving to the back. Charlie is completely passed out. He unbuckles her and picks her up, cradling her to his chest before closing the door and walking to the front door.

He waits as I unlock it and toes his shoes off in the entryway before making his way up the stairs and straight to Charlie's room. I lean against the door frame as I watch him pull back the covers and gently place her in bed before tucking her in. He leans in and whispers something to her before meeting me in the hallway. As we walk down the stairs, my stomach tightens. I'm not ready for him to go.

"Do you want some coffee or something else to drink?" I ask in an attempt to get him to stay longer.

He smiles at me. "I should probably head out."

I feel the change on my face, and I know Caleb notices it too because his hand comes up and finds the nape of my neck, giving it a quick squeeze.

"Bailey, trust me, I'd love to stay, but I don't think I could hold myself back from you if I did. So I'm going to go and I'll text you and we can plan another date. I don't want to skip a bunch of steps with you, Bailey. I want to get to know you. I want to get to know your amazing little girl. I want to do this right and in order to do that, I think I have to leave. Okay?"

Heat fills my cheeks, and I nod.

"Good," he says before leaning forward until his lips hover over mine, and I hold my breath. "Can I kiss you good night?" His breath brushes over my lips as he whispers the question.

"Yes," I exhale, and his lips are on mine.

He kisses me softly, seductively. I moan into his mouth, wanting more, but he doesn't take it. His lips move slowly over mine, no tongue, just his lips brushing mine. He pulls back and gives my lips a couple of pecs before he says, "Good night."

I watch as he makes his way to his truck then I close the door, lock it, and lean against it. Tipping my head back, I close my eyes. I can still feel his lips on mine. I push myself off the door and quickly make my way up the stairs and into my bedroom. I strip and climb into bed, placing my phone beside me before reaching into my nightstand drawer and pulling out a rabbit vibrator.

I turn it on and drag it over my breasts, allowing it to vibrate on my nipples. The sensation causes them to stiffen. I continue down my body before positioning it at my entrance. Closing my eyes, I picture Caleb kissing me, picking me up and holding me against the wall in the hallway. Him leading me up the stairs and into my bedroom. I feel his lips on mine. Feel them brush across my skin and down my neck.

I pinch my nipple, imagining it's his teeth. A guttural groan leaves me. I'm so turned on.

I increase the speed of the vibrator, and my back arches off the bed. I moan Caleb's name as my body tightens. I imagine him hovering over me, removing my underwear and pushing down his boxers before thrusting inside me. That sends me right over the edge. I come calling his name as my back arches off the bed, my toes curl into my feet, and my hands reach for anything they can grab onto.

I turn off the vibrator as I hear a ding from my phone. Ignoring it, I go into my en-suite washroom and turn the shower on. When I'm done, I return to my bed and check my phone.

CALEB

God, Bails, that was fucking hot.

You're fucking killing me.

You should know listening to that had me coming harder than I ever have. I can't wait to get my hands on you.

I don't think I'll be able to walk away with just a good night kiss next time.

FUCK!

I scroll up and see I accidentally sent Caleb a voice recording of my entire masturbation session. He heard me moaning and calling his name as I came. I don't think I'll ever be able to face him again. I ignore the messages, plugging in my phone and setting my alarms for the morning.

Bailey

In the morning, I'm woken up by Charlie climbing into bed. She bounces on her knees as she says, "Mommy, you need to get up. Someone's at the door."

I groan and roll towards her, pulling her down and into my body to stop the shaking of the bed. She wiggles in my hold. "Mommy, someone's at the door. You said I can't open it until I'm a big girl. You need to open the door."

I groan, knowing my relentless daughter won't stop anytime soon. Rolling out of bed, I grab my robe then head downstairs. Charlie follows happily behind me. As I reach the bottom of the stairs, I hear the knocking.

"I'm coming," I grumble.

I grumpily pull open the front door and see a smiling Caleb on the other side. I slam the door closed and lean my back against it.

Why is he here? I can't face him after he listened to me last night. He'll get the hint and leave, right? I saw him and closed the door. That's a universal sign for *I don't want to see you*. Right?

"Mommy?" Confusion is all over her face.

"Yeah, Baby Girl?"

"Why did you close the door on Caleb?"

I don't know how to explain this to her, so I say, "Why don't you go into the kitchen, and I'll join you in a bit."

She gives me a quizzical look before she turns and leaves. My daughter is too observant for her own good, and pretty soon, it's going to bite me in the ass.

Another knock on the door. "Bails, I'm not going to leave, so you might as well open the door."

I bang my head on the door a couple of times before reaching back and rubbing the spot. Maybe I shouldn't have done that. Making sure my robe is tied tightly, I pull open the door and plaster on a fake smile.

"Hi, Caleb. What are you doing here?"

He gives me a stupid shit-eating grin that says he remembers last night as much as I would like to forget it.

"I thought I'd bring you and Charlie breakfast," he says as he holds up a brown takeout bag. His eyes rake up my body, pausing slightly at my chest and, likely, my nipples poking through the thin fabric.

I eye him, wondering what he's getting at. His smile just gets bigger, and I huff. Charlie saw him, and it would be more difficult to explain why I sent him away than it would be to put on my big girl panties and invite him in. I open the door more and usher him in. He steps inside before toeing off his shoes and making his way into the kitchen. Charlie calls his name the second he appears in the entryway.

I close my eyes and take a deep breath before following behind him. I beeline to the coffeemaker, putting on a pot while Caleb and Charlie chat at the kitchen table. Heat surrounds me as Caleb leans around me, and goosebumps scatter across my skin from his proximity. He grabs plates for everyone and takes them back to the table. I press the last button on the coffeemaker when I hear my phone alarm going off upstairs.

I turn and mumble, "I'll be right back," as I escape upstairs.

Making it into my room, I close the door, grab my phone, and silence the alarm. I grip my phone as I stand in the middle of the room, trying to figure out how I'm going to get out of this mess I've created. I decide the first thing I need to do is change into more appropriate clothes. Once I'm changed, I head back downstairs and see Caleb not only got us breakfast and set the table, but he's poured Charlie a glass of orange juice and each of us a cup of coffee and set the milk and sugar on the table.

My insides twist and turn as my mind races. As much as I'm embarrassed about last night and want to protect both mine and Charlie's hearts, I can't help but admit this man is chipping away at me and my shell is beginning to crumble. I want to walk over, kiss him, and say thank you for all of this. I want to open up to him and tell him my entire life story and believe he will hold it all safe.

I slide into my seat and smile at them. Charlie and Caleb continue their conversation as Caleb pushes the milk and sugar my way and they begin to eat. I make my coffee and take a deep sip, savouring the taste on my tongue. I eat and listen to the conversation. When Charlie is done, she asks if she can be excused before carrying her plate to the kitchen counter, leaving Caleb and me alone.

I avoid eye contact, picking at my food and sipping my coffee. He leans in close, his hand reaching forward and tucking a stray piece of hair behind my ear.

"I kind of wish you had kept the robe," he says softly.

My cheeks warm as a blush fills them. When I still don't meet his eyes, he puts two fingers beneath my chin and lifts my head, forcing me to make eye contact with him.

"Bails, you're embarrassed, aren't you?"

I nod.

"Don't be. Last night was hot. I'm glad it happened." He leans in so close that his lips brush over the shell of my ear. "Do you know how hot it is knowing you think of me when you get yourself off?"

I shiver.

"Would it make you feel better knowing I think about you when I jerk off? That I think about you on your knees and your pretty lips wrapped around my cock. How good I know you're going to taste on my tongue and how hot and wet your pussy will be when I finally get to have you. Bailey, this isn't one-sided."

He pulls back and continues drinking his coffee like nothing happened. My entire body is flushed, and I feel like I'm about to start sweating. I think I might need to change my panties after breakfast because the images his words created in my head have me wet and wanting to beg for all of it. I've never been one to want to give a blow job, but I'm sitting here wanting nothing more than to get on my knees and let this man use me for his pleasure. I squeeze my thighs together, trying to quench the ache growing between them, but it does nothing.

I take a long sip of my coffee to try to wet my suddenly dry mouth and throat. This man does things to me that no other person ever has, and I'm completely speechless. I finish my breakfast and take our plates to the sink, rinsing them before putting them in the dishwasher. When I close the dishwasher, I feel Caleb behind me. I turn to face him, and his arms go to either side of me, caging me in.

"Let me spend the day with you two. I want to spend time with you. No expectations."

Before I can think, "Okay," escapes my mouth.

He smiles before leaning down. "Good," he whispers across my lips before he places a soft kiss on them. He pulls back and asks, "So, what are the plans for today?"

"I have to go grocery shopping and Charlie needs to go to the mall and grab a gift for her Secret Santa at school. I need to meal plan for the week, do laundry, make sure Charlie has done her homework, call the mechanic and schedule my oil change and tire rotation, and clean the house," I ramble.

"Okay, so it sounds like we have a full day. Why don't you call your mechanic while Charlie and I review her homework?"

I nod, and he calls Charlie into the kitchen and asks her to bring in her homework. While they do that, I grab my phone and call the mechanic and schedule an appointment for next Saturday morning. I smile as I watch how good Caleb is with Charlie as they go over the letters she has been working on at school.

When I'm done making my list, we all bundle up and head outside. Caleb insists on driving, so he buckles Charlie in his truck before helping me up into the passenger seat.

We head to the mall first. He pulls into a parking space near the front of the mall, and we all hop out. Charlie begins to walk towards the mall, and I sternly call her name. She stops and turns to me.

"Yeah, Mommy?"

"What have I said about parking lots and cars?"

"To always hold an adult's hand," she mumbles.

"Are you doing that?"

She shakes her head before walking up to grab Caleb's hand. She's obviously annoyed at me, probably for correcting her in front of Caleb, but as long as she holds one of our hands, I'm happy. Caleb gives me a warm smile and reaches his free hand out for me. I hesitantly place mine in his, and he gives it a reassuring squeeze. Together, we walk into the mall and head into the closest store that I think may have something Charlie can take to school.

We wander around looking at different things, but nothing catches either Charlie's or my attention. On our way out, I stop at a glass showcase and take in a beautiful gold locket on display. I've always loved the idea of wearing a locket with pictures of those you love most in the world in it, but I've never been able to afford one I've liked. I hold back a groan as I see the price of the one inside the case. $250.00. Yeah, that's a no. Not this close to Christmas. I can't afford to splurge on myself like that. I walk away from the case, and we make our way through the mall. Charlie and Caleb spot the Build-a-Bear and both beeline for the store.

I know this bear is going to cost me a lot.

When I make it into the store, they are browsing the different animals. Caleb shows her the ones from *Star Wars* and is shocked when she says she hasn't seen it. He decides to make one for himself too and chooses a brown bear, and Charlie chooses a cow. I stand back as they go through the whole process of having them stuffed, whispering a wish to the animals' hearts, and then dressing them. Charlie helps Caleb pick the clothes for his bear, and they name them. Caleb keeps his name a secret, and Charlie names hers Princess.

When they finish, I join them at the register, pulling my card out to pay for Charlie's, but Caleb pushes my hand away and tells the cashier to put them together. I try and protest, but Caleb just looks at me and says, "Bails, you're not going to change my mind, so arguing over this is pointless. Let me buy her the cow."

I see in his eyes that he's serious.

"Fine," I huff. I let him pay, but I'm not happy with it at all.

When the new Build-a-Bears are in their little houses, we find a store to quickly grab Charlie her Secret Santa gift before we make our way back to the truck and head to the grocery store.

When we get to the store, Caleb grabs a cart and follows behind me. I have a very specific way I do my shopping. I start with produce, grabbing everything and putting it in the top part of the cart. I then move to the meat department at the back, then to the dairy, and then up and down every aisle.

When I've grabbed everything, the cart is overflowing and I have to say I'm glad Caleb is here because this would take me multiple trips inside when we get home. He and Charlie decide to be in charge of bagging, and I watch as he teaches her that the heavy stuff needs to go in first.

They load the cart, and I pay for the groceries before we head back to the truck. When we get home, Charlie grabs the two little houses and runs inside after I unlock the door. I grab a handful of bags and make my way inside with Caleb following. Everything gets placed on the kitchen counter, and I turn to go back to the truck, but Caleb stops me.

"Bails, I've got it. Why don't you just start putting everything away, and I'll bring it all in?"

I nod and get to work, putting everything in its proper place. When I finish, I go into the living room and find Caleb and Charlie cleaning up and putting her toys away. Caleb somehow has a thing of Lysol wipes and is wiping down my coffee table, side tables, and even the window sill.

I think I may start crying. I've never had this kind of help around the house without begging for it, and even then I almost always had to do everything myself. I return to the kitchen, lean against the fridge and take deep breaths, trying to centre myself again. When I open my eyes, I meet Caleb's assessing gaze.

"Thank you," I whisper.

He steps forward, and his hand comes up to my face. "Bailey, you keep thanking me for things I'm choosing to do. I want to help you. I don't want my presence in your life to make it more difficult. I want to make it easier."

His words are my undoing. I wrap my arms around his neck and pull him down for a kiss. I kiss him hungrily, trying to show him just what he does to me. I lick the seam of his mouth, and he moans into mine, granting me access. I've never taken control of a kiss like I am with him, and it's invigorating. He kisses me back, meeting my tongue stroke for stroke. I could fall into him and this kiss for the rest of my life.

A crashing sound from the other room has us pulling apart and running into the living room. Nothing looks broken, but I head straight for Charlie.

"Are you okay, Baby Girl?"

She nods. "Yeah, I just put the jeep in the box," she says.

I turn and see her Barbie Jeep stacked on top of all her other toys and figure she just threw it in and that was the crashing sound.

"Mommy, I'm hungry."

"Okay, what do you want?"

She holds her finger to mouth like she's thinking; I have no idea where she got that from. "Grilled cheese and tomato soup," she says.

I pat my thighs before getting up off the floor. I turn to the kitchen, but Caleb stops me.

"Why don't you go do the laundry you said you needed to do and I'll make lunch?"

"I've got it," I say.

"I know you do, Bails, but let me help. I make a mean grilled cheese."

He grins, and I relent. I make my way upstairs, gathering both Charlie's and my laundry before heading downstairs to the laundry room. After I'm finished, Charlie and I play in the living room while Caleb makes lunch.

Caleb

Today has been eye-opening. I don't think I fully appreciated my mother the way I should have after my dad passed. I always knew she did a lot and there was no one around to help her with a lot of it, but today, listening to the list Bailey had on a Saturday, made me appreciate both women so much more. I make a mental note to drop by my mom's place and do something for her so she knows how much I appreciate her.

I butter the bread and get everything ready to make lunch. Bailey thinks she needs to do everything herself because she has for so long, but I'm going to show her that if I'm around, it doesn't have to be that way.

Once the food is cooked, I get the table set and call the girls. We settle at the table, and Charlie makes a loud *Mmmmmm* as she takes a bite of her grilled cheese.

Bailey dips her sandwich into her soup and moans. I close my eyes as I remember her moans from last night. That voice message surprised me, but in the best way. The first moan I heard had me pushing down my boxer briefs and pulling out my cock. I jerked off to her sounds and hearing her call my name made me even harder. Listening to her come drove me over the edge, and it took everything in me to not just get in my car and drive over to her place right that minute. I had to settle for bringing her and Charlie breakfast and finessing my way into their day.

I clear my throat and take a spoonful of soup as I push the memories out of my mind. We sit and eat in relative silence, but it feels natural. I can't think of anywhere I'd rather be than sitting at this table with these girls.

It pisses me off to think that Bailey's douchebag ex gave all of this up. That he laid his hands on such an amazing woman. That he had such a lack of concern for his smart and loving daughter. I clench my fists, but the feel of Bailey's hand on my arm immediately has them relaxing.

I grab her hand and smile at her. She smiles back, and we continue eating. When we finish, I clear the table and load the dishwasher, turning it on.

"Caleb, will you watch a movie with me?" Charlie asks.

"Yeah. What movie do you want to watch?"

She jumps up and down on her tiptoes. "*Inside Out!*" she cheers.

"How about some popcorn, then?" Bailey asks.

"Yay!" Charlie squeals as she runs into the living room.

I follow behind her, settling on the couch. Charlie climbs into my lap, and I pull the movie up on Disney Plus. A few minutes later, Bailey joins us, sitting right beside me with a bowl full of popcorn, and I press play. We watch and pick at the popcorn until we reach the bottom of the bowl. Bailey puts the bowl on the coffee table then comes back and cuddles into my side.

I'm content. Charlie cuddled in my lap and Bailey cuddled into my side. When the movie finishes, Bailey sits up and I immediately miss having her so close.

"I should go transfer the laundry," she says before getting up and leaving the room.

"Caleb," Charlie whispers.

"Yeah, Little Bear?"

"You won't hurt Mommy, will you?"

My heart breaks in my chest at this wonderful little girl asking me that question. No child should have to ask someone if they'll hurt their parent. I wrap my arms around her, pulling her as close to me as possible, and kiss the top of her head.

"No, Little Bear, I'll never hurt you or your mom. I promise you that. And if anyone ever tries to hurt you, you tell me, okay? I'll always protect you."

And I mean that with every fibre of my being. No matter what happens between Bailey and me, I will always protect this little girl. I would protect both of them with my life if I had to.

She wraps her arms around me as much as she can and squeezes. I bury my nose in her hair and inhale her scent, allowing it to ground me from the anger that wants to take over my entire body for what these two have gone through. Bailey comes back into the room, and Charlie climbs off my lap and plays with her toys. I check my watch and see it's already almost 7 p.m. and decide I should head home and allow them to enjoy the rest of their night. I'm sure Finn would like his evening walk.

I pat my hands on the top of my thighs and push off the couch.

"I should head home," I say.

Charlie jumps up and wraps her arms around my legs. I run my hand over the top of her head and say, "I'll see you soon."

She nods and returns to her toys.

Bailey walks me to the front door but before she can open it, my hand goes to the back of her head. I pull her close and kiss her. She melts into me as my tongue invades her mouth, wanting to taste every inch of her. Her hands fist in my shirt, and it takes everything in me to not push her against the door and take her right now.

When we break the kiss, we're both panting, working to catch our breath. I rest my forehead against hers.

"I have a game tomorrow afternoon. Will you come?"

She licks her lips before nodding. A breathy, "Yeah," escapes her.

I kiss her forehead and make my way out the front door and to my truck.

When I get home, it feels empty. The walls aren't full of pictures. There's no mess of toys in my living room, and there isn't a feminine smell filling the air. The sound of Finn's claws on the hardwood floors seems to echo more. I never realized I was missing anything until recently, but I wasn't missing just anything.

I was missing Bailey and Charlie.

I take Finn on his walk. Coming home, I make myself a quick and easy dinner before settling on the couch and watching the game. The minute the game finishes, I feel restless. I text Grayson to see if he's up for a beer. When he responds, I head out.

I push the door open to our favourite sports bar, and the smell of stale beer fills my nose and the sound of music fills the bar. I find a couple of empty stools at the bar and take a seat, ordering a pint of a local pale ale. I watch the sports highlights as I wait for Grayson to join me. I'm pulled out of my concentration when a hand comes down on my shoulder, and I look over and see Grayson grinning at me.

"Hey, man. Thanks for joining me. I needed to get out of the house," I say as he pulls out the stool next to mine and waves down the bartender.

He orders, and when his drink is delivered, he goes right for it. "So, what's wrong?"

"What makes you think something's wrong?" I ask.

"Man, you're only this desperate to get out of the house when something is wrong. So spill. What's up?"

My shoulders sag as I release a sigh. "I'm kind of freaking out. I'm falling for Bailey and Charlie and I'm worried that if we do this, she's going to leave me, or I'm going to fuck it all up." I take a large sip of my beer before continuing. "She kissed me the other day and every kiss I've had with her has been the best kiss of my life. She does something to me. I've held off from sex, but I'm not sure I can any longer. Last night she accidentally sent me a voice message, and let's just say there will be no getting that out of my head anytime soon."

We sit in silence for a minute before I turn and look at my best friend. He's just grinning at me like an idiot.

"What?"

"I'm going to win that bet," he says, taking a sip of his beer. "You're going to marry that woman."

The thought goes through my mind. Being able to come home to both of them every day, growing a family with them, watching Charlie go to prom, graduate high school, decide what college she wants to go to, what she wants to major in. I want that, but I don't know if I can have it.

It feels so out of reach. I always thought I'd settle down and have a family, but being told by a partner that they can't handle certain parts of you does something to you. It flipped a switch in me. Even after we'd both said I love you, she just packed a bag one day and left. That had me deciding I wasn't going to try again because what's the point?

Grayson pats me on my shoulder. "See, I told you. Just enjoy it, man. If you have something good, explore it, see where it leads, and have fun."

We sit in silence for a while, and after we finish our beers, we each throw some cash on the bar and make our way outside. On the way home, I let Grayson's words sit with me. Maybe he has a point and this is worth exploring. I can't help but feel light, like a major weight has been taken off my shoulder and I can breathe easier at the thought of having Bailey and Charlie in my life permanently.

I decide I'm going to give this my all and see where it goes. I want that life with Bailey and Charlie, and I'm going to fight for it.

The next day, I do my own household chores before grabbing my bag and heading to the rink. As I'm walking towards the dressing room, I hear Charlie call my name. She runs at me with a Build-a-Bear house in her hands. I drop my bag and crouch. She drops the box in front of me, wrapping her arms around me, and I hug her back.

When she pulls back, she grabs the box and thrusts it at me. "You forgot your bear last night. Mommy said I could bring it to you today," she says.

"Thank you, Little Bear."

She gives me a big toothy grin, and I look up and see Bailey standing behind her. I stand to my full height and open my arms.

"Bails, you gonna hug me too?"

A blush colours her cheeks as she walks into my arms.

I wrap my arms around her tightly and lean down, to whisper in her ear. "Next time, I'm going to kiss you hello and I don't care who sees it. We're doing this, Bailey. You need to let me know if you don't want it."

She nods, and I pull back and look into her eyes. "Yes, you want this or yes, you're letting me know you don't?" I ask.

"Yes, I want this," she says.

I'm about to kiss her when Charlie calls, "Aunty Liv." I watch Charlie run towards Liv, who is standing with a group of people watching us. Bailey ducks her head and tucks a piece of stray hair behind her ear. I put a couple of fingers under her chin and lift her head.

"Are you ashamed, Bailey?" I whisper.

Her face fills with shock. "No, of course not. Why would I be ashamed of you?"

"Just checking," I say before leaning down and dusting my lips over hers. "Because I really wanted to do that."

There's a smile on both of our lips as we pull apart. I reach down and grab my bag and the Build-a-Bear box.

"I'll see you after, right? You'll stick around with Liv until I'm done?"

"Yeah, we'll stick around."

She smiles at me, and I turn around and face Charlie, who is with the group that's been watching us, but it looks like Olivia has kept her entertained with her back to us.

"Little Bear," I call, and she turns around. "How about another hug before I go change?"

She smiles and runs at me, wrapping her arms around my legs.

"I'll see you after, okay?"

She nods and runs back to join Liv. With one last smile to Bailey, I push open the door to the dressing room and head to my usual spot, dropping my gear.

I place the Build-a-Bear box on the top shelf of my dressing area and begin to check my sticks. Deciding to re-tape one of them, I rip the tape off and wrap it in a ball, throwing it in the garbage can in the centre of the room. Just as I finish applying tape to the bottom of my blade and begin to wrap it, a group of people stop in front of me. I look up and am met with a grinning Grayson, a smirking Matt, and a quizzical Josh.

"So, one beer last night and now you're kissing her for the world to see," Grayson remarks, and I go back to taping my stick.

"What's it to you?"

"Well, you see, I'm just curious how 'Mr. I Won't Ever Get Serious'"—he uses his fingers to make air quotes—"decides after one beer with me that he's now going to start kissing the single mom in public?"

I grunt.

"That's all you're going to give us? A grunt," Matt pushes.

"Seems like Caleb here might need a little incentive. Is it serious man, or should we get her number from Liv? Because I heard Luke saying how hot he found her."

My head shoots up, and I glare daggers at him. "Don't. You. Fucking. Dare." I emphasize each word as I grit my teeth. "You cross that line and I will help Hannah use every legal means possible to fuck with you."

Matt laughs. "Man, you really got under his skin if he's threatening you with Hannah." He claps Grayson on the shoulder.

"You're serious about her," Josh finally says.

I sigh. I've never been one to talk about my emotions, but it seems like it may be the only way to get them to back off a little. I disregard my stick and lean back against the wall.

"I tried to stay away. I tried to put space between us, but she just pulls me in. They both do. I can't even tell you what it is that pulls me in."

Now Grayson and Matt have sombre looks, but Josh is grinning like an idiot. He claps me on the shoulder before saying, "I'm happy for you, man."

"What's that supposed to mean?" Grayson asks him.

"That's exactly how I've always felt about Olivia. Even before my feelings for her became romantic. I couldn't be in a room with her without gravitating towards her. I always had this nagging urge to talk to her. To be near her. To hear her laugh or see her smile. It's still that way. Every time I walk into a room, I find her immediately. I still want every one of her smiles and laughs directed at me."

There is a softness to his features that's only present when he talks about Liv. You can see he has affection for his sister when he talks about her, but with Liv, he completely melts. I know in every part of myself he would die for her if he needed to.

I lean my head back, close my eyes, and allow his words to sink in. I'm falling for this woman. I'm falling for a woman I barely know, but it's not just her I'm falling for, it's her daughter too. I think I'm royally fucked because I don't see a way to stop it, and I'm not sure I want to.

Bailey

Charlie is completely enraptured by Olivia, allowing Hannah to pull me aside to chat. The other girls weren't able to come out tonight, so it's just Liv, Hannah, Charlie, and me cheering on the team today.

"So, I heard from a little birdy that Caleb kissed you outside the changing room before the game," she says with a shit-eating grin. "I guess you decided to take my advice and go for it."

I blush, remembering all the events that have gotten Caleb and me to this specific spot. Hannah's finger does a circular motion in front of my face. Her smile grows larger and her eyes light up.

"Okay, spill because women don't blush like that for nothing."

Olivia catches the motion and comes to sit beside us as Charlie decides she's going to run an entire lap around the boards. I can see the entire thing, so I let her. It will help wear out some of her energy and hopefully make putting her to bed tonight easier.

"Okay, spill," Hannah says, nudging me.

I sigh. I've only met Hannah recently, but I know she's relentless and I'm not going to get away with saying nothing.

"So, I ended up working a flu vaccine day at his precinct, and he was our liaison. He caught one of the guys flirting with me, and honestly, I wasn't not flirting back. But Caleb came up and was all alpha and told the guy to get back to work and basically, without actually saying it, said I was off limits. So when he took me to his locker to give me back the container his cookies came in and I saw a photo of him and Charlie in his locker..." I trail off. "I may have jumped him and kissed him." I rush the last words out as quickly as possible.

Their mixed expressions of amusement and pride tell me they heard.

"He then told me he promised to teach Charlie how to skate. That night, I invited him over for dinner. Then we went on a date Friday, and it was good." I blush, thinking about it. I'm still embarrassed about it, but it also turns me on knowing how much Caleb enjoyed receiving it.

Hannah's eyes narrow. "More happened. You're not telling us everything. We want everything."

I cover my face with my hands as I say, "I may have accidentally sent him a voice message of me masturbating while thinking about him and calling his name." My hands are pulled away from my face, and I'm left staring at their shocked expressions.

"I'm sorry, I'm going to need you to repeat that," Olivia says. "Because I believe you just said you accidentally sent Caleb a voice message of you masturbating and calling his name."

I nod, and both girls break out into uproarious laughter. I shove their shoulders.

"This isn't funny. I was mortified. I found out I sent it because he texted me about it. Then, to top it off, the fucker showed up at my house Saturday morning with a cat-who-ate-the-canary look when I answered the door. If it wasn't for the fact that Charlie had seen him, I'm not sure I would have answered the door after I slammed it in his face. He used my daughter and breakfast to weasel himself into the house."

The girls continue to laugh so hard they clutch their stomachs. After a few seconds, their laughter dies down and they wipe at the tears leaking from their eyes.

"So glad you two can have a laugh at my expense," I huff.

"Girl, when Josh and I had just started to date, I woke up on the couch one day and he was sitting there reading on my Kindle. He had opened up one of my dark mafia romances. I was mortified. But it did turn out good in the end because he's now taken to finding inspiration from my books. He's not intimidated by them, he uses them to his advantage." She rubs her hand lovingly over her belly. "I wouldn't be surprised if one of those inspiration nights made this little one."

The guys walk out and begin to make their way towards the ice. Just as Caleb walks past, Hannah calls, "Hey Caleb, I hear you have a fondness for voice messages."

I elbow her in the side, and Liv covers her mouth, trying to suppress her laugh.

He grins mischievously. "From Bails, hell yeah. Think they might be my favourite." He winks at me before he steps onto the ice and does a lap.

A blush covers my entire body at this point.

I know I need to steer this conversation somewhere else. I pat my thighs and ask Liv about the baby until it's time for puck drop.

Charlie cheers loudly for Caleb every time he's on the ice. Near the end of the second period, he goes on what Liv says is called a breakaway towards the other team's goal. He fakes a pass across the ice to the left, sending the goalie following the movement, and then he shoots into the top corner. I jump and cheer as he skates towards where we're sitting and points at me, mouthing, *for you*.

I sit back down, and Liv bumps my shoulder.

"That means something," she whispers.

I look at her, not sure how that could mean something. She must be able to read the question on my face because she says, "In high school, the guys would point to whoever they were trying to impress, and it usually meant nothing. Then, as the guys got older, they didn't do it anymore, but Josh did it for me when we started dating. No one knew we were seeing each other. That was the first time I had seen him do it. I watched his college games sometimes, and he never did it during those." She analyzes my expression as her eyes bounce around my face. She smiles softly. "It's a good thing, babe. It's definitely a good thing."

I spend the third period absorbing her words. When the game horn buzzes, the score is 4-3, and Caleb's team wins. The guys come off the ice, and I watch as Josh and Caleb make their way to us. When Caleb's close, Charlie runs to him. He picks her up, and she wraps her legs around his middle.

"You won!" she calls as she jumps in his arms.

He smiles at her. "We did."

Caleb puts her down, and she joins Liv and Josh while he makes his way to me. I stand and smile at him. He smiles back before bending and placing a kiss on my lips. Despite how PG the kiss is, the effect is the complete opposite. It leaves me wanting more. I want to wrap my arms around him, pull him in, and taste his mouth. But I don't.

"I think I need a kiss before every game to make sure we win," he says with a grin.

I bat my lashes up at him. "We'll see." I rise on my tiptoes and whisper in his ear, "You'll have to be a good boy to make sure."

He groans, leaning his forehead on my shoulder and gripping my hips, giving them a squeeze. "Woman, you're killing me."

When he lifts his head, I take a step back, hoping the distance will prevent me from doing something I shouldn't.

"I, uh, should take Charlie home. I have to get dinner ready and get her ready for school tomorrow."

His eyes search mine. Apparently finding what he's looking for, he nods and says, "One more kiss for the road?"

I smile and wrap my arms around his neck, going up on my toes to kiss him. His arms wrap around me, and his hand finds my ass, squeezing it. This second kiss begins to cross the line of PG as he licks at my lips before giving them a nip. A throat clearing behind Caleb has us tearing apart.

"As much as I'm greatly enjoying the show," Grayson says grinning at us, "But, I'm not sure how much longer Liv is going to be able to distract Charlie. I think Liv has started her 'I gotta pee' dance."

I turn and look over my shoulder and see Liv bouncing from foot to foot, and yup, I remember doing that dance.

"Charlie, say your goodbyes. It's time to head home."

"But, Mommy, I want to spend more time with Aunty Liv," she calls.

"I know, but you'll see them soon. Let's get you home and fed so we can go to bed."

She gives me a pouty face. I know how much she wants to stay. Caleb squats down.

"Come here, Little Bear."

She walks right into his arms and hugs him. He whispers something to her, and she nods against his shoulder. When they pull apart, Charlie walks up to Olivia and hugs her before meeting me and taking my hand. I mouth a silent *Thank you* to Caleb before calling and waving my goodbyes.

Over the next few weeks, Caleb and I text daily. He checks in with me. He asks about Charlie and her school. He invites us to his games. And with Olivia also asking us to go, I can't say no. I can't stay away from this man for some reason. I thank my lucky stars that I don't hear from Derek. I'm not going to actively seek him out about his visitations with Charlie because I'm not sure what I'm going to do when I'm forced to see him again. Caleb has been my rock, and that scares the crap out of me. The last time I leaned on a man this much, it didn't turn out well.

Charlie loves seeing Liv and Caleb and going to all these games. She has this new support system of people who genuinely care about her, and it feels as though a weight has been lifted off my shoulders. I'm just not sure how long this peaceful feeling in my life will last.

CHAPTER 15

Caleb

Having Bailey and Charlie at my games over the last few weeks and talking to Bailey has provided a levity in my life I didn't know I needed. The stress from work falls aways when I'm with them. I'm mentally present with them too. My mind doesn't wander the way it does in other situations. I don't sit at home and allow my thoughts to wander to the what-if places they tend to go. I feel like I'm more myself, like the me before my last tour.

I shower and change relatively quickly after the game. I want to make it home to take Finn for a decent walk tonight.

"You down for a beer?" Grayson asks as I shoulder my bag.

As I open my mouth to respond, my phone rings. I pull it out and smile when I see Bailey's picture and name on the screen.

"Hey, Bails."

"Caleb." Her voice shakes with fear, and my entire body stiffens on alert.

"Bailey, what's wrong?"

"He left a note on my door," she whispers and takes a deep breath. "He said he's going to come back."

I immediately drop my bag and sticks and begin running towards the door.

"Bailey, get in your car, lock the doors, and drive somewhere public."

I yank the dressing room door open and run at a full sprint

through the rink and out to my truck. When I get in, I tear out of the parking lot, not caring about the speed limit. I need to make it to Bailey. She stays on the line with me as she drives to the strip mall a few blocks from her place.

A few minutes later, I pull in right beside her car and jump out, jogging right up to her door. She unlocks it, and I pull it open. She undoes her seatbelt and wraps her arms around my neck. The contact allows me to finally release the breath I've been holding. I peek in the back and see Charlie peacefully asleep.

I hold her tightly as her tears hit my shoulder. We stay like that; me crouched there holding her close for a few minutes. When she seems to gather herself, she pulls away and I wipe my thumbs over her cheeks, taking the stray tears with them.

"Thank you," she whispers.

"You don't have to thank me, Bails." I lean forward and place a kiss on her forehead. "Are you okay?"

She takes a deep breath before nodding. "Yeah, the note just scared the shit out of me."

"Okay, why don't we go grab some of your stuff? I'll go with you and I'll call the guys to meet us there, just in case. Then we can head to my place."

"I can call Lily and see if we can stay with her."

I force her to meet my eyes so she knows just how serious I am when I say, "Bailey, I'm not letting you and Charlie stay anywhere other than my place. I'm not going to change my mind about this. I need to know you guys are safe and the best way to do that is to have you with me. Okay?"

Another tear falls down her cheek, and I wipe it away. She smiles a sad smile and nods.

"Okay. Let me talk to the guys and then we'll head over to your place."

I grab my phone and move to the back of my car.

CALEB

I need you guys to meet me at Bailey's.

Shared contact: Bailey

GRAYSON

On my way.

MATT

Be there in 10.

JOSH

"Okay, they're on their way. You okay to drive? I'll be right behind you."

"Yeah, I'll be okay."

I tap the top of her car before she closes the door. I head to my truck and follow her back to her place. When we get there, I open Bailey's door for her and place my hand out, palm up.

"Give me your house keys. I'm going to check the house before you two come in." She places the keys in my hand. "Lock the car, only open it for me or one of the guys, okay?"

When she nods, I jog up the front steps and unlock the door. I cautiously make my way through each room. Confirming it's empty, I go back and join Bailey. As I'm opening her door, Grayson and Matt pull up. I open the back door, unbuckle Charlie, and help her out of the car.

I crouch in front of her. "Little Bear, can you go and pack a bag? You and Mommy are going to do a sleepover at my place for a bit. I'll be inside in a minute."

She nods with a smile and runs inside cheering, "Yay, sleepover!"

"Bails, I'll be right in. Go get your stuff. We'll be right out here. Just shout if you need anything." I kiss her cheek before she heads inside and turn to face the guys.

Josh's car pulls up, and he joins us.

"So, what's up? Bailey and Charlie are going to stay with you?" Grayson asks.

I sigh and run my hand through my hair as I try to tamper down my anger. "Yeah, Bailey's ex apparently left a note on her front door. She saw it when she got home. He said he'd come back, and I'm not risking anything. I need to know they're both safe."

"We've got you, man," Josh says. "Go inside with them. We'll hang out here until you guys are ready to go."

"Yeah, go," Grayson adds. "Is your truck unlocked? I've got your bag in mine."

"Yeah, thanks, guys. I appreciate it."

They lift their chins, and I turn and hustle inside. I make my way up the stairs and into Charlie's room, finding both girls working on packing for Charlie. I place my hands on Bailey's hips, and she tenses. When she looks over her shoulder and sees it's me, her body relaxes and she leans into my touch.

"Bails, go get yourself packed. I'll help Charlie, okay?"

She lets out a sigh, like me doing this is such a relief. "Thanks, I've got her underwear and socks packed and I started on her pants, but she still needs everything else."

"Sounds good."

Bailey leaves, and Charlie and I get to work on packing her clothes. I pack as much as I can, not knowing how long they'll be staying with me.

"Why don't you put together some toys you'd like to bring? Make a pile and I'll find a box to put them in, okay?"

Finishing in Charlie's room, I pop my head into Bailey's. "Bails, pack for a while. I want to err on the side of caution."

She nods as she continues packing, tension filling her shoulders. This is stressing her out.

"I'm going to run Charlie's bag downstairs. I'll be back," I say.

I head out onto the lawn, putting Charlie's bag in my truck. "Hey, I have a favour to ask of your wife," I say to Josh as I move towards the guys.

"Shoot."

"Can you have her, or maybe one of the girls, put together a relaxing basket? Bath bombs, Epsom salts, candles, tea, hot chocolate, some snacks. I'm going to order us dinner, but Bailey needs something to relax."

Josh's fingers fly across his phone screen as he texts Olivia. "She says she'll have it to your place in the next thirty minutes."

"Thanks."

I run inside and help Charlie pack her toys and Bailey carry her luggage downstairs. Everything gets packed into the back of my truck. As I'm closing the tailgate, a car pulls up and stops across the street. I immediately recognize the driver, and I'm completely on alert. My hand instinctively goes to my hip where my gun sits while on duty, but I feel nothing.

"Bailey, take Charlie inside and lock the doors. Don't come outside for anything."

I don't hear anything, so I look over my shoulder and see her looking at me. When the door to the car across the street opens, her eyes widen and fear fills her face. She grabs Charlie and runs inside.

Derek approaches the house, but before he can step onto the property, I call, "You're not welcome here. I think you should go back to your car and leave."

He eyes me, and a look of disgust spreads across his face. "And who do you think you are to tell me when I can see my wife and daughter?" he spits, anger lacing his voice.

"Ex-wife," I correct.

"Bailey doesn't know what she wants. She'll be back with me as soon as I talk to her."

My body heats, and I clutch my hands into fists as anger rises through me. Over my dead body will this man talk to Bailey.

My Bailey.

"You're not going to talk to her. Like I said, you're not welcome here. You need to leave before I call the cops."

His eyes widen, and he lifts his hand and snaps his fingers like he's just made the world's biggest discovery. "I knew I recognized you. You're the officer that showed up when my daughter accidentally called 911," he says like it's the juiciest bit of gossip. "What do you think your superiors would say if they knew you're hanging out at the house of one of the calls you responded to?"

"That call wasn't an accident," I say, choosing to ignore his question.

He takes a step towards me and as he does, the guys move in closer, silently supporting whatever move I decide to make. Derek stops in his tracks as his eyes bounce between the four of us. None of us are exactly small, and there's no way he could take on all of us.

"This isn't over," he spits. "Let that little whore know that she'll be mine again."

I snap, grabbing him by the collar and holding him against my truck. "Don't you ever disrespect her like that again," I growl in his face. "I also don't recommend threatening her in front of me, either."

I lean forward so my head is beside his and lower my voice so only he can hear me. "I may be sworn to uphold the law, but you don't want to see just how quickly I'd be willing to break any and every law to protect those two girls. I served. I have all the training to back me up. So, I recommend you climb your ass back into your car and drive away before I show you just how serious I am."

I shrug off of him and take a step back, allowing him just enough space to slide out from between me and the truck. I watch as he climbs into his car and peels down the street. It's not until I can no longer see his brake lights that I turn back towards the house. Climbing up the stairs, I unlock the front door with Bailey's keys that are still stashed in my jeans pockets.

"Bails, it's me," I call as I make my way up the stairs. I head straight for Bailey's room and slowly push the door open. "Bailey, it's me. He's gone."

Movement out of the corner of my eye catches my attention, and I see she had positioned them in the corner of the room behind the door so she could see the entire room and would be hidden from anyone who enters.

It hits me like a stab to the gut that she knows that tactic. No person should have to know to do that to protect themselves. I fall to my knees in front of them and pull them both straight into my chest. We stay like that for a few minutes, just holding each other.

When I pull back, I meet Charlie's scared eyes and I crack even more.

"Is Daddy going to hurt Mommy again?" she whispers.

I hold her face on either side, making direct eye contact with her. "Little Bear, I promise I will do everything I can to protect you and your mom. I promise I will always do my best to make sure that nothing happens to either of you."

I kiss her forehead, keeping my lips pressed there as I try not to let my tears fall. I'm not a crier, never have been, but these two have me doing things I never in my life thought I would.

I move back and rest on my ankles, forcing a smile onto my face. "Now why don't we go back to my place and order pizza for dinner?"

They both nod, and we get up. We make sure we have everything, and I do another walk-through of the house to make sure all the windows and doors are closed and locked. When that's done, we gather on the lawn. The guys all push off my truck as we make our way towards it.

"Thanks guys, I appreciate you being here."

They all say, "Of course," and "Anytime," before hopping into their own cars and heading out. I text Bailey my address so she has it in her GPS, but she follows behind me the entire way. I religiously check my rearview mirror to make sure she's there. The tension in my body doesn't start to ease until we pull up outside my place.

I round the truck and grab their bags. Before unlocking the front door, I say, "My dog Finn is inside. He's big, but he's friendly and I'm sure he's going to love the company. I guess I should have asked if you're allergic."

"Nope," Bailey says as she shakes her head.

Charlie looks at me with a wide smile. "You have a dog?"

"Yup. He's a black lab. His name is Finn. He loves treats, pets, and walks."

An excited squeal escapes Charlie. As I put my key into the lock, I hear Finn's excited paws on the other side of the door. I push open the door and usher them in, locking the door behind us. Charlie is immediately loving on Finn, and he's licking her face.

I take in my living room and am thankful I took yesterday to do a deep clean, otherwise, there would be dust everywhere. I may also be guilty of leaving my socks in the living room after a long day of work. I lead the girls up the stairs, Finn following, and into the guest room that's set up. I have three bedrooms, but I only have one set up and ready for guests.

I push open the door and take their bags to the bed. Finn runs and jumps on the bed.

"Finn, down."

He looks at me, tilting his head, but I continue to stare at him. He relents and jumps off the bed. I lead him into the hallway, closing the door behind him.

"Sorry about that. If he does it again, just kick him off and close the door. He likes to sleep on my bed, so he's used to just jumping up."

"It's all good. It's his house. Don't worry about us. We appreciate the place to stay." Bailey smiles at me, but it's an uncomfortable one. I know she doesn't like being in a situation where she needs help, but I'm going to give it to her because, for some reason, I can't walk away from these two.

"Charlie can crash in here, I'll take the couch, and you can have my room. Tomorrow, I'll get your room set up."

"We can stay in here together. You're already offering us a safe place to stay. I don't want to put you out anymore."

"It's not a problem, Bailey. I've been meaning to get it set up for a while now."

She sighs, too tired to fight me. "Fine, but for tonight, I'll stay in here. You're not sleeping on the couch for me."

Not wanting to push her anymore, especially after what she's gone through today, I relent. "Okay. Well, I'm going to order us pizza. Why don't you girls get settled while I grab the rest of the bags?"

When I open the door, Finn is lying across the floor in the hallway. He sits up, and I scratch the top of his head before making my way to the truck. I grab the last couple of bags and as I'm making my way up the front steps, Olivia pulls up to the curb. She climbs out of her car and grabs a basket from the back seat, carrying it up to me. I smile as I take in just how full the basket is. I can see all the things I listed to Josh and much more. Liv has gone all out with this relaxation basket.

She stops in front of me, offering me the basket. "I got everything you suggested. Great suggestions, by the way. Plus, I added some more things I thought she might enjoy. I also added some things for Charlie in there."

"Thanks, Liv. This means a lot. I'm sure she's going to love this."

"Of course. Please let her know that if she needs anything, she can call me." She looks around me before she continues. "Is she doing okay? I'm guessing she's a little overwhelmed right now. I know what it's like having to pick up and move somewhere you weren't expecting to."

"Yeah, I don't think the part about leaving her place is what's bothering her the most, though. It's thinking they're putting me out. That's the last thing I want her to worry about. There is no other place on Earth I'd want them right now. It's just going to take her some time to adjust."

I feel Olivia's accessing gaze. She's scrutinizing me and my words.

Finn walks up to her and nuzzles against her leg. She reaches down and scratches his head while still looking at me. My stomach tightens. I'm worried she's going to think the girls would be better off somewhere else, maybe at her place, but then a smile spreads across her face and my stomach loosens.

"You're falling for her," she says wistfully.

My entire body straightens. I run a hand through my hair and grip the back of my neck, not sure what to say.

She reaches forward and grips my arm. "Caleb, you don't have to say anything. I'm happy for you. For both of you. She deserves someone as great as you."

"I'm not sure about that."

"Now what in the world makes you say that?"

I sigh. "Liv, you know I love you like a sister. You're my friend's sister and my other friend's wife, but there is some shit I'm just not going to share."

She squints at me. It's like she's trying to will the information out of me, but I don't budge. She squares her shoulders and stands taller before crossing her arms over her chest. She inhales a deep breath, letting it out slowly.

"When Josh and I started dating, I had just gotten out of a relationship where I walked in on my boyfriend cheating on me. He then continued to make me feel bad about myself so I'd go back to him, because in his words, 'No other man would be able to love me because of my size.' I carried that baggage around all throughout the beginning of my relationship with Josh, and it still affects me. Do you think Josh would be better off without me and my baggage? Do you think I should have walked away from the man I love because of it?"

Her words hit me like a sledgehammer. I had no idea she had gone through all that. I wish I hadn't let her ex off with a warning at the summer barbeque and had just arrested him for harassment.

"Liv, first, I had no idea things with your ex were that bad. And second, I would never say Josh is better off without you. You two are perfect together. I've never seen Josh as happy as I have since you two got together."

"So if you wouldn't say that to me, then why would you say it about yourself?"

I open my mouth to respond, but before I can say anything, she begins backing away.

"Well, I need to get home to my husband. He's cooking dinner."

She turns and heads back to her car, and I'm left there staring at her retreating back. I continue standing there even after her car pulls away until Finn nudges me. It pulls me out of my staring, and I head inside.

CHAPTER 16

Bailey

I'm standing on the stairs when Caleb comes inside with his arms full of our bags and what looks like a basket filled with goodies. I rush down the stairs to meet him. When I reach for my bags, he turns so they're out of my reach.

"Come on, Caleb, let me help you. You're going to drop something."

He grunts and makes his way up the stairs. I follow closely behind him. He turns into the guest room he's set us up in. The room is nice, especially for a guest room. A queen bed is set in the middle of the room. It's covered in a soft grey comforter and matching sheets. Two matching nightstands are on either side, and a dresser that matches the nightstands sits at the end of the bed. A chair sits in the corner to the right of the bed. A decent-sized walk-in closet is beside the dresser. The room feels welcoming.

Caleb places our bags on the bed and then turns, handing me the basket he brought in.

"I asked Liv to put this together for you. She added some of her own ideas as well. I figured after dinner, you could take a bath to unwind from today."

I look inside the basket and see bath bombs, candles, tea, and hot chocolate. There are also colouring books and crayons for Charlie. I smile at him.

"You really are the best."

I think I see the tips of his ears turn pink. He rubs his hand over the back of his neck before reaching for the bin of Charlie's toys.

"Charlie, why don't we find a good place downstairs to get you set up before dinner gets here?"

Charlie excitedly follows him down the stairs, and I fall wistfully back on the bed. This man. I'm not sure how he could be more perfect. He dropped everything the second I called him about Derek. I could hear him running as soon as I told him, and he stayed on the phone with me until he was standing right in front of me. And now he had a friend make a care basket for Charlie and me.

I wipe at the tears that have started running down my cheeks. Have I really been so neglected that these acts of kindness from Caleb are making me cry?

The doorbell rings, and a minute later Caleb calls, "Bails, food is here."

"Coming," I call and wipe away the last few tears.

I stop in the washroom and make sure I'm presentable before joining them downstairs. Finn is eating in the corner of the kitchen while Charlie is helping Caleb put plates on the table. He opens the large pizza box in the centre of the table. Turning, he goes to the fridge, returning with a bottle of ranch. He has a beer and a glass of wine already poured and on the table. I pull out a chair across from Charlie, and we eat our dinner.

When we finish, I go to clean up, but Caleb grabs my wrist gently, stopping me. "Leave it. I'll take care of this. You get Charlie ready for bed so that we can get you a bath drawn."

He pushes away from the table, gathering all the dirty dishes and making his way to the kitchen sink. I watch him for a second. The simple movement of rinsing the dishes has the muscles in his back rippling.

He looks over his shoulder, catching me staring, and smirks. I duck my head and tuck a stray piece of hair behind my ear, attempting to hide my blush.

"Come on, Charlie, time for bed."

She follows me, and we make our way upstairs. I draw her a bath and get her pyjamas ready. We make tonight a quick one because it's already much later than I was hoping to get her to bed. As I'm tucking her into bed, Caleb appears in the doorway.

"Do you have a book for bedtime?" he asks her.

"Can you read *Llama Llama Red Pajama* again?"

He hops onto the middle of the bed and Charlie curls into his side as I pass him the book.

"Say good night to your mom. She's going to go have a bath," he says, his way of dismissing me.

I lean down, kiss my girl on the forehead, and say good night before retreating into the washroom and turning on the hot water. I pull out the bottle of lavender bubble bath and pour a generous amount in before I strip.

Something in the bottom of the care basket catches my eye, and I do a double take. Sitting at the bottom, under everything else, expertly hidden, is a box with an image of a bullet vibrator. My eyes widen. Sneaky Liv putting this in here. I flip the box over and in all capitals written at the bottom of the box is WATERPROOF. My eyes bounce between the bath and the box. I grin to myself; Caleb did say to take a bath to relax. What better way to relax than an orgasm?

I take the bullet out and slowly dip my feet in the water, adjusting to the warm temperature before completely submerging my body. When the water and bubbles completely cover me, I turn the bullet on and run it over the skin of my neck, down to my right nipple. I hold it there until it hardens and then slowly move the bullet across my chest, doing the same to the other. The vibrations travel through my nipples, and my core clenches.

Slowly, I drag it in a zig-zag pattern down my stomach and between my legs, finding my already sensitive clit. My back arches at the sensation that travels through my entire body. The moan that's torn from my body reverberates around the tiled washroom. I bite my lip, hoping to hold back anymore noises.

Closing my eyes, I lean my head back and allow images of Caleb to flood my mind. I remember his kisses that leave me wanting more, the feeling of his body pressed against mine each time we've hugged, and the tenderness and protectiveness in his voice when he rushed to my side today

I'm on the edge, every muscle in my body begins to tense, ready for the relief that will flood my system when I finish. A knock on the door has me jolting slightly.

"Bails, can I come in?"

I reach down to turn off the vibrator, but accidentally turn it up. Sensation rushes through my body. My back arches, my toes curl, and I reach for the edge of the tub. "Yes," I moan as the vibrator keeps going, winding me tighter. I come, calling, "Caleb!"

The door opens, and my chest leaves the water as my entire body lifts from the orgasm tearing through me.

"Fucking hell," Caleb says.

I reach down and immediately remove the bullet as I slide back under the water.

I look towards Caleb, his head is thrown back, and his throat moves as he swallows. His erection pressing against the zipper of his jeans is visible, and despite the orgasm that just tore through me, the sight of it has me aching for more. I want to reach out and grab it.

His head comes down, and our eyes meet. His pupils almost take up his entire eye as he stares at me. He licks his lips, and I find myself doing the same, imagining my tongue is his as I trace my lips. Placing the towels he brought me on the counter, he stalks towards me, kneeling beside the tub. He settles, resting his hands on his thighs as his eyes stay on mine.

"Show me," he says.

I reach into the water and find the still-vibrating bullet, and hold it up for him to see.

He grins.

"Use it on your nipples."

His order turns me on, and I do exactly as he says. I watch him while his eyes follow the bullet. When I find my right nipple, I thrust my chest up, cresting over the water, giving him a perfect view of my breasts. His breath hitches when I use my free hand to tweak my other nipple. His eyes flick to mine.

"You dirty girl." He leans forward slightly. "You enjoy me watching you touch yourself. Is that what you wanted? Did you want me to come in here and watch you come as you play with yourself?"

It may not have been my initial thought, but I'm glad it happened, so I nod.

"Do it. Put that bullet on your clit and make yourself come. I'm going to watch you come with my name on your lips without me even touching you."

I do as I'm told, moving it down my body and finding my clit. I close my eyes to enjoy the sensation.

"Eyes on me," Caleb growls. "You're going to watch me. Watch me as you give yourself pleasure."

His words have another orgasm building. He's taking command, but not touching me. His words say he's in control, but his actions say I have the final say. It provides me with a sense of freedom I didn't know I needed.

I keep my eyes on his as my second orgasm builds. When I'm close, I reach out and grip the edge of the bathtub. I come, calling his name while holding eye contact. My eyes want to roll into the back of my head. I can't fight it anymore, my eyes close as the orgasm continues to ripple through my body.

As I come down from the high, opening my eyes, I'm met with a view of Caleb adjusting himself in his pants. The view and the continued pressure from the vibrator have me coming again. I have to clamp my hand over my mouth as I almost shout Caleb's name. I remove the bullet and turn it off. My entire body goes limp as I relax back into the water.

Caleb groans. "Fucking hell, woman. You're gorgeous. I could watch you like that every day for the rest of my life."

My body is too limp and satiated to be embarrassed. The click of the door has me turning my head and seeing he's left.

CHAPTER 17

Caleb

I had to leave that washroom before I reached out and touched her. I had no plans to do that. I wanted to give her the towels and then I was going to leave and retreat back to my room. She's been through enough tonight. I didn't want to cross any lines, but seeing her like that, flushed from her orgasm, my name on her lips as she came. My resolve snapped, and I needed to take some control.

I head straight to my en-suite washroom and turn the shower on cold before stripping and stepping under the water. It does nothing to calm my erection. I lean forward, bracing myself on the wall with one arm and reaching down with the other. I wrap my hand around my cock, giving it a good stroke. I groan as I remember the view of Bailey's breasts as they came out of the water when she climaxed. I hear her breathy moans; her calling my name. I groan and stroke myself faster. I imagine what it would feel like to have her hot pussy clench around my cock when she comes. The thought alone has me tumbling over the edge, calling her name as I come.

I finish my shower and climb into bed, staring at the ceiling, I toss and turn before I finally fall asleep.

My hands are red and they slip as I try to hold pressure on the wound.

"Stay with me!" I yell.

Tyler screams in pain as his eyes begin to roll back. I push harder on the wound with one hand, quickly tapping the side of his face with the other.

"Tyler, you fucking stay with me. You're not dying on me."

I watch the life slowly drain from him. His eyes roll back, and his eyelids start to close. His body relaxes into the ground. The sound of gunfire surrounds me. The sand is irritating my nose. I'm sweating like crazy in my gear. I continue to hold pressure despite him slipping away. I look up to call for help, but my eyes are met with the barrel of an AK-47.

I jolt awake, my body covered in sweat and my legs tangled in the sheets at the end of the bed. Finn tends to leave the bed during my nightmares, so I'm not surprised I don't feel him near my feet. A hand reaches out and touches my forehead, and I'm immediately on alert. My head snaps in the direction the hand came from, and striking blue eyes stare at me.

"You're okay, Caleb. It's just me. You had a nightmare."

She continues to brush my hair off my forehead, and the tension slowly leaves my body. I lean back on my pillow and let out a deep breath. The feeling in the air changes when Bailey walks away. Noise comes from the washroom and then the bed dips as she climbs next to me. The feeling of a cool washcloth on my forehead has me closing my eyes. She stays quiet, patting it along my forehead as I lie here silently, allowing it to happen.

I begin to drift back to sleep. The bed moves as she moves to climb off, but my hand reaches out and grabs her wrist.

"Stay, please," I ask.

She comes back and curls into my side, throwing an arm around my middle as I wrap mine around her, holding her to my side. I can't remember the last time I held someone as I fell asleep. I've never asked someone to stay like I just did. Bailey is slowly chipping away all these preconceptions I had about how my life was going to be. I quickly fall into a dreamless sleep.

I wake up wrapped around Bailey. A sense of contentment washes over me, feeling her so close. I turn and look at my phone and see it's

6:30 a.m. I slip out of bed and quietly make my way downstairs, Finn following behind me.

I decide to whip up some French toast, eggs, and bacon. I put Finn's food in his bowl before I hurry upstairs. I pop my head into my room and see Bailey still wrapped in the covers in the centre of the bed. I quietly walk over to the bed and climb in beside her. Brushing the hair that's covering her eyes behind her ear, I smile. It feels like I've done this a million times before.

"Bails," I whisper, and her eyes flutter open. A smile spreads across her face as she snuggles deeper into the bed. "Bailey, it's time to get up."

A groan escapes her. "No."

I chuckle. "Yes, I made coffee and breakfast."

She opens one eye. "Coffee?"

"Yeah, I'm going to wake Charlie up. You think you can make it down on your own?"

"Yeah." She rolls over and stretches.

I smile as I make my way towards the guest room. The door is cracked, probably from when Bailey made her way into my room last night. I give it a little nudge and see Charlie is curled in the centre of the bed, exactly like her mom was just curled up in mine. Like mother, like daughter.

I brush her hair back in the same way. "Little Bear," I say, and she rolls and stretches. "It's time for breakfast. I made French toast."

The mention of food seems to wake her up quicker than I ever would have thought.

"French toast?"

"Yup, and eggs and bacon."

She climbs out of bed, and we make our way downstairs and into the kitchen. I get a plate made for her with a glass of orange juice and then make my coffee. A minute later, Bailey makes her way into the kitchen, rubbing her eyes.

"Morning."

"Good morning, Mommy," Charlie says around a mouth full of French toast.

"Good morning, sleeping beauty," I say as I push a cup of coffee towards her.

She cradles the cup between her hands like it's the most precious thing. I chuckle as I make her plate and leave it on the table. After I make mine, I join them. Charlie's too busy eating as much food as she can to talk, and Bailey is very focused on her coffee. Finn's positioned himself at Charlie's feet, hoping to steal whatever she may drop. We eat breakfast in silence. When Charlie and I finish, I clear our plates and she runs upstairs to brush her teeth and get ready for school. I smile as Finn chooses to follow her upstairs.

I sit across from Bailey and make sure she makes eye contact with me before I say, "About last night."

A blush tinges her cheeks, but I'm not talking about what she thinks I am.

"I'm sorry if my nightmare scared you. That was the last thing I ever wanted. Thank you for checking on me, though."

She places her coffee cup down and reaches across the table, taking my hand. "There's nothing to apologize for. You didn't scare me. Are you okay, though?"

I squeeze her hand. "Yeah, I've had them for a while. I'm used to them by now."

"You called a name out last night," she says quietly, almost too quietly. "You kept saying Tyler."

I sigh and look over her shoulder at a blank spot on the wall. She must take this move as me pushing her away, but I'm not. I just don't think I can look at her while I retell this story.

"It's a lot to process. Are you sure you want to hear this story?" I force myself to look at her so I can gauge her response.

I can see the steeliness in her eyes, and she squeezes my hand. "Yeah, Caleb. I want to know whatever you're willing to tell me. About anything."

I lean back in my chair, and my eyes find that blank spot again. I haven't told anyone this. The thought that I'm willing and about to tell Bailey shows me I feel safer with her emotionally than I have in any other relationship in my life.

"Tyler and I served in the same unit. He became my best friend. We spent our leaves together, met each other's families, and had each other's backs. Always. During our last tour, we were patrolling a small village in Iraq. We were on our way to see a family who claimed to have information for us. We were ambushed on our way to their home. All hell broke loose as gunfire rained on us."

I can hear the sounds of the guns going off and the cries of people as bullets hit them. The smell of sand fills my nose and lungs. My breath starts to come faster and more shallow. Bailey squeezes my hand, and I close my eyes, taking deep breaths and counting. After three counts of eight in and eight out, I open my eyes again. Bailey's eyes catch mine. There is no fear in them, just empathy. It gives me the strength to continue.

"One of the bullets went straight through Tyler. At first, I thought the bullet got stuck in his plate carrier. There was no blood. I waited for him to sit up, but then the blood started to appear and it came fast. I held pressure on the wound. I tried to keep him awake so we could get him loaded on a chopper. I kept talking to him. I did everything I could."

My words get caught in my throat, and heat builds behind my eyes. Leaning forward, I rest my elbows on my thighs. I rub my eyes with the heels of my hands, the pressure helping to hold back the tears.

"I could see him fading. I saw his life leaving right before my eyes. When I went to call for help, I was met with the barrel of an AK-47. I swore I was a dead man. In those three seconds, I had resigned myself to my fate. But just as his finger was about to twitch and pull the trigger, a shot rang out and a bullet went straight through his head. I felt relieved I hadn't been killed. Then the guilt flooded me. I was kneeling over my dead best friend and I was feeling relieved. What kind of person kneels over their dead best friend and feels that way?"

I can't look at her, I can't see the disgust I know will be written all over her face. She squeezes my hand, and I continue to look at the floor between my legs. Her chair scrapes across the floor, and the next thing I know, she's kneeling between my legs, making eye contact with me. I don't see disgust on her face, though. I see sadness and empathy.

She reaches up and places her hands on both sides of my face. "You had every right to feel relieved in that moment. Any normal person would feel relief. I can see you, touch you, smell you. I know that you're right here. You're with me, but hearing you tell that story, I felt relief when you said the man holding the gun to you was killed. Your feelings don't make you less than. They don't make you a bad person. They make you human. You, Caleb Sutton, are a good man. Please don't question that."

She lifts herself up, and her lips brush over mine. I close my eyes at the contact, savouring the feeling. My entire body hums with electricity. I reach out and wrap my arms around her, holding her to me. She places soft kisses on my cheeks, eyelids, forehead, nose, and neck. Each time her lips touch my skin, it sends another hum of electricity through me, but they also calm me. And not just my body, but my soul. I've been more open with her than I've been with anyone else in my life. No one has heard the full story. The military got a very technical recall for the KIA report. Grayson, my mom, and Max know that Tyler was killed during my last tour, but they don't know any specifics. Especially not the feelings I felt over it.

I sometimes still wonder about what his life would be like if the roles were reversed. He and his girlfriend were talking about trying for a baby. He wanted a daughter so badly. He kept talking about how cool it would be to be a girl dad. The two of them loved each other fiercely. Would the world be better if I was the one that was shot instead? Would Tyler and Tayna be married? Have a few kids running around?

"Stop that."

Bailey's words rip me from my thoughts.

"I can see you're going somewhere dark. A what-if place. Don't."

She holds eye contact with me until I nod.

"Please don't think less of yourself over any of this, Caleb. I don't see you as less than." She gets up, standing between my legs. "I need to check on Charlie and get ready for work." Her hand runs through my hair a few times. "Thank you for sharing that with me. It means a lot to me."

She leans down and kisses my forehead before making her way upstairs. I need to shower, so I make my way upstairs too. I shower quickly and change into my uniform, taking my gun from the safe in my room and securing it on my hip. I jog down the stairs and fill two to-go mugs with coffee, making one for me and one for Bailey. I meet her and Charlie in the entryway as they're putting on their jackets. I hand Bailey the mug and a spare key to the house.

"This works on the front door. If you have any issues, just text me. Finn should be good for you when you get home. Let me know if you have any issues with him."

She smiles and says, "Thank you."

I nod before crouching in front of Charlie. I make sure her jacket is zipped up and she's bundled warm.

"Have a good day at school, Little Bear." I kiss her forehead before standing and doing the same to Bailey. "Have a good day at work," I say as I open the front door.

"You too, and be safe."

I smile at her over my shoulder. "Always."

CHAPTER 18

Bailey

I watch Caleb as he makes his way towards his truck before I lock the front door and Charlie and I walk to the car. I drop her off at school before heading to work. I'm fifteen minutes early, so I head into the kitchen and text Lily. I haven't told her about any of the craziness of late and I feel bad for not keeping her updated.

BAILEY

Hey, you free for lunch today? Lots to catch you up on.

I text Liv next.

BAILEY

Thanks for the package yesterday. I appreciate it.

LIV

Of course. Let me know if you need anything at all. I'm always just a text or call away.

BAILEY

Thanks.

LIV

Did you find the little surprise at the bottom of the basket?

BAILEY

...

LIV

I'll take that as a yes. Did a replay of that Friday
night happen???

A girl's got to know.

BAILEY

More like a live remake of Friday.

I bite my thumbnail as I watch the bubbles pop up on the screen
then disappear, then come back again. This continues for a minute
before her message finally comes through.

LIV

We need a girls' night.

Liv has added you to the group Badass Bitches

I chuckle at the name, assuming Hannah named the group chat.

LIV

Girls, we are in desperate need of a girls' night.
Bailey has some tea that needs to be shared.

HAN

Happy hour tomorrow. Meet at the Clover, 5 p.m.

ZOEY

Sounds juicy, I'm down.

LIZ

I'll be there.

HAN

Welcome to the group chat, by the way, Bailey.

BAILEY

Thanks. I'm guessing you named it.

HAN

Of course I did 😏

Just as I'm about to put my phone away, Lily responds.

LILY

Sounds good. Meet at the usual at 11.

BAILEY

I pocket my phone, head out to the reception desk, and get to work on my morning tasks. The office is pretty busy today, so time flies by. At 10:45 a.m., I grab my purse and start the walk to the corner deli to meet Lily.

When I get there, Lily has already gotten us a table in the corner for more privacy. I wave at her before going to the counter and ordering myself a sandwich and a cup of coffee and join her.

Taking a sip of my coffee, I relax in my seat. Lily picks at the muffin in front of her. When I don't say anything right away, she leans forward.

"Okay, so you said you had lots to catch me up on. Catch me up."

"Charlie and I are staying at Caleb's," I blurt.

She leans back in her chair, eyes wide and mouth agape. "I think I need my hearing checked, or are we living in some new crazy world? Did you just say that you and Charlie are staying at Caleb's?"

"Yeah. When I got home yesterday, there was a note from Derek on my door. I freaked. The last visit didn't exactly go well, so I called Caleb. He ran to us and stayed on the phone with me until he was standing right in front of me. He then insisted we were staying with him. When I said I could check with you, he refused. He said the only place he was comfortable with us staying was with him, so he could ensure that we're safe. So, yeah, we're staying with Caleb."

As soon as I finish my rambling, I take a bite of my sandwich. Lily continues to sit there quietly, just watching me. I keep taking bites, trying to make sure my mouth stays full so I don't share more.

She squints at me and leans forward. "There's more. You're hiding something, you're doing that thing where you do whatever you can to ensure you don't blab. So blab."

I take another bite of my sandwich, but she grabs it from my hand, grabs the plate, and moves them in front of her.

"Fine." I pick up my coffee cup and mumble into it, "He may

have watched me use a vibrator in the tub last night." Embarrassed, I hide behind my cup.

"So let me get this straight. In the last two months, you have spent four days straight with each other, you sent him a voice message of you masturbating, and I'm guessing coming too, moved in with him, and he watched you masturbate in the tub? Am I getting all that?"

I nod. "Well, except last night, he kind of told me what to do."

She throws her head back and groans. "How are you so lucky? How did you find this alpha man who respects you, but also wants to take care of you and your daughter? Like it doesn't get much better."

She's right; he's basically perfect. On top of everything Lily's said, he's opened up to me too. I know the story he told me this morning was not easy for him to tell me. It means the world to me that he did. That he was vulnerable with me. But I also wonder how long things can really be this perfect. Because I've been burned before, and that's the last thing I ever want to go through again.

"You're doing it again," Lily says as she continues to eat her muffin in little bite-sized pieces.

"Doing what?"

"Doing the whole worst-case scenario, what-if thing. Stop. All that's going to do is keep you from a good thing."

"I'm attached," I admit. "He's opened up to me too. We haven't even had sex, and I'm attached. Like if we were to go days without talking or seeing each other, I'd be sad, attached. Like things remind me of him and I smile attached. It has only been two months, how has it gotten to this point? I don't trust men. There's a reason I haven't so much as gone on a date since the separation." I down the remainder of my coffee. "I'm screwed, and if I'm like this"—I motion my hand over myself—"I know that Charlie's attached. It will kill me if something happens and she's caught in the middle."

Lily gives me a look of sympathy. She leans forward and grabs my hand. "This is all part of life. All are part of being human. You can't always think worst-case scenario. He's done nothing but show you he's a good guy. Keep relying on what he's showing you. It will all work itself out in the end."

I nod and grab my sandwich back from her, finishing it before hugging her and returning to work. I spend the day powering through paperwork and thinking about the last thing that Lily said.

It will all work itself out in the end.

When three o'clock hits, I grab my purse and head to Charlie's school to pick her up, and we head back to Caleb's house.

I'm in a daze on the way home, surprised to see that Caleb is already home when I pull into the driveway. I open the door, and Charlie goes and finds Finn in the living room while I follow the sound of a drill up the stairs and into the second guest bedroom. Caleb is in there putting together a bed frame. I see he's already put together a nightstand and dresser.

"Hey," I say when the drill stops.

He looks over his shoulder and smiles at me. "Hey, how was work?"

"It was good. What are you up to?"

"I told you I would get this room set up for you, so I'm putting together the bed frame. The mattress is being delivered in about an hour. It will be all ready for you shortly."

I'm speechless. He's gone through all this trouble to get this set up for me. He's bought brand new furniture.

I walk up to him, placing my hand on his shoulder. "You didn't have to do all this, but thank you."

"Of course, I needed to do this, Bails." He smiles at me over his shoulder. "Charlie home with you?"

"Yeah, she's playing downstairs in the living room with Finn before I make her do her homework. I was actually thinking about heading to my place. I have a bunch of perishables that I bought to make dinner this week and wanted to grab them so they don't go bad."

Caleb stiffens as he finishes putting the last screw in before standing up.

"Why don't you give me your house keys and I'll go pick up anything you need. Just give me a list. I don't think you should go there by yourself right now. Have you thought about filing a restraining order to prevent him from showing up at the house?"

"The last time I considered one, I was told a judge wouldn't grant one because I didn't have any proof he had hit me or Charlie. I'm guessing because of Charlie's age she can't be a witness, and I don't want to subject her to that, so I don't really have any options right now. I guess I'm just going to have to look for another place to move. I'm going to have to see him eventually, he does have court-mandated visitation with Charlie."

"You guys can stay here as long as you want or need. I won't be pushing you guys out. I can understand your point on the restraining order, but for the visitations, I want you to make sure you always have someone else with you. Me, Lily, Liv, and I know that any of the guys would be willing to be there. I don't want the two of you alone with him."

I know he has a point, so I just nod. "I would appreciate it if you could grab the groceries from my place. I'll write a list. I guess I should probably let everyone know that dinner on Saturday is cancelled."

"Why? We can have everyone here. Just let me know what ingredients to grab from your place and I will. We've got the space here for everyone, so just tell them there's a change of venue."

I can't wrap my head around how accommodating he's being about everything. Derek would have never gone for people invading his space the way that Charlie and I have Caleb's. He wouldn't just provide an easy solution like having all my friends over for dinner because the original place didn't work anymore.

I stare at him in disbelief. I reach forward and poke him in the peck. He doesn't even flinch. I do it again, this time harder. He reaches up and rubs the spot.

"What gives, Bails?"

"How are you real?"

His brows pinch together. "What do you mean?"

"How are you real? You've taken in Charlie and I, you're offering to host the people I invited for a dinner party, and you've bought new furniture for this room for me. Again, how are you real?"

He places his hands on either side of my face. "Bailey, I'm slowly realizing I'd do anything for you and Charlie. I can't think of anything I wouldn't do for you two. I'm real. I'm right here, and I have no intentions of going anywhere anytime soon."

I stare into his eyes, getting lost in the sincerity in them. I go onto my tiptoes, and as my lips brush his, the doorbell rings. He rests his forehead against mine and groans.

"That's probably the mattress. I should go let them in."

He kisses my forehead before retreating out of the room, and I follow behind him. He opens the door, and sure enough, there are two guys in delivery uniforms on the other side. They take the mattress upstairs while I help Charlie start on her homework and write my list. When the delivery guys leave, Caleb joins us in the kitchen.

"If you give me your keys, I'll head over there now. I should be back in time for us to start dinner."

Grabbing my keys from my purse and removing my house key, I hand it to him along with my list. Charlie and I finish her homework, and I work on unloading the dishwasher and cleaning the kitchen counters. My phone buzzes on the counter, and I smile, thinking it's Caleb asking a question about the list. I check my phone and the blood drains from my face. It's not Caleb. It's Derek.

> **DEREK**
>
> Bailey, I stopped by your place yesterday and you weren't home. I'd like to see you and my daughter.

I knew this was a possibility. I just told Caleb it was, but seeing the proof in front of me makes my heart race and not in a good way. I stare at my phone, not knowing what to say. I choose to ignore the text for now and deal with it later.

By the time I finish, Caleb is returning with bags full of groceries. He puts them on the counter, and I separate what I need to make stir fry and put the rest away.

I watch Caleb and Charlie draw at the kitchen table while I cook. He's so good with her, taking an interest in her hobbies even though she's only five. While the sight fills me with warmth that Charlie has a male role model who has taken an interest in her, I'm so unbelievably worried he's going to leave just as quickly as he showed up in our lives.

As we're eating, I say, "You should invite Grayson for dinner, and anyone else you want to. Just tell me how many so I know how much food to make. I already told Liv to invite Matt, and I've invited the girls and Lily."

"Sounds good. Let me know if you need me to grab anything for the dinner."

"I think we have everything."

We finish eating, and Caleb sets Charlie up in the living room with Disney Plus before he comes back and helps me with clean up. We work together in silence and then head into the living room to join Charlie. He sits in the corner of the couch, and Charlie climbs right into his lap. He wraps an arm around her and pats the seat beside him, and I sit. As the movie plays, I slowly inch closer to him until my head is resting on his shoulder. His arm comes down and pulls me closer to him.

I inhale deeply as his scent wraps around me like a safety blanket and I relax into him further. The next thing I remember is being lifted off the couch and carried up the stairs. Caleb places me gently into bed and kisses my forehead before leaving the room. I dream of him. I dream of all the things I now want with him, but am not sure I'd ever ask for.

I'm woken by the sounds of Caleb's nightmare. I pad to his bedroom, slowly opening the door and making my way to him. It pains me to see him like this as he thrashes in bed, calling the name of his friend. I wake him gently like I did the last time and grab a cold washcloth from the washroom using it on his forehead as he falls back to sleep.

We find a routine throughout the week. Caleb hangs out with Charlie while I cook dinner, we watch a movie or a show together, take Finn for a walk, and then we all head to bed. Derek reaches out a few times throughout the week, but I continue to ignore him. On Thursday, Caleb has a game, so it's just Charlie and I at home because it's too late for Charlie to go. I leave him a covered plate on the table with a note before I head to bed.

Every night, I go into Caleb's room and use a washcloth on his forehead when he wakes from his nightmare. Once he falls back asleep, I make my way back to my room and wish I could find a way to take away his pain.

CHAPTER 19

Bailey

Everyone is confirmed for dinner tonight. There should be eleven of us in total, so I'm making two lasagnas. I've seen how these guys eat and I want to make sure we have enough food. I'm also making garlic bread, a tossed salad, and a chocolate cake for dessert. I get to work on making the cake in the afternoon while Caleb's at work. I allow Charlie to watch TV while I get the table in the dining room, which Caleb apparently never uses, set up for dinner. I lay the tablecloth I bought on the table and set all the place settings. I also got some candles and candleholders and put them along the centre of the table.

I've got the lasagnas and garlic bread ready to go into the oven and am chopping vegetables when Caleb comes behind me and says, "Smells good," as he reaches out and grabs a piece of cut pepper.

I look at him with a smile. "Thanks."

"I'm going to head upstairs and shower. I'll be down shortly to help with whatever you need."

"I think I've got everything," I say as he leaves the kitchen.

I toss everything in the salad, and then the doorbell rings. I grab a dish towel and wipe my hands before I make my way to the front door, calling, "I'll get it."

I excitedly pull open the door and smile at Olivia and Josh on the other side. "Come in. Caleb is just upstairs in the shower."

Olivia pulls me into a hug as she steps inside. When we pull apart, she hands me a bottle of red wine. "I may not like wine or be able to drink, but that doesn't mean you guys can't."

I smile at her.

Josh gives me a side hug as he comes in and says hi before making his way into the kitchen. I grab a couple of wine glasses and pop open the bottle.

"So, how is living with Caleb going?" Liv asks.

"It's going well. We seem to have found a routine. I'm just eternally grateful he's letting us stay here."

A smile spreads across Liv's face, and she nudges Josh with her elbow. "You know, this reminds me very much of you and me," she says, and he starts coughing on the baby carrot he's chewing. She looks back at me.

"In May, I caught my boyfriend cheating on me. We were about to sign a lease on a new place. I had given my landlord notice I was moving out and everything. I needed to find a place to live, and Josh offered me his spare room. I moved in and shortly after, we started dating, in secret at first. Josh and I have been friends for years, but he's also my brother's best friend, and I didn't want our relationship to ruin the relationship the two of them have. Our relationship eventually came out at a hockey game, of all places." She laughs. "But everything turned out all good. Josh proposed that night, and then we found out about the baby. We found out at our wedding that everyone knew about us and they had a whole bet going."

"Yeah, Zoey raked in on that one," Caleb says as he joins us. "Did Liv tell you about her punching a guy on the ice at one of our games?" he asks as he pops a piece of cut pepper and ranch into his mouth.

I'm shocked. "You punched a guy at one of their games?"

A blush spreads across Liv's cheeks, and she moves in closer to Josh, who wraps an arm around her and kisses the top of her head.

"Yeah, she did. The guy had cross-checked Josh and his head hit the ice. When Josh didn't get up, she ran onto the ice to check on him. When he finally opened his eyes and got up, she turned around, hauled one back and punched the guy. It was pretty great to watch." Caleb chuckles. "We had all suspected they were together for a while, but that and the fact that Josh had to pull her back and talk her down while calling her 'babe' just confirmed it."

I cover my mouth with my hand, trying to hold back my laugh. I can't help it. I let it out. "You ran onto the ice and punched a guy in full hockey gear?" I can't stop laughing, imagining what that would look like. "Remind me to never get on your bad side," I say.

The doorbell rings, and Caleb excuses himself to answer it. Liv goes to find Charlie.

"You know he cares about you and Charlie, right?" Josh asks.

We stand there in silence, his question hanging in the air.

"He doesn't let people in. Matt and I met him after his last deployment, but Grayson knew him before. None of us know anything about his time in the service. He's always there for us. I would trust that man with my life, with Olivia's life, with the life of our child. His moving you guys in here is a big step for him, though. He's had us over for poker nights, but he likes to have a safe space. A place to retreat. You guys mean something to him if he's sharing that with you."

I don't have time to process his words before a large group files into the kitchen. I'm greeted with hugs, and then I put the lasagnas in the oven, setting a timer. I watch as Charlie rotates through people. Some draw with her, and the girls sit on the floor and play Barbies with her for a bit before she decides she wants to hang out with Caleb. She asks him to pick her up, and he does, positioning her on his hip as he holds her. She just rests on him as he continues his conversation with Grayson and Matt, and my heart squeezes. This is what I always wanted for her, a family. I turn towards the kitchen sink and wipe at the tear that's escaped when an arm wraps around me.

The smell of Lily's perfume has me leaning into her.

"What's wrong?" she asks, worry filling her voice.

"Nothing." I sigh, gathering myself. "This is just what I always wanted for Charlie, this little chosen family."

She squeezes me close. "You've got that now, hun."

I nod and turn into her, holding her in a real hug. "Thank you for standing by me this whole time. You've been there for everything. I don't think I would have survived the last six years without you."

She holds me tight. "Always. I'll always be here."

The timer goes off, and we separate. I put the garlic bread in before topping off my wine. Lily and I chat until the timer goes off again, and it's time to take the food to the table. Everyone filters into the dining room, but Caleb stays behind. He grabs one of the lasagnas and takes it in before returning for the other one. I take the garlic bread, and we join everyone in the dining room. Charlie insists on sitting between Caleb and Olivia, so I sit between Caleb and Hannah.

Everyone helps themselves to food, and the conversation flows.

"So, I was thinking about doing another group camping trip this summer," Olivia says.

"You mean you want more freaky in the woods time," Hannah says with a laugh, and Josh starts choking.

Liv pats him on the back as he clears his throat. His cheeks and the tops of his ears are both red, and it's adorable. Not a word I ever thought I'd use to describe Josh, but it is.

"You told them?" he asks.

"Yes, but also it doesn't take that long to do dishes and Liv was extremely happy when you guys returned to the campsite," Hannah says.

I laugh. I can't help it. I love the way they all give each other shit.

"Laugh it up, miss voice message," Liv says.

My laugh stops immediately, and heat fills my cheeks. I reach forward and take a sip of my wine. Questioning looks from the guys are directed at me, and there is noticeable silence coming from Caleb. His expression has me knowing he's thinking about that message and likely the other night in the washroom.

Grayson seems to be the shit disturber of the guys because he asks, "Miss voice message?"

"It's nothing," I rush out.

A shit-eating grin takes over his expression. He's going to dig, I know it. "No, there's more to it. What types of voice messages are we talking about?"

"One's I'm sure you never get," Hannah says, tension radiating between them.

He smirks at her. "You sure about that?"

Hannah opens her mouth, I'm sure to say some smart-ass response, but I know it's going to out more information than I want, so I elbow her.

"Ow, what was that for?" she asks with a shocked expression.

"I'm sorry, I didn't mean to," I say with a sickly sweet smile

"So, where do you want to go camping?" Liz asks, jumping in and changing the subject.

"Oh, I was thinking we could all take a trip to the interior this year. Maybe Kelowna or Osoyoos."

"A lake," Zoey says, pointing her fork at Liv. "That is my only requirement. Otherwise, just tell me where we're going and I'll be there."

"Just remember that little one will be here then, so just be sure you want to go camping with them," Liv says as she rubs her belly.

"We can take the little one in the water and read books. It's going to be great."

"Bailey, you and Charlie will have to join us. It was a blast last year. We rented two side-by-side campsites and spent a long weekend camping and swimming in the ocean. We barbequed and sat by the fire. We even got these guys to listen to a romance audiobook," Hannah says.

That surprises me. "You got them to listen to a romance book?"

"Yeah, and Josh even listens with me sometimes."

"What did they listen to?"

"*The Deal*," Liz says.

"It wasn't as bad as I thought it would be," Grayson says.

"So you'd listen to the rest of the series?" I ask.

"With the right motivation, yeah." He winks at me, and I swear I hear Caleb growl.

When I turn and look at him, he's glaring daggers in Grayson's direction. I don't know why I decide to poke the bear, but I do.

I lean over the table, look at Grayson, and ask, "And what would the right motivation be?"

His eyes widen for a second like he wasn't expecting that response, but then he grins. "Baby, I could think of a number of things that could sufficiently motivate me."

Another growl comes from Caleb, and I hold back a smile. I sit back in my chair, enjoying Caleb's reaction.

"So I'm guessing you're familiar with the book?" Zoey asks.

"Yeah, I've read the whole series. I loved them. I'm a Dean stan," I say.

"What about Garrett?" Liv asks.

"Don't get me wrong, I love Garrett, but there's just something about Dean. He became a total simp for Allie, and you see it even more in *The Legacy*. Plus, you gotta love the whole Winston thing," I say with a laugh.

The girls all stare at me mouths agape, and then they look at each other and every one of them bursts into laughter.

"You have to name it Winston now, Bailey," Hannah wheezes out.

"It's baby blue and small, though," Liv says between her fits of laughter.

"What is baby blue?" Matt asks, confused by the sudden uproarious laughter.

"What about Winnie, then?" Zoey asks.

"How about we don't name it," I say, shaking my head, completely embarrassed they have decided to name my vibrator at the dinner table.

"What in the world are you trying to name?" Grayson asks.

"Nothing," I say, reaching for my wine.

Josh, either being super intuitive and not nosy, or knowing he may get information out of his wife later, helps move the conversation along. "So, Bailey, how's work going now that it's flu season?"

"It's good. We've done a lot of flu shots, but other than a couple of people, most people stay home when they're sick. I've had a few helicopter parents bring their kids in, but that's about it."

"What do you do?" Matt asks.

"I manage a medical practice office. It's mainly paperwork and some face-to-face with patients at reception, but I also deal with the doctors and nursing staff."

"Grayson and Hannah both work at Vancouver Memorial in the ER. You enjoy working in a smaller place?" Matt asks.

"Yeah, I like the predictable schedule and flexibility. Being a single parent, I often need the time to take Charlie to her appointments or grab her after school on days she gets out early. I enjoy working for the doctors there."

Caleb reaches out and grabs my leg under the table, squeezing it, and I smile at him. Despite the group of people here, I wish I could crawl into Caleb's lap. His reaction to Grayson's comments earlier has me wanting to tell him he's the only one I want. That he's the only man I think about when I touch myself. I want to stake my claim on him. I want to show him how much I want him.

We finish eating, and Caleb and I clear the table. While we're in the kitchen, I quickly check my phone and see another missed text from Derek.

DEREK

Bailey, stop ignoring my texts. I have a right to see my daughter.

Fuck. He has a point; he does have a court-ordered right to visitation. But I don't want to see him and I don't want to subject Charlie to his toxicity.

Caleb comes up behind me. I lock my phone and leave it on the counter while he grabs the chocolate cake and I grab the vanilla ice cream out of the freezer.

With the exception of the text from Derek, the night is relaxing. Everyone chats and laughs, and Charlie is included in conversations. This group has completely accepted the two of us, and it fills me with gratitude.

After dessert, we move into the living room and queue up some music and chat. After a while, I notice the time and tell Charlie it's time to get ready for bed.

Olivia pats her legs and stands. "Guess that's our cue," she says to Josh.

He smiles at her with an expression full of love and affection.

"We're going to take Charlie with us," she announces as she makes her way to the entryway where I see Charlie's bag is already waiting. "We packed that earlier when we were playing," Olivia informs me, noticing my gaze.

"Um, what's going on?"

"I decided Charlie needed a sleepover with Aunty Liv and Uncle Josh, so we're going to take her home with us and then you can grab her from the game tomorrow afternoon. We will feed her breakfast and lunch. It's going to be a blast," Liv rambles on.

I turn to Charlie who has an excited look on her face as she stares up at me. "You really want to go, don't you, Baby Girl?"

She nods and does her excited toe-jumping.

"Okay, but be a good girl for your Aunt Liv and Uncle Josh, and you can always call me if you need me to come pick you up."

"I won't, Mommy, and I'll be super good! I promise!"

I pull her into a hug and hold her tight before she gets her shoes on and leaves with Liv and Josh. Everyone shuffles out behind them, leaving just Caleb and me. He's staring at me with a look so intense the air crackles around us.

He takes a step towards me, and my breath catches. I can smell him. His cologne intoxicates me. He continues to advance on me, and I slowly back into the wall. When he's standing toe to toe with me, his hand comes up to my hair, gripping it tightly at the base of my skull, and I just may melt into a puddle at his feet.

"Do you know how hard it was to contain myself in there? The pretty pink that covered your cheeks reminded me of watching you come in the tub."

I squeeze my thighs together and whimper as his nose runs along the length of my neck. He nips at the sensitive skin.

"We're alone," he whispers against my neck, making goose-bumps erupt over my entire body. "I plan to use this time to make you scream my name."

I squeeze my thighs so tightly my muscles strain as he nips at my neck before licking the sting away.

I arch my neck to the side, granting him more room, and he takes it, trailing his lips up to my jawline before they're on mine. He kisses me with an urgency that I reciprocate. He lifts me by my thighs, and I wrap my legs around his waist. He presses me between him and the wall as he devours my mouth. I nip at his bottom lip, causing him to groan as he rolls his erection into my centre. My legs tighten around him, trying to draw him closer.

He pulls us away from the wall and climbs the stairs and heads into his room, his lips staying on mine as he does. He turns the lights on before lowering me to the ground and taking a step back, his eyes tracing my entire body.

"Strip."

I go rigid at the command. The last person to see me naked was Derek, and near the end, I only took my clothes off with the lights off. After having Charlie, Derek only said nasty things about my body. He pointed out the stretch marks on my stomach and breasts, the extra skin that was now around my waist, and the fact that my breasts weren't as perky as they once were.

I wrap my arms around my middle, dropping my eyes from Caleb's.

"Can you turn the lights off?" I ask, almost in a whisper.

I watch his feet as he draws closer. His fingers come below my chin, and he lifts my head, forcing me to make eye contact.

"Bailey, I want to see every inch of your body. I want to enjoy all of it. So, we are going to keep the lights on and you're going to strip for me."

My arms tighten around my middle. "Caleb, I don't look like the women you're probably used to."

His grip on my chin tightens. "Bailey, I don't ever want you to mention another woman when we're like this. I want you. I want to see you. Do you want this?"

I nod.

"Then you can either strip for me, or I'm going to tie you to the bed and rip your clothes off so I can feast on you. Your choice."

His eyes are filled with determination, and I know he's not lying. If I don't do as he's said, he'll do it for me. I take a step back and lift my shirt over my head, dropping it to the floor beside me. Avoiding eye contact, I undo the button of my jeans and work them down my hips before stepping out of them. I'm now standing in front of this gorgeous man in only a black lace bra and a pair of matching panties.

CHAPTER 20

Caleb

My eyes take in Bailey and her beautiful skin as she stands before me in nothing but a lace bra and panties. Her tits are perfect, just over a handful, and she has hips that are perfect for holding onto as I take her from behind. Hesitance fills her face and body language as her eyes avoid me and she attempts to cover her stomach.

"Everything. I want it all off," I say.

She reaches behind her and undoes her bra, sliding it down her arms and dropping it with the rest of her clothes before she does the same with her panties. I watch each of her movements, enraptured by her. When she's completely naked, I walk up to her and kiss her, enjoying her taste. I move my lips along her jaw and neck, continuing to move down her chest until I capture a nipple in my mouth. I flick my tongue over the hardened bud, and she moans as her hand comes to my hair. Her grip is tight as my tongue plays with her nipple. I kiss across to her other breast, teasing her the same way.

My teeth scrape over her nipple as I release it and drop to my knees, kissing down her stomach as I go. I lick across each of her beautiful stretch marks, nipping my way to the apex of her thighs. I smell her arousal and groan, wanting a taste, but needing to tease her first. I continue licking and nipping across her stomach, hip to hip, and the top of each thigh. Her grip tightens on my hair, and she mewls at each of my movements over her sensitive skin.

When I finally decide I've built her up enough, I help her spread her legs and kiss up her thighs and lick her from entrance to clit. She bucks into my face, and I grip her thigh, throwing her leg over my shoulder for better access. Her flavour erupts on my tongue, and I groan around her clit. She arches, calling my name as I continue to use my tongue. I add a finger, slowly circling her entrance, teasing her.

"Please," she begs.

I grin; I like hearing her beg for me.

I continue to tease her, circling her entrance and then slowly inserting my finger before pulling out and repeating the same motion. She yanks my hair as she tries to shove my face away from her dripping pussy.

"Caleb, I need to come," she mewls. "Please." Her voice comes out in a breathy plea.

I push my finger fully inside her, finding that sensitive spot. I scrape my teeth over her clit before pulling my finger out and adding another as I continue to work her. I move my hand and tongue faster. She bucks her hips into my face, seeking her pleasure, and I give it to her. I use my teeth over her clit one last time and it sends her over the edge. Her pussy clamps down on my fingers, and she chants my name over and over as she comes.

When I've pulled every last drop of her orgasm from her, I withdraw my fingers and rise to my full height. Making eye contact with her, I lick her off my fingers. She reaches for me, and I kiss her, forcing her to taste herself on my lips.

She works to undo the buttons of my shirt then pushes it off my shoulders. Her hands roam over my chest, and her eyes widen as she moves them slowly down my stomach. She drops to her knees in front of me, working to undo my jeans. My head drops back, and I groan. The sight of her before me on her knees is almost too much. When she gets my jeans undone, she pulls them and my boxer briefs down until my cock springs free. Wrapping her hand around it, she leans forward and licks the tip with a mischievous grin. I'm too on edge to have her tease me like a brat.

My hand grips her hair, pulling her head back so I can look into her eyes. "Don't fucking tease me, Bailey. Now open that pretty little mouth of yours."

She opens, and I slowly feed my cock between her lips.

I groan as her hot mouth wraps around me. Her hand helps work the part of me that can't fit. My hips buck as she hollows her cheeks, her free hand coming up and rolling my balls. This woman is bringing me to the edge faster than I ever have before. The telltale tingling sensation at the base of my spine lets me know I'm close. I pull her off me, a popping sound echoing around the room.

I lean over her, my lips hovering over hers. "I want to come with your pussy wrapped around my cock. Now be a good girl and get on the bed."

She swallows but does exactly as I say. I smile to myself. She's good at taking orders.

I shove my jeans and underwear the rest of the way off and step out of them before climbing on the bed between her legs. I kiss my way up her body slowly, flicking my tongue over each of her nipples and pulling them with my teeth. I kiss her, slowly this time, savouring it. The way she meets my tongue, the feel of her lips, the way she surrenders to me.

She reaches between us, running my cock through her slick pussy. She's completely soaked. I groan and place my head on her shoulder.

"Condom." I barely get the word out as her grip tightens around me.

"Birth control, I'm all clear," she pants.

Her words are almost my undoing. My hips buck closer to her. I've never even considered going without before, but Bailey has all my usuallies flying out the window.

"Me too. I was just tested."

That's all she seems to need as she positions me at her entrance and begins to wrap her legs around me. I grip the sheets beside her head in a fist as I slowly push inside her, her pussy stretching around me. She feels like fucking heaven. I could die right now and be a happy man.

"Fuck, you're tight," I groan into the spot between her neck and shoulder. When I'm fully seated, I stop, allowing her to adjust. She bucks into me as she moans.

"Move, please, Caleb."

I nip at her shoulder, lifting and watching her face as I pull out of her slowly. When just the tip is still inside, I thrust my hips forward, hard and fast. Her back lifts off the bed, and she mewls when I hit that sensitive spot inside. I continue to slowly thrust my hips, finding that spot each time. She meets every one of my movements. My left hand wraps around her throat while my right finds her clit. I watch her eyes roll back as she moans my name.

Her hands move up to her breasts, and she plays with her nipples.

"Fuck woman," I groan.

She smiles as she meets my eyes and continues to play with herself.

I tighten my grip on her throat slightly, remove my hand from her clit, and slap it. The sensation sends her over the edge, and she clamps around my cock. Her hands fly out, gripping my forearm as she comes.

When she comes down from her high, I remove my hand from her throat and pull out of her. "On your knees."

She moves as quickly as she can, getting on all fours. I push down on her shoulders as I line myself up with her again. Gripping her hips, I thrust forward, and she moans as she fists the sheets. I'm able to get deeper in this position, and it's driving me crazy. I don't take my time, I fuck her fast and hard, watching her ass bounce every time I hit it.

I slap her right cheek, leaving a nice pink mark, and her legs begin to give out. She's close. She tightens around me, and I grip her hips so tightly she might have bruises tomorrow as I fuck her harder. Faster. The tingling starts at the base of my spine again. I need her to come. I reach around and find her clit. Two flicks of it and she's coming around me. I follow, emptying myself in her as my thrusts become jerky and I call her name.

I roll off of her and her legs go out. She lies there, flat on her stomach. She smiles at me, and I tuck a piece of hair behind her ear. We're both panting as we just stare at each other. I'm trying to wrap my mind around everything. I've never felt so out of control during sex as I did with Bailey. She had me wanting to consume her, destroy her, and leave her forgetting about anyone but me.

"Best sex I've ever had," she says breathlessly.

I grin, leaning over to kiss her. "Me too."

We lie like that for a minute, staring at each other. I can't ever remember a time after sex when I've just wanted to stare at a woman.

I finally lift off the bed and pick her up. She giggles as she wraps her arms around my neck. I kiss her nose as I walk us into the washroom, placing her on the counter before I turn on the shower. As the water warms up, I step between her legs and kiss her slowly.

There is zero urgency to this kiss. It's intimate. Exploring. Savouring. With my hand in her hair, I pull her head back, allowing me a better angle. She goes with the movement and wraps her arms and legs around me. Her nails gently scrape my back and it gets me going. I feel myself hardening between her legs.

I pull back and lead her into the shower, allowing her to get under the water first. When she's good and wet, I grab the bar of soap and begin washing her. I start on her back, moving my way slowly down to her ass, massaging each cheek, before moving down her legs. I turn her and stand back up. I massage each of her breasts, tweaking her nipples, and she throws her head back with a moan. I walk her back as I work my way down her stomach and kneel before her.

I throw her leg over my shoulder, giving myself a perfect view of her pussy. It's pink and wet, and not from the shower. I grin up at her as I lick her lazily. Her hand immediately goes to my hair, and I grin. I eat her like a man starved, tasting every part of her. She's still sensitive from her earlier orgasms. I suck on her clit twice, and she detonates.

When she's come down from the high, I stand and she wraps her arms around my neck before jumping up. I grab her legs as she wraps them around my hips. She reaches down and positions herself before sliding down my cock. She's fucking soaked, and I slide in easily.

"Fuck, woman, you're going to be the death of me."

She grins as she continues to work herself on me. I grip her ass tightly and take over, bouncing her on my cock as she grips my shoulders and throws her head back. Her tits bounce with each thrust, and I lean forward, capturing a nipple between my teeth and tugging on it before laving it with my tongue.

We keep a relentless pace as she clenches around me. A couple more bounces and she comes. As soon as she clamps down around me, I come. I'm breathless as I hold her against the wall. She slowly unwraps her legs from around my hips before she grabs the bar of soap and begins washing me. She takes her time as she washes every inch of me, and it's the most intimate I've ever been with a woman.

I shut off the water and step out of the shower. I wrap a towel around her and then my waist. I slowly dry her body before offering her one of my shirts to wear to bed. I slip into a pair of boxer briefs and go to climb into bed. I look up and see Bailey still standing in the middle of the room. She looks hesitantly between the bed and the door.

"Bails, come to bed."

"I can go back to my room," she says as she plays with the hem of my shirt.

I walk around the bed and stop in front of her, gently placing my hands on each side of her face. "Bailey, I want you in my bed. I want you beside me. You're not going back to that room unless it's what you want."

She looks into my eyes for a few seconds before she nods and walks around me, climbing under the covers.

I round the bed and climb in behind her, wrapping an arm around her middle and pulling her into me. "You're not sleeping all the way over there," I say as I drop a kiss on her temple.

She wiggles back into me, and I hold her tight. Her hand comes to mine, and she interlaces our fingers. I listen to her breathing as it slows, and she falls asleep in my arms.

I wake up in the morning to Bailey draped across me and I smile. Her hair is spread across my chest and shoulder, her arm is wrapped around my stomach, and her leg is over mine like she was worried I'd run away. There is no way that's going to happen.

I turn and check the time and see it's almost 9 a.m. I didn't wake up in the middle of the night. The only thing I can think of that caused that is Bailey. I run my fingers through her hair as she snuggles into me. Her eyelashes flutter across my skin before she looks up at me with a smile.

"Good morning," she says.

I tuck her hair behind her ear. "Good morning."

I lean down and kiss her. She pulls back from the kiss and throws her leg all the way over me to straddle my hips. She looks at me with an expression full of lust as she reaches down and pulls my shirt over her head before pushing my boxer briefs down and pulling my cock out. She sits over me, her blonde hair cascading down her front and back. I groan as I grip her hips. She has a mischievous smile as she lifts, positioning herself before sinking down on my cock. She goes slowly, allowing each inch to stretch her. I throw my head back, gripping her hips as I try not to just thrust mine up. When she's all the way down and our hips meet, she leans her head back, her hair going with as she grinds herself on my pelvic bone, working her clit against me.

She swivels her hips before lifting up and slamming down. She works herself up then she leans forward, planting her hands on my chest.

"Play with my clit," she moans while continuing to ride me.

I let her take the lead this morning. I don't usually take orders, but seeing her like this, so unrestrained, has me doing exactly as she asks. I reach between us, finding her clit. With each swipe of my thumb, her nails scrape at my skin. When she comes, her nails dig in, leaving marks. I love it.

I remove my hand and hold her hips as I thrust, finding my own release. She collapses on top of me, and I brush her hair back before kissing her forehead.

"Breakfast?" I ask, and she nods against my chest.

She rolls off me, and I make my way into the washroom, cleaning myself off before returning to the bedroom with a warm washcloth and cleaning Bailey. I give her a quick kiss before tossing the washcloth into the laundry basket.

Opening the bedroom door, I see Finn lying in front of it. He lifts his head, giving me an expression that tells me he's not happy about not being able to sleep on the bed last night. I reach down and scratch the top of his head.

"Come on, boy. Let's get you some breakfast, and I'll let you out to pee."

He follows me down the stairs and into the kitchen. I turn on the coffeepot then fill Finn's bowl. Once he starts chowing down, I begin scrambling eggs and putting bacon into a frying pan. As I finish plating breakfast, Bailey wanders into the kitchen wearing only my shirt. I hand her a cup of coffee and kiss her.

I enjoy being able to kiss her whenever I want and I'm going to take advantage of it. She smiles at me before settling into a chair at the kitchen table.

"What do you want to do today?" I ask her.

"I don't have any plans."

"So you're saying that I can keep you naked until we need to leave for the game?"

She smiles and blushes.

"I love that colour," I say.

She raises an eyebrow, and I reach forward and brush the backs of my fingers over her cheek. Leaning down, I whisper, "The pink your cheeks turn when you blush."

Goosebumps erupt over her skin as my breath dusts over the shell of her ear, and I grin at her body's reaction to me.

When we finish eating, I lift Bailey into my arms as she giggles and wraps her legs around me then I rush us upstairs. We spend the next few hours in bed, either exploring each other's bodies or talking.

She tells me about her parents and their deaths and how that left her with no other family as her parents were only children and her grandparents had already passed. Lily was the only friend who stuck by her when she got pregnant.

It takes everything in me to not ask for names and addresses to go over and give these people a piece of my mind. Who abandons their friend just because they get pregnant? I could never imagine pulling away from Josh and Olivia or from Max and Sarah because they're expecting.

I tell her about my father dying overseas while I was a teenager and how my mom raised Max and me by herself. She listens, taking in every word. I almost tell her how I've been requesting records from the military to find out more about my father's death, but I'm not able to work up the nerve. I haven't told anyone yet, not even my mom or Max.

At 3 p.m., we get up and get dressed before heading to the game.

I have Bailey hook her phone up to the car stereo and I find out she listens to a lot of pop, particularly a lot of Taylor Swift. We ride there with my hand on her thigh as she sings along. When we get there, I kiss her before she joins Olivia and then make my way to the dressing room.

Bailey

As Caleb heads to the dressing room, I join Olivia on the bleachers. Charlie is sitting beside her with paper and crayons and seems content with drawing. She doesn't even notice me sit down.

Olivia smiles at me before she leans in and whispers, "You've got a post-orgasmic glow."

I blush and make a zipping motion over my lips.

"You don't have to say anything, but at least tell me, was it good?"

I blush even more before I lean in and whisper directly in her ear, "Best sex of my life."

Her head turns to me with wide eyes and a slack jaw.

"Yeah," I say, confirming.

"Good for you!"

She tells me all about her night with Charlie, and it sounds like they had fun. Charlie eventually notices me, jumping up and hugging me. I bury my nose in her hair, enjoying her smell. Charlie doesn't spend nights away from me often. With it only being the two of us and Lily, there haven't been many opportunities.

"Did you have fun at Aunty Liv and Uncle Josh's?"

"Yeah, lots. I want to go again," she says excitedly.

I chuckle. "We'll see."

The guys come out and make their way to the ice. When Charlie spots Caleb, she runs at him, calling his name. He hears her, and a smile spreads across his face as he crouches to meet her. The whole scene has me melting. This man is genuinely happy to see my daughter. My entire body is warm as I look at him, and all I want to do is be closer to him. I think I've fallen in love with him. But it's only been two months. How could I have possibly fallen in love with him that quickly?

When he and Charlie separate, he smiles at me before jumping onto the ice. They end up losing the game, 2-3, but the guys still seem to be in good moods when they come off the ice. He waves as they make their way to the dressing room, and Olivia, Charlie, and I head upstairs.

We order dinner, and I text Caleb to get his order so he can join us. Charlie colours while Liv and I talk. Josh, Caleb, and Matt join us as our food is delivered.

"So, what are your plans for Christmas?" Olivia asks me.

"Oh, I don't know. I don't have any family, so it's usually just Charlie and me," I say as Caleb says, "She'll come to my mom's with me."

His hand comes to the back of my neck and gives it a quick squeeze before adding, "You two aren't going to spend the holidays alone."

My stomach knots. That's a big deal. Being invited to meet someone's family is huge, but to spend the holidays with them is major. I just stare at him. I don't know what to say.

"That's great," Liv says, her voice full of excitement. "We're having a big friend's Christmas on Boxing Day. You'll have to join us. And for New Year's Eve too."

I use my napkin to wipe at my mouth before turning back to Liv. "That sounds great. We'll be there."

We finish eating and say our goodbyes before we make our way to the truck. When we get back, I take Charlie upstairs and get her ready for bed before reading her a bedtime story and tucking her in. Finn is sitting patiently beside Charlie's bed. I look at him, and he gives me this pleading look I can't ignore.

Charlie notices and asks, "Mommy, can Finn sleep with me?"

"Yeah. I'll double check with Caleb, but for now, he can join you."

"Yay!"

I pat the spot beside her, and Finn jumps up, spinning in a circle twice before he cuddles up beside her. When I leave her room, I find Caleb leaning against the wall across from her door.

"My daughter stole your dog."

He smiles and reaches out for me, pulling me towards him and forcing my legs onto either side of his outstretched ones. His hands rest on top of my ass.

"That's all good. If Charlie and Finn want to sleep together, it's all good with me." He gives me a quick peck before his expression turns sombre. "I'm sorry," he says, and I stay silent. I'm not sure what he's apologizing for.

"For?"

"If I overstepped in saying you guys will be joining my family for Christmas. I understand if you don't want to, but I want you to know I meant it. I don't want you guys spending Christmas alone and I would love to take you to my mom's. I know she'll be so happy to have you. She keeps nagging me to bring a woman home to meet her," he says with a grin.

"I don't want to impose," I start, but his finger comes to my mouth and he leans down.

"Bailey, you and Charlie are never an imposition. I want you there."

"We'll go," I say as his lips descend on mine.

He kisses me in a way that has me thinking he's saying more with this kiss than he ever could with words. When we finally break apart, he whispers, "I want you in my bed tonight."

I nod, and he lifts me, carrying me into his bedroom.

I love that he carries me everywhere. I could easily walk, but it's like he needs to have me close, and I love it. He drops me on the bed and follows me. We work to undress each other, his lips dusting over every inch of my exposed skin. He kisses my stretch marks, slowly taking time to show them each love. Tears gather behind my eyes. I've never felt as cherished as I do with Caleb.

He works his way down my body to the apex of my thighs. Taking his time tasting me. I arch my back as his finger enters me and his tongue flicks my clit. I fist the sheets, needing something to ground me. The pleasure radiating through my body is almost too much. His teeth scrape my clit, and it sends me over the edge. The tears fall as I come.

He works out every ounce of my orgasm before he slowly kisses his way back up my body. When he makes it up to my face, he pulls back and brushes a stray hair back from my face. His face is full of concern. "What's wrong?"

I shake my head. "Nothing," I whisper.

"Baby, you're crying. What's wrong?"

As I stare into this man's eyes, I realize I'm completely lost for him. I went and jumped straight over the edge and fell for him. For his protective side, for the way he loves my daughter, the way he cherishes me, and the way he's pulled me into his life and hasn't let me go. The tears start in earnest.

"Nothing's wrong. Everything is perfect," I say, wrapping my legs around his hips.

He leans down and kisses my tears away. It's gentle and full of affection. He positions himself at my entrance and slowly pushes in as I stretch around him. He holds eye contact, and I feel this unwavering connection with him. His movements are slow. He holds my hand beside my head as he kisses me and takes his time. The build is slow, but when I explode, it's the best orgasm I've ever had. The tears start again. I don't ever want to lose this. I don't ever want to lose him.

He follows shortly behind me, his thrusts becoming more choppy as he calls my name into my neck and finishes. He rolls off me, taking me with him. He stares at me like he's searching for some hidden meaning, some secret. And I guess there is one. I've fallen in love with him and I'm not sure I'm ready to tell him.

He gives me a quick kiss before making his way to the washroom then returning with a washcloth. He cleans me up and then climbs back into bed, pulling me into him and kissing the top of my head as he whispers, "Good night, baby."

Bailey

When I wake up in the morning, Caleb isn't with me. I roll out of bed and make my way downstairs and find Caleb in the kitchen drinking a cup of coffee and making breakfast. He sees me and smiles, pouring another cup before bringing it to me and kissing me.

"Morning, Bails. Sleep well?"

I smile. "Yeah, you?"

"Like a baby. Breakfast is almost done. I was just going to go wake you and Charlie up."

"I'll go get her."

I take a sip of my coffee and place it on the counter before going to Charlie's room. I push open her door and see her curled up in the middle of the bed, cuddling Princess and Finn. I walk up to her slowly, enjoying how peaceful she looks.

Finn stirs first, giving his head a shake as he watches me.

I kiss Charlie's forehead. "Baby Girl, it's time to get up. Caleb made breakfast."

She rolls and stretches, pulling Princess back into her as she curls back into a ball.

"Baby Girl," I say again, and her eyes flutter open.

She yawns and smiles up at me, "Morning, Mommy."

"Morning, Baby Girl. Caleb has breakfast downstairs."

She does another cat stretch, causing Finn to stand and jump off the bed. She rolls out of bed and follows me downstairs with Finn hot on her heels. She settles into a chair at the kitchen table, and Caleb sets a plate and a glass of orange juice in front of her. She thanks him and digs in. I grab a scoop of Finn's food and fill his bowl, placing it right beside Charlie as he doesn't seem to want to move. I grab my coffee and pull out the chair across from her, and Caleb joins us, giving me a plate.

"So, I was thinking about going and getting a Christmas tree tonight. Do you guys want to come?"

Charlie perks up at the question. "A real tree?" she asks, her voice full of wonder.

"Yup, a real tree." He smiles at her.

She looks at me. "Mommy, can we?"

We've always had a fake tree. It was easier because I couldn't carry and set up a real tree by myself. Growing up, we always had real trees. My parents and I would go and pick one out, and Dad would carry it in and set it up in the living room. Mom and I would then decorate the tree together. She would let me put my ornaments wherever I wanted and then, when we were done, Dad would lift me and I would put the star on the top. I always wanted to share that tradition with my own family, but Derek wasn't interested and could never be bothered to help decorate for Christmas.

I smile at her. "Yeah, we can go."

Caleb smiles at me. "Sounds good. I was thinking we could leave here at 5:30, does that work for you guys?"

"It's perfect."

We finish eating, and I take Charlie upstairs to get ready for work and school.

Caleb waits for us downstairs. He helps Charlie into her jacket, helping her zip it up before placing a kiss on her forehead. "Have a good day at school, Little Bear."

He stands and passes me a to-go mug of coffee and gives me a quick kiss. "Have a good day at work."

That's the first time he's kissed me with Charlie obviously watching us. I don't have a problem with it. She needs to know that Caleb and I are seeing each other and seeing me in a healthy relationship will be good for her.

"You too," I say, and he makes his way out the front door. I make

sure Charlie and I have everything, and we make our way to the car. I drop her off at school and make my way to the office.

When Charlie and I get home that night, I work on her homework with her as we wait for Caleb to come home. He walks through the front door and straight into the kitchen, kissing me and then Charlie's forehead before he goes upstairs to change. Charlie and I clean up and meet him in the entryway. Once everyone is bundled up with jackets, scarves, gloves, and boots, we head out to his truck. The winter weather is rolling through now. We've had a few days with a little dusting of snow, but nothing major yet. We've mainly had to deal with ice.

Charlie asks for Christmas music as we drive to the tree farm, and Caleb agrees. She is so excited when we get there. Caleb unbuckles her, and she jumps in place as she stares at all the trees. Making our way inside, Caleb directs us straight to a little kiosk and buys us each a hot chocolate.

He hands them to Charlie and me. "You can't shop for a Christmas tree without hot chocolate."

We wander around a few trees nearby, Charlie using both her hands on her cup. I stick my nose near a few trees, inhaling the scent. I love the smell of Christmas trees. When I pull my nose out of one, I turn and see Caleb watching me with a smile. I blush and tuck a piece of hair behind my ear. I know it's a little weird to just shove my face in the trees, but I missed this. I miss the house smelling like the tree during Christmas. I miss being in a house that truly feels like Christmas during the holidays.

He tosses his cup into a nearby garbage can and comes up to me, whispering in my ear, "You're fucking adorable." His lips brush my cheek, and he grabs my hand.

As soon as Charlie finishes her hot chocolate, she asks to hold Caleb's hand too, and the three of us walk through the trees. After twenty minutes of wandering, I find the perfect tree. I stop in my tracks and stare at it. It's the perfect height and is uniform all around, with a nice wide base.

Caleb looks at me, a smile lighting his face. "That's it, huh?"

I nod, and he squeezes my hand. I walk up to it, running my hand lightly over the branches while Charlie and Caleb go find an attendant to get the tree shaken and loaded in the bed of the truck. They return, and Caleb and the attendant chat, figuring out logistics before the guy grabs the tree and we follow him to the shaker.

We wait nearby. Charlie is in Caleb's arms when a familiar voice calls my name. I freeze. My back stiffens, and my blood runs cold. I see Caleb stiffen too, prepared for whatever may be coming.

I turn and come face to face with Derek. He smiles and takes a step towards me. I retreat backwards. His smile drops and a look of frustration crosses his face.

"You've been ignoring my texts," he says, and the energy in the air changes.

"Yes, I'm sorry. I've been busy."

"I would like to see you." He looks over at Charlie before he adds, "and my daughter."

I can see he's holding back his anger. His cheek is twitching the same way it would before he grabbed or hit me.

"I will contact you when I can find an appropriate time and place. Right now, we are out and this is not the place. I would like you to leave us alone." My words come out stronger than I thought they would, but I think that's because I can feel Caleb's presence behind me.

"I work here," he says before looking back at Caleb.

"Why are you holding my daughter?" he asks, venom lacing his voice.

"Because she asked me to. Now, I believe Bailey just asked you to leave her alone, so why don't you move somewhere else on the lot while we finish up here."

Derek stares daggers at Caleb and grips his hands into fists. "I would like to see my daughter."

I turn and look at Charlie cuddled in Caleb's arms. She's hiding herself. She has half her face covered and is only looking at Derek with one eye. Derek takes a step closer to us and holds his arms out for Charlie.

"Hey, Char, why don't you come see your dad?"

She shakes her head and snuggles deeper into Caleb's chest. Caleb, being the protective man he is, brings a hand to her back and rubs it while adjusting his position so that Charlie is further away from Derek.

"She said no, I think we're just going to take her home," he says as he moves towards the truck where the attendant is securing the tree.

"You can't keep my daughter from me," Derek calls.

The anger in his voice is evident, and I'm on high alert. I move to catch up with Caleb as he begins to buckle her into the backseat. I don't even make it two steps before a painful sting radiates up my arm. I look down and see Derek gripping my forearm. I try to pull my arm away, but his grip is too tight. He yanks me closer and gets in my face.

"You can't keep her from me. You can't replace me with that loser. Soon enough, both of you will be back with me, where you belong." He steps so close I feel his breath on my cheek as he says, "And when you're back with me, I plan to fuck your pussy hard and fast. So, you better be keeping your legs closed because you don't want to know the consequences if you've opened them for someone else."

I want to puke. Tears gather behind my eyes, and I blink, trying to stop them from falling. I know he means it. He'll follow through with his threats if he ever gets me alone. I'm scared not just for me, but for Charlie. I feel the world around me closing in. My hand goes up to my throat, and I take deep breaths, trying to centre myself.

Derek is ripped away from me as Caleb shoves him away. "You keep your hands off of her. You don't contact her until she contacts you."

Derek's entire face is dark red as he stares up at Caleb. Their height difference is so noticeable like this; Caleb has a good four inches on Derek.

"You can't tell me what to do," he spits.

"I can and I will because I protect what's mine and I will protect those girls until my last dying breath. So, believe me when I say you don't want to cross me." Caleb stares him down for another second before coming over and grabbing my hand, squeezing it reassuringly.

I follow him to the truck. He opens the door, helps me up, and buckles my seat belt before quickly rounding the truck and hopping in. The air in the truck is tense despite the Christmas music playing.

When we get back to the house, he helps Charlie out and carries her inside. "Hey, Little Bear, can you head to your room and play for a bit while Mommy and I talk?"

She nods and runs up the stairs.

I make my way into the kitchen, the place furthest from the bottom of the stairs in case she decides to come down while we're still talking. Caleb follows me, crossing his arms over his chest and planting his feet shoulder-width apart in an intimidating pose. He's probably used this pose in the military and at work, I realize. I know I'm in for an integration and I guess I deserve it. I hid the texts from him.

"Why didn't you tell me?" His voice isn't filled with accusation, but more pain. It's like he's hurt I didn't tell him.

"I wasn't sure what to do. I didn't want to see him. I still don't want to see him and I don't want Charlie to see him. But he does have court-ordered visitation, and I don't know how to deal with it or how to do it," I rush out.

"I can help you, Bailey. You're not alone anymore. I want to know why you didn't tell me. Why did you think you couldn't tell me?"

I look up at the ceiling, holding back my tears. The emotions running through my body are a lot right now. When I look at him, they slowly fall down my cheeks. "Because you've already done so much for us. I don't want to just be a burden on you. You're always saving me."

His entire body relaxes, and he steps towards me, framing my face with his hands and wiping way my tears.

"Bailey, you're not a burden. You and Charlie could never be a burden to me. I like being the one saving you because you're saving me, too. I've never opened up to someone the way I have with you. When you sleep next to me, I don't have nightmares. You're saving me just like I'm saving you, and that's okay. Let me save you. Let me support you."

My tears fall in earnest, and he pulls me into his arms. With him wrapped around me, I completely relax into him, feeling safer than I ever have. He rubs his hand over my back and places kisses across my temple and the top of my head, soothing me as I cry. I've felt so lost since losing my parents and ending everything with Derek. While I knew Lily was there for us, I didn't want to rely on her too heavily. To have him ask to be able to do that for me means everything.

It takes me a few minutes, but I'm eventually able to gather myself and pull out of his embrace. He doesn't let me get far as his hands come back to my face, brushing the stray tears away.

"Will you let me help you come up with a plan?"

I nod, and he kisses me softly. It's not sexual; it's intimate. It's a kiss shared by partners.

"Okay, why don't I bring in the tree and we can order dinner? I'll get the tree set up and we can decorate it tomorrow."

I smile, and he kisses the tip of my nose before heading out the front door. I make my way upstairs and into Charlie's room, where she's happily playing with Barbies and Finn on the floor. I join her, sitting beside her. She looks at me and then back at her Barbies.

She's quiet for a minute before she softly asks, "Mommy, are we going back with Daddy?"

"No, Baby Girl, we aren't. Do you want to?"

She shakes her head but doesn't look at me. "No, I want Caleb to be my daddy. He doesn't hurt you like Daddy does. He's nice, and he plays with me."

My heart breaks for my little girl. She's been through more than anyone her age ever should. I pat my lap, and she climbs into it. I wrap my arms around her, holding her close. "I will do everything in my power to keep you safe, Baby Girl. Caleb and I are going to talk about what to do with your daddy. I don't want you to worry. Just know that Mommy loves you loads."

I rock back and forth with her in my lap, and she lets me hold her. I absorb every second of this time because I know in the future, she won't let me do this anymore.

A creaking noise has me turning my head to see Caleb leaning against the door frame, smiling at us. I smile back. Charlie notices my movement, lifts her head, and climbs off my lap, running towards Caleb. He picks her up and she nuzzles into him and he rocks her.

"You won't leave, right, Caleb?"

He kisses her forehead. "No, Little Bear, I'm not going anywhere."

We stand in Charlie's room, the silence and heaviness of the moment wrapped around us.

"What do you girls want for dinner?"

"Nuggets," Charlie says.

"We can do that," he says, rubbing his hand over her back.

"Sounds good to me," I say as we head downstairs.

He settles on the couch with Charlie in his lap and Finn at his feet. Pulling his phone out, he opens a delivery app and hands it to me. I order some nuggets and fries for Charlie and a burger for myself. Caleb finishes the order before we get comfortable and watch a Christmas movie.

Caleb pulls me into his side, and I snuggle in. Right here is where I feel safest. I could spend the rest of my life in this man's arms with my daughter.

Our food is delivered, and Caleb gets everything settled for us on the coffee table so we can continue the movie. Charlie falls asleep before the movie finishes, and Caleb carries her upstairs, settling her in her bed as Finn joins her. I wait for Caleb in the hallway, and we make our way to his bedroom.

"You okay to talk?" he asks.

"Yeah."

"This is my view of everything. You don't have to do this. This is all your decision. I want you to know I'm not going to pressure you into anything. Derek has court-ordered visitation. I say the three of us meet him somewhere in public. We let him see her, but we start the process of getting a restraining order and revoking his visitation. We don't want to give the court any reason to side with him, so that means going with the order."

I soak in his words, knowing he's right.

"Okay, let's do that."

"Okay. We should file a police report about tonight so that you have it in writing. I'm your witness."

I nod and strip out of my clothes and climb into his bed naked. He does the same and pulls me to him. He places soft kisses on my temple and cheek before whispering good night.

CHAPTER 23

Caleb

We go through our regular morning routine. The difference this morning is Bailey meets me at the station after she drops off Charlie. I sit with her as we get the police report filed about last night's incident with Derek.

When we finish, I walk her out to her car, giving her a quick kiss before she drives to work. Back inside the station, I gather my stuff to begin my patrol shift. While I'm out on patrol, I stop by the courthouse and pick up some information packets for Bailey about getting a hearing to have the decision of Derek's visitation rights overturned. On my way home after shift, I stop at the store, grabbing some more Christmas decorations so we can spend the entire evening decorating the house. I don't own a lot of decorations because I never felt the need to decorate with it always being just me. Mom always decorates her place, so I help her.

While I'm at the store, I text the family group chat to let them know I'm bringing the girls.

CALEB

I'm bringing two people with me to Christmas dinner.

MAX

Two?

CALEB

Yeah.

MAX

Who?

MOM

Any dietary restrictions?

CALEB

No allergies that I know of. They aren't super picky.

MOM

Okay. Can't wait to meet them.

MAX

Again, who? You just bringing some friends with you?

CALEB

Nope.

MAX

Now I've got to know. You have two girlfriends and you're bringing them both to dinner? 😏

CALEB

WTF? No. It's my girlfriend and her daughter. You really think I'd do that?

MAX

Just giving you shit.

MOM

You're seeing someone? And she has a daughter? Why don't you bring them for dinner this weekend? I'd love to meet them.

CALEB

I'll ask.

MAX

Count Sarah and me in too.

As I'm finishing my bagging, a man walking by bumps my shoulder. Lifting my head, I see it's Derek. He's standing there glaring at me.

"They're mine," he growls.

I ignore him. I don't want to start a scene in the middle of the store, especially while wearing my uniform.

"You just going to be a pussy and not say anything?"

He steps right into my personal space. I take a step back, but he follows.

"You're not man enough for her. She's mine, always has been, always will be."

I'm done. I snap. "She's not yours. She's not a possession to be owned. She's a person, and she chooses who she wants to be with and seeing as she divorced your ass, that obviously isn't you. You need to leave her and I both alone before you wind up back in jail." I turn and leave the store before he can say anything.

When I get home, Charlie is playing with toys in the living room and Bailey is dancing to Taylor Swift while cleaning the kitchen. Her black leggings hug her curves and show off her perfect ass. Her T-shirt rises slightly, showing just a sliver of skin as she reaches across the kitchen counter with a rag and shakes her ass to the music. I lean against the doorjamb and smile as I watch her.

This view makes me realize I want to come home to this every day for the rest of my life. I don't know how it happened, but I've completely fallen in love with these two girls. That thought also scares the crap out of me because I'm not sure how long I'm going to be able to keep them.

Bailey turns and when she sees me, she yelps as she jumps before laughing. My smile grows as I walk up, wrap my arms around her back, and pull her into me before leaning down and kissing her. She melts into me when our lips touch. Her arms wrap around my neck. I kiss her slowly, taking my time. Charlie's in the living room, so I have some time with just Bailey. I lick across the seam of her lips, coaxing her to open for me, and she does. Our tongues meet, and I grab her ass before breaking the kiss.

She smiles up at me. "Welcome home."

With her head tipped back like this, her beautiful blonde hair cascades down her back. I run my fingers through her long strands, enjoying the feeling of it between my fingers.

"How was your day?" I ask.

"It was a day. Nothing special. You?"

I sigh, knowing I need to tell her about my run-in with Derek, but not wanting to ruin the mood or upset her. I hold her tight to me. "I ran into Derek at the store on my way home."

Her hands fist the back of my uniform shirt.

"He still seems to think he has a chance with you. He tried to warn me away from you and Charlie."

Her face is etched with worry.

I tuck her hair behind her ear and kiss the tip of her nose, forehead, cheeks, and lips. "But I'm not going to do that. I'm not going anywhere. You need to be watchful when you're out. If I had it my way, you wouldn't leave the house without me. I know I can't do that, so I want you to be vigilant. Program speed dials, make sure you always have your phone on you, and try to stay in super public places. If you can, I'd like for you to be with other people as much as possible."

"I'll be careful, but what about you? I'm worried that he'll take it too far."

"I'll be okay. I'm trained to be vigilant and protect myself."

She looks deep into my eyes, concern filling hers, but mine outmeasures hers tenfold. I've been in worse situations and been able to handle myself, but this is completely new for both her and Charlie.

"I grabbed some Christmas decorations on my way home. I thought we could decorate together."

Seemingly thankful for the subject change, she smiles, and her face lights up. I let go of her and move to the bags I brought in and pull out some Christmas ornaments and other nicknacks. As she pulls out each item, her excitement increases. I love seeing this side of her.

We take everything into the living room, and I say hi to Charlie, giving her a hug and forehead kiss and listening as she tells me about her day at school. The two of us decorate the tree, and Bailey puts the other decorations in their place.

When we finish, I take a step back. My house now feels like a home. I've noticed that ever since the girls moved in. I walk in the door and everything feels warmer, happier. I used to love the solitude of my place; it was where I could escape the noise of the world. I never would have let someone move into my space. Then I met Bailey, and she pulled me in with her strength and resilience, her determination and independence, her capacity for love and understanding, her beauty and intelligence. Charlie pulled me in the same way. She has all the best traits of her mother, and they both have me wrapped around their little fingers. I would and will do anything for them.

When we finish decorating, Bailey and I make our way into the kitchen and get started on dinner. Tonight, I'm making a quick pasta and Bolognese and Bailey is making a salad.

"My mom invited us for dinner this weekend," I say, stirring the sauce.

Silence fills the room. I no longer hear the subtle sound of the knife hitting the cutting board. Turning, she looks at me with a strange look on her face.

"You okay?" I ask.

"Yeah." She clears her throat and continues to cut the tomato in her hand. "So, your mom invited you to dinner this weekend."

"No," I correct. "She invited us. You, me, and Charlie."

"What do you mean?" she asks.

I'm not sure how I'm being confusing.

"My mother invited the three of us to dinner at her place on Saturday," I say the sentence slowly.

"I'm understanding what you're saying. I'm just confused as to how this happened," she says with an adorable little huff.

"I texted my family group chat and said I'd be bringing two people to Christmas dinner. My brother, being my brother, decided to try to give me shit about it. I cleared it up by saying I'd be bringing my girlfriend and her daughter. Mom wants to meet you, so she invited us to dinner on Saturday. I said I'd ask you."

"Girlfriend." The word is full of awe. It's light and breathy, and I smile at the sound.

"Yeah, girlfriend."

"Really?" There's confusion on her face now.

I take a deep breath. "I'm going to try my best not to be an ass here, Bails, but yeah, girlfriend. What the fuck?"

She closes her eyes and takes a deep breath, setting her knife on the cutting board. I watch her, worried I've fucked this all up.

She lifts her head and makes eye contact with me, a light sheen over her eyes. "It's just a lot. After the divorce, I never thought I'd get serious with anyone. One, I never thought someone would want to be with me. I have a crazy ex-husband and a daughter who demands a lot of my time and energy. And two, I never thought I'd be able to trust another man after everything I went through. It's still just a lot to wrap my head around."

I hold her eyes for a few seconds before turning the burner to the lowest setting and rounding the kitchen island. I place my hands on each side of her face. "I want you. I want Charlie. I want all your baggage. You're not just a quick fuck. I'm in this. I would like you to come meet my family on Saturday if you're up to it."

Tears slowly fall down her cheeks, and I wipe them away with my thumb. I rest my forehead against hers. "Please don't cry, baby. I hate seeing you cry."

A rush of air passes over my cheek as she takes a deep breath and releases it.

"You just make me happy. These are happy tears."

I kiss each cheek before pulling back. "You okay?"

She nods, and I return to the stove and finish dinner. When everything is done, the three of us sit at the table to eat.

"Mommy, can I go to Aunty Liv's on Saturday?"

"I'm sorry, Baby Girl, but we're going to Caleb's mom's on Saturday."

I smile, happy she's taking this step with me.

"Really?" Charlie asks.

"Yeah, she's super excited to meet you," I say. "But I do have a hockey game in the afternoon. I'm sure you can see Aunty Liv there."

Bailey reaches out and places her hand on my forearm. "I actually have a doctor's appointment Saturday afternoon, so I won't be able to make your game."

"Okay, well, I can take Charlie with me for the afternoon and see if Liv will hang with her while I'm changing. If you finish early enough, you can meet us there. If not, we'll meet back here and head to Mom's."

Bailey stares at me. She opens her mouth, closes it, and then does it again. "You'll take Charlie?"

"Of course." I look at Charlie. "You okay hanging out with me while your mom goes to the doctor, Little Bear?"

She nods as she continues to eat her pasta.

"See, sounds like a plan."

"Thank you," Bailey says, affection filling her voice.

"You don't have to thank me for spending time with Charlie," I say, meaning every word. I enjoy spending time with Charlie. It's not a chore, it's a privilege.

She stares at me with a soft smile, and it's one I want to see on her for the rest of my life.

Caleb

After breakfast on Saturday, Bailey leaves for her doctor's appointment and Charlie and I take Finn for a walk around the neighbourhood. The entire walk, Finn sticks to Charlie's side. Any time someone approaches us, he positions himself between them and Charlie. When we get back, I make sure he has some water before I grab my bag and get Charlie loaded in the truck, and we head to the rink.

She tells me about the characters in her show as we make the drive. When we get there, she insists on carrying my sticks for me. She drags the blades across the cement because of her height. I'll have to re-tape them, but to see how happy she is to help me with something so simple makes it worth it.

When we get inside, I tell her the number of the rink we're playing on and she already knows the way. I follow behind her as she happily makes her way through the hallways. When we get to the dressing room, I knock on the door and call out to ensure everyone is still dressed before pushing the door open and leading Charlie inside. I show her where she can lean the sticks and then head to my usual spot in the dressing room and drop my bag.

The door opens, and Mac, our goalie, steps inside. He's been out of the country for a few weeks due to work, so we had to find someone as backup for our last few games.

"Hey, man." I lift my chin at him.

He lifts his chin back, and his eyes catch on Charlie. "This your girl?" he asks in his British accent.

Mac doesn't hang out after the games. He usually showers quickly and leaves, so we don't talk. He doesn't know much about us and vice-versa. So his question doesn't catch me off guard.

I look at Charlie, and the words come out of my mouth before my brain even processes them. "Yeah, this is Charlotte." I place my hand on top of her head. "Charlie, this is my friend Mac."

She smiles at me before looking back at Mac and offering him a shy wave. When I first met Charlie, she was so open and receptive to me, but I've noticed she wasn't that way with everyone. Even with the guys, she didn't open up to them at first. It took spending time around them to be more comfortable with them. The girls were a different story, though. She didn't need as much time to warm to them, and I wonder if she witnessed more between Bailey and Derek than Bailey knows.

I hold Charlie close to my side as these thoughts race through my mind. I don't want to think about what Charlie's witnessed. That would also lead me to having to think about what Bailey's endured, and I'm not sure I have the strength to not hunt down Derek right now.

I lead Charlie out of the dressing room and towards the bleachers. I take a seat, and she sits beside me. I feel her eyes on me. She looks at me hesitantly as she chews her lip the same way her mom does when she's thinking about something. I shift so I'm facing her.

"What's up, Little Bear?"

"Mac asked if I'm your girl. You said yes."

"I did. Does that make you upset?"

A vise squeezes my heart as I wait for her answer. I didn't realize how important her answer was until now. I feel as though I'm sitting on the edge of a cliff and her answer could send me over the edge, crashing to the bottom. My breath catches in my lungs as I wait for her answer.

"No," she says. "I wish you were my dad."

The last part is whispered so quietly I barely hear it. My heart cracks at her confession, and all I want to do is hold and protect her from the world and anyone or anything that may try to hurt her. I open my arms for a hug, and she climbs right into them. I hold her tightly to my chest.

"I'll always be here for you. Always. No matter what you want or need, you can always come to me. I want you to believe that. I will always be here for you," I say into her hair.

I start to pull back, but she holds me tighter, and her tears run down her cheeks and soak into my shirt.

"Why doesn't Daddy love us?"

I'm at a loss for words. I don't want to overstep something that should be Bailey's territory, but I'm the only one here right now, and I need to say something.

I clear my throat. "Sometimes people don't know how to show their love. I think your dad loves you. He just doesn't know how to show it."

As much as I hate what Derek has done to these girls, I don't doubt he believes he loves them.

"I love you, Caleb," she whispers into my chest.

I hold her tighter. "I love you too, Little Bear."

I continue to hold her for a minute before we pull apart and she gets settled with a few toys. When I see Liv, she smiles at me. Something on my face must give away how difficult the last few minutes have been for me because her smile drops and she waits at the edge of the hallway for me to join her.

"What's wrong?" she asks in a hushed tone as I approach.

"She asked some hard questions about her dad," I say, running a hand through my hair.

A look of sympathy crosses her face. "What'd she ask?"

"Why her dad doesn't love them."

Her hand goes to her chest, and heartbreak spreads across her face. "That poor girl."

I nod. "Yeah, I told her I'm sure he loves her and that some people just don't know how to show love, but I don't know what else to say. I don't want to overstep my boundaries. I'm just her mom's boyfriend."

Olivia reaches out and grips my forearm, squeezing it. "Don't downplay your position in Charlie's life, or Bailey's. You may be Bailey's boyfriend, but you have also become a safe space for those girls. They have not had it easy. You have provided them a place of safety. I know they aren't just sitting around waiting for the ball to drop when it comes to you. That's a huge thing when it comes to people in these situations. You're doing great with them."

I smile at her, appreciating her words.

Grayson calls my name and motions towards the dressing room, and I nod and him.

"Thanks, Liv, and thank you for hanging with Charlie during the game."

"Of course, any reason to spend time with Charlie is a good one."

Walking into the dressing room, I make my way towards my gear. I get dressed in silence, letting my thoughts run wild as I replay what Charlie and Liv said.

I wish you were my dad.

You have become a safe space for those girls.

Thankfully, the guys let me sit in my thoughts before we head to the ice. My head isn't in the game. I miss passes and I don't make the hits I usually would. At the start of the third, I notice Bailey sitting with Liv and Charlie. She smiles and waves, and I wave back. I feel a little more grounded being able to see her, but my thoughts are still in the clouds. We lose the game, 3-1, and I know that's partly because of me, but I can't muster the energy to care about it right now.

When we make it into the dressing room, the guys have decided to stop letting me brood.

"Okay, what gives?" Grayson says, dropping down beside me.

I sigh, and Josh and Matt join us. I lean against the wall and tilt my head back. "Charlie asked me why her dad doesn't love them and then proceeded to say she wishes I was her dad."

Silence. That's all I get. I drop my chin and see the guys watching me.

"I thought you said she was your girl," Mac says as he drops to the bench across from me.

I watch the guys as they tamper down their grins.

"She's technically my girlfriend's daughter," I say.

He nods and leans down to undo his skates. He stops partway through and looks at me. "As someone who comes from a fucked up family, and if I'm right in assuming her dad has done some fucked up things, it's going to take her a lot to be able to trust new people who come into her life. If she trusts you, if she feels safe with you, you earned that. Don't take it for granted. Our parents can do some real damage to us."

I think that's the most Mac has opened up to anyone on the team about his personal life, and I take his words to heart. He obviously knows what he's talking about.

"When Liv tells me about her time with Charlie, she says Charlie only has great things to say about you. I think you just keep doing what you're doing and see where things go. You obviously love and care for her. There is nothing anyone can do about the past," Josh says.

"I do care for her," I say, my voice serious. "I would do anything for that little girl. I want to give her the world."

"Not all families look the same," Matt says. "Just love her and everything will fall into place." He claps me on the shoulder and moves to his bag and strips out of his gear and Josh does the same.

"They're lucky to have you," Grayson says.

I turn to him and shake my head. "No, I'm the lucky one. I never thought I'd have so many happy days. I enjoy going home to them, watching Charlie's movies on the couch, coming home and seeing Bailey dancing to Taylor Swift while cleaning the kitchen. I just worry about what I'm going to do when she feels safe enough to go back to her place."

"Then show them they're meant to stay with you."

Grayson's words cement an idea in my head, and I know the first step of my plan to make sure they stay right where they're supposed to be.

With me.

CHAPTER 25

Bailey

I text Caleb that I'm going to take Charlie back to the house and change before he comes to pick us up for dinner at his mom's. Charlie raves about her day with Caleb, and a small weight is removed from my shoulders. I've only left Charlie with Lily and the one time Olivia decided to take her. Knowing that Charlie enjoyed her time with Caleb is a big deal.

When we get back to the house, I run upstairs and change into a nice pair of dark-blue jeans and a dressy red blouse. I want to make a good impression on Caleb's family. I know it's a big deal to introduce a partner to your family, and Caleb and I are so new. I don't want to screw this up.

"Mommy, can I wear my red dress?" Charlie calls from her room.

I quickly check my hair in the mirror and decide to pull the top layer back so my face is more visible before making my way to Charlie's room. She's pulled out her favourite red dress with black bows printed on it.

"That's a really nice dress," I say, taking a seat on her bed.

She plays with the hem of the dress, avoiding my eyes. "I want them to like me," she whispers.

I reach out and run my fingers through her soft blonde hair. "Baby Girl, they're going to like you."

"But, Mommy, if they don't like me, won't Caleb leave us?"

Her question breaks my heart. She's grown so close and attached to Caleb, and I worry what will happen if things with Caleb don't work out. I pull her into my arms and rock her slightly.

"No, Baby Girl, Caleb won't leave us because they don't like you. But it doesn't matter because they are going to love you."

I hold her close for a minute before helping her into her favourite dress. As I finish braiding her hair, I hear the front door open and close.

"I'm home," Caleb calls up the stairs.

"In Charlie's room," I call back.

The sound of his footsteps up the stairs carries through the air. I look up and see Caleb leaning against the door frame smiling at us.

"Well, now don't you two look beautiful," he says.

"Thank you," I say as he makes his way towards us. He gives me a quick kiss before kissing Charlie's forehead.

"I guess I should change, since you two look so nice. You know it's a casual family dinner, right?"

I blush, not wanting to admit I'm nervous about meeting his family and I put more effort into my looks to make a good impression.

"Yeah, just thought it would be nice to dress nicely," I say, hoping my nerves don't show through.

He holds my eyes for a few seconds before nodding and heading into his room. He comes out a few minutes later dressed in a pair of jeans that hug his muscular thighs and tight round ass that has me wanting to sink my teeth into it like a juicy apple. His navy button-down is pulled tight across his muscular chest, and if I look hard enough, I think I can count his abs under it.

"I take it you approve," he says with a chuckle.

My eyes snap to his, and he's grinning like an idiot.

"Yeah," I breathe out.

He checks his watch quickly and looks back at me. "We should probably head out. I don't want to be too late."

I nod and usher Charlie to follow me downstairs where I step into my knee-high, black heeled boots, bundle us each in a jacket, and grab my purse. Like always, Caleb is the one who gets Charlie situated in the back seat after he opens my door for me.

When he gets settled in the driver's seat, I ask, "Can we make a quick stop at the store on our way? I'd like to grab something."

"Of course, baby. What are you wanting?"

"I just want to grab something for your mom."

Caleb stays with Charlie while I hurriedly make my way into the store and grab a bouquet and a bottle of red wine. When I make it back, Charlie is telling Caleb all about her favourite *Paw Patrol* character. He's fully engaged in the conversation with her, listening to what she's saying and asking questions. It only has my love for him growing.

We make our way to his mom's place, and he lets Charlie and I listen to Taylor Swift the entire way, no complaints as Charlie and I sing along.

Caleb's mom lives in a charming residential neighbourhood. Every house has nice front yards, many filled with kids' toys. Christmas lights from the houses light the entire street. I smile at the yards filled with Christmas decorations and giant blow-ups. He pulls in front of a house halfway down the street.

Bright Christmas lights wrap around the top of the house and up the pillars of the front porch. A giant Christmas welcome sign leans to the left of the door, and light-up reindeer are placed all across the yard. This looks like the house of someone who enjoys Christmas.

Caleb rounds the front of the truck and opens my door, helping me down before moving to the back and helping Charlie. I grab the flowers and wine while he holds Charlie's hand, and we make our way up the front walkway. Despite the chill in the air, nerves have my hands starting to sweat.

"Caleb." Charlie's voice comes out soft. "Will your mom like me?"

Caleb stops dead in his tracks and crouches in front of her. He holds both of her hands as he says, "Little Bear, she's going to love you almost as much as I do. You are an amazing little girl. Don't worry about what anyone thinks about you, just keep being the amazing little girl that I've fallen in love with and everything will be okay."

He pulls her into a hug and kisses her temple. She wraps her arms around him, and I have to tip my head back to prevent the tears from rushing down my face. This man is wrecking me for any other man, and I think I'm perfectly okay with that.

They break their hug, and we make our way up the steps. He doesn't knock, just walks right in the front door. He leans down and helps Charlie out of her shoes before taking his off and setting them against the wall. I do the same, and he leads us inside the house calling, "We're here."

We end up in the kitchen where a woman in her late fifties stands over a stove stirring something. She turns at our entrance, and I'm met with Caleb's steel-grey eyes and a warm smile that has my entire body relaxing. She drops her spoon on the counter, wiping her hands on a towel as she makes her way towards us.

"Oh, how lovely to meet you," she says as she pulls me into a hug.

When she pulls back, I hand her the flowers and wine. "These are for you."

She smells the flowers and smiles back at me. "Well, these are just lovely. Aren't you sweet."

Caleb chuckles beside me. "Mom, this is my girlfriend, Bailey, and this is our girl, Charlotte. Bailey, Charlie, this is my mom, Loraine."

She waves her hand in front of her. "Oh, where are my manners? You can call me Mom or Gran. Why don't you guys grab a seat? Your brother and Sarah should be here soon. Dinner is almost done."

I'm stunned by her words. She already wants me to call her Mom and Charlie to call her Gran? I feel like I've stepped into some alternate reality. This doesn't happen. You don't just show up at your new boyfriend's mom's house and she just accepts you as part of the family like that. And not just me, but my daughter too.

The feel of Caleb's hand at the small of my back rips me from my daze. I look up at him, and he smiles. "You okay?" he whispers, quiet enough that only I can hear him.

"Yeah," I whisper back.

Charlie and I make our way to the kitchen table.

"Baby, you want a glass of wine?" Caleb asks, and I want to melt into the chair. The way the word baby sounds rolling off his tongue does things to me.

"Yes, please."

He opens the bottle I brought and grabs three wine glasses from a cabinet over the counter. "Little Bear, would you like some milk or some juice? I think there is orange juice in the fridge."

"Milk, please."

He passes his mom a glass of wine and kisses her on the cheek before pouring a glass of milk for Charlie and handing it to her. He goes back to the kitchen and returns with our wine. Charlie is on my right and there's an open seat to my left, but she looks up at me. "Mommy, can you please move? I want to sit beside Caleb."

I shuffle to the empty seat on my left so Caleb can sit between us. He places my wineglass in front of me and kisses my temple once he gets settled. After adjusting a setting on the stove, Loraine comes and joins us.

The front door opens, and two sets of footsteps make their way towards the kitchen. I turn and see a man who looks just like Caleb. His big frame takes up much of the doorway, and his facial features are just as prominent as Caleb's. His hair is a darker shade of blond, almost brown, and his eyes are hazel, but there's no mistaking they're brothers.

Beside him stands a stunning brunette. She comes to his upper chest, and her hand rests on her very visibly pregnant belly.

"You must be the woman my brother has convinced to put up with him," the man says.

I smile because, honestly, there isn't much to put up with. He's the one who's had to put up with a lot of crap since meeting me.

"I think you've got that the wrong way around," I say.

He walks up to his mom and kisses her cheek before holding out a hand to me. "I'm Caleb's older brother, Max, and this is my wife, Sarah."

I shake his hand. "Bailey, and over there is my daughter, Charlie."

I look around Caleb and see she's trying to hide in his side, and he's got an arm wrapped around her. Sarah reaches her hand out next.

"It's so nice to meet you and Charlie. Max here hasn't been able to shut up about how excited he's been to meet you two."

"Really?"

"Yeah, the first woman my little brother has ever brought home to meet the family, colour me intrigued."

My eyes cut to Caleb, and a slight blush colours his cheeks. He never mentioned never bringing a woman home before. Sarah walks over to Charlie and crouches beside her chair.

"Hi, Charlie, my name is Sarah," she says in a soft, sing-songy voice.

"Hi," Charlie says in a small voice. This is a lot to take in for her. Sarah, realizing Charlie isn't going to give her any more, stands and takes a seat across from Caleb. Loraine gives Charlie some colouring sheets and coloured pencils. She quietly says thank you and starts to colour.

"So, Bailey, how did you meet my brother?"

I blush and fidget with my fingers in my lap. I reach for my glass of wine and take a sip before clearing my throat. "He responded to a 911 call at my house." I can see the shock on their faces, but no judgment. "Charlie wanted to make him cookies after they talked about Thanksgiving at school and thanking people we appreciate, so we made them and brought them to the station. Charlie invited Caleb to lunch, and then a meddling friend of Caleb's invited Charlie and I to a game, and it kind of went from there."

I look over at Caleb, and he's smiling down at me. His arm comes around the back of my chair, and his thumb runs in soothing motions over my shoulder. I relax into him.

"Which meddling friend was this? I think I should send them a thank you cake," Loraine says.

"Olivia," I say, taking a sip of my wine.

"Oh, Josh's wife. How lovely. How are they? How's her pregnancy going?" she asks.

We sit around the table, and I tell her about how Liv is doing before she makes her way to the stove.

"Can I help with anything?" I ask.

She waves me off. "No, dear, you just sit and relax."

"So you're coming here for Christmas dinner. Any other exciting plans for the holidays?" Sarah asks, leaning back in her chair and rubbing her belly.

"I'm planning on taking them to Fly Over Canada," Caleb answers.

"Oh, that sounds like fun. Do you mind if we tag along? I've been meaning to go, but we haven't found any time yet."

"That sounds fun. There's a Christmas market right there I want to go to too," I say.

"The German one? That would be great. I might need to find a bench to sit partway through and get off my feet for a bit, but I'd love to go."

"I remember what that's like. When I was pregnant with Charlie, I swear my ankles swelled to twice their size. I think just before I gave birth, you couldn't tell the difference between my calf and my ankle."

"Do you want more kids?"

Her question catches me off guard. Caleb and I haven't talked about it. We haven't talked about the future much at all, I realize. I feel his eyes on me, waiting for my answer. His thumb continues its movements up and down my shoulder, relaxing me slightly.

"Yeah. I've always wanted a big family."

Sarah and Max both smile at me before exchanging looks with one another.

Loraine comes back to the table with a hot pot of spaghetti. She puts it in the centre of the table and retreats to the kitchen, then she comes back with garlic bread and salad. Once everything is set, we dig in. Caleb makes Charlie's plate, and we pass the food around the table.

I ask Sarah and Max questions, learning that Sarah is a paralegal at a law firm downtown and Max is an architect. Loraine was a bookkeeper for a few different businesses, offering her the flexibility needed to raise the two boys on her own. For dessert, we eat a homemade apple pie Loraine pulls out of the oven and some vanilla ice cream.

Throughout the night, I notice Charlie become more comfortable being here and being with new people. During dessert, she talks with Sarah about her favourite shows and what she likes most about her school.

When we finish, I help Loraine clear the table. She tries to wave me off, but I ignore her. I'm not going to let her take my daughter and me in for a meal and let her cook and clean by herself. We finally agree that I'll wash and she can dry and put away.

I'm arm deep in warm soapy water when she says, "Thank you."

I smile at her. "Of course, I don't mind helping out with dishes. You cooked an amazing meal."

She gives me a sad smile. "No, I mean with Caleb. He's been closed off since his dad died. It's nice to see him so happy. I was worried he'd never get that."

"He's done much more for me than I have for him," I say, continuing to wash the dishes. "He's taken us in after some stuff went down with my ex. I'm not sure how I'll ever repay him for it, or what I'll do when he decides that he's ready for us to move out."

My stomach knots at the thought of leaving Caleb's place. I love my home. I inherited it from my parents when they passed. But it's not my safe space anymore. Derek took that from me. Maybe I need to list it and find a new one. One with new memories. Make a new safe space. The thought doesn't undo the knots in my stomach.

"Don't rush to any conclusions," Loraine says, interrupting my thoughts. "My boys are both stubborn. They don't do anything they don't want to. Remember that. I can see your brain is over there telling you things that may not be true."

"I've learned to never make assumptions and to rely on myself."

Before I know what's happening, I'm being pulled into an all-encompassing hug. I'm stiff at first, not knowing what to do, but when she doesn't release me, I melt into her. I wrap my arms around her slender frame and allow the smell of her perfume to invade my senses.

"You're not alone anymore. You have us. You have a family to support you."

Her words crack me. It's like the shell I've had surrounding me for the last few years has slowly been chipped at and her words are the final undoing. The pieces of my shell fall to the ground around me and the tears fall. The tears are a relief, as though they're washing away all the pain and heartache I've had to protect myself from.

They don't stop; they turn from light crying into soul-wrenching sobs that have my entire body shaking. Not once does Loraine release me. Her hand rubs soothingly over my back as she holds me.

"Baby?" Caleb's voice breaks through the air.

His mother steps back, allowing him to see me. When he does, the look of pain on his face has me sobbing even more. It's written all over his face how deeply seeing me cry hurts him. He pulls me against him, and I rest my head on his chest, allowing the sound of his beating heart to soothe me. His fingers run through the ends of my hair in the way he's learned has a calming effect on me. When my sobs finally subside, I lean my head back and he places his hands gently on either side of my face.

"I'm sorry," I whisper.

He leans down and gently kisses over the remaining tears on my cheeks. "Don't ever apologize for feeling your feelings, baby."

He stares into my eyes, and I stare right back, memorized by the softness in the steely colour.

"What happened?"

"Your mother is amazing."

He smiles at the remark. "She is, but what caused you to feel so much that you needed to cry?"

"She said I don't need to only rely on myself now, that we have a family to rely on."

"She's right. I know you've spent so much time only being able to count on yourself and Lily, but that's not the case anymore. You have me. Always. You have Liv and Josh, and you might not realize it yet, but you also have Zoey, Hannah, Liz, Matt, and Grayson. You have my family. You're not alone anymore."

I fist his shirt in my hands. "I hear your words, but after doing everything on my own for so long, it's hard to realize the truth behind them."

"I know, baby, but I'll spend the rest of my life showing you how true they are."

He leans down and kisses me. It's soft and intimate, one that's meant to be just a kiss, with no other goals or intentions. The idea that we're in a place where we can kiss each other with no need to take it further warms my soul. It's not a lack of desire, but rather a sense of contentment that a single act of affection brings each of us.

When his lips leave mine, he holds me for a few moments, allowing me to absorb the feeling of safety I have when in his arms. When I've gathered myself, I wipe under my eyes and make my way into the living room where Charlie's sitting, reading a book with

Sarah. Max and Loraine sit on the couch talking, but I notice how he watches his wife, his gaze full of affection.

I walk up to Loraine and hug her before saying, "We should probably head home. I need to get her in a bath and ready for bed."

She nods. "Okay, well, we will see you for Christmas dinner. Don't forget what I said, either."

"I won't, thank you." Looking over at Sarah and Charlie, I see they're just about done with their book. "Baby Girl, when you two finish that book, it's going to be time to go."

She looks up at me, and I can see the tiredness all over her face, but she's trying to be a trooper and stay awake.

"Okay, Mommy."

When they finish, we make our way to the front door.

"Thank you so much for having us," I say to Loraine.

"You're welcome whenever you'd like."

"I'll get your number from Caleb to set up the trip to Fly Over and the Christmas market," Sarah says before pulling me into a hug. "It was so nice to meet you both. I'm happy Caleb was able to find you two," she whispers in my ear softly.

"You too," is all I manage to say through the lump in my throat.

Caleb has Charlie in his arms, and she's almost passed out with her head resting on his shoulder.

"Thanks, Mom. I'll call you before Christmas to confirm what we need to bring." He leans in and kisses her cheek and then Sarah's before shaking his brother's hand and leading me out the door.

The drive back to the house is quiet. Music plays softly in the background while I stare out the window. Caleb has his hand on my thigh the entire time, his thumb moving softly up and down.

It's hard to think that in just ten short weeks I've gone from being a single mom with only myself and Lily to rely on to having this huge group of people who want me to rely on them. Who want to be in our lives. It feels too good to be true. I'm waiting for the other shoe to drop, for the world to spin on its axis and everything to go back to normal. The problem is, I don't want things to go back to normal. I want everything to stay the way it is. I want these people in my life, in Charlie's life. I want to come home to Caleb, a man who cares about me and my daughter. This is the life I want to build. But the ground has fallen out from under me before. I think if it happens again, I won't be able to survive it the same way. I don't know that I can put that shell around myself now that all these people have cracked and destroyed it.

Arriving home, Caleb carries Charlie upstairs, and I decide to skip the bath tonight and just tuck her into bed.

CHAPTER 26

Caleb

When we get home, I can tell that the day has been emotionally exhausting for Bailey. After tucking Charlie into bed with Finn cuddled at her feet, I head into our room and straight into the washroom to run her a bath. I pull out some candles I have stored in the bottom drawer, light them, and drop a lavender-scented bath bomb into the water. While the water runs, I head into the room and silently lead Bailey into the washroom.

Neither of us says anything as I slowly take off each article of her clothing then mine. I turn off the water and step into the bath, offering her my hand. She takes it, stepping into the bath in front of me, and we both sit. We sit in silence, her back to my front and the only sound the gentle sloshing of the water anytime we move.

The warm water and the feeling of her body pressed against mine has me completely relaxed. I could fall asleep right here, perfectly content.

After a few minutes, I feel her chest heave. Opening my eyes, I see her biting her lip as she tries to hold back tears. One arm holds her tighter while the hand of the other reaches up and brushes away a stray tear that's fallen. I place gentle kisses on her temple and cheek, showing her my quiet support. Those kisses seem to break her because she stops holding the tears back and allows herself to cry in my arms. I hold her, allowing her to release all these pent-up emotions. She grips my arms tightly, and her entire body fully relaxes into me. As her sobs subside, I kiss her temple and whisper against her skin, "When you're ready to talk, I'm right here."

I watch the flickering of the candle lights and listen to her breath as it evens out.

Just when I think she's fallen asleep, she says, "I've never felt this supported and cared for. It's so much, it's overwhelming."

I don't say anything, giving her the space to continue.

"When I was with Derek, I did everything around the house, even when I was pregnant. He didn't come to any of the doctor's appointments. He didn't help decorate the nursery. I felt so alone despite being married and living with my husband. Then Charlie was born, and I was still left doing everything. Derek started coming home later, and that's when the hitting really started. He swore up and down he loved me and it was my fault that he hit me. I wasn't keeping Charlie quiet, wasn't keeping up on the cleaning. I didn't have dinner waiting for him every night. He was my first for every-thing. When we got married, I swore we were this great love story and we would spend the rest of our lives together. It was the broken bones that made me finally leave."

I tense at her words. Picturing her in a hospital room with cuts, bruises, and broken bones has my chest burning. I close my eyes, lean my head against the side of hers, and take a few deep, steadying breaths.

When I've gathered myself I say, "That's not love. I don't ever want you thinking that's love again. Someone who loves you supports you. Protects you. Treasures you. You've found a family that will do all of that. Don't question whether you're worthy of it because you are, and so much more, Bailey. You deserve the world."

She turns her head and looks at me. I lower my mouth to hers. I kiss her slowly, reverently, affectionately. She turns in my arms, the water sloshing around us as she straddles my lap. Her lips leave mine and trail my jaw, down my neck, across my chest, and up the other side. I groan as she takes her time, dragging her lips over my skin. She rocks against me, and I harden beneath her. I grip her hips, trying to get her to stop.

Her lips find my ear. "I want you," she whispers.

I groan as her teeth scrape across my ear lobe. Reaching between us, she grips my cock in her hand, giving it a couple of pumps. My hips jerk to match her movement. My grip on her hips tightens, and a sly smile spreads across her lips as she positions me at her entrance. As she slowly sinks down, she holds my eyes. The eye contact is more intimate than what we're doing physically.

When she's all the way down and her hips are flush with mine, she stays like that. I relish the feel of her stretched around me. I lean forward and kiss her. I want every part of our bodies connected. I need it. Her hands find their way into my hair, her nails scraping across my scalp since my hair is too short to grab. She slowly circles her hips and moans into my mouth. She lifts herself and slams down, causing both of us to moan and water to splash over the edge of the bath. She moves to lift herself off of me, but I stop her. My toe finds the plug and lifts it to allow the water to begin to drain.

She leans in and kisses me again. Her hands find my shoulders as she slowly lifts herself. My hips meet hers as she comes down.

"Yes," she moans as her head falls back, her chest pushing out towards my face.

I take advantage and lean forward, my mouth latching around a nipple. My tongue flicks over it, and I kiss my way across her chest, doing the same to the other.

She clenches around me. I use my thumb to find her clit and apply pressure. As my teeth scrape over her nipple, she comes, calling my name. She's breathless as she rides out her orgasm. When she stops clenching around me, I lift her and we step out of the tub. I pick her up and carry her into the bedroom. Tossing her on the bed, I watch as her breasts bounce with her.

Groaning, I stroke my cock a few times as I stare at her. "Fuck, you're sexy," I growl as I drop to my knees in front of her.

She pushes up on her elbows and watches as I push her legs apart and position myself between them.

"So pink and wet for me," I say, staring at her pussy.

She bites her lip. I lean forward and take my first taste of the night. I groan. I've never tasted anything as good as her. As my tongue flicks her clit, she drops onto the bed. Her hand finds the top of my head, grabbing the longer hair there. I grin as I bring a finger to her entrance and tease her. I slowly insert it, only going as far as one knuckle before pulling it out. I continue to tease her. I take my time, slowly building her up until she's just about to fall over the edge, and then I stop.

I continue teasing her until she squeezes her thighs around my head and locks her ankles behind my back. I grin against her, sucking her clit into my mouth and using my tongue and teeth to bring her over the edge. Her back arches so high that only her shoulders and hips touch the bed. I work every last bit of her orgasm out of her. Playing with her until she's pushing my face away.

I wipe my mouth with the back of my hand before I climb onto the bed and up her body, slowly kissing my way up until I reach her lips. She kisses me back, and it's such a turn-on that she doesn't shy away from her taste on my tongue. Breathless, she breaks the kiss.

"On your hands and knees, baby."

She slowly rolls over and gets on all fours. My hand between her shoulder blades pushes her chest to the bed. I'm not gentle as I slam into her. She quivers around me. She whimpers as I hit her G-spot with each thrust. Her arms move above her, pressing against the headboard, trying to stop her body from scooting higher on the bed.

I spank her, and she mewls. I do it again, and she clamps around me. I love her response to me. Reaching forward, I grip her hair and pull her head back. Her eyes roll backwards, and she comes around me. My hips move faster, and I watch as her ass bounces every time they slam into it. Heat builds at the base of my spine. I pull out of her and flip her onto her back. Gripping my cock, two pumps is all it takes before I'm coming all over her stomach and chest. I fall back onto my heels as I work to catch my breath.

I stare at her, and she stares back, a satiated smile on her face. I lean over and kiss her.

"You look good like this. You look like mine," I whisper against her lips.

I leave the bed, making my way into the washroom and grabbing a wet washcloth to clean her up before we make our way back into the shower. This time, only using it to clean ourselves. After we dry off, we climb into bed and I hold her close. I kiss her temple softly and listen to her breathing slow as she falls asleep in my arms.

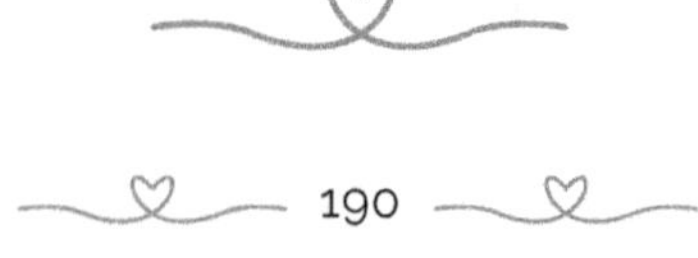

I wake up before Bailey and slowly climb out of bed, making sure not to wake her. I quietly get dressed before heading downstairs, throwing on a pair of shoes and grabbing a jacket. I step onto the back porch and call Liv, hoping she and Josh won't be too pissed about me waking them up.

"Caleb?" her groggy voice comes through.

"Hey, Liv. Sorry for waking you, but I have a favour to ask of you."

"Okay, what's up?" Her voice sounds a little more clear now.

"Who is it?" Josh asks on the other end.

"Caleb."

"Why the fuck is he calling you at this time?" he grumbles.

"He has a favour to ask." I smile as I listen to them. Josh obviously isn't happy I woke them up.

"Sorry, Caleb. What's up?"

"I was hoping that you'd go to the spa with Bailey today. I think she could use it. I'll pay for it but thought she could use the company."

"Spa day? I could go for a spa day. Everything okay with Bailey?"

"Yesterday was just an emotional day. I want her to relax and recharge today."

"You're sweet," she says softly. "Yeah, I can pick her up in an hour."

The sound of sheets rustling travels through the phone.

"Maybe make that an hour and a half," she says with a laugh before the phone goes dead.

I head back into the kitchen and turn on the coffeepot. Just as I pour myself a cup, Charlie walks into the kitchen, rubbing her eyes. Finn is hot on her heels.

"Good morning, Little Bear," I say.

"Morning," she mumbles and walks up to me, wrapping her arms around my legs.

I run my hand over the top of her head. "So, I was thinking about making your mom breakfast in bed and then you and I can spend the day together. Just you and me. How does that sound?"

She looks up at me with a huge grin.

"How do pancakes sound?"

"Yum, pancakes!"

I chuckle.

I quickly open the sliding glass door in the kitchen for Finn before filling his bowl and gathering the ingredients for breakfast. Charlie helps me make the batter and lay the bacon on a baking sheet before I stick it in the oven and get to work on the pancakes. Charlie puts some fruit in a bowl, and I find a tray to take up to Bailey. After loading the tray with the food and a cup of coffee, Charlie and I head upstairs. When I open the door, Bailey's still peacefully asleep in bed.

Placing the tray on the nightstand, I run my hand through her hair. "Bailey, baby, we made breakfast."

She mumbles something and snuggles into the bed.

Charlie climbs on behind her. "Mommy, we made pancakes."

Bailey cracks an eye open and looks at me. I hold up the cup of coffee, and she smiles before sitting up, holding the top sheet to her chest.

"We made breakfast, and Olivia will be here in an hour to pick you up. You two have plans, and Charlie and I have plans today, so eat up."

She looks at me, confused. I smile and give her a quick kiss before I usher Charlie back downstairs. We sit at the table and eat our breakfast together before I clean up while she plays in the living room. Bailey comes down and joins me in the kitchen while I finish cleaning the counters.

"So, these plans I have with Liv, what's going on?"

"I thought you could use some time to relax and recharge, so you two are going to the spa. I have plans with Charlie, so all you have to do is take your sexy little ass and go relax. I've got dinner covered tonight, too, so you have nothing to worry about."

She stares at me, not saying anything. I shake the rag out over the sink before refolding it and placing it beside the sink.

"You really organized this for me?" she whispers.

I walk over to her and wrap my arms around her waist. "Of course, baby. Liv should be here soon, so please go with her and relax." I reach into my jeans pocket and grab my wallet. I pull out my credit card and hand it to her. "Use this to pay for both of you."

She shakes her head. "No, it's fine. I don't need your card."

"Baby, take it or I'll just give it to Olivia and make sure she uses it. Go get a massage and have lunch with Liv. Put it all on here. I want to do this for you."

I can see the reluctance in her eyes, but she knows I'll give it to Liv, so she takes it and puts it in her back pocket and thanks me. The doorbell rings, and Charlie goes running towards the door.

"Little Bear, where are you going?" I call after her.

"To see who's at the door," she calls as she continues to run.

"You know the rules. Let your mom or I answer the door."

She stops and turns to me, a sad look on her face, but she nods. I make my way to the front door, and she lifts her arms up as I get close. I pick her up and prop her on my hip as I answer the door.

A smiling Olivia is on the other side. "Good morning," she says in a chipper voice. I don't want to think about what led to that.

"Good morning," I say, taking a step to the side so she can come in. "We have a couple pancakes if you're hungry."

She shakes her head. "I'm all good, thanks. Josh fed me before I left."

She follows me into the kitchen where Bailey is working on her second cup of coffee. I place Charlie on the kitchen counter while the girls say their hellos and hug.

"Spa day! Are you excited because I am," Liv says.

"Yup," Bailey says, popping the p sound.

"I'm excited for a girls' day. You joining us, Charlie?"

Charlie shakes her head. "No, I get to hang out with Caleb," she says with a huge smile.

"That's right. A Caleb and Little Bear day," I say, running my hand through her hair.

Liv and Bailey smile at me.

Liv claps her hands and says, "Well, we should get going."

Bailey rinses her coffee cup before putting it in the dishwasher and giving both Charlie and me a kiss.

"I'll check the card," I call after her and Liv as they make their way to the front door.

Turning back to Charlie, I say, "Why don't you get dressed and then we can head out?"

She nods, and I help her off the counter and she runs upstairs. When she comes back down, I help her bundle up, and we take Finn on his walk before loading up in the truck. I get her settled in the back and put on Taylor Swift, knowing she loves it, and make my way to the hardware store. I decided that today we are going to pick out a colour to paint Charlie's room and maybe some new furniture for her.

I grab a cart, and we head inside. Charlie holds onto the side of the cart as we make our way to the paint section. I watch as she takes in our surroundings. I didn't tell her what we're doing today; she was just excited to spend the day with me. This amazing little girl didn't care what we did, she just wanted to spend the day with me. I realize more and more each day just how blessed I am to have these girls in my life.

I stop the cart in front of the colour selection and crouch in front of her. "Do you know what these are?" I ask while pointing to the wall of colours.

She shakes her head.

"These are paint colours. I thought today you could pick a colour to paint your room. Any colour you want."

Her eyes widen.

"I can paint my room?"

"Yeah, any colour you want."

She lunges herself into my arms, and mine instinctively wrap around her, holding her close. When she pulls back, she rushes over to the section of pinks. I smile, not surprised. I pull out a couple of options, and she picks a pastel pink. I put it in my pocket, and we make our way down the aisles. I grab the primer and a couple of cans of paint and all the supplies we need before we make our way to the mixing station.

Once I give them the paint and the colour choice, I pick up Charlie, so I can show her how they are making the colour for her. The entire process fascinates her.

When I finish paying, we make our way back to the truck. In need of some more coffee, I hit a drive-through and grab Charlie a hot chocolate. Our next stop is a furniture store. I lead us straight towards the children's bedroom section.

"So, you've picked out your paint colour. Now it's time to pick out a new bed."

She runs over to a loft bed and climbs up the ladder and settles on the mattress. "Can I have this one?"

I walk up to her and rest my arms on the side of the bed. "Yeah, Little Bear, you can have this one."

She wraps her arms around my neck. The smell of her strawberry shampoo fills my nose, and I realize how much it relaxes me because smelling it means she's close by and she's safe.

"You're the bestest," she whispers in my ear.

I continue to hold her, soaking in this feeling.

She pulls back and climbs down. I take note of the information for the bed so we can get it ordered, and we wander through the rest of the store.

I grab a chair, a couple bookshelves, and a small table to add to her room. She finds some glow-in-the-dark stars she wants to add, so we grab those, too. We make our way to the checkout, and I pay for everything. They say they can have the bed delivered today around 5 p.m.

Charlie is excited the entire drive home. When we get there, I carry everything inside and have her go up and move her toys into Bailey's old room. Once everything is inside, I head upstairs and disassemble the bed in Charlie's room while she watches a show in the living room. When I come down to get her, she's excited to help me. She helps me lay the plastic sheeting on the floor, and I open the primer. I give her a brush and a small section to paint while I get to work. She asks for music, so I grab my Bluetooth speaker. I smile as she sings and paints.

While the primer dries, I make us an early lunch. After, I put together one of the bookshelves before heading back into Charlie's rooms and start the first round of painting. I spend the next few hours putting together furniture and doing laundry before finishing the last coat.

Her bed is delivered shortly after I finish the last coat of paint, and I begin setting it up in the middle of the room. Once the walls are dry, I can move it. I texted Liv earlier in the day to keep Bailey out of the house as long as possible. I call in a delivery order of Chinese food and while we wait for it, Charlie and I put some finishing touches on her room. I've moved her bed, and Charlie is sitting on my shoulders sticking stars to the ceiling when Bailey walks in. Her gasp is what draws my attention. She's standing in the doorway, mouth agape, staring at us.

"Wow," she whispers.

"Hi, Mommy. Caleb let me paint my room and he got me a new bed and these really cool stars."

Bailey smiles up at her. "I see that, Baby Girl. Did you have fun with Caleb today?"

"Uh huh, lots. He got me hot cocoa and made grilled cheese and tomato soup too. Aaaaaannnnd we get Chinese food for dinner," she says excitedly.

I lift her off my shoulders and set her onto the ground. Charlie gives her mom a hug and then runs off to the new table with her collection of colouring materials, and I lead Bailey into the hallway.

"You did that for her?" she asks.

I cup her face and lean down for a quick kiss. "Yeah, I did that for her. I wanted to make it more her room instead of my old guest room. So I took her shopping. We had fun," I say with a smile.

She reaches up and wraps her arms around my neck. "You're amazing," she says before she kisses me.

Her tongue licks at the seam of my lips, and I happily open for her. My tongue comes out to meet hers as my arms wrap around her. My hands find her ass, grabbing it and pulling her closer. I nip at her bottom lip, but as I go to deepen the kiss, the doorbell rings.

I groan, leaning my forehead against hers before kissing it and making my way down the stairs. We settle in and enjoy our dinner while Charlie tells Bailey more about our day.

When we finish, Bailey takes Charlie upstairs and gets her into the bath while I clean the kitchen. When I'm done, I go back upstairs, to ensure all the final touches are done in Charlie's room before heading into my washroom and jumping in the shower.

CHAPTER 27

Bailey

I'm filled with so much gratitude as I listen to Charlie tell me all about her day with Caleb.

Derek would never spend an entire day with Charlie, let alone take her shopping and do all the work that Caleb did today. He never cared for me enough to realize I needed a day of relaxation, let alone do everything to ensure I got it.

I've fallen for this man, but something is still holding me back from telling him how I feel. I'm still worried the ground will be ripped out from under me. Not by Caleb, but rather some outside force.

When Charlie finishes her bath, I help her get dressed, and we head into her room. I have to stand beside her bed to read her a bedtime story now. When I finish, I kiss her forehead before heading into Caleb's room.

Stepping into the room and closing the door, the sound of the shower running has a smile spreading across my face. I walk into the washroom, strip out of my clothes, and step into the shower with Caleb.

He grins, wrapping his arms around me and pulling me into the stream of water before leaning down and kissing me. He kisses me deeply, and I melt into him, feeling his erection pressing into my stomach. When we break apart, I immediately drop to my knees in front of him. He groans as I reach forward and grab his hard cock in my hand, pumping it twice.

One hand reaches out and steadies him while the other comes to my head. I feel so powerful right now, holding this man in the palm of my hand, being in complete control of his pleasure. He's allowing me to be in complete control. My breathing quickens as this heady feeling rushes through me. I squeeze my thighs together, trying to quench the ache growing between them.

Leaning forward, I lick him from base to tip, flicking my tongue over his slit. His grip on my hair tightens. I tease him, slowly licking the other side and flicking my tongue the same way. I tighten my grip slightly as I give him another pump before my other hand finds his balls and rolls them.

"Fuck, you're a naughty little minx, aren't you?" he says as his hand flexes in my hair.

A devilish grin spreads across my face as I nod and lean forward, taking as much of him in my mouth as I can. I moan around his length. He hits the back of my throat and I need to use my hand to work the rest of him. His moan wraps around me, filling me with pride as I bring him pleasure.

I continue to work him slowly, drawing out every last bit of his pleasure. His thighs tense, and I can tell he's close.

"I'm going to come, baby," he says as his grip on my hair loosens, allowing me the freedom to move.

But I don't want to. My hand leaves his balls, and I find his taint and massage it. His grip on my hair tightens again and his hips buck. Within seconds, he's coming. He groans my name as my mouth continues to move along his length.

When he's finished, I release him with a pop and use my thumb to collect any stray drops from my lips before licking them off. As he watches me, his eyes fill with hunger. His hands come under my arms and he lifts me. He spins us so I'm pressed against the cold tile of the shower wall before his lips descend on mine. He has no hesitations about tasting himself as his tongue invades my mouth.

His kiss is full of power and control, and I completely turn myself over to him. I follow his lead as he adjusts the angle of my head to kiss me deeper. I moan as his hand comes up and tweaks my nipple. This man is consuming me in the best ways possible, and I'm not sure I'm going to survive it.

He drops to his knees in front of me. "My turn," he says with a grin.

Before I can even say anything, he's spread my legs and his tongue has found my clit, flicking it. It's so sensitive my back pushes off the wall at the one touch. He chuckles between my thighs, lifting one leg over his shoulder to give him better access.

He's not slow like he's been in the past. He devours me with quick and relentless strokes of his tongue. His fingers join in, and within minutes, my legs are giving out as I come, calling his name.

He slowly kisses his way up my body until he's standing at his full height. He stares at me, his eyes full of emotion as he tucks a stray piece of hair behind my ear.

"You're stunning," he whispers.

I hold his eyes and see nothing but truth in them. If I've learned anything about this man, it's that what he says, he means.

He reverently kisses my forehead, cheeks, eyelids, nose, and then leaves a feather-light kiss on my lips. He rests his forehead against mine, closing his eyes.

"How are you real?" he asks.

I chuckle, and his eyes open.

"I could ask the same thing about you," I say.

We stare at each other for what feels like minutes before he reaches out and grabs my shampoo. He puts a generous amount in his hand before twirling his finger, and I spin. He slowly massages the shampoo into my scalp and down through my hair.

As his fingers work, he says, "You've chased the nightmares away." His voice is soft as he says it, as though he's scarred to put the words into the universe.

I don't say anything, waiting to see if he's going to say more.

"Before you started staying in my bed, I had nightmares every night. I would wake up in a sweat, my heart pounding out of my chest. Ever since you started spending every night in my bed, I haven't had a single one. You've saved me."

He rinses the shampoo out before working the conditioner into my ends and grabbing the bar of soap, washing every inch of my body. He's gentle with me. There's nothing sexual about this it's so much more. It's a simple act of taking care of me.

When he finishes, I do the same to him before he washes out the conditioner from my hair. He dries me off before drying himself, and we climb into bed together. As I snuggle into him, I realize that right here in his arms is the place I feel safest in this world, and that scares the shit out of me. What happens when this ends? Will I be able to find that place of safety with just myself?

"Stop overthinking," he whispers against my temple before kissing it.

"What?"

"You're overthinking about something. Stop."

"How'd you know?" I whisper.

"Baby, I know you. I can read your body, your feelings." His grip around me tightens as he holds me as close to him as possible. "Whatever you're thinking, it's all going to be fine."

He kisses my temple again, and I do my best to relax into him. His thumb runs over the skin under my left breast and the movement has me relaxing even more. He's learned all my tells and what relaxes me in such a short time. I fall asleep to the movement of his thumb and his steady breathing.

The sound of the door creaking open wakes both Caleb and me. He sits up, and I follow. Charlie is standing in the doorway, clutching her Princess.

"Caleb, can I sleep with you? I had a bad dream."

"Of course, Little Bear. Can you give me one minute?"

She nods and steps outside the door, and he quickly jumps out of bed and pulls on a pair of grey sweats and a black VPD shirt before opening the door and picking up Charlie. He carries her back to the bed before climbing in and bringing her with him. She nuzzles her way into his side, and he rubs a hand up and down her back. He leans down and kisses the top of her head, and my heart skips a beat.

"Do you want to tell me about it?" he asks her.

Silence fills the room. I think she's not going to say anything until her barely there voice comes out. "I had a dream you left and I never got to see you again."

Her little sob at the end of her sentence echoes around me.

His hand stops moving on her back. "Little Bear, can you look at me."

She moves her head so she's looking right at him.

"I will never leave you. You will always have me. No matter what happens, you can count on that. You can call me day or night. You can always talk to me. You will always have me. As long as you want me to be here, I will."

I have to brush away my own tears as I listen to him. That's such a big promise, yet I know he means every word of it. If he didn't, he wouldn't say it. He holds her tight to him and his other arm finds me, pulling me closer with Charlie positioned between us. He holds my hand over Charlie's back as she stays cuddled into his side.

"I will always love having my girls in my arms," he says before we drift asleep.

On Wednesday, I walk to the café on the corner for lunch. While I'm waiting in line, the hairs on the back of my neck rise, and I stiffen. I slowly move my head, looking for something, but I'm not sure what. I make my way to the front of the line and order a sandwich and a peppermint mocha. Grabbing my items, I move to a table that places my back in the corner and provides me a view of the entire café.

I scroll through the group chat finalizing plans for Boxing Day. As I read Olivia's last text, the chair across from me is pulled out, and someone sits in it. I don't have to lift my head to know who it is. My grip on my phone tightens, and I position it in my lap, out of his view. I look up and work to keep my face even. Derek looks at me, a look of triumph on his face. Cold washes through me as I look around to see if anyone is paying attention to us.

Derek leans forward. "Hi, honey. It's been so hard to get a hold of you. Is your phone not working? I've texted you several times."

I hear the restrained anger in his voice. It has me on high alert.

"I've been busy." My voice comes out weaker than I had hoped.

"You can't be too busy for me. I've wanted to see you, and Charlie, of course."

He stares at me, and it makes me want to push my chair as far away from him as possible. I force myself to stay put. Pushing away would just provoke him. My eyes dart down to my phone, and I select Caleb's number, making sure I turn the sound down on my phone so the ringing isn't audible.

"Well, I've got you here now. I want to spend Christmas with you. Why don't I come by Christmas Eve and spend the night and then we can do a whole thing on Christmas Day." He sounds so sure, like I couldn't possibly say no.

"We have plans for Christmas." My voice comes out stronger this time. The call timer on my phone appears, showing Caleb's picked up. Knowing he's on the phone gives me a sense of strength. "We can plan a supervised visit for you and Charlie at a park or somewhere next week."

His gaze hardens, and his hands that are resting on the table ball into fists. I flinch at the movement. He wouldn't do anything in public, would he?

"Cancel your plans. You should be spending the holiday with me." The anger and demanding tone of his voice cause me to shiver, and this time I do move my chair back.

"I can't and won't cancel. I made a commitment. Like I said, we can set something up for you and Charlie next week. Now, I'd like you to leave. I would like to finish my lunch in peace."

He pushes his chair back, placing his fists on the table as he leans in close. "You are my wife. You will spend Christmas with me. I won't give you a choice."

"Ex-wife." Caleb's voice sends a wave of calm through me.

I watch a look of absolute hatred cross Derek's face as he stands to his full height, puffs out his chest, and turns to face Caleb.

"This is none of your concern," Derek spits.

"You're currently harassing your ex-wife. If that didn't make it enough of my concern as an officer of the law, the fact that you're harassing my girl does." Caleb is taller and broader than Derek, but that doesn't seem to deter him from stepping closer to him.

"She will always be mine. I had her first, and I'm not letting her go." He spins and looks at me. "You really whoring yourself out for this thick skull? You really have lowered yourself, Bailey. I'll forgive it this one time, but know that I don't take kindly to cheating."

Caleb steps closer, forcing Derek to take a step back. He continues until Derek's back is pressed against the wall. Derek seems to lose his vibrato for a second before puffing out his chest again.

"She is your ex-wife. You don't get to make any decisions about her life. You'd be smart to leave her alone. Like she said, we can arrange for you to see Charlie next week. She will contact you when she's ready to set that up." Caleb leans in close and says something that has all the blood drain from Derek's face. When Caleb steps back, Derek walks towards the door, leaving without a second glance.

Caleb crouches in front of me, and I instantly wrap my arms around his neck. His head dips and his lips find the side of my neck while his arms wrap around my waist.

"Are you okay?" he whispers against my skin.

I nod against him.

He pulls back and his hands come to the side of my face as he tucks my hair behind my ears. "You sure?" Worry laces his voice as his eyes take me in.

"Yeah," I say before checking my phone. "I need to head back."

He nods and grabs my food and bag. We walk into the parking lot, and he leads me to his cruiser, opening the passenger door for me. We ride in silence for the few minutes it takes to get back to the office. When we arrive, he jumps out and opens my door. Before I can get out, his lips come to mine as he dusts a light kiss over them. Resting his forehead against mine, he whispers, "Thank you for calling me."

I stare into his eyes, reaching up and running my fingers through his hair. "Thank you for showing up," I whisper.

"Always," he says before kissing my forehead.

He helps me out, and I make my way into the office. I spend the rest of my shift on edge, worried that every time the door opens, it's going to be Derek that's walking in.

I power through the rest of the week. Once the weekend comes, I know Derek isn't going to be able to find me at Caleb's. Caleb and I agree to try to set up a meeting on the eighteenth. Caleb's off work and can go with us so I don't have to do it alone. Knowing he's going to be there makes it more bearable to think about.

Caleb

Derek never showed up to the scheduled meet-up with Charlie last week, so we spent time in the park just the three of us. Then I took the girls to get ice cream to take Charlie's mind off the fact her dad never showed. We took notes and recorded everything to help Bailey build her case to have Derek's visitation rights revoked.

We decided to spend Christmas Eve at home, just us. Bailey shares their traditions with me, an easy dinner in before baking cookies and watching Christmas movies with hot chocolate.

Bailey hands me a wrapped gift, and I look at it with furrowed brows. "I thought we were doing gifts tomorrow."

"We are, but this is the Christmas Eve gift," she says with a wide smile as she hands another gift to Charlie and takes one herself. They begin to unwrap theirs, and I open mine. My heart skips a beat as I see what she wrapped. I hold my pair of matching pyjamas in my hands and close my eyes.

Matching pyjamas is something families do.

This small gift means more to me than anything anyone else could get me. I reach out and pull both girls into a hug, kissing the tops of their heads and hoping my tears don't fall. I don't cry, but being pulled into this family—and being wanted—is making me more emotional than I've been since my dad's death.

Charlie secures the matching bandana around Finn's neck before we head upstairs and change. Bailey insists on getting a photo of the four of us, so I hold Charlie on my hip while Bailey uses her phone for the picture. We take several, some nice and some silly. I watch as Bailey selects one of me kissing her temple and Charlie kissing my cheek and makes it her lock screen.

I lean down and whisper in her ear, "Send me those, please."

She smiles and nods before we bundle up on the couch. Charlie insists on sitting on my lap, and Bailey tucks into my side. Contentment washes over me.

After Charlie falls asleep, I carry her upstairs and get her settled in her bed. I meet Bailey in the hallway, and we begin taking gifts out of our closet and bringing them downstairs, placing them under the tree. I stuff Bailey and Charlie's stockings while she fixes some of the gifts. When she gets up and turns to them, tears fill her eyes.

"You stuffed them," she whispers.

Her eyes find mine, and I stride right for her, wiping the tears as they fall. Her eyes close, and she leans into my touch.

"I always had to stuff all the stockings," she says. "I didn't stuff my own at first. And as Charlie got older, she would ask me about mine and I had to tell her Mommy didn't get one. I decided to stuff my own after that first year so she wouldn't ask me about it."

Anger rises in my chest. Who doesn't stuff his wife's and child's stockings? At least his wife's, if she does his and their kid's. Standing here, I vow to myself that I will make sure her and Charlie's stockings are stuffed every year.

"You don't need to worry about that anymore," I say, giving her a quick kiss. "I'll take care of it from now on."

She closes her eyes, and I lean my forehead against hers. After a minute, we make our way upstairs and I hold her close as we fall asleep.

After breakfast, we head into the living room and open stockings. Charlie is ecstatic about all her chocolate. She pulls out her new crayons, card game, and socks with bears printed all over them. She ignores everything else and brings the socks right to me.

"Look Caleb, Santa brought me socks with bears. You call me Little Bear. It's so cool," she says excitedly.

I smile at her and run my hand over her hair. "That is really cool. So, you like your new socks?"

She nods vigorously. "They're my favourites."

She goes back to her stocking, slowly putting everything back inside before helping Finn take everything out of the stocking Bailey insisted we get him. He excitedly plays with his new toys, and I set the treats on the side table. Once his stocking is done, Charlie puts everything back into it, like she did hers, and comes over to Bailey.

"Mommy, I cleaned up my stocking. Can we open presents now?" she asks as she clutches her hands together and places them under her chin in a pleading motion.

Bailey smiles at her. "Yeah, Baby Girl, we can open presents."

Bailey drops to the floor in front of the tree and hands a gift to Charlie. "This one's for Caleb," she says, and Charlie runs the gift to me.

I thank her as she runs back to Bailey, grabbing her own gift before settling on the floor in front of me.

I look down and read the gift tag.

To: Caleb
Love: Charlie

I open the gift, and inside is a hoodie that says, *It's okay if you don't like hockey. It's kind of a smart people sport* with crossed hockey sticks in the middle. I laugh, and have Charlie come over so I can hug her and thank her for my gift. She shows me the new dress her mom bought her and then she opens another gift. She sits in my lap as she pulls out the giant haul of books I bought her. Her voice is full of excitement as she pulls each one out.

She turns in my lap and hands me a book. "Will you read this one to me?" she asks, and I chuckle.

"I will, but how about we open the rest of the presents?"

"Promise?"

"Promise," I say.

Bailey hands her another gift and then she hands me one. She looks hesitant as I take it from her and slowly take the wrapping paper off the box. When I open it, I see a digital photo frame as well as additional frames underneath. I pull them out and see a photo of me with the guys at a game. There's one of me and Charlie the first time I took her on the ice, one of the three of us Christmas tree shopping, one of me and Finn in the backyard. I continue to go through the stack until I come to one at the bottom. It's of my dad and me at a hockey game when I was a kid. I stare at it, stunned. I don't know how she managed to get her hands on this.

"I asked your mom for that picture," Bailey whispers beside me.

I raise my gaze and meet hers. She gnaws on her lip as she stares at me.

"You don't have a lot of pictures, and I thought that maybe adding a few might warm the place up a bit," she says as she fiddles with her fingers in her lap.

I reach out, my hand going to the back of her neck, I pull her in for a slow kiss. This gift was not about the material, but rather she put a great deal of thought into it. She melts into me as she kisses me back.

I break the kiss and whisper, "Thank you," across her lips.

She smiles and whispers back, "You're welcome."

"Open yours," I say when we pull apart, and she goes back to the tree and pulls out two individually wrapped boxes with her name on them. She opens the smaller box first, and inside is a pair of drop earrings with an amethyst stone in each. She stares at them for a minute before her eyes come back up to mine.

"They're amethyst. It's Charlie's birthstone."

"They're gorgeous," she says as she takes them out and immediately puts them in, not caring that she's currently wearing pyjamas with Santa printed all over them. It's adorable.

I hand her the other gift, and she opens it with a smile. Inside is a gold locket. It's open to a picture of Charlie. I caught her staring at one during our trip to the mall, so I went to a jewelry store and found one worthy of her. She holds it reverently before she hands it to me and turns, lifting her hair so I can secure it around her neck.

She kisses me. "Best gifts I've ever received," she whispers, and pride washes over me.

She snuggles into my side as we watch Charlie open the rest of her gifts. She opens a set of American Girl dolls I got her as well as clothes she can dress them in. There are a few games and movies too.

She seems elated by all of it. Charlie goes over to the tree and grabs the last gift. It's from Charlie to Bailey. I helped her wrap it and put it under the tree.

"For you, Mommy," she says.

Bailey sits up, taking the gift. She looks over her shoulder at me and then back to the gift. She carefully opens the box, and her jaw drops as she looks inside and then back at me.

She pulls out each vinyl album in awe. When I asked Charlie what she wanted to get her mom for Christmas, she told me Taylor Swift, so I did some research and we got her all the albums on vinyl.

"Do you like them, Mommy?" Charlie asks.

Bailey's eyes jump up to her daughter's. "Yeah, Baby Girl, I love them."

She sets the box aside and hugs her. I pull my phone out and snap a picture of the two of them. They both turn and look at me, and I snap another, then set it as my lock screen.

When Charlie goes back to her toys, I say, "My mom has my dad's old record player. She doesn't use it and said we can bring it home with us tonight after dinner."

"You're not real," is all she says before returning to her position at my side.

I wrap my arm around her as we sit and watch Charlie play with her new toys.

We eventually clean everything up and head upstairs, getting changed before heading to dinner at my mom's place. We load the gifts for my family into the back of the truck before heading over. When we get there, Bailey insists on helping in the kitchen and Sarah wants to hang out with Charlie, so Max and I sit on the couch in the living room, each with a beer in our hands.

"You love her," he says.

My head whips to him, and he looks at me with a shit-eating grin and chuckles.

"Never thought I'd see the day when my baby brother was head over heels for a woman, but I've got to say, I'm happy for you, man."

I take a deep breath and lean my head against the back of the couch. After a minute, I lift my head and look towards Bailey through the entryway between the kitchen and living room. "I'm not sure she's ready for the words," I say. There's no point in denying my feelings because he's right. I've fallen for both of these girls, but I'm not sure Bailey is ready to be loved again, no matter how much I want to.

"Don't give up on her." Max's voice is soft as he says it.

I look him dead in the eyes. "Never. I will never give up on her. She will always have me." My voice is full of conviction.

He pats me on the shoulder. "Good," he says before pushing off the couch and making his way over to his wife. He kisses the top of her head then heads into the kitchen.

"Dinner's ready," Mom calls from the kitchen.

Dinner is relaxed, and everyone laughs as we eat and talk. When we finish, we move into the living room for our gift exchange. Mom has completely spoiled Charlie. Bailey grips my hand as she watches Charlie unwrap everything.

"It's too much," she whispers.

I kiss her temple. "Mom wouldn't do this if she didn't want to. Don't worry about it," I say.

"I thought you could keep some of these new toys here, for when you come and visit Gran," Mom says, and Charlie nods excitedly.

Mom got Bailey a peacoat and a scarf, and brings out the record player for her. Bailey fawns over it, and it has both Mom and me smiling.

Max is looking at us like his every suspicion has been confirmed. I get up and make my way into the kitchen to grab a glass of water when Mom joins me. She jerks her head towards the stairs, and I follow her up them. She leads me into her room and makes her way into her closet before returning and handing me a small velvet box.

"Your brother wanted to buy a new one when he proposed, but I have a feeling that your Bailey will like the sentimentality of this one. Your father would have loved both her and Charlie. He'd be so happy for you," she says.

I look down at the box in my hand and open it. Inside is my mother's engagement ring. It's a simple white gold band with a round stone in the centre. It's not overly showy, but big enough to be a statement piece. It was for years. It represented my parents' love for one another. I know Mom's right, this is the perfect ring for Bailey when it's time.

"I see it in your eyes," she says softly. "The way you look at them both. I see your love and devotion for both of them. I know you'll spend the rest of your life protecting and loving them. Your father would be so proud of the man you've become."

I take a deep breath and close my eyes as I wrap my arms around my mom. There's something about a hug from her that centres me, even at almost thirty years old.

"Thanks, Mom."

She pats my back and pulls away. "I'm happy for you, Caleb."

Her hand comes up, and she gives my cheek two light taps before she leaves her room. I stare at the ring for a minute before stuffing the ring box into my pocket and heading downstairs.

CHAPTER 29

Caleb

Boxing Day morning is easy and relaxing. We sleep in, eat breakfast, and cuddle on the couch while watching Christmas movies. Josh and Liv are hosting us for Boxing Day dinner, so after lunch, we load gifts into the car and drive to their place.

Charlie is so excited to spend the day with her Aunty Liv. When we get up to their place, Liv shows us to the Christmas tree where we leave all the gifts. Charlie starts telling them about all the new gifts she got. Once everyone arrives, the girls head into the kitchen and work on dinner together while the guys and I hang in the living room. We brought some toys for Charlie, and after a while, she brings over one of her new books and asks, "Caleb, will you read it to me?"

I smile at her. "Yeah, Little Bear, climb right up."

She climbs onto the couch and snuggles into my side while I open up the book and start reading. I notice the room has quieted and the guys are watching me. It doesn't stop me from reading or doing voices, just like Charlie enjoys.

When I finish, she takes it and returns to her toys on the floor.

"You're good with her," Grayson says.

I look at him with a smile. "She's a good kid," I say.

He shakes his head. "Nah, man, it's more than that. You engage with her. You don't just brush her off when she's looking for your time and attention. That's important."

I mull his words over. I feel like that's just part of being human. Kids are human too. They deserve respect, to be listened to. Charlie's kind and smart. She's strong and resilient. It doesn't take much from me to pay attention to her when she asks for it.

I push off the couch and make my way into the kitchen to grab something to drink. The girls are huddled in the corner talking. When I enter, the chatter stops. I chuckle as I make my way to the fridge.

"Spilling secrets now, are we?" I ask as I grab a beer from the fridge and a juice box for Charlie.

I turn and face them. They're all staring at me with smiles, except Bailey, whose cheeks are flushed and she's tucking her hair behind her ear. I have a feeling she's been the one spilling secrets. I grin at her, placing the drinks on the counter before I stalk over to her. I crowd her, my right hand going into her hair and gripping it, pulling her head back so her eyes meet mine. Her eyes go wide as she stares at me, and I just grin before my lips meet hers. Her entire body melts into mine as I kiss her deeply. This kiss is far from PG, but right now, I couldn't care less.

Her hands fist the front of my shirt, and a moan escapes her. My left hand finds her ass, giving a quick squeeze before I smack it. Having the freedom to touch her when I want has only intensified the need to touch her. When I break the kiss, my lips trail along her jaw until they find the shell of her ear. "So you have more to brag about."

With one more smack on her ass, I turn and grab the drinks. Out of the corner of my eye, I see Hannah pulling her hands apart as Bailey says, "Biggest I've ever seen."

I don't think she knows I heard her. I shake my head slightly and make my way back into the living room. Josh looks at me as I enter and grins. I give him a quick chin lift before putting the straw in the juice box and handing it to Charlie.

"Thank you," she says with a large smile.

I lean down and kiss the top of her head before settling back on the couch. The guys are talking about how the season is going for the Vancouver Cyclones, our local NHL hockey team. I fill them in about Bailey's run-in with Derek the other day. Tension is written on all of their faces. They're all fiercely protective of those they love and, by extension, those each of us loves.

"If you need anything, let me know," Josh says.

"Thanks, man. We're trying to set something up for this week after he missed the last one. So we'll see how everything goes."

"Dinner," Liv calls, and we make our way into their large dining room.

Olivia has gone all out with the decorations. A table runner spans the entire length of the table. An elaborate Christmas-themed centrepiece sits in the middle with candles spread out among the abundance of food.

Everyone finds seats around the table and I make Charlie's plate as the conversation around the table flows.

"The decorations are gorgeous," Josh says to Liv. It's an odd thing for him to say, but I attribute it to his being head over heels in love.

"Thanks, babe," she says, smiling at him.

"You're whipped," Grayson says from the other end of the table.

Josh just grins at him. "Call it what you want, but I call it love."

"Sure."

"Just wait, you'll find your love story, and when you find the one, you won't be saying any of this," Josh says.

Grayson groans, leaning his head back, but Josh continues. "You'll meet a girl and you'll say you noticed sparks fly and they'll be yours forever and always."

"Okay, enough with this lovey-dovey stuff," Grayson says.

"You a little sour puss because you can't keep a girl?" Hannah says in a high mocking tone. This girl really likes to get under Grayson's skin. I'm not sure what he did to her, but I wouldn't want to be on Hannah's bad side.

"Do I need to teach you how you get the girl?" Josh prods, and something in my head clicks, making me groan. I use my napkin to wipe my mouth as Josh says, "You should be fearless and ride in on your white horse and say you're enchanted by her and that long story short, she's your end game."

I groan so loud that everyone looks at me. "As much as I enjoy messing with Grayson, and I'm not sure who this says more about, you or me, but you can stop with the Taylor Swift song titles," I say.

Olivia throws her arms up and pushes off her chair before she runs around the table and wraps her arms around me from behind. "I love you, thank you. I just won a bet," she says.

"You're welcome," I say, confused.

As she rounds the table, Matt stares at me. "Really dude, you had to say something?"

"What? Josh said like twelve song titles, it was getting to be a little much."

Matt, still confused, says, "You were able to identify twelve Taylor Swift songs in that?"

"Yeah."

"How?" Matt asks.

"My girls love Taylor Swift. I'm constantly hearing it," I say with a shrug.

Grayson laughs. "You really are fucking pussy whipped."

I glare at him. "Watch your language in front of my daughter," I growl.

The entire table goes silent, and Grayson's eyes widen. He puts his hands up in a placating manner. "Sorry, man. I'll watch the language, but that doesn't mean it isn't true."

"Josh is right too. When you find someone you love, you'll do anything for them. You won't be saying this stuff then."

Grayson continues eating. "Not going to happen," he grumbles. "Sure."

I turn the conversation to Liv, who apparently was the mastermind of this bet. "Okay, so what exactly was this bet?" I ask.

She grins. "Well, Matt and I got into a little debate about how popular Taylor Swift is, so we made a bet. I said if Josh could throw song titles into a conversation and not get called out on it, I would let Matt find out the sex of the baby." She rolls her eyes, and I can see the unease on Josh's face. "But, if I won, I get to set him up on a date with someone and he has to go on at least three dates with her."

Bailey's hand comes to my thigh, and her thumb gently strokes over the fabric of my pants. I look to my left, my eyes meeting Bailey's tear-filled ones. My hand instantly goes to her face. "What's wrong, baby?"

She closes her eyes and leans into my touch. When she opens them, an electric shock runs through my body.

"Your daughter?" she whispers.

When I nod, she whispers, "I love you."

Her voice is so quiet I almost don't hear her. A smile spreads across my face as my entire body feels light and warm. I lean my forehead against hers.

"I love you," I whisper before giving her a quick kiss.

I never thought I'd utter those words to another woman. But I've never felt this soul-deep love that I do for Bailey. I'm always aware of her presence. Just stepping into her embrace can have all the tension leaving my body. My hand goes to her thigh as we continue eating.

I'm over the moon as we finish dinner. I've got my friends around me and, most importantly, I have my two girls. And Bailey just told me she loves me. I didn't think she would be the one to say it first, not that it matters. All that matters is she feels the same about me.

I'm not sure I deserve the love of someone as amazing as her. She calms my soul. She's pulled me from my nightmares on several nights. She's so unbelievably strong, and I know I will spend the rest of my life working to be worthy of her love.

Charlie, my beautiful little Charlotte, is so resilient. She has seen things most children will, and should never, see. She continues to be a happy girl who laughs and gets excited about the little things in life. The way she has accepted new people into her life over these last few months and bonded with them makes my heart swell.

When we finish eating, I help Josh clear the table. As we make our way into the kitchen, Matt and Grayson join us.

"Your daughter?" Grayson says, leaning against the kitchen counter with his arms crossed over his chest.

"Yeah, my daughter," I say.

The kitchen is silent except for the sound of the dishes as we place them in the sink. I turn and look at Matt and Grayson. Matt's got a quizzical expression while Grayson's got his eyebrow quirked.

"What?" I ask, a little irritated these fuckers won't just spit it out.

"That's just a big declaration. Have you discussed this with Bailey? Are you going to adopt her? What about her biological father? Does Charlie want this? It just seems like there are a lot of other things that need to be addressed with this declaration," Grayson says.

"Are they permanently moving in with you? Is Bailey getting rid of their place?" Matt adds.

I leave the dishes in the sink and turn to face them, spreading my legs shoulder-width apart and crossing my arms over my chest. I look at Josh, who's remained silent this entire time.

"Anything to add?" I grind out.

He holds his hands out in front of him, palms out. "Nope, unlike these fuckers, I know what it's like to be head over heels for your girl. I also know what it means when you'll do anything for them. You may have me beat by falling for two of them, but I know the feeling."

I nod at him and move my stare over to Matt and Grayson. "First, no, I hadn't discussed it with Bailey, it just came out. I love both of them, and I plan on marrying Bailey one day. And if they both say yes, I do plan on adopting Charlie. She may not share my blood, but I will always see her as mine. I will do whatever Charlie and Bailey are comfortable with. Whatever they want. As for her biological father, the man is only looking to get back with Bailey. I don't believe he has an actual interest in his daughter. Which is a damn shame because she's an amazing little girl. As for their place, I have no plans on them ever moving out of my place unless I'm moving with them." I run a hand through my hair, allowing the next words to really soak in. "They have ingrained themselves into me so much that I'm not sure I'd live if they left me. Those girls saved me. I don't think they'll ever be able to truly understand just how much they saved me. Because of them, I wake up looking forward to the day. I'm no longer just going through the motions."

The three of them nod, knowing I just told them more about my emotions and how I've been since coming back than I ever have. I make eye contact with Grayson.

"I told her about Tyler," I say.

His jaw drops. I haven't even told him about what happened with him. He met Tyler one of the times we were home on leave and he knows he didn't come back, but that's all he knows.

CHAPTER 30

Bailey

I'm entirely in my feelings as I process how Caleb — in front of his friends, the people closest to him — claimed my daughter as his. No questions about it, called her his daughter. He's brought so much into our lives. A new friend group that's more like family. His family has embraced us wholeheartedly, and he makes me feel safe. He brought us into his home after one of the worst experiences of my life. I don't think I could love this man more.

Needing to show him just how much he means to me with more than words, I change into black lace lingerie after I finish my shower and stand at the foot of the bed. Caleb steps into the room. His eyes hungrily eat up the sight of me, and it sends a thrill through me.

His pupils dilate, and he licks his lips as he takes measured steps towards me. My chest is rising and falling so quickly I can feel the hem of the babydoll grazing across the tops of my thighs.

"Fucking hell," he rasps as his finger reaches out and trails the edge of the fabric covering my breasts.

His slight touch sends goosebumps across my skin. I watch as his eyes trail the movements of his finger. His pupils are so large I almost can't see the steel grey anymore.

"What do you want to do?" I ask breathlessly.

His eyes snap to mine, filled with hesitation. "I'm not going to do those things. I don't want to cross a boundary that will scare you."

His features soften as he says that, but I know deep in my bones this man would never hurt me. In the same way I know the sun will rise tomorrow, that two plus two is four, and I need oxygen to breathe, I know Caleb will never hurt me.

Resolved, I say, "What do you want? I trust you."

He stares at me intensely before he gives his head a slight shake. He opens his mouth, and I blurt, "Pineapple."

His brows draw together in confusion.

"My safe word. Pineapple. I promise that if something goes too far, I'll use my safe word."

His eyes widen, and I reach across my body, slowly pushing one strap of the babydoll down.

His eyes are stuck to the movement.

"Please, tell me what you want." My voice is soft, and it seems to snap something in him.

His hand comes to my neck as he grasps it, not tightly, but in a possessive manner that sends heat radiating through me and has my pussy clenching.

He brings his mouth to my ear. "I want you naked and on your knees while I see just how well you take the biggest cock you've ever seen. I want to watch your pretty lips stretch around me as I fuck your mouth until I hit the back of your throat. Then I want you tied to my bed, spread eagle, so you can't move while I eat your pretty pussy."

My head falls back as I picture it.

"I want you so on edge that the moment I thrust into your tight little cunt, you come for me. Then I want to flip you over and spank your ass until it's covered in my pink hand marks. I want to fuck you so hard you can't walk. I want you screaming my name so much you won't remember your own. I want you to know that you're mine."

I'm soaked. The way he growls the word mine has me questioning my sanity because I've never wanted to be possessed the way I want Caleb to possess me.

I squeeze my thighs together, trying to quench the ache between them. I can feel my arousal on the inside of my thighs. Fuck, it's embarrassing how turned on I am just from his words.

His teeth scrape my ear lobe. "Does that make you wet, Bailey?"

I've lost the ability to speak, so I nod. When he pulls back, I lift my head to meet his gaze. His is hungry. No, it's ravenous.

Not wanting to wait any longer, I throw the babydoll over my head and push my panties down before dropping to my knees in front of him. I reach for his jeans, undoing the button and pulling the zipper down.

"So eager," he says, and my mouth waters as I slowly pull his jeans and boxer briefs over his ass and watch his cock pop free.

I grip the base in one hand, lean forward, and lick him from base to tip. He groans, his hand coming to my hair. His words about fucking my mouth come back to me. My hand meets his on top of my head as the other finds his thigh, and I relinquish control to him.

He tightens his grip on my hair. "If it's too much for you, tap my thigh twice," he says.

I nod as much as I can, and his hips thrust forward.

He truly fucks my mouth. My hand goes back to his base, working what I can't with my mouth. When he hits the back of my throat, he slows.

"Relax for me, baby."

I do exactly as he says and I'm able to take more of him. I feel him coming undone as he thrusts faster and incoherent noises leave him. I move my hand from his thigh to his balls and roll them once. That's his undoing. He thrusts a few more times as he empties his release down my throat.

When he's done, he removes himself before reaching down and lifting me into his arms. He kisses me as my legs wrap around his waist and he walks us to the bed. When he places me on the bed, he does it softly, with reverence. No matter the situation, this man makes me feel like I'm the most precious thing in the world.

He retreats to the closet and comes back with four ties. The knowledge of what he's going to do with those only turns me on more. I hurriedly scurry to the middle of the bed and position myself so he can wrap the ties. Lying spread eagle like this is exposing. My every extra ounce of fat, every stretch mark, every flaw is there for him to see. But with Caleb, I don't feel self-conscious or unsafe. I feel worshiped. Desired. Coveted.

He takes his time wrapping the ties around my wrists, securing them to the bed frame before doing the same with my ankles.

When he's finished, he stands at the end of the bed and slowly removes his clothes. I watch with bated breath as he exposes every carved muscle of his chest. As he finishes shoving his jeans off, I take in his massive, muscular thighs.

This man could easily overpower me, but knowing he never will fills me with a sense of power I never knew I could feel. One simple word, and he would stop. Knowing that with one word, this could all end makes me feel more powerful than I ever have in this life.

Caleb crawls up my body slowly, his eyes never leaving mine. When his face is level with mine, his lips crash into mine. His kiss is all-consuming. I pull at my bindings, wishing I could wrap my arms and legs around him and pull him closer. But something about him being in complete control makes the kiss that much hotter.

I melt into the bed, and he follows me down. His hand comes to my hair as he adjusts my head, allowing him to taste more of me. When his lips leave mine, I'm breathless. His lips are soft as they trail down my neck, over my breasts, and across my stomach until he reaches the apex of my thighs. I sigh as I lift my hips, looking for his mouth. He places soft kisses from hip to hip before his tongue finally tastes me. I'm so on edge, so built up, that the single sensation of his tongue over my clit has me moaning his name.

His tongue works fervently, bringing me to the edge, and as soon as I'm about to come, he stops. I groan, needing to fall over the edge, needing to come, but he refuses. His mouth returns, and he continues to work, licking and tasting. Each movement of his tongue has my body tightening. I pull at my bindings as I moan his name.

When I'm on the cusp of an orgasm, he pulls away, this time kissing up my body. His teeth scrape over my sensitive nipples. I hold my breath as the sensation rushes through my body. He continues to drag his lips up my body until he's hovering over me.

"You're so beautiful, all pink and wound-up for me," he murmurs against my lips before kissing me. I taste myself on him, but it doesn't matter. All I want is that connection to him. His hand comes to my breast, and he gives it a squeeze before pulling my nipple. My chest thrusts up to meet his hand, but I don't find release.

He smiles as he grips his cock in his other hand and uses the tip to play with my sensitive clit. I'm panting as I watch him. Positioning himself at my entrance, he thrusts inside me in one motion, stretching and filling me completely.

I shatter.

My pussy tightens around him as I grip my bindings as best I can to ground myself. It doesn't work.

Caleb fucks me through my orgasm. His face in the crook of my neck as he murmurs, "Such a good girl, taking my cock like this," and, "So fucking sexy."

But the words that send me into my second orgasm, so intense that tears fall, are, "Mine. Mine to fuck. Mine to protect. Mine to love."

He kisses me passionately through the orgasm. I ride it for what feels like forever. I've never come so intensely. It's as though every ounce of stress has been removed from my body. I'm limp. He pulls out of me and unties my hands and feet before helping me roll onto my stomach. He lifts my ass and thrusts into me. I grip the sheets, tears still staining my cheeks, but I find the strength to meet his thrusts.

His hand comes down and meets my ass, sending a shockwave of pleasure through me. It only takes three spanks before I'm coming again. He has to hold my hips as my legs give out from under me. My orgasm sends him over the edge, and he calls my name before he collapses on top of me.

He catches his breath and moves to lie beside me, tucking my hair behind my ear. His gaze is heistant. Mustering all my strength, I move closer to him, throwing my leg over his and bringing my hand behind his neck. I pull him in and kiss him. It's nothing like the kisses we shared during sex; this one is more emotional. I kiss him slowly, savouring him. He kisses me back just as softly.

"I love you," I whisper against his lips.

He smiles against mine, whispering back, "I love you more."

We lie like that, kissing each other and whispering I love you for a few minutes before he rolls off the bed and picks me up. He carries me into the washroom, settling me on the counter before drawing a bath. I use the bathroom before we settle in the warm water. His thumb skates in slow movements over my stomach and it lulls me to sleep.

I barely wake up when Caleb lifts me out of the tub, dries me off, and carries me to bed. As I'm drifting to sleep again, I think I hear him whisper, "I'm going to marry you," before placing a kiss on my temple.

In the morning, I wake to an empty bed. Climbing out, I wrap my robe around me before making my way downstairs. The sound of Caleb in the kitchen has me smiling. That man is mine. I've never been so proud to be able to say that about a man, but with Caleb it's like I've landed a prize I never thought I'd get.

Before I step into the kitchen, Charlie says, "I have a question." She can't see me from here, so she must be talking to Caleb.

"Okay, what's your question?" I can hear him cutting something.

Charlie doesn't say anything for a minute, and when she does, her voice is soft. "Yesterday, you said you love Mommy."

I hear him place the knife down and his feet move across the floor before the sound of a chair being pulled out travels through the air. I press myself against the wall and listen with bated breath.

"I do love your mommy, and I love you too," he says. Hearing those words from him will never get old.

"You do?" Charlie's voice is so hesitant. It breaks my heart knowing she questions his love, and I know it stems from her father.

"Yeah, I do. Charlotte, I will spend the rest of life showing you how loved you and your mom are."

I hear the shuffling of a chair again.

"Charlotte, what can I do so you know I love you?"

I love that he communicates with her like she's a person who can think for herself. Not many people would ask that question, let alone ask a child.

"I don't know," Charlie says.

"What about a hug?"

She doesn't say anything, but I assume she nods because I hear her get out of her chair. Deciding I've done enough snooping, I step into the kitchen and call, "Good morning."

Caleb's still holding Charlie in his arms as he smiles at me and says, "Good morning." Placing a kiss on the top of her head, he asks, "Do you want to go see your mom?"

She holds on to him for a few more seconds before she walks up to me and hugs me tightly.

"I love you, Mommy."

"I love you more, Baby Girl," I say, leaning down and kissing the top of her head. Caleb sits and watches us before coming over and kissing me.

"How'd you sleep?" he asks.

"Like a baby."

"Good, well, I'm making breakfast, so I hope you're hungry."

I grin at him. "Ravenous."

He returns to his cutting board and the fruit he was cutting while Charlie and I settle at the kitchen table. Caleb brings me a cup of coffee with a chaste kiss before giving Charlie her orange juice and kissing the top of her head.

As Charlie draws, I think about all the times he's kissed the top of Charlie's head or ran his fingers through her hair. Every time he's kissed me just because he was nearby. He makes us breakfast every morning and makes sure Charlie and I are properly bundled up before we go outside. Caleb shows his love through acts of service and physical touch.

I'm an emotional wreck as I hold back my tears. I've cried more being with him than I did during the entirety of my relationship with Derek. But these tears aren't sad. They're freeing tears because I know I'm safe. That Charlie is safe. I can show my feelings around Caleb, and it won't feel like the world is crumbling around me because he's right there to hold it all for me.

After breakfast, Caleb says, "So, I was thinking we could go to the aquarium today."

"Yay!" Charlie cheers.

"That sounds amazing. Charlie, why don't you head up and get cleaned up and changed, okay?"

She slides out of her chair and says, "Okay, Mommy," before running upstairs.

As soon as she's out of sight, Caleb lifts me out of my chair so that I'm straddling his lap. I giggle as he moves me. My arms instantly go around his neck, and I settle in his lap. His arms wrap around me, and he grabs my ass, making sure I don't fall.

"Morning, beautiful," he says as he brings his lips to mine.

I grin back. "Morning, sexy." I lean in and kiss him.

"I hope you don't mind me planning this little family outing," he says, and my grin gets wider. I'm glad he planned something for all of us to do together, and him calling it a family outing makes it so much better.

I shake my head, and his smile begins to drop, but my words bring it back. "Caleb, I'm glad you planned something. You wanting to do things with us will never upset me."

Giving me another kiss and a slap on the ass, he says, "I'm glad. Now why don't we go upstairs and change so we can take our girl to the aquarium."

I shuffle off his lap and run up the stairs, Caleb right on my heels giving me love taps on my ass the entire way up, causing me to giggle.

I can't pinpoint when it was exactly or how long it took him, but Caleb, at one point, started slowly moving my things from the guest room into his. When he does laundry, he does both of ours, and he started putting my things away in his closet.

I make my way into the closet and undo my robe, hanging it beside the door. I turn to grab a bra and panties. Out of the corner of my eye, I see Caleb leaning against the door frame, watching me.

"Can I help you?" I ask, amused.

"Nope. I'm just enjoying the view of my very sexy, very naked girlfriend."

I chuckle as I put on my bra and panties.

"What's the laugh for?" he asks, his voice sounding annoyed.

"Because I know that only half of that statement was true."

I pull on a pair of jeans and a red, long-sleeved shirt. When I turn to him, he looks angry. I've never seen that look directed towards me before.

"Bailey, please don't tell me I only meant half of what I said. I meant every word." He stalks towards me, grabbing my hand as he places it over his very hard cock. "This is what you do to me. This is the reaction I have to you. If you don't want to believe the words, believe this very physical proof." He leans in close, his breath dusting over my ear, sending goosebumps across my skin. "Next time you think I don't find you to be the sexiest thing I've ever seen, I'll bend you over and fuck you so hard and long that your pussy will never forget just how much I crave you."

He palms my ass and pulls me closer. "This ass is fucking sexy as hell. It gets me hard every time I see you dancing in the kitchen while you clean."

He drops to his knees in front of me, pushing up my shirt. He kisses my stretch marks. "These show me your strength and sacrifice to grow our beautiful girl."

Standing up, he grabs my breasts and says, "And don't get me started on how much I love these. In fact, I plan on fucking these tonight just to prove to you how much I love them."

He kisses me and steps back as if he didn't just say life-altering things to me. He then hooks his thumbs into the waistband of his sweats and pushes them down his legs, his erection springing free. I stare at it, licking my lips, which causes a guttural groan to escape Caleb.

"Baby, if you keep doing that, we won't be leaving here anytime soon, and we promised our girl a trip to the aquarium. So, get your sexy ass out of the closet while I get changed, so we can leave."

I nod and quickly shuffle out. Caleb smacks my ass as I pass him.

In Charlie's room, I find her wearing a shirt Caleb got for her for Christmas. It's pink, and the front says *Ice Princess*. I smile at how she went straight for a shirt he got her.

"Baby girl, you ready?" I ask, leaning against her doorframe. She looks up at me while putting her socks on.

She nods. "I just need my shoes."

"Okay. Let's go downstairs and put those on so we can go see the fish."

She hops up, and we make our way downstairs. As I finish putting on our shoes, Caleb comes down the stairs. He moves with precision as he takes each step. I watch the flex of the muscles in his thighs. When he reaches the bottom, he smirks, and I know he caught me checking him out. He ensures both Charlie and I are properly bundled with gloves, scarves, and toques before we head to the truck.

Arriving at the aquarium, Charlie insists on holding Caleb's hand, and he smiles as he takes hers. He holds mine with the other, and we get in line to purchase tickets. I go to reach for my wallet, but his hand instantly goes to mine and he gives me a hard stare and shakes his head.

"Bailey, you're with me. When you're with me, my girls don't pay. I've got it."

He taps his card before grabbing my hand again. When we step inside the door, he shuffles us off to the side quickly. His hand leaves mine, and his arm wraps around my middle, pulling me in close. He looks down at Charlie with a soft smile, then back at me.

He speaks to both of us. "I don't want you two to need, want, or worry about anything. That means, when we go out, I pay. You need something, you tell me, and I'll get it. I will always take care of my girls. I promise you that." He looks down at Charlie, his arm dropping from around my waist as he crouches in front of her. "Charlotte, my Little Bear. You know you can always count on your mom, but I want you to know you can come to me with anything too."

She nods and wraps her arms around his neck, hugging him. "I love you," she whispers.

"I love you more, Little Bear."

Of course, this conversation is happening in the middle of a very public place and I'm now on the brink of tears.

He stands up and pulls me into him. His lips dust over my temple. "I want to take care of you. You're not on your own anymore."

He kisses me softly, and we move towards the entrance for the tropical fish. As we get closer, Charlie pulls her hand free and starts to run forward.

"Charlotte," Caleb calls, and she stops in her tracks and turns to him with a perplexed look. He never calls her by her full name.

He crouches. She steps closer, and Caleb takes her hands.

"We're going to set a couple of ground rules, okay?" he asks, and she nods.

"I want you to have fun today, but I need to know you're safe. There are lots of people here. You don't have to hold our hand the whole time. You're a big girl, but we need to be able to see you. So you can't run too far ahead. You need to make sure you can see us too. If you can't find us, you find someone wearing a uniform that says security or a blue shirt with the aquarium logo and you have them call us and we will be right there. Okay?"

She nods again, and he leans in and kisses her forehead.

"Okay, let's go see some fish."

She grins, turning and making her way to the tank filled with blue fish. Pressing her hands to the glass, she stares inside with a look of pure joy.

A fish swims towards her, and her eyes light up. Bouncing on her toes, she turns towards us. "Daddy, it's Dory. Come see Dory."

I freeze. Is Derek here? And if he is, how did he find us? My head swivels, and my eyes are peeled, looking for that familiar frame of the man I used to love. Charlie, impatient, runs up to us, grabbing Caleb's hand and pulling him. "Daddy, come see Dory."

All the emotions that rush through me at once are overwhelming. Relief that Derek isn't here. Love for my daughter and the relationship she's built with Caleb. Gratefulness to Caleb that he's been such an influence in my daughter's life. Joy that we have a man in our lives who genuinely cares for both Charlie and me.

A tear runs down my cheek, and I quickly brush it away before going and joining them in front of the fish tank. Charlie drags us around the entire aquarium, making sure we see all her favourite things. When we finally finish our rounds, we stop for a quick lunch at a nearby restaurant. On our way home, Charlie begs us to watch *Finding Nemo*, and Caleb, being the softy he is for her, agrees.

We spend the rest of the day as a quintessential family day, and as we sit eating dinner, I realize the three of us do make a family. Caleb has made me feel safe when I wasn't sure I ever would in a relationship again.

Caleb

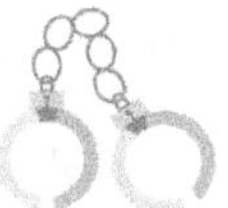

Once we put Charlie to bed, I lead Bailey into our room with every intention of keeping that promise I made to her this morning. Closing the door behind me, I lean against it, taking in Bailey's beauty. My eyes slowly trail up her body, taking in every glorious inch of her.

"Strip." My voice is low, demanding.

I watch as she does as she's told. Her arms instinctively come in front of her, and she clasps her hands together. Her reflex is to hide her body, and I'm not having any of that shit. Leaving her standing there, I make my way into the closet and grab a tie.

Stepping out of the closet, I ask, "Do you trust me?"

She nods.

"Good," I say as I walk behind her. Leaning forward, I slowly trail my nose across her shoulder and up her neck until my lips find the shell of her ear. "You don't hide from me, Bailey. I want to see every inch of your sexy body."

Reaching around her, I grab her wrists and pull her arms behind her back, securing her wrists with the tie. I walk around her, trailing my fingers over her skin. Goosebumps erupt behind the movement. I grin at the effect I have on her.

When I'm standing in front of her, I pinch each of her nipples, and she drops her head back as a moan leaves her.

"Eyes on me."

Her head snaps to face me as a blush creeps across her skin.

Taking a step back, I sit in the chair in the corner of the room and stare at her. My eyes eat her up. I take in every inch of her skin. She squirms under my gaze and pulls at her bindings. I just sit, taking her in as she's forced to stand there completely exposed to me with her hands tied behind her back.

"When I bring you pleasure, your eyes will be on me. When you come, you will call my name."

I watch her throat bob as she swallows and nods.

"Now, who makes you wet and needy, Bailey?"

Her eyes close, and I immediately miss the bright blue. When she opens them, the air that fills my lungs feels fresher.

"You." Her voice is breathy, revealing just how turned on she is.

I watch her as silence fills the air. Bailey presses her thighs together, but from the look on her face, it does nothing for her.

Pushing up from the chair, I stalk towards her and drop to my knees in front of her. I help her spread her legs before leaning forward and inhaling her scent.

"You smell almost as good as you taste."

I revel in the sight of the goosebumps that spread across her thighs. My hand finds the back of her knee, and I lift her leg, throwing it over my shoulder. My tongue dives in, and I taste her. I groan as I feast on her like a starved man. Like she's the last meal I'll ever eat.

My tongue thrusts inside her before finding her clit and flicking it. Her breathy moans tell me she's close, but I want her falling over the edge of ecstasy. I pull back, not letting her come, and she whines. I grin as my tongue circles her clit, playing with it. I suck it into my mouth, scraping my teeth over it and sending her straight over the edge.

My name on her lips is the best thing I've ever heard.

My hand finds her bindings behind her back, holding her close to me so she doesn't fall. When her orgasm subsides, I stand to my full height.

Her chest, neck, and cheeks are tinged pink, her chest rising and falling rapidly as she recovers from her orgasm.

"What did I tell you I would do tonight?"

"Fuck my tits."

I nod. "Why did I say I would fuck your tits?"

"To show me how much you love them."

I reach around her and undo the tie securing her hands. "Now, be a good girl and get on the bed."

She quickly climbs on, lying on her back. Her eyes are full of heat as she watches me undress. I take my time, slowly removing each item, starting with my socks then my shirt. She squirms when my fingers reach for the button of my jeans as I tease her with each new inch of skin I expose.

"Caleb," she moans, and I grin.

"Patience."

I push the button through the hole slowly then pull the zipper down at a pace that has the sound of the prongs coming undone echoing through the room. When it's all the way down, I hook my thumbs into the waistband of my jeans and push them down my legs. Bailey licks her lips as I grip my erection through the fabric of my boxer briefs. I stride towards her, stopping right beside her head. I push my underwear down and off and grip my length.

"Open."

Her jaw immediately drops, and I feed my cock into her mouth. I groan as her hot mouth takes me. As I slowly pull out, her eyes pout at me. Climbing onto the bed, I straddle her.

"Hold your tits," I say.

Using the wetness her mouth left behind, I slowly push my cock between her tits. Her skin is soft, and I relish in the feel of it. I pick up the pace, the head of my cock hitting her lips. Her tongue darts out and flicks across it, and I groan.

"Your tits are fucking amazing," I growl as my hips work at an unrelenting pace.

I'm close. She opens her mouth and as the head of my cock enters it, she sucks, sending me over the edge. I lean forward, bracing my weight on my hand as I come all over her chest, lips, and chin. She smiles at me as she moves her hand from her tits and uses her thumb to collect my cum off her chin and sucks it off. I close my eyes, the sight so intense I'm nearly hard again.

I roll over and lie beside her to catch my breath. As I close my eyes, the bed shifts and the next thing I know, Bailey is straddling my lap with my cock in her hand. My eyes fly open as I watch her take charge of my body. She grins down at me as she runs my cock between her folds, and I'm instantly hard again feeling how wet she is. With a devilish grin, she slowly sinks down until I'm fully inside her.

She swivels her hips as she holds eye contact with me, and it's the sexiest fucking thing in the world. Leaning forward, she braces her hands on my chest, and the feeling of them sears into my skin as she slowly lifts herself up before dropping back down. She clenches around me, and I toss my head back as my eyes begin to roll back in my head.

"Eyes on me." A mocking tone fills her voice.

My eyes fly open, and I stare at her as my hands find her hips, gripping them tightly. "You really want to tease me right now?" I ask, and I see a little glint in her eye.

I quickly roll us so I'm on top. Sitting up, I grab her legs and pull them together in front of me as I push them to her chest. A loud moan leaves her as I fill her deeper and fuck her harder.

"This is your lesson not to mock me, Bailey. I own your pleasure." I groan and lean forward. "I own your pussy."

I nip at the side of her legs, my teeth scraping across her skin. Her body quakes beneath me. Wrapping one arm around her legs to hold them in place, I use my free hand to grab her left breast. "I own these pretty fucking tits, Bailey."

She nods vigorously as her eyes roll back and she comes around my cock. Her pussy clenches around me so tightly it has me coming with her. My thrusts become erratic as I empty my release inside her. I roll off her, allowing her legs to drop onto the bed. When I've caught my breath, I get up and make my way into the washroom, cleaning myself up before wetting a cloth and taking it out to Bailey. Once she's clean, I offer her my hand to help her up, but she shakes her head.

"Baby," I say.

"My legs are jelly. You had me all bent like a pretzel and coming so hard my legs are jelly," she says as she burrows into her pillow.

I push the stray hairs from around her face behind her ear, and she smiles at my touch. "Baby, you've got to get up. I'll carry you to the washroom."

She looks at me with heavy eyes before she nods.

With an arm under her legs and the other behind her back, I gently lift her off the bed and take her into the washroom. I turn on the shower, and she does her business before joining me. I stare at her. Her eyes are closed, and she leans her head backwards as the water rushes over her. She looks so relaxed as the steam builds around us. I help her wash her body and hair before giving myself a quick scrub, turning the water off, and carefully drying her off.

The second her head hits the pillow, she's out. I chuckle to myself as I watch her for a minute. Grabbing a pair of sweatpants from my dresser, I pull them on and make my way downstairs, making sure all the lights are off and the doors are all locked.

As the front door's lock clicks into place, a loud bang sounds outside. My body is instantly on high alert. My head swings back and forth as I look for something to ground me. The air filling my lungs feels sharper and the walls feel like they're closing in around me.

My eyes catch on a picture of Charlie and on I on the mantel. I use all the energy I have to focus on it.

Her blonde hair. Deep breath in and out.

Her blue eyes, just like her mom's. Deep breath in and out.

Her smile as she has her arms wrapped around my neck. Another breath.

The air doesn't feel as sharp anymore.

I see my smile. Another breath.

I haven't smiled like that, with pure unadulterated happiness, in years.

My body relaxes, and I fall back, sitting on the couch. My head falls into my hands, and I run my fingers through my hair. I thought I was past this. I haven't had a visceral reaction like this in months. Leaning my head on the back of the couch, I keep my eyes closed as I continue my breathing. Deep breath in and out. Before I know it, I'm fast asleep.

The hot sun beats down on us as we walk along the side of the road. Sweat pools under my helmet, and the weight of my C7A2 pulls on the strap resting on my shoulder. Tyler walks beside me as our squad makes their way towards the house of a family who claim to have information about a recent attack.

Something about this doesn't feel right. The people on the street seem to keep a greater distance from us than usual.

We're a street away from the road we need to turn down. Out of the corner of my eye, I see two different houses close their windows. This isn't right. We shouldn't be going to this house.

As I'm about to call out to the men in front of us, the sound of a gunshot echoes through the air. My instincts and training kick in. I find the first place I can that has cover, pressing myself against a half wall that separates two houses. I listen, trying to identify where the gunfire is coming from. It definitely came from the direction we were walking towards. Looking around, I see very few people on the street, and I know that's no accident.

This was an ambush.

I radio in our coordinates and the situation. The radio beeps as they tell me support's five minutes out. Closing my eyes, I look to the sky and count to three. When I'm done, I look around the wall, trying to find another member of my team. I spot Tyler at the same time he sees me. He's positioned between two cars just up the road. He does a quick look around and, still crouched, makes his way towards me. The surrounding gun fire gets loud. When he's half a meter away from me, he staggers as a bullet hits his chest. He manages to make it all the way to me before collapsing.

There's no blood, so the bullet must be stuck in his plate carrier. I try to sit him up, but he's not doing anything to help me. His breathing is ragged as he lets out a scream.

"Tyler, help me out."

He looks right through me. Pulling open his vest, I see the blood starting to pool.

FUCK!

Putting pressure on the wound, I talk to him. "Stay with me," I yell as his eyes roll back. Pushing harder on the wound with one hand, I use the other to tap the side of his face. "Tyler, you fucking stay with me. You're not dying on me."

Fuck, fuck, fuck, fuck. I'm losing him.

"Caleb," a woman's voice calls, and something cool touches my forehead.

I look down, and Tyler is still lying there.

"Baby, you're safe." I know that voice. The stress in my body starts to subside. Looking down, I don't see Tyler anymore.

"Caleb."

My eyes flutter open, and I'm met by the most beautiful set of blue ones. Bailey smiles softly as she uses the wet washcloth on my forehead.

"You're safe." Her voice is soft as she continues smiling down at me while gently patting the cool cloth on my skin.

I take in my surroundings, noticing I'm in the living room and not our bedroom. Bailey is wearing nothing but her robe.

"I'm sorry." My voice comes out weak and shame washes over me. I once again woke her up with one of my nightmares. Did I wake Charlie? This can't happen again. This is exactly what caused Gina to leave me. She couldn't put up with constant nightmares and me waking her from her beauty sleep.

Bailey shakes her head. "Baby, there's nothing to be sorry about."

My hand comes up and wraps around her wrist. My thumb stroking her pulse point. Her skin is soft under my touch and it grounds me even more now that I've woken up.

"I woke you up with my nightmare."

Dropping the cloth on the coffee table, she straddles my lap and runs her hands through my hair. Her nails gently scrape at my scalp, soothing me. Every little thing she does keeps me in the present and away from that nightmare. Bailey has saved me in more ways than she will ever know.

"And that's okay," she says.

"Charlie?" I ask.

"Fast asleep in her bed."

We continue to sit as I lean into Bailey's touch. My eyes grow heavy.

"Come to bed," she whispers as she climbs off me and offers her hand.

I rise from the couch and follow her upstairs. Climbing under the covers, Bailey comes right into my side and rests her head on my chest. Her nails gently scrape over my chest, my abs, and across my arm. I watch the movement of her delicate fingers as they trail over my skin. On her fifth trail, my eyes begin to close. I inhale deeply, the smell of Bailey's shampoo filling my lungs, and I melt into the bed.

Home. That's what I feel right now. I feel at home, that one place in the world where you feel safe. Bailey is that place.

CHAPTER 32

Caleb

A knock at the bedroom door wakes me up. I'm wrapped up in Bailey as I groggily call, "Yeah."

The door creaks open, and Charlie stands there holding Princess with a sleepy look as she rubs her eyes. Finn stands behind her, his head tilted as he watches Bailey and me. He's been sleeping in Charlie's room every night, so he hasn't seen that his place has been taken over.

"Can I cuddle?" Charlie asks.

I lift the blanket, and a smile spreads across her face as she makes her way to my side of the bed and climbs in. She cuddles right into my side, and I lower the blanket, holding my two girls as close to me as possible.

The bed shifts as Finn jumps up and gets settled at my feet. He rests his head on my legs, staring up at me, and a small smile ghosts my lips. I'm lying here with the quintessential family. The only thing that could make it better would be a little baby lying on my chest.

Since my deployment, I've never thought of having children. That was until meeting Bailey; she's turned my world upside down.

Bailey stirs and brushes her hair out of her face, smiling up at me as she whispers, "Good morning."

"Good morning, baby."

"Good morning, Mommy."

Bailey's eyes widen for a second before she looks over and sees Charlie cuddled into my side.

"You snuck into bed with us, I see." Her voice is tinged with amusement.

Charlie nods against my chest. "Yeah, I wanted cuddles, and Daddy said I could."

There's that word again. That name. The name I never thought I'd hear directed at me. The girls smile at each other, but where Charlie's is carefree, I see the worry behind Bailey's.

"Okay, Baby Girl, you need to go get dressed and pack your bag. We've got to leave soon to meet up with Aunt Lily," she says, and I stiffen underneath them.

Why does Charlie need a bag? Was last night's nightmare too much and she's leaving me just like Gina did? Is she scared to have Charlie around me now? Is she upset that Charlie called me dad and I didn't stop it? Questions swirl around my head as my breathing quickens. My chest tightens. Fuck, I think I'm having a panic attack.

Charlie's voice sounds far away as she says, "Okay, Mommy."

The bed dips as she climbs off and makes her way out of the room. Finn stays behind, his eyes staying on me as Bailey's lips dust over my cheek before she follows suit and makes her way into the washroom. I rub the sheet between my fingers as I close my eyes and focus on the sound of the water running in the washroom and steady my breathing.

Deep breath in. Deep breath out.

I continue to focus on those things as I try to ground myself.

The sound of the washroom door opening carries through the room, and my eyes fly open. I watch as Bailey makes her way into the closet and comes out dressed in a pair of jeans, a T-shirt, and a cardigan. But the thing that catches my eyes is the bag she brings out with her. She places it on the bed as she sits on the edge and puts her socks on. I want to ask her so many questions, but my breath is caught in my lungs.

This feels all too familiar. My ears are filled with a whooshing sound as she rounds the bed, leaning over and giving me a chaste kiss. I can see her lips move, but I can't process what she says before she moves into the hallway. The door opens again, and Charlie comes back in, climbing onto the bed as she gives me a hug before leaving.

The sound that pulls me back to reality the front door closing. Since they've moved in, they haven't left without me being downstairs to say goodbye, giving them each a kiss goodbye.

Does this mean that it's the end? Did Bailey rush out of here because she didn't want to tell me she was leaving me? I lie in bed, staring at the ceiling, not wanting to move. Finn nudges his nose against my face before resting his head on my chest, watching me. The pressure on my chest calms me a bit. Reaching up, I scratch his head. He whimpers as he continues to watch me.

I pat his head then move out from under the blanket and make my way into the washroom, Finn on my heels. I turn on the shower and stare at myself in the mirror. I take in the sunken look in my eyes as I process the last twelve hours. I know it isn't from lack of sleep, but from the realization of what's happened.

My nightmare last night scared away Bailey.

The only thing that packing a bag and staying somewhere else could mean is they're leaving me, and my soul cracks. I'm not sure how I'm supposed to move on from this. How do you move on from two people who have taken over every part of your being?

My life before them was routine, the same things day in and day out. Get up and walk Finn, eat breakfast and drink coffee, work, home, workout, walk Finn, dinner with a game on the TV. The only difference was the nights we had games, when that replaced my workout, and poker night on Saturdays. When they walked into my life, I found more things to enjoy. I laughed more. Smiled more. I woke up with a smile and looked forward to the day. I'm not sure how I'm going to go back to my boring routine.

I step into the shower, and the scorching water washes over me. I hope the heat will help my tight muscles relax, but it doesn't. Realizing it's useless, I turn the water off and wrap a towel around my waist. Finn watches me from his spot on the floor. I leave the washroom, and he follows. Making my way into the closet, I stare at all of Bailey's clothes hung up on her side. It doesn't look like she took much. I run my fingers over the soft material of the light-blue blouse she wore that day at the station.

That day will forever be seared into my brain.

The look in Bailey's eyes the minute she decided she was going to kiss me. The feeling of her lips against mine was like nothing I had ever experienced. I'm almost thirty, and I've been no monk, but her lips pressed to mine had my heart racing and skin heating. Something took over my mind, body, and soul that had my hand in her hair and my mouth devouring her as though the world around me would burn in flames at any second. Her soft little moan seemed to snap all control I had as I lifted her and her legs wrapped around my waist. I knew I needed to taste more of her when my lips found her neck.

Her and Charlie were everything I never knew I needed. They are everything I need.

I move to the drawers where I keep my sweats and hoodies. Slipping into a pair of grey sweats and a T-shirt, I reach to the bottom of my hoodies and go looking for the one where I hid Mom's engagement ring. I can't find it. I had it in the one we ordered when our team won the championship a few years ago, but it's not here.

I rip out every hoodie, throwing them to the floor before moving to my sweats and doing the same thing. My hands move to my hair, pulling at the strands. The last fucking thing I need right now is to have lost Mom's ring. I search through my jeans, moving through my closet until everything is in a pile on the floor.

I abandon the closet and move into the bedroom, heading straight for my nightstand. I pull out the drawer and dig through its contents. It's not there.

With my hands on top of my head, I stare out into nothingness. I take a deep, steadying breath.

I jog down the stairs and head into the kitchen. I pull open the junk drawer and dig through it. Again, it's not there, but I do find some interesting papers tucked in the back. They're house listings in the area of Bailey's house. They all seem to be similar to her place, the number of rooms and washrooms, square footage, and yards. If their packing bags wasn't a sign, this has to be. She was looking for a place to buy and never told me.

Was I moving too quickly for her? Has she been planning this since my nightmares in the beginning, just buying time until she could get a place? Was Charlie calling me Dad her tipping point? I brace my hands on the counter, and my head drops between my shoulders. I need a drink.

I move to check my cabinet for the bottles I usually keep there, almost tripping over Finn on my way. When I open the cabinet, there's nothing, and I remember we finished them at the last poker night and I never re-stocked.

Grabbing my car keys, I call Finn, and he follows me out to the truck. I drive to the closest liquor store and grab a twelve pack of beer and a bottle of Jack. The cashier is a blonde woman in her late twenties. She smiles at me as her eyes roam my body. I don't even have the energy to smile politely. I toss some cash on the counter, grab my items, and make my way out to my truck.

When I get home, I check the mail on my way in, tossing it all on the counter. I decide to go for the Jack first, opening the bottle and tipping my head back as I take a swig.

When my head comes back down, my eyes catch on one of the envelopes from the mail. It's from the National Defence Headquarters in Ottawa. Placing the bottle on the counter, I rip open the large manilla envelope and pull out the documents inside. *Sutton, Simon H.* is written across the top of the first document, and I know exactly what it is I'm holding.

It's my dad's KIA report I requested from the military earlier this year.

Grabbing the bottle of Jack and the papers, I make my way to the couch. I take a large sip of the whiskey before I begin reading, needing to steel myself.

It's all a daze. As I read, I continue to drink, each sip larger than the previous. The package isn't small. There are several reports inside, and I work my way through each one. At some point, I decide to order myself lunch. Grabbing it off the front porch, I settle onto the couch and continue reading.

At the end of the report, there's a stack of pictures, and they break me. I can't remember the last time I truly let myself cry, but this does it. I drop the pictures and papers, and they scatter on the floor around me as I hold my head and cry. My chest heaves as every little painful thing escapes my body. I stay like this for what feels like an eternity.

I barely register the sound of the front door opening, but a gasp has my head shooting up. Bailey is standing at the entrance to the living room, her mouth agape as she looks at me.

When her eyes meet mine, she rushes to my side, cupping my face as she uses her thumb to wipe away my tears. The simple touch has me crying harder. Now that it's started, I can't seem to stop it. She straddles my lap, pushing me back into the couch as she wraps her arms around me and buries herself into my chest. My arms instinctively wrap around her.

I take a deep breath, trying to gather myself, and vanilla and jasmine fill my nose. It causes a mixed feeling in me. It relaxes me in a way nothing else can, but it has me anxious because I don't know how long I'll have this.

What is she doing here? She took a bag with her this morning.

When my breathing calms, she pulls back. My hands fall to her hips, and she runs her fingers gently through my hair. I close my eyes, enjoying the feeling. Her thumb traces over the last of my tears. Her lips dust over the same place and then my eyelids. Her simple touches bring me peace.

When she pulls back, my eyes open, and I'm met with her brilliant blue ones. They are filled with concern. But she doesn't say anything, just waits for me to begin.

"What are you doing here?" I ask in a whisper.

"I live here," she says with a soft smile.

Her fingers move from the top of my head, where my hair has some length, to the back and scrape at my scalp. She looks around the room, taking in the fast food bag, scattered papers, and half-finished bottle of Jack sitting on the side table. She slowly climbs off my lap and collects the papers, putting them into a neat stack.

I see her eyes scan the top page, widening at certain places. Her eyes dart to mine. "Is this about your dad?"

I nod.

"Oh, baby, I would have been here with you when you read this. You should have told me."

My eyes sweep over her, trying to process her words.

"Will you tell me what it says?"

I nod, and she settles on the floor, her attention fully on me.

"Dad was deployed overseas, working in a joint operation with American forces. He was stationed in a remote village that was being used as a small base when he was killed. They were tasked with developing a relationship with the locals in the hopes they could obtain information from them that could be useful." I swallow as I try to continue. "Dad had thought one of the guys was paying a little too much attention to some of the local young women. One night, he followed him and saw him going into a house. It wasn't long before he heard a woman scream. He entered the house, weapon drawn, and found the soldier attempting to rape her. Before Dad could do anything, the guy shot him. He must have thought the woman was too scared of him, because he left her alive. She ended up at the base where she told them everything. They decided their mission was too important to tell the family it was friendly fire, but with the mission well over now, they released the information at my request."

Bailey's eyes are wide as she stares at me. Reaching forward, she grabs my hand and squeezes it. "I'm sorry, Caleb. Truly. I'm sorry that happened to your father, and I'm sorry you had to read it."

She places the stack of papers on the coffee table as she moves to stand. Her eyes catch on something, and she pulls out one of the house listings I must have grabbed with the report when I came in here.

"What are you doing with these?" she asks. Her voice doesn't sound accusatory, rather, she sounds worried.

"I was looking for something in the junk drawer and found those stuffed in the back. I must have grabbed them when I grabbed the others." My voice sounds dull and emotionless, even to me, and I can tell Bailey notices it too.

"I can explain," she starts.

She settles back on her heels as she scratches at her jeans. I watch her nails scratch over the material, leaving little lines of changed colour in their wake.

"So, at some point after we moved in here, I decided I want to sell my place. The good memories of my childhood have been taken over by the bad ones, and most of Charlie's memories there aren't good ones. So, I thought we need a fresh start. And I know that living with you wasn't a permanent invite, but I figured I could list it and we could find a small place to rent until my place sold and I found a place I could afford. I don't want us to overstay our welcome. And I know Charlie has said some big things the last few days, and she didn't say anything to me about it, so I was just as surprised as you." Her words are rushed, and her cheeks pinken as she avoids my eyes.

"Overstay your welcome?" I ask.

Her gaze shoots up to mine, and her mouth opens and closes a few times before she takes a breath and pulls her shoulders back. "I know you only brought us here because of Derek showing up at my place, and I want you to know how much I appreciate that."

"Did I do something wrong? Was it the nightmare?" I ask.

Her brows pull together in confusion. "No. Why would you ask that?"

"You packed a bag."

Her brows drop, and her shoulders sag. "We had a girls' night planned with Lily. Every year, we pick a day during Charlie's winter break to watch movies, play games, and do a sleepover at Lily's. It was just an overnight bag." Her words don't completely relax me.

"You didn't wait for me to come down and say goodbye this morning."

"I thought you wanted to stay in bed. I didn't want to drag you out of bed on your day off," she says.

"The way you rushed out of bed this morning."

She blushes slightly. "I wasn't ready to have the conversation about Charlie calling you Dad, not once, but several times. I wimped out and decided to run." Her gaze darts around the room everywhere, but my face.

"I like it."

My words have her head snapping to me so quickly, I'm surprised I don't hear it pop.

"What?" Her words are breathy and quiet.

I slide onto the floor in front of her, my hand grasping her chin. "I like it."

Her eyes widen.

"I never thought I'd hear someone call me that. I love that Charlie was the first one to. And you're not overstaying your welcome. Why do you think I helped Charlie paint and decorate her room? That room is hers. I want her to be comfortable in it and down the road when she grows up and wants to change it, we'll change it."

A tear falls down her cheek, and I release my grip on her jaw to use my thumb to wipe it away.

"You weren't leaving me?" I ask softly.

"What? No!" she practically yells. "Why would I leave you?"

I lean forward, our breaths mingling. "Can I kiss you?"

"You never have to ask," she says as she leans forward, her lips finding mine.

My hand finds her hair as I hold her head so I can devour her. The kiss heals me in a way I never knew a kiss could. Bailey, being right here with me now, has brought peace to my soul. She's not leaving me, and when she walked into the house and saw the mess I was, she still chose to comfort me. She's not letting last night's nightmare run her off.

She's choosing to stay.

She moves to straddle my lap, and I help her, gripping her hips and lifting her. She moans into my mouth and the sound steals my breath. I want to hear that sound for the rest of my life. I want to be the cause of that moan. My lips leave hers as they trace down her neck. Wanting more access to her neck, I reach for the hem of the hoodie she's wearing, and that's when I realize she's wearing the one I was looking for earlier. The one that had the ring in the pocket.

"You stole my hoodie," I breathe out.

She bites her bottom lip, it's sexy as fuck, and nods. "I wanted something that smelt like you."

"I was looking for it this morning, but it looks good on you."

She worries her lip between her teeth as her hand reaches into the front pocket. "I'm guessing you were looking for this," she says as she pulls out the ring box.

My hand goes to the back of my neck, and I rub it as I clear my throat. "Yeah."

"It's beautiful."

Her eyes hold mine, and it's like the air between us stills.

"It's my mother's," I say. "She gave it to me at Christmas."

"Christmas," she whispers.

I nod. "Yeah, she said she knew I'd want to use it soon."

"Do you?" Her eyes bounce between mine.

"Yeah, soon."

A tear falls down her cheek, and she places the box in my hand. "When you're ready," she whispers before she kisses me again. She takes control of the kiss, but I have a question I want answered before we continue.

"It doesn't scare you?"

She holds my gaze, and I see the full conviction in her eyes as she says, "Nothing about being with you scares me. You saved me in more ways than one. You are my safe space. So, no. It doesn't scare me, but I don't want to rush anything either. So, when we're ready."

"Bailey, you're saving me every day."

Another tear falls down her cheek, and I kiss it away before I reach for the hem of the hoodie, pulling it over her head and tossing it on the floor. Her smile is blinding. She grabs my shirt and pulls it off, tossing it in the same direction. We quickly work to get our pants off. When she's completely bare in front of me, I allow my eyes to eat her up before I slide flat on my back across the floor.

"Come ride my face, Bailey."

Silence fills the air. I lift my head to look at her, and she's staring at me with her mouth slightly open.

"Bails, come ride my face."

She slowly makes her way to me. When she's right beside me, she swings a leg over my chest, straddling me. Impatiently, I grip her hips and pull her forward, positioning her right over my face.

"Sit," I growl, and she lowers herself slightly as my tongue darts out and tastes her.

Her taste bursts over my tongue, and it's even better than it's been in the past. As though those last little barriers I had up, the worry that had plagued me, had dampened everything when it came to being with her.

She continues to hover, so I wrap my hands over her thighs and pull her down. Her legs spread outward as her centre comes closer to my mouth.

"I plan to feast Bailey, don't make me work by having me go to my meal. Bring it to me."

With that, my tongue begins to work furiously as I taste and tease her. My tongue thrusts in and out of her pussy before it moves to her clit, circling it slowly. She shivers above me as I take my time with the most sensitive part of her.

I do everything I've learned that sends her over the edge. Her body falls forward as she braces one hand on the edge of the couch and the other goes to my hair. She grips it tightly as she calls my name. I grin against her. She moans as I bring her to the edge. I make her cling to the razor thin edge between orgasm and pure torture. But when she falls, she'll thank me for it. She'll come so undone for me and it will be a sight to behold.

I suck her clit into my mouth. It sends her crashing over, and I'm not disappointed. She throws her head back so forcefully her body follows. Her hand finds my stomach as she attempts to hold herself up. Her creamy white skin is now a deep shade of pink. Her mouth is open, but no sounds escape as she allows the orgasm to tear through her.

She takes a breath, and I help her slide down my body before she lies on the floor beside me. Rolling, I prop myself up on an elbow, using my free hand to brush her hair from her face. Her satiated smile captures everything beautiful in this world.

Leaning in, I brush my lips over hers, and she lazily kisses me back. I nudge her legs wider as I move, positioning myself between them while never breaking our connection. I thrust my hips forward slightly, allowing the tip of my cock to tease her clit. She moans into my mouth. Her hips move up, seeking more. I break the kiss and sit back on my heels as I reach and grab a pillow off the couch. Placing the pillow on the floor beside her, I spread her legs more, pulling her body closer to me so her legs sit on my hips, and move the pillow under her ass.

Her eyes are wide as she stares up at me. I grip my cock and give it a few strokes before I slap the tip on her clit. Her mouth drops open as the sound of her sharp intake of breath fills the air. I do it again, and she squirms.

"Play with your tits, Bailey. I want to watch while I fuck your tight cunt."

Her hands move up to her breasts, her thumb and forefinger finding her nipples and pulling them slightly. I position myself at her entrance and press into her slowly. It's torture not just for her as she attempts to bring her hips up to meet mine, but for me too. The look on her face as she bites down on her bottom lip while she watches my cock disappear inside her is worth it, though. When I'm fully seated, I lean forward as a groan leaves my chest.

"You're fucking perfect," I growl into the junction of her neck and shoulder before I nip her.

She clenches around me, causing me to moan. I push myself back up, grabbing her right thigh while my free hand finds her clit. My thumb plays with it, and I watch the effect it has on her. Her hands continue to play with her tits as her breathing quickens and her eyes close, her head thrashing back and forth. She's a fucking sight to behold.

I fuck her hard and fast, relishing in every noise that escapes her. I watch as my cock stretches her.

"Look at yourself. Spread open for me, taking my cock like my dirty girl. Do you like being spread out for me, Bailey?"

She nods slightly, but I want words. I want to know just how much she likes it.

My hand slaps against her clit, and her eyes widen.

"Tell me, Bailey. Do you like being spread out, naked, and taking my cock like my dirty girl?"

"Yes." Her voice is barely above a whisper.

I grin at her as my hips move faster. "You look so good, baby."

She moans and tightens around me. She loves being praised while I talk dirty to her. I feel the telltale sign of my orgasm building. I need her to come.

"Come for me, Bailey. Soak my cock as you call my name. Show me you're mine." My voice is possessive.

She moans when I pinch her clit, sending her over the edge. Her hands leave her tits as she reaches out, looking for anything to grab. I pinch her clit again, and her back shoots off the floor. She clenches around me so tightly I feel like I might completely lose circulation. It has me coming harder than I have in my life.

I'm breathless as I come down from the high. I stare down at my beautiful Bailey and see tears slowly running down the side of her face as she lies beneath me. My hand reaches forward, and I carefully brush them away as a weight sits on my chest.

"Baby, are you okay?" My voice is nothing more than a whisper, but the concern that fills it is more than evident.

She nods delicately, and a smile spreads across her face. "Yeah, baby." Her voice catches in her throat, and I watch as her chest rises while she takes a deep breath and slowly exhales it. "I'm perfect."

Pulling out of her, I lie beside her and pull her into my side, feeling all the emotions of the day fade away as I drift to sleep.

CHAPTER 33

Bailey

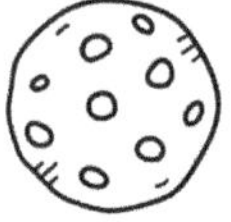

Caleb's soft little snores carry through the living room as we lie on the floor. I grab a blanket off the couch, draping it over us before reaching for my phone. I text Lily.

BAILEY

Can Charlie stay with you? I think I'm going to stay here tonight. I don't want to just up and leave him right now.

LILY

Of course, hun. You take care of what you need to. I've got her, just let me know when to drop her off.

BAILEY

You're the best 

I settle back into Caleb's side, resting my head on his chest and listening to the mixed sounds of his heartbeat and snoring. I should have known something was up with Caleb this morning. He always meets us downstairs and says goodbye, even if he's not working that day or leaving after us. I guess I thought it was all a reaction to Charlie calling him dad. It could have been part of it, but he claimed her as his with his friends. My heart and mind are still a mess as I process everything.

Charlie, Lily, and I are about to settle in and watch some movies when I grab Caleb's hoodie out of my bag and throw it on. Snuggling into it and inhaling Caleb's scent, I put my hands inside the pocket and find something square and hard inside. Pulling out the box, I look down, and I swear my heart stops because I'm holding a ring box.

The velvet is soft under my fingers, and my mind races a mile a minute. I open the box, and my entire world freezes. Nestled inside is a gorgeous diamond ring. A white gold band with a small, round diamond sitting in the centre. It isn't ostentatious; it's perfect. Something I could see myself wearing.

"Ummmm, whatcha got there?" Lily's voice pulls me out of my thoughts.

"I don't know. It was in the pocket of Caleb's hoodie."

My eyes leave the ring, and I meet her gaze as a shit-eating grin spreads across her face.

"That, hun, looks like an engagement ring." Her voice is full of excitement.

"We haven't even been together that long," I say, but I also really want it to be just that. The thought of marrying Caleb one day doesn't scare me. It fills me with joy and excitement. I'm not ready for that step yet, but one day in the near future, I'd love to be engaged to him. To marry him.

"Go talk to him."

I shake my head quickly. "No, tonight is our annual Christmas girls' night."

Lily shakes her head, her smile still on her face. "I know you. You're going to spend the rest of the night with your head filled with questions about what that ring means. You won't mentally be with us. So, take the ring and go talk to him. Charlie and I will hang out here."

I worry my lip between my teeth, knowing she's right. "Fine, but I'll come back after."

"Don't worry about us," Lily says as she pushes me towards the front door. "Charlie, come say bye to your mom."

The sound of Charlie's pounding footsteps carries through the house until she stops in front of me.

"Why are you leaving, Mom? We were going to watch a movie." She's more confused than sad.

"Mommy's got to go talk to Caleb. I'll be back as soon as I can." I pull her into a hug and kiss the top of her head.

"Okay." That seems to be enough for her, because as soon as I release her, she runs back into the living room.

"Don't rush," Lily says as she ushers me out the front door, handing me my purse and keys.

"I'll text you when I'm on my way back," I say as I step outside.

"Don't worry about us."

I hurry to my car, unlocking it and making my way back to Caleb's. As I drive through the neighbourhood, it hits me just how much I don't want to move, but I really don't want Charlie and I to overstay our welcome at Caleb's. I've started researching listing my place and apartments we can move into.

Pulling into Caleb's driveway, I turn off the car and sit for a minute. Going inside and talking to Caleb has the possibility to change everything. Taking a deep breath, I open the door and as soon as I step inside, the sound of heart-wrenching sobs fills the air.

Oh, my poor Caleb.

Rounding the corner into the living room, I see the state of it and gasp. Caleb sits on the edge of the couch with his head in his hands as he cries. Papers are scattered over the floor in front of him, takeout containers litter the coffee table, and a partial bottle of Jack sits near him.

Caleb's head flies up, and when our eyes meet, I see the absolute torment in his. I rush to his side, cupping his face and brushing his tears away the same way he's done for me on so many occasions. He cries harder, and I move to straddle his lap and hold him as best as I can. When his arms come around me, he holds me so tightly it's like he thinks if he holds me any looser, I'll somehow disappear. This man doesn't seem to know that I'm not going anywhere.

He has become my home.

He is the one place I always want to be.

He is the light in the darkness that had become my life, and I never want to give that up.

When his sobs subside and he pulls back, his words come out barely above a whisper. "What are you doing here?" His words are like a slap, but I still smile at him because if he truly didn't want me here he wouldn't have held me like I was his lifeline.

"I live here."

I'm pulled from my thoughts as I feel Caleb's hand run through my hair, and I smile up at him.

"What are you thinking about so intently?" he asks.

I shake my head. "Nothing."

"We should talk." Those three words have my entire body on edge. *We should talk* are not words anyone wants to hear.

I hold the blanket to my chest as I sit up and lean against the couch, and Caleb follows suit.

"Okay. What do you want to talk about?"

"First, I want to talk about your place."

My eyes search his face for any clues about what he's going to say, but I can't find anything.

"If you want to sell it, I support you. I don't want you and Charlie to move out, though. I thought I was showing you that, but I guess I need to say it too. I want you and Charlie to move in permanently. What you do with your place is your choice. If you want to list it, I'll help you find a realtor. If you want to rent it, I'll help you find a property management company so you don't have to be super hands on if you don't want. If you want to renovate it, I'll be there with you every day doing everything I can." He reaches for my hand and squeezes it. "I want to go back and grab all of your things so you and Charlie are properly moved in."

I move and straddle his lap, taking his face in both hands. I lean forward and kiss him softly. "Of course we'll move in Caleb."

His arms wrap around me.

"Second?" I ask.

Removing a hand from my waist, he tucks a piece of stray hair behind my ear. "How do you feel when Charlie calls me dad? This isn't just about how I feel. You're her mom and have a say in this. If you don't want her to call me that, then I'll sit down and have a talk with her, but I meant what I said earlier. I like it. I will always be there to love and protect her. If she wants to call me dad, then she's more than welcome to. But if it makes you uncomfortable, then we'll stop it."

I run my hands through his hair, feeling the strands between my fingers before moving my hands down the sides of his face and across the hard muscles of his chest. He looks at me quizzically as I continue to move my hands, trying to confirm that this magnificent man in front of me is real. Leaving my left hand on his chest, I move my right to pinch myself. His brows furrow.

"Baby, what are you doing?" he asks as he takes my hand in his, kissing the top before holding it.

"Making sure you're real and I'm awake because how in the world did I manage to get this lucky? I went from being in an abusive relationship I had to fight my way out of, to managing being on my own and a single mother, to finding you. A perfect supportive man who loves my daughter as fiercely as I do. You have brought us into your family and friend group, all of them accepting us." I take a deep breath, hoping to hold back the tears that are fighting their way to the surface. "I fall in love with you more and more every day, Caleb Sutton. I don't know how you're still single."

"Baby, we both have baggage. You are so unbelievably strong and resilient. You saved and protected yourself and your daughter. You then came into my life and saved me without even trying. Having you in my life is a privilege I will spend the rest of my life working to earn, and I'm not single. I'm very much taken by a stunning, strong, intelligent blonde woman who surprises me every day."

He leans forward, his lips dusting over my cheek then my forehead. I close my eyes, savouring his gentle touch. His lips move over each eyelid, my nose, and other cheek before he pulls away. I open my eyes, meeting his. The look in them takes my breath away. If his words weren't enough, which they were, the look in his eyes would be.

They're full of love.

"You never answered my question," he says with a small smirk.

"If that's the relationship you want with her, I'm not going to stop it. Charlie has decided she wants that with you. You have done nothing but love and care for her since we bulldozed into your life. You are an amazing role model for her. I can't think of a better person for her to call dad."

I watch the tears gather behind his eyes. One slips free and makes its way down his cheek. I kiss it away and take a deep breath.

"Aren't we just a mess?" I say on a laugh.

He smiles at me softly. "There's no one in this world I'd rather be a mess with than you."

He wraps his arms around me and pulls me into his chest, and I inhale the smell of him. I'm just about asleep wrapped in his arms when his chest moves as a light laugh escapes him.

"Baby, as much I love holding you like this, I need to get up. My ass is starting to fall asleep."

I laugh and move to get off him, taking the blanket with me and exposing him. My eyes devour him, and he groans.

"I would really love to fuck you senseless again, but I really need a shower," he says as he pushes off the floor, offering me a hand. I take it and he pulls me up until my body is flush with his. Heat radiates off him as he stares at me. After a few seconds, he takes a step back. Still holding my hand, he leads me upstairs and into the en-suite washroom, starting the shower. He tests the temperature with before bringing me in with him. I allow the water to wash away the craziness of the day.

When we leave the washroom and head into the bedroom, Caleb asks, "Do you need to head back to Lily's? I can give you a ride."

I shake my head. "No, Lily offered to take Charlie for the rest of the night and she'll drop her off tomorrow."

"So you and me, curled up on the couch with dinner and a movie?"

I smile. "That sounds perfect."

Caleb

I'm awoken by the sudden need to sneeze and something tickling my nose. Slowly opening my eyes, I smile to myself as blonde hair fills my vision and I realize I have Bailey draped across me. I inhale deeply, taking in the smell of her, it's always hints of vanilla and jasmine. Reaching up, I brush her hair away from my nose and tuck stray pieces behind her ear. She nuzzles her face into my neck, and I chuckle. She's so freaking adorable.

I watch as her eyes open and she stretches before looking at me.

"Good morning," she says with a sleepy smile.

"Good morning."

We stare at each other for what feels like minutes. Last night was full of heavy and important conversations, and being able to just hold her as we lie in bed means everything to me. I can see all the thoughts swirling around her mind as she looks at me. Her smile grows even bigger, her eyes crinkling at the corners with the magnitude of it.

"I want to sell," she says.

It takes me a second to wrap my head around the comment, but when I do, my smile matches hers.

"You want to sell?"

She worries her lip as she nods, and I couldn't be more ecstatic. Her choosing to sell means she's not looking for some backup plan to get out of this relationship. She's all in.

I roll us so that I hover over her. "I love you," I whisper before I lean down and kiss her cheeks, then her forehead, nose, and neck, before landing on her lips. It's an intimate kiss that conveys more for me than words could. She completely relinquishes herself to it, following my lead and allowing me to take control. I savour every second of it before I break the kiss, resting my forehead against hers.

"Why don't we go get our girl?"

Bailey nods, and I climb out of bed and make my way to the closet. Joining me, Bailey gasps as she takes in the mess I left the closet in yesterday. I rub the back of my neck as I turn and look at her.

"I kinda tore it apart looking for Mom's ring last night. I'll put it all back tonight. Don't worry about it."

She walks up to me and wraps her arms around my neck as she smiles up at me. "I'm not worried about it. I'm sorry I scared you yesterday." She rises onto her tiptoes, and her lips brush against my cheek so softly that if I hadn't watched her do it, I would have guessed I dreamed it.

We get dressed and head downstairs. Bailey lets Finn out while I make us coffee. When she comes back in, we grab our to-go cups and head to the entryway. As we are putting our shoes on, Bailey asks, "Do you mind if we stop by a realtor's office? I'd like to get some information for listing the house."

"Yeah, I can text the guy that helped me buy this one. I'm sure he can help you out."

I pull out my phone and text him. He says to stop by his office and he'll get us started. Our meeting there is quick and then we are on our way to Lily's to pick up Charlie.

When we arrive, Bailey lets herself in, and I follow behind her.

"We're here," she calls, and I smile at the sound of Charlie's running.

"Mommy! Daddy!" she calls just before she barrels into my legs.

I reach down and hook my hands under her arms, lifting her. I hold her close to my chest, closing my eyes and appreciating the feel of her in my arms. Her arms wrap around my neck, and I start to sway a little as I just hold her. This little girl helped save me, and I'm not sure she knows it.

"Daddy, you can put me down now."

I chuckle as I kiss her cheek and put her down so Bailey can hug her. Down the hallway, Lily is leaning against the wall with her arms crossed over her chest and a smile.

"Hey, Lily," I say with a head nod.

"Hey, Daddy," she says.

My neck and cheeks heat.

"I was a little worried when I heard Charlie call that when you guys came in." She walks towards us and runs her hand over Charlie's head as she takes the three of us in. Her smile only gets bigger. "I have to say, I like this development."

"Me too," I say.

"Thank you for hanging out with Charlie," Bailey says.

"Oh, you don't need to thank me for hanging out with my girl here."

"Well, next time you should come over to our place. I can make myself scarce at Josh and Liv's for a few hours for you guys to have a girls' night," I say.

Lily's eyes bounce between Bailey and me before landing on me. "You're a good one."

I rub the back of my neck as I say, "Thanks."

"So, um, Lil. If there's anything at my place you might want, just let me know. I'm listing it, so you're welcome to whatever you want before I sell it. I'm only keeping the sentimental photos and stuff, so all the furniture and pretty much the entire kitchen is up for grabs."

Lily stares at Bailey, wide-eyed. "You're selling your parents' place?"

"Yeah. I think the negative memories have made too much of an imprint on the place, and we don't need it anymore."

Lily doesn't say anything, she just nods. Bailey leaves us as she takes Charlie to go gather their things. Once they've walked away, Lily pulls me into a hug.

"Thank you," she whispers. "Thank you for loving them the way they deserve to be loved. You're a good man, Caleb Sutton."

She releases me, and I make sure to hold her eyes to ensure she knows just how serious I am about what I'm going to say.

"I will love those girls until my last dying breath. They are the best thing to ever come into my life. I will spend the rest of it knowing just how amazing they are, and how lucky I am that they chose me."

Lily tips her head back as she wipes at a tear that falls down her cheek. "That's all I've ever wanted for them," she whispers.

Bailey notices Lily wipe away her tear as she comes down the hallway with Charlie's bag thrown over her shoulder. Her eyes are filled with worry as she looks at me and then back to Lily.

"What's wrong?" she asks.

Shaking her head with a chuckle, Lily says, "Nothing. Absolutely nothing. I'm just so happy for you."

Bailey pulls her into a hug before we make our way to the truck.

When we get home, Finn doesn't greet us at the door like usual. I make my way through the house, calling out for him. When I walk into the kitchen, the breeze that sweeps through alerts me to the open sliding glass door.

Bailey's gasp travels through the kitchen. My head swings to her, and I see the tears forming in her eyes. I make my way to her, but she moves past me and heads straight outside. She frantically calls Finn's name as she moves through the yard. When he doesn't turn up, she runs up the side of the house and Charlie and I follow. Bailey's frantic.

None of us find him. When Charlie and I catch up to Bailey, she turns towards us, completely distraught as she works to catch her breath. With her hands on her hips, she tips her head back and takes deep breaths.

Charlie walks up to her and wraps her arms around her legs.

"Mommy, are you okay?"

Plastering on a smile, Bailey looks down at her. "Yeah, Baby Girl, I'm okay. I'm just worried because we can't find Finn."

"Mommy, it's okay. Finn's a good doggy. He'll come home."

Bailey's eyes leave the little girl wrapped around her leg and meet mine. She's fighting to hold back tears. I slowly approach her like a scared animal, worried that going too fast will have her breaking before my eyes.

"Bails, it's okay. We'll find him. Charlie's right, he'll come home."

Her tears slowly fall as she gives up the fight.

"How are you so calm? I lost your dog. I swore I closed the door all the way before we left, but I guess I left it cracked and Finn pushed it open more and ran out. We don't know how long he's been gone and how far he's gotten."

She's out of breath as she rambles, and I wrap my arms around her and hold her, kissing the top of her head.

"Bailey, breath for me. It's all going to be okay. Finn knows the neighbourhood from our walks. We are going to go inside, and I'm going to grab his leash and walk around the neighbourhood looking for him. You two can stay here, and I'll let you know when I find him."

Her hands fist my T-shirt as she cries into my chest. "I'm so sorry," she mumbles against me.

"Bails, this stuff happens. Everything is going to be okay."

She nods and pulls back, her head leaning back as she looks up at me. "Okay, but we're going with you. I created this mess and I'm going to help fix it."

Determination fills her eyes, and I know there's no way I'm talking her out of this, so I nod before kissing her forehead and stepping back. The three of us make our way into the house, and I grab Finn's leash, along with a bag of treats, and stuff them into my pocket. I watch as Bailey makes sure the sliding glass door is closed and locked before we head out the front door.

We head down the road in the same direction I usually take Finn on his walks. Every few minutes, one of us calls Finn's name. We make it to the park that marks the halfway point of our walk, and there's still no sight of him. I stop by the dog park, but he's not there either. We ask if anyone has seen him and no luck. It's starting to wear on Bailey. Her shoulders are starting to hunch as she walks with her arms wrapped around her middle. Charlie doesn't seem phased the way her mother is. She is positive Finn will come back.

We are almost home when one of our neighbours, Mr. Price, walks out and greets us on the sidewalk. I give him a nod as he approaches us.

"Hey, Caleb," he says, reaching a hand out and shaking mine. "Your boy Finn was having a blast running up the street a little bit ago. I tried calling him, but he just kept going."

Bailey perks up. "How long ago?"

Mr. Price smiles at her. "Probably about twenty minutes ago. He was running towards your place."

Bailey reaches out and squeezes his arm as she says, "Thank you, thank you, thank you." Turning to me, she says, "Let's go. Maybe he's at the house."

Hope fills her eyes, and I smile at her.

"Thank you, Mr. Price. My girl here was very worried about him," I say.

He looks at her with a soft smile. "I can tell. You go find your dog."

Bailey immediately starts speed walking towards the house. I follow behind her, making sure I keep pace with Charlie, who jogs beside me. Bailey frantically calls Finn's name as she makes her way closer to the house. When the house is within view and Bailey calls his name, Finn comes running at full speed towards us. Bailey drops to her knees in the grass as he barrels up to her, licking her face. Charlie joins her and giggles as Finn moves on to giving her kisses.

I join them, kneeling beside Bailey. She has the largest smile as she looks at me, and it sucks the breath out of my lungs. She throws herself at me as she wraps her arms around my neck.

"I'm so sorry, Caleb," she says again.

I pull away from her and grip her face between my hands. "Bailey, please listen to me. You don't have to apologize anymore. It was an accident. I know you wouldn't do it on purpose. Bailey. Everyone is alive and safe. That's all that matters."

As I stare into her eyes, I realize just how much damage Derek did to her. She's always so worried that something small is going to cause a huge blow up. I know I will spend the rest of my life showing her and Charlie the love they should have had this whole time.

Kissing her softly, I stand and hook Finn's leash to his collar. Charlie asks to hold it. Finn is good and walks right beside her as we make our way home. When we get inside, Charlie feeds Finn, and I hold Bailey on the couch. I know just how much she needs the affectionate physical touch after being starved of it for so long. Charlie comes and joins us, cuddling into her mom's side, and I put on a Disney movie.

The sound of a stomach rumbling has me looking over to the girls. They're both completely passed out. Not wanting to disturb them yet, I order us takeout. Finn comes up to me and rests his head on my knee as he stares at me.

Scratching his head, I say, "You caused quite the scare there, boy."

He tilts his head as I find that spot behind his ear he likes so much.

"You can't be running out like that. You nearly scared Bailey off, and we can't have that. We have to make sure both these girls stay forever." His head moves in their direction before he leaves me and jumps on the couch beside Charlie and curls up, his head resting on her hip as he stares at me. I guess that means he agrees.

I can't help my grin as I take in the sight of the two girls and Finn all cuddled on the couch. Four months ago, it was just Finn and me with a hockey game on, a bottle of beer, and a pizza. I wouldn't trade this for anything in the world.

Bailey

Charlie and I spend the next two days as low key days at home while Caleb worked. Finn has been attached to my side the whole time, like he can tell that the emotions of the last few days completely wrecked me.

For New Year's, we have plans to go over to Josh and Liv's for the night. I'm not sure Charlie will make it to midnight, but Liv assured me she can always crash in one of the rooms at their place, and Caleb and I can too if we need.

Caleb works during the day but is home in time to shower before we leave. Charlie is super excited as she bounces in her booster seat while Caleb buckles her in. When we arrive at Josh and Olivia's place, Liv pulls me into a big hug before doing the same with Charlie. Charlie runs over to a corner where I see toys set up for her. Liv really has gone all out to ensure we feel welcome in her home and their lives.

As we enter the living room, I see the snacks Liv has spread out over their coffee table. There's even more in the dining room.

"Are you feeding an army tonight?" I ask her as Josh comes and wraps an arm around her middle, kissing her temple. Her body relaxes into his as he holds her. Mine does the same as Caleb comes behind me, mirroring the same position. For years I've missed the simple affectionate touches of a man, and to have that with Caleb now means the world to me.

"My cravings have been all over the place, and I know these boys can eat me out of house and home, so I figured I'd have lots of options," she says with a laugh.

"I remember the crazy cravings. When I was in my third trimester, I was obsessed with Blizzards."

Olivia's eyes twinkle as she stares at me for a second. A smile stretches across her face ear to ear as she asks, "Do you want more kids?"

Caleb's hand moves and settles on my stomach as he leans down and kisses my temple again. The question doesn't throw me the way it did when Sarah asked.

"Yeah, I'd like another."

"Maybe a few," Caleb says.

I look over my shoulder, holding eye contact with him as he smiles down at me. He's all in, and it makes me melt for him even more. I never thought I'd feel this safe and content with a man again after Derek, but Caleb has proven to me that you can trust and rely on people. That not everyone is putting on a facade to gain things from you.

"They'd be gorgeous kids," Olivia pipes in.

"Whose kids would be gorgeous?" Hannah asks as she joins our little huddle.

"Caleb and Bailey's."

"Oh, yes, they would. Those kids will grow up to be heart-breakers for sure. When are you getting started on that?" Hannah asks with a hip bump.

My jaw drops as I stare at her.

She reaches forward and, using two fingers, pushes my jaw back up. "Oh, babe, you can't be that surprised," she says, amusement filling her expression.

"We haven't even been together that long. We are just settling into a life together. I think throwing a kid right into the middle of that is a little pre-mature," I say.

Hannah's eyes move from me, up and over my shoulder, to Caleb. "Caleb, when do you want kids?"

Hannah really has embraced the shit disturber role in this group.

Caleb's grip on me tightens. "When Bailey's ready. For now, we have a beautiful little girl."

I physically melt further into him, which I didn't think was possible.

"What did you do to him?" Grayson asks from beside me, and I jump a little, not realizing he'd joined us.

"What do you mean?" I ask.

"You have turned Mr. Hard-and-Doesn't-Talk-About-His-Feelings, into"—he reaches out and moves his hand up and down in front of Caleb—"this."

I look up at Caleb again and I'm not sure what he could possibly mean. The entire time I've been with Caleb, he has been completely emotionally available to not only me, but Charlie too. He has helped me process feelings I didn't know I had buried deep down and come out the other side. He's held me while I've cried. He's listened to and communicated with Charlie in difficult emotional situations and shared deep traumas with me.

"And now you're going gooey." I can hear the eye roll in Grayson's voice.

"When you find someone to love, you'll go gooey too," I say, my eyes never leaving Caleb.

He leans down until his lips hover over mine. "I love you, Bailey Emerson." His breath dusts across my lips with his whispered words just before he kisses me.

"I never thought Caleb would be the soft kind," Grayson says, and we break the kiss.

I turn in Caleb's arms and face the group again.

"I think that's because you lack emotional maturity," Hannah says.

"Just wait, he'll find a woman who brings him to his knees," Caleb says, and I feel the chuckle that leaves him reverberate through my body.

Lifting his beer to his lips, Grayson shakes his head. "Nope, not going to happen."

Thoughtfulness fills Olivia's eyes as she looks at Grayson. "Why?" she asks in a soft voice.

The tension that fills Grayson's shoulders fills the room too. A hardness fills his eyes as he looks at us. Every interaction I've had with Grayson so far, he's been super laid back, always laughing and poking fun at his friends. This look in his eyes is one I haven't seen before. The hardness carries a sense of detachment.

His voice is void of any emotion as he says, "I learned my lesson a long time ago."

Confusion fills Josh's face, and Caleb says, "Never say never."

Grayson looks at Liv and asks, "Where are your brother and Zoey? I thought they'd be here by now."

Reaching for Josh's wrist that rests on her pregnant belly, she turns it and reads his watch. "I'm not sure. I thought they'd be here too."

The front door opens, and in walk Matt and Zoey, both with flushed cheeks. Zoey seems a little out of breath as everyone stands watching them. She releases a breath, trying to blow the stray strands of hair that fell in front of her face out of the way.

"Hey," Matt says with a smirk.

Out of the corner of my eye, I see the large smile that overtakes Olivia's face.

"Hey," she says. "What were you two up to?"

"Nothing," Zoey says as her cheeks turn bright pink.

Matt chuckles. "Oh, when she says nothing, she means I just caught her basically dry humping some guy outside your building."

"Zoey!" Olivia exclaims.

Zoey punches Matt in the arm. "I told you to keep your mouth shut," she hisses at him.

"Oh, Zo, you really think I wasn't going to watch the look on my little sister's face when I told her?"

A saccharine smile overtakes Zoey's face as she bats her lashes up at him. "Just remember, as her best friend and someone who grew up around you, I know all the best stories. And I also know where she keeps those 'in case of emergencies' photos she has of you."

He leans down and whispers something in her ear. The blush that was only in her cheeks has now covered her entire face and spread down her neck and chest. He pulls away, smirking before making his way over to us. He claps Josh on the shoulder and hugs his sister before moving to the food and making himself a plate.

We all disburse and make plates or join conversations as we wait for midnight. Caleb makes Charlie a plate, and she clings to him throughout the night. She's either sitting right beside him with a toy in hand or in his lap.

"She really loves him," Hannah says as she sits beside me, watching Caleb and Charlie.

"Yeah, we both do."

She nudges my shoulder with hers. "See, I told you to go for it."

Everyone was supportive of a relationship between Caleb and me, but I think Hannah was the one that pushed it the most, telling me it was the twenty-first century and just make a move myself.

"You were right," I say.

She grins. "I know. I usually am."

I watch as her eyes drift to Grayson and her look changes to one of deep concentration, like she's trying to solve some deep puzzle. Then anger takes over her expression as she shakes her head.

I notice Charlie has fallen asleep in Caleb's arms, so I make my way over to them so I can move her into one of the spare rooms. I reach for her, but his arms tighten around her.

"What are you doing?" he asks.

"I was going to take her to a spare room."

He shakes his head. "I've got her."

"Caleb, you don't have to hold her for the entire night."

"Baby, I missed five years of her life. I missed five years of getting to hold her. I'm not missing anymore." His words have me melting and sitting beside him.

"How are you so perfect?" I whisper.

He turns to face me. "I'm not perfect. I've just realized that I have everything I could ever need in the two of you, and I'm never going to take that for granted. I'm going to soak it all in for as long as you'll have me."

I pinch my thigh, and when the sting registers, I smile.

"This is real," he says on a laugh.

I settle into his side, and we join back into the conversation around us. As the time hits 11:55 p.m., Caleb gently wakes Charlie.

"Little Bear, it's almost midnight."

She yawns and burrows into his chest as she rubs her eyes.

He slowly runs his hand up and down her back. "Little Bear, time to wake up."

Her eyes crack open, and she looks up at him. The smile that over takes his face is blinding. How this man found Charlie and I, I will never know, but I will spend the rest of my life eternally grateful.

We all stand, and Caleb holds Charlie as we watch the the start of the fireworks at the Space Needle and prepare for the countdown. As the countdown appears in the bottom corner of the screen, we all start shouting the numbers. With each number, Caleb bounces Charlie, and she giggles. As zero comes and the clock strikes midnight, we all shout, "Happy New Year!"

Caleb's lips immediately find mine as he kisses me deeply. When he breaks the kiss, he rests his forehead against mine and whispers, "Happy New Year, baby."

"Happy New Year, Caleb."

He kisses my forehead and then plasters kisses on Charlie's cheeks and forehead, making her giggle. "Happy New Year, Little Bear."

"Happy New Year, Daddy."

We stand there with Caleb's arms wrapped around both Charlie and me. The three of us our own little family.

We say our goodbyes and gather our things so we can get Charlie home and tucked into bed. She starts school again on Tuesday, and I know I need to get her back onto her school sleep schedule. When we get home, Caleb carries her upstairs, and she climbs up her ladder and into her bed. Once she's settled, he grabs my hand and leads me into our bedroom. He stops us at the foot of the bed and turns to face me. Lust fills his eyes as they travel up and down my body.

He leans down until his lips are right beside my ear. No part of his body is touching mine, but the heat radiating from him and the feel of his breath skating over my ear have me wet already.

"I'm going to slowly make love to you Bailey. And then once you've come calling my name, I'm going to fuck you. I'm going to have you feeling me for the rest of the week. I want you to remember just how real you and I are."

My knees almost buckle. He reaches for the hem of my shirt and slowly drags it up my body before tossing it in the hamper outside the closet. His finger slowly and softly drags over my exposed skin, starting at the tops of my breasts before jumping down to my stomach. Goosebumps erupt over every inch of my skin.

I want more. I need more.

I reach for him, but he takes a step back.

"No, Bailey. I plan to take my time with you."

I groan, and he chuckles. His finger resumes its movement over my bare stomach until it reaches the waistband of my jeans. He deftly undoes the button and zipper before pulling them down my legs and falling to his knees in front of me. He presses his face into the fabric of my panties, and I feel his deep inhale almost as much as I hear it. He nips me through the fabric as he growls, "Mine."

That one word has me fucking soaked. His eyes find mine as he looks up my body while still on his knees.

"You like that, Bailey? You like being told that you're mine? That no other man will ever touch you, or make you come like I do?"

I nod, unable to speak. I want to collapse to the floor and let this man do unspeakable things to my body. He is the only man who has ever had me this turned on. I have never craved sex the way I do with him.

His fingers find the waistband of my panties, and he pulls them down my legs slowly. He stands and reaches behind me as his fingers undo my bra. He pulls the bra off and drops it to the ground, taking a step back.

"Perfect," he says.

My skin heats as the blush spreads across it. No one's ever complimented me the way Caleb does. My arms go to wrap around my stomach instinctively, but when I see the hardened look in his eyes, I keep them at my sides.

With a quick step forward, he drops to his knees in front of me again and kisses across my stomach. "Bailey, I will spend the rest of my life showing you how much I love you. How much I love your soul. Your brain. Your heart. Your body. You brought the most wonderful little girl into this world, and I hope that one day, hope-fully soon, you'll bring another little one into this world. Don't hide your beauty from me."

I nod, and he smiles. "Good, and now I plan to feast."

His head moves to my centre, and my hips buck as he tastes me. My hand grips his hair for stability. I think he moans more than I do. My body tightens as I feel myself building. I'm close. I try to push his head away, but he grips my hips and holds me tight. He becomes more persistent as his tongue moves faster and his fingers join in his effort.

I come with his name on my lips as the tightness in my body fades. Caleb continues to work every last bit of my orgasm from my body until I'm nothing but limp limbs.

He slowly stands to his full height, his arms wrapping just under my ass as he takes me with him. He moves us until the back of my legs hit the edge of the bed, tossing me on it, and I giggle as I bounce. He grins as he reaches behind his head with one hand and pulls his shirt off in one swift movement.

I hungrily eat up the sight of him. My eyes take in each cut of muscle on his chest. He quickly undoes the button and zipper of his jeans, pushing them down with his boxer briefs. I watch as his erection pops free, licking my lips at the sight of it.

He groans. "Woman, you are going to be the death of me."

Stepping out of his jeans, he climbs onto the bed. I spread my legs, giving him ample space. His eyes are full of heat as he slowly climbs between them until we're eye to eye.

He holds my gaze saying, "I love you."

I wrap my arms around his neck and pull him down to me, kissing him as I hook my legs around his waist. His hand comes to my hair and he fists it then positions himself at my entrance. With one swift thrust, he's fully seated inside me. A guttural groan leaves me, and he absorbs it with the kiss.

He takes his time with each movement of his hips. His lips trail across my skin, licking and nipping, and I feel like I'm in heaven. He finds every spot that elicits a reaction from me. He continues to learn every inch of my body each time we have sex. He will be the only man to know every inch of me. To know what gets me going and what completely turns me off. The knowledge that Caleb enjoys learning with his lips, his fingers, and his eyes has me falling over the edge again.

I bite my hand as an all-consuming orgasm rips me to shreds. My heart continues to beat out of my chest as I come down from the high.

"Fuck," Caleb groans into my neck. "You're so fucking perfect. So fucking mine," he growls as he gives into his release. He holds me tight as his hips buck erratically.

He pulls out and rolls over, pulling me with him.

I move to straddle him and kiss every inch of his stomach. "You are amazing," I whisper against his skin before moving up to his chest. "And special." I continue to kiss across his chest. "Cherished." I move up to his neck. "Loved." I kiss across his throat. "Wanted." I move up the side of his face to beside his ear. "Needed." I kiss his forehead. "Strong." I move across and down to his other cheek. "Kind." My lips drag across to his other ear. "Smart." My lips find his. "Desired."

He kisses me deeply. My entire body melts into his as I lie on his chest kissing him. When I break the kiss, we're both breathless.

"What was that for?" he asks.

"You're always making sure I know you're in this for the long haul. That you want me. I need you to know that I feel the same. That I want to be with you. That I love you."

I watch as his gaze softens while he looks into my eyes.

"Thank you," he whispers.

He holds me, and I feel him harden between my legs. I push up so I'm sitting. I grin as I lift myself and position him at my entrance before slowly sinking down. I relish the feeling of him stretching me. His hands immediately find my hips. Once we're hip to hip, he rolls us, and a small shriek escapes me.

He grabs my right leg and pushes it up to my chest. "I told you I was going to fuck you," he says, a smirk pulling at his lips.

He adjusts the position of my leg, allowing him to hit that sensitive spot deep inside me. My eyes roll to the back of my head as he continues in hard, slow thrusts, dragging the head of his cock over that spot each time. He releases my leg and grabs two pillows, positioning them under my ass.

Once I'm settled, his hand finds my throat as he continues to fuck me. I grip his arm, not wanting him to remove it, but needing something to hold on to. He holds my eyes as his hips thrust into me in a punishing rhythm. I tighten around him as my orgasm builds again. His free hand comes and slaps against my clit, sending sparks through my entire body. My back arches off the bed as I allow the sensation to take over me. He does it again, and this time it sends me over the edge, and he falls with me.

Falling with him is such a blissful feeling. That we trust each other so fully to give ourselves to one another completely is freeing.

In the morning, I wake to an empty bed, but with a note on the nightstand.

Good Morning, Baby.
I had to go into work this morning. There is coffee in the coffeepot, and I'll be home for dinner.
Love you,
Caleb

I grin at the note and hold it close to my chest. Derek never would have been thoughtful enough to leave me a note if he left before me. I fold the note in half and tuck it into the bedside drawer before grabbing my robe. Phone in hand, I make my way downstairs. I pour myself a cup of coffee. It's not as hot as I'd like, so I pop it into the microwave and text Caleb.

BAILEY

Thank you for the coffee. You good with BLT's for dinner?

CALEB

You're welcome. I'm good with whatever you want.

I grin at my phone.

BAILEY

BLT's it is.

CALEB

Ok, let me know if I need to grab anything from the store on my way home.

Charlie and I go to the park during the day. When Caleb comes home, we eat dinner together as a family and finish our night with a movie before bed.

Caleb

The days following New Year's Day are blissful. We settle back into a routine as Charlie goes back to school and Bailey gets everything ready for the sale of their place. We've gone over and started packing up the sentimental items she wants to keep and figuring out what she wants to sell. Lily is supposed to go with us this weekend and decide what she wants to take, and then the guys and I will deliver it to her place.

On Friday morning, I'm pulled into my staff sergeant's office. I take a seat in one of the leather-back chairs across from his desk, clasping my hands in my lap.

His head swivels from his computer to me, and he settles back into his chair. I watch as he twists the edge of his grey moustache. He sighs heavily before bracing his arms on his desk.

"Sutton, I'm going to need you to lead the elementary school event today. Bell called out."

"Of course. Is there anything I need to know?"

He grunts as he adjusts himself in his chair. "No. You're just doing a basic presentation on safety. There's a manual you can take with you. I'll have someone else cover your patrol for the day."

I nod. "Of course, sir. What school am I heading to?"

"Dogwood Elementary." I grin to myself as he says the name, because that's where my little girl goes to school.

I slap my hands against my thighs and push up from the chair.

"I'll grab that binder and the other guys and head over there right away."

He nods as I make my way out of his office and into the bullpen. I find the binder and gather the guys, and we figure out rides. I decide to take my truck, and Officers Whitmore and Haas join me. Haas jumps in the front, and Whitmore opens the back door and stands there for a second.

"Whitmore, in or out, let's go," I call.

He pulls himself in, and his head pops up between the front seats. "Sutton, why do you have a booster seat back here?"

"Because my daughter needs it," I grunt.

Both men's heads swing to me as their jaws drop.

"Daughter?" Haas asks, seeming to gather his wits first.

I nod.

"Ummm, not to seem rude or anything, but when the hell did you get a daughter? She's obviously older if she's in a booster seat."

"My girlfriend has a daughter with her deadbeat ex."

Both men nod and sit back as I drive us towards the school. Haas reaches forward and presses play on the stereo, and Taylor Swift blasts through the speakers. I quickly reach and turn down the volume.

Whitmore breaks out laughing, and I glare at him through the rearview mirror. He works to tamper down his laughter as I change the music. Nineties rock fills the car, but I can still see the amusement in their eyes.

Finally pulling into the parking lot, I park, and we make our way to the front office. There will be five of us doing the presentation today. The receptionist leads us to the auditorium and informs us the students will be arriving shortly. I place the binder on the podium and quickly peruse it as the guys stand in the corner chatting.

A door at the back of the room opens, and the sound of children talking carries into the space. I watch as teachers shuffle in with lines of kids behind them and lead them to rows of seats. I've just closed the binder and am standing in the centre of the stage when I hear Charlie's voice ring through the room, "Daddy!"

I grin and jump off the stage as she comes running at me full speed. I pick her up as she wraps her arms around my neck and kiss her cheek.

"What are you doing here, Daddy?"

"Working. Some of Daddy's friends are going to do a presentation for your classmates."

She looks over my shoulder and waves her hand furiously at them. I turn and look at the four officers standing on the stage staring at us, obvious interest on their faces. They all wave back.

"Can I say hi?" she asks.

I look back at the auditorium and see students still funnelling in. I make my way to the stairs, climbing them two at a time to join the guys. Their conversation stops immediately as they watch us approach.

"Charlie, these are Officers Whitmore, Hass, Jones, and Lazar," I say, pointing at each of them. "Guys, this is my daughter, Charlotte."

They all wave and say, "Hello."

Charlie says, "Hi," and then asks me, "Daddy, why aren't they at your games like Uncle Josh, or Matt, or Grayson?"

"Because they play on the same team, I don't play with people from work."

"Are we not good enough for ya, Sutton?" Whitmore jokes.

"I'm not sure you could keep up," I say with a laugh.

"I'm sure I could keep up with you, old man," he says, even though he's only three years younger than me.

"My daddy is really fast," Charlie says, smiling.

All four of the guys look at her with soft smiles as Whitmore says, "I'm sure he is."

The sound of the back door closing has me turning to face the crowd of students and teachers gathered. I watch as the final students find their seats. "Little Bear, time to go join your class."

"Are you taking me home, or is Mommy coming?" she asks.

"If I'm still here, you can go with me. I'll let you know when school is done."

She nods as I put her down and then runs to join her class.

We go through our presentation and answer questions from the students about when to call 911 and what police officers do. When we finish, Charlie waves at me as her class leaves the auditorium. The guys and I make our way to the front office and go over the basics of what they're supposed to do in case of an emergency. When we finish, I check the time and see that classes will be out in half an hour. I decide to make my way to the Timmies across the street and grab a coffee and bagel while I wait for Charlie to be done with school. I send a quick text to Bailey to let her know I was here for a presentation and will bring Charlie with me.

Five minutes before the bell, we all make our way back to the school. I head into the office and ask that they tell Charlie's teacher that I'm in the office when she's ready.

Confusion fills the secretary's face as she looks at me. "Charlotte Porter was picked up about five minutes ago by her dad."

The blood drains from my face. Derek hasn't wanted anything to do with Charlie. His sole goal has been to get Bailey back, so why would he take Charlie? He's only allowed supervised visitation with her, so he shouldn't be taking her from school, ever. I need to find my little girl.

"Call her mother right now, tell her Caleb says it's an emergency and she needs to get here ASAP. Then you need to shut the campus down. No one in or out until I say so," I order, my training kicking in.

The secretary's face blanches.

I turn and see all four of the men with me are ready to do what I order. "Haas, you take the southwest corner, Whitmore the southeast, Jones the Northwest, and Lazar the Northeast. I'll take the parking lot. Haas, radio in a potential child abduction. The suspect is Derek Porter, he has a record for domestic abuse."

They nod, and I jog towards the parking lot, making sure to keep my eyes open for both of them.

I have never felt the panic that I feel right now, not knowing where Charlie is. At least when I was deployed and now at work, everyone else is trained. Charlie is defenceless.

I do everything I can to push that feeling aside as I work to find her. I push open the door to the parking lot, and the brisk winter air hits my skin. Adrenaline has my blood pumping through me so quickly the cold barely registers.

I meticulously make my way up and down the rows of cars, looking for the familiar make and model. I check each license plate, hoping to find him. I'm halfway through the parking lot when I hear

Charlie's cries. That awful sound makes me freeze, but it's going to help me find her.

Crouching, I listen for where it's coming from. I can tell it's to my left and a few rows back. Still crouched, I slowly make my way in the direction of her cries. Each row I move through has the sound getting louder and my heart racing faster.

"I don't want to go with you," she says through her sobs.

Frustration fills Derek's voice as it sounds like he pounds his fist on a car. "When your mommy gets here, everything will be better," he says.

"You hurt Mommy," she says.

"Only because she deserved it. Now, if you don't stop that crying, I'll give you something to cry about."

I see him five cars down from me as I come to the last row. He's gripping Charlie's arm as he drags her to the car. I carefully grab the radio on my shoulder and say into it, "I found them. Last row at the back of the parking lot, south side. He's driving a red Honda civic." I turn the radio down to ensure it doesn't alert Derek.

As the beep of him unlocking the car fills the air, I unclip my gun from my side, flicking the safety off and standing to my full height. Luckily, he hasn't noticed me yet. I put one foot in front of the other and slowly approach the vehicle.

When I'm just one car away, I say, "Put your hands up and step away from the girl."

Red crawls up Derek's neck, and he turns to face me. His grip tightens on Charlie, creating white marks on her skin. That poor girl is going to have bruises to remind her of today.

"Release the girl," I say, my voice coming out calmer than I feel.

He shakes his head. "I'm not listening to the likes of you," he spits.

This isn't going to be easy. I steel myself, knowing I need to remove the emotional aspect to ensure a positive outcome.

"Why don't you tell me why you took Charlie," I say.

That seems to have him loosening his grip on her. I watch her blood flow rush to the spots that had turned white from his fingers.

"Because it seems to be the only way to get Bailey's attention. She's selling our house. I saw the sign. I needed her to talk to me."

"Did you really think that kidnapping her daughter would have her see you in a positive light?"

His brows pinch together as his face flushes red. "That bitch doesn't realize how lucky she had it with me."

His words have me wanting to punch him. How could he possibly think she was lucky being scared of her husband? I push the anger down with three deep breaths. I will not fuck this up. I will not lose Charlie.

"Man, I can't let Bailey come here until you let Charlie go. I need to make sure she's safe," I say.

Out of the corner of my eye, I watch as Haas and Lazar make their way through the cars in an attempt to get behind Derek. I take a step to the side, forcing Derek to turn towards me more so they can sneak past without him seeing.

"Please let me go," Charlie says as she sniffles, and my heart breaks watching her.

Derek shakes her arm. "Shut up," he grits at her, and I watch as tears fall down her cheeks.

I take a step towards them, and Derek reaches behind his back and produces a 9mm hand gun, pointing it at me.

"Don't take another step," he says as he shakes the gun at me. The way he holds the weapon shows me he's had no training on how to use a gun, but that only makes it more dangerous.

I stop in my tracks, keeping my weapon trained on him.

"Okay. Let's talk this out then. What will it take for you to let her go. You're hurting your daughter."

He looks down at her, his face lacking any emotion. My anger grows, but I work to keep it tamped down. I don't understand how he can look at her with anything other than love.

"Get me Bailey," he says. "I wanna talk to Bailey."

"I can't bring her out here. How about I call her?" I offer.

His eyes narrow for a second before he nods and gestures his gun at me as if to tell me to get on with it. Reaching into my pocket, I pull my phone out and dial Bailey. She answers after one ring.

"Caleb." Her voice comes through soft and worried.

"Bailey," I say, as Derek shouts, "Put it on speaker!"

Pulling the phone away from my face, I click the screen, putting it on speaker.

"Bailey, I'm here with Derek. He has Charlie and says he wants to talk to you. Is that something you can do for me?"

The sound of her muffled sob and deep inhale travel through the line. "Yeah." Another deep breath. "Yeah, I can do that."

"Derek, I'm going to come closer so you can talk. Okay?"

He nods erratically, and I cautiously approach him, holding the phone in an outstretched hand.

"Bailey," he yells at the phone.

"Yeah." Her voice comes out stronger than it did just a second ago.

"I had to get your attention. I knew Charlie was the best way," he says, as if that explains away his behaviour.

"You have it," she says.

"Honey, you need to come back to me. We need to be a family again."

"Charlie is scared right now. We can't do that if Charlie is scared. Please let her go," Bailey pleads.

I watch as Haas positions himself behind Derek and puts a finger to his lips the second Charlie spots him.

"If I do that, then you won't come see me."

Just then, Haas wraps an arm around Charlie and pulls her away. He quickly turns his back to Derek to shield Charlie, leaving Derek standing there, mouth open. Derek spins, the gun moving to follow Charlie before he trains it on me as he yells. The vein in his neck pulses.

"You did this," he shouts as he takes a step towards me. "You turned her against me. You took her from me. You can't take her from me."

He aims the gun right at my head. Without a thought, I aim for the shoulder of the arm holding the gun, and my finger pulls the trigger. The shot echoes through the air as Derek stagers back from the impact. He drops the gun, and Lazar comes behind him, securing his hands in handcuffs before holding pressure to the wound.

The second I know Derek is contained, I run to look for Charlie. I find her at the edge of the parking lot with Haas. I rush to her and pull her into my arms, holding her as she cries into my neck and squeezes me tight. Haas leaves us and joins Lazar, radioing the situation and getting an ambulance to attend to

Derek's wound. I make my way towards the building. Just as I'm about to reach the doors, they fly open and Bailey comes running out.

She spots Charlie and me and makes a beeline towards us, wrapping her arms around us as she cries. I hold both of them as close and tight as possible. It takes everything in me not to break down with them, but I know they need my strength right now. The sound of sirens nearing draws my attention. Releasing my hold on the girls, I turn and watch as the ambulance pulls into the parking lot, two cruisers right behind it.

I'm still holding Charlie, her arms tightly wrapped around my neck, as I tell Bailey, "We're going to have to give them our statements. They'll want one from Charlie, too, but you'll be allowed to be with her."

Bailey nods as she wipes away her tears.

I pull her into me again, kissing the top of her head as I whisper, "I love you" into her hair.

When I turn back towards the cruisers, I'm shocked to see my staff sergeant approaching us.

"Sutton," he says, his voice its usual gruffness.

"Sir," I say with a nod.

"Haas and Lazar have the subject detained and are getting him medical treatment. I'm going to need your weapon, and then McKinnon will take your statements."

I nod and try to pass Charlie off to Bailey, but she shakes her head and tightens her grip on me. I withdraw my weapon and pass it to staff sergeant Cook, barrel pointing down. He clears the chamber and removes the magazine before depositing it into a clear evidence bag.

McKinnon steps up beside us and nods at the Staff Sergeant, who then leaves. He extends his hand to Bailey, and she shakes it before wrapping her arms around her middle.

"I'm Officer McKinnon, I'm going to ask you a few questions now, while everything is fresh," he says, and she nods.

He looks at me as though dismissing me, and Bailey must notice, because she says, "I'd rather Caleb stay."

McKinnon raises an eyebrow at her. "Caleb?" he asks.

"Bailey's my girlfriend," I say, and he nods.

"Okay, Bailey, can you start by giving me your full name and your relationship to the assailant."

McKinnon goes through all the basic questions with Bailey before moving to me and, eventually, Charlie. She answers all his questions as best as possible, all while staying in my arms. When he's finally done, he hands Bailey a business card and shakes my hand before joining the rest of the guys.

I turn and look at Bailey, seeing the exhaustion in her eyes. Using my free hand, I cup her cheek. "Let's head home."

She nods against my hand, and I lead them towards my truck. I'll come back for her car or send someone later, but I'm not letting her drive right now. As soon as we pull out of the parking lot, Charlie is passed out in the back and Bailey holds my hand tightly. When we arrive home, I carry Charlie inside and lay her on the couch, covering her with a blanket and grabbing Princess and Vanilla from her bedroom.

Bailey and I settle at the other end, and I hold her as we watch Charlie sleep. The exhaustion eventually takes over for both Bailey and me, and we fall asleep on the couch.

I'm woken up when Charlie climbs into my lap, bringing her blanket and bear with her. She settles in, and I hold her as she falls asleep again.

In the morning, I make us all breakfast before we head upstairs for showers and fresh clothes. After pulling my shirt on, I settle on the edge of the bed and grab the stuffed bear that's sitting on the dresser across from the foot of the bed. I stare at it as I remember the day that Bailey, Charlie, and I went to the mall and Charlie helped me make it. That day, I didn't know just what those girls would become to me, but I knew they had forever affected me.

I look up at the sound of the door opening and see the girls standing there. Charlie comes in and climbs onto the bed, settling into my side as I wrap an arm around her and kiss the top of her head.

"What's its name?" Charlie asks, and I smile.

"Charlotte," I say, and her eyes go comically wide.

"We have the same name," she says.

"She's named after you."

"Really?" Her voice is filled with wonder as she looks at the stuffed bear in her princess dress and tiara Charlie chose the day we made our bears.

"Yup. I knew you were special, and I always wanted to keep a part of you with me. So I made this bear to be my Little Bear at home."

She smiles up at me and snuggles into me. "Why do you call me Little Bear?" she asks.

I tuck a strand of hair behind her ear and run my fingers through her blonde strands the same way I've learned her mother likes.

"Did you know bears represent courage and strength?"

She shakes her head.

"When we first met, you were strong and courageous when you called 911, just like a bear. Not only that, you remained a happy little girl, showing just how strong you are. So, you're my Little Bear."

"I like it," she whispers into my chest, and I hold her close as I watch Bailey wipe at her tears. I pat the spot beside me on the bed, and she joins us. I wrap my arm around her and we sit there as I hold my girls.

I'm on leave at work for the next little bit while they run an investigation to ensure my shooting was justified. Bailey takes some much-needed time off as well, and we keep Charlie home from school. We spend our days at home, just the three of us, plus Finn. We get Charlie registered for therapy to make sure she works through everything that happened, and Bailey schedules herself an appointment. I have department-mandated sessions with a therapist through the department.

We get Bailey's house completely packed so she can be done with those bad memories, and the guys help me get rid of the furniture. The next few weeks are filled with more interviews at the precinct, to ensure all the details are straight, and court dates. Luckily, our friends are there, supporting us through everything. I can see how much having people around who truly love and care for her helps Bailey. She's never had it before, and I'm so glad she has it now.

I use the time off to turn the den that wasn't being used into a split space. I add bookshelves and a comfy chair so Bailey can use part of the room as a reading getaway. In the other half, I set up all of Charlie's toys so she has somewhere other than the living room to play.

I spend every day grateful to have been the officer that responded to that 911 call and to have met Bailey and Charlie. I know I will spend the rest of my life ensuring they are happy and cared for, and one day I will make sure they have my last name and know I'm never letting them go.

CHAPTER 37

Grayson

our Months Later
      Fucking hell.

I groan as I read my email while sitting at the bar waiting for Caleb. Next weekend, one doctor and one nurse from the ER department are being sent to Vegas for an annual conference, and I've just received an email confirming that I'm going. Not only am I going, but I'm going with the one person in the entire department that absolutely hates me.

The thing that gets to me the most is she seems to think I don't like her either, but that couldn't be further from the truth. I learned long ago that long-term happiness isn't for me. It was a harsh lesson to learn at only eighteen, but I learned it.

Caleb claps me on the shoulder, pulling me out of my thoughts.

"Hey, man," he says as he lifts his chin at me and takes the bar stool next to mine.

"Hey," I say, taking a sip from my beer.

I pick at my beer label as he places his order with the pretty brunette behind the bar. My eyes take in the sight of her. Ample hips and a generous chest. Her jean shorts are so small I can see the bottom of her ass cheeks peeking out of them. She notices me checking her out and offers me a flirtatious smile. I smirk at her before she turns around and grabs Caleb's drink.

"So, what had you so enthralled when I got here?" Caleb asks.

"I just got an email confirming that I'm going to Vegas next weekend for a work conference."

He looks at me in the way that Caleb does when he wants more information but isn't going to go digging for it. I hold my ground, taking a sip of my beer.

He concedes. "A weekend in Vegas. That sounds right up your alley. I'm sure there will be plenty of woman for you to have fun with between events."

I've never tried to change my friends' ideas that I have a different woman in my bed every night. Up until about two years ago, they were right. I enjoyed a good fuck, often with a different woman each time, and I didn't let a woman get attached. I haven't corrected their impression over the last two years, though.

"True," I say, although I can hear the lack of conviction in my voice.

"What's got you all wound tight about it?" he asks.

I don't want to go more in depth about the situation, so I say, "No, you're right. It will be great." Needing to move the subject along, I ask, "What's new with you?"

The grin that over takes his face is one that's still weird to see. Caleb never grinned like this before Bailey and Charlie came into his life, and I'm happy for him. He seems so much lighter and happier now.

"I'm taking Charlie to her first daddy-daughter dance on Friday."

"And when are you going to make that official?"

"As soon as Bailey is ready. I have the ring, and then we can talk about me adopting her."

Caleb and I talk for another hour before he says he needs to get home to the girls. I wave the bartender over and ask for the bill. She brings it, smiling flirtatiously at me, and when I look down, I see a phone number written in pen across the top with a note that says *I'm off at 9*. I open my wallet and leave cash on the bar before making my way home, trying to figure out how the hell I'm going to make it through next weekend with a woman who hates me. A weekend in Vegas with Hannah Smith. What could go wrong?

Epilogue

BAILEY

Tonight is the daddy-daughter dance at Charlie's school. A year ago, I never would have thought that would be something Charlie would be able to go to. When she mentioned it at dinner a few weeks ago, Caleb was so excited to take her. He handed me his credit card that night and told me to get Charlie whatever dress she wanted. I tried to hand the card back, but he refused, insisting he wanted to treat her.

Once the dress was purchased and I tried to give him the credit card back, he told me to keep it. I've tried to sneak it into his wallet several times, but it always ends up back in mine. I think he's been sneaking random cash into my wallet, too, because there have been times when I've known I didn't have cash, only to open my wallet and find a twenty-dollar bill.

I help Charlie get ready for the dance, doing up her hair in a few French braids that looked like a crown on top of her head. When she comes downstairs to meet Caleb, who has a corsage for her, I swear I see a tear fall down his cheek.

We've settled back into our life since the incident. Charlie gets the occasional nightmare and climbs into bed with us. I've updated all the information at the school so that Derek can't pick her up. Caleb and I are the primary contacts with Lily and Caleb's mom being the emergency contacts. Derek is still in police custody, but we don't know what he'll do when he's released.

I'm looking forward to my night in curled up in the chair in my little reading nook Caleb created for me while he and Charlie are at the dance. I'm currently reading a recommendation from Hannah. I had mentioned I was in a bit of a reading slump, so she recommended a mafia romance with a plus size FMC and an obsessed mafia man. I'm devouring it.

Needing a little break, I close my Kindle and head up to our bedroom to put away the laundry. Once everything is put in its spot, I make my way over to Caleb's nightstand, opening the drawer and grabbing the familiar black velvet box before settling on the bed. Opening the lid, I stare at the beautiful ring inside.

A few weeks ago, I was looking for an extra phone charger, and Caleb said he had one in his nightstand. When I opened the drawer, I saw, sitting in the front corner, the ring box that was in his hoodie a few months ago. Now, every once in a while when he's out of the house, I'll open the box and just stare at it. It's still surreal to think that after only two meetings with his mom, she gave him this ring to propose.

I know when we discussed it that night I came home to find him in the living room we decided we would wait, but now I'm wondering if I want to anymore. Caleb has only proven over and over he's a man that can be trusted. That he will be there through thick and thin, supporting Charlie and me.

I tilt the box in my hand, looking at the ring at different angles, as the light hits the stone.

"You could take it out of the box."

Caleb's voice startles me. I close the box quickly and look up to see him leaning against the door frame, smirking at me.

"You're home," is all I manage to squeak out.

He nods. "I am." He continues to watch me, not saying anything else.

My skin heats with embarrassment, and I squirm under his unwavering gaze.

"I'm sorry," I say.

His brows furrow in confusion. "For?"

"Snooping and looking at the ring."

His face relaxes, and he pushes off the door frame, closing the door and making his way to me before sitting on the bed in front of me. Reaching forward, he grabs the box from my hand and opens it, looking at the ring before placing it on my knee, facing me.

"Bails, there's no need to apologize. I've already told you this ring will belong to you one day. It's just a matter of when you agree to marry me." He reaches forward and tucks a piece of stray hair behind my ear. "We said when we're both ready. I'm ready when you are," he says as he leans forward and kisses my cheek.

I lean my head back and blink away the tears gathering behind my eyes. Taking a deep breath, I look at Caleb. "Yes," I say, as a smile over takes my face.

He stares at me wide-eyed for a second, and then a matching grin spreads across his face. "Yes? Yes, you'll marry me?" he asks, his voice unsure.

I nod vigorously. "Yes, I'll marry you, Caleb Sutton."

His hands come up to my face, and he kisses me deeply. Each kiss with Caleb is soul consuming. It doesn't matter how long we've been together, each kiss feels like Caleb is burying himself into my soul so deeply that he'd take a piece of me with him if he were to leave.

When we break apart, he immediately finds the ring box and slides the engagement ring onto my finger. I stare at it, marvelled by how perfectly it fits. When I look at him again, his eyes are filled with hunger. He stands and wordlessly grabs my ankle and pulls me down the bed so I'm lying on my back.

"Charlie is asleep, so I'm going to have some fun with my fiancée," he says.

His eyes drag over my body as his fingers find the waistband of my leggings and panties. He pulls them down in one fell swoop so I'm laid bare for him. He quickly pushes my shirt up my body, but leaves it wrapped around my wrists. I watch as he undoes the front clasp of my bra and my tits pop free. I'm surprised he even noticed it was a front clasp, but I guess nothing gets past him.

Caleb stands there staring at me for a minute, causing heat to rise in my body. I squirm. I watch as he leaves his position and moves around the bed to my nightstand. Opening the bottom drawer, I hear him grab something and then watch as he drops a vibrator and some lube on the bed.

My eyes widen, and a sexy smirk spreads across his face as he untucks his dress shirt from of his slacks and begins slowly undoing the buttons, exposing his hard chest with each button. I lick my lips to prevent myself from actually drooling as I watch him. I will never stop relishing in how sexy he is, or the fact he's chosen me.

When the last button is undone, he takes off the shirt, dropping it to the floor before he undoes his belt and slacks and drops those along with his boxer briefs. I moan at the sight of his erection popping free, and the chuckle that leaves Caleb has me instantly squirming for more. I've learned he likes taking his time to wind me up. I can't complain, because when he does, the orgasms are mind blowing.

He slowly climbs onto the bed, positioning himself between my legs as he drags his nose delicately over the inside of my right leg, nipping as he goes. I'm embarrassingly wet.

When he finally reaches the apex of my thighs and I feel his breath over my extremely sensitive clit, I moan.

"Please."

"So needy tonight, Bails." He chuckles.

"For you, always."

I look down my body, making eye contact with him as he holds my thighs open and his tongue darts out, tasting me. It's his turn to groan. I watch as his eyes roll back, and I feel the blush in my cheeks deepen.

"Best fucking thing I've ever tasted," he says before going back in.

He takes his time, using his tongue to explore and taste every part of me like it's the first time. His hand holds my pelvis down as I squirm. He finally takes mercy on me, inserting a finger and massaging my G-spot, sending me over the edge. He doesn't stop as I come.

His lips trail up my body until he reaches my breasts. He nips at my left nipple before salving the sting with his tongue and repeats it with the right one then moves to hover over me.

"What's your safe word?"

I swallow, knowing this means tonight is going to be intense.

Caleb always checks in with me to make sure he's respecting my boundaries, so this question tells me we're trying something new.

"Pineapple," I say, licking my lips.

"Good girl."

Sitting back on his heels, he grips my hips and flips me onto my stomach. His strength still amazes me, but he never uses it in a negative way or one that makes me feel unsafe.

He lifts my hips and reaches beside me. The click of the cap on the lube is my only warning before the cool liquid drips between my ass cheeks. He uses his thumb to gently massage my puckered hole, and I moan. The sensations are all new to me. His thumb gently breaches the ring of muscle as he slowly pumps it in and out of me.

When I begin rocking with the movements, he withdraws then adds a second finger. I stiffen at the new feeling of stretching.

"Relax, baby. I've got you," he coos behind me. His words do their job, and he's able to get both fingers inside me now.

The lid of the lube bottle clicks again as his fingers leave me.

"Are you okay?" he asks.

I nod, and when he doesn't respond, I say, "Yes."

The head of his cock presses there now, and I tighten, squeezing my ass cheeks together. I know how fucking big his cock is, he completely stretches my pussy. Imagining what he'll do back there is unnerving.

"Bails, if you want me to stop, I will. If not, I will make sure we take this slowly and you're ready for me. You have no idea how much I want to claim your perfect little ass."

The head of his cock massages me again, and I relax a little.

"Keep going," I say.

He pushes forward a little, notching the head inside of me, and I stretch around him. The buzz of the vibrator turning on travels through the room just before he presses it to my clit. I bite the pillow beneath me as I try to muffle the moan that's ripped from me as he slides further in. He takes his time until he's fully inside me, and I've never felt so full.

He stays like that, allowing me to adjust to the new feeling and sensations. When my breathing slows, he begins to move. Each movement has me building in a way I've never felt before. I'm on the edge of an orgasm already. A click of a button, and he has the vibrator speed picking up.

My pussy is soaked and my ass is full, but it's not enough. A noise of discontentment leaves me, and Caleb picks up the pace of his thrusts. He fucks me relentlessly until I'm screaming into the pillow beneath me. My entire body is fucking jelly as I come. His thursts become erratic as he comes. I can't hold myself up any more as he pulls out of me and my hips drop to the bed.

He's pulled all the energy out my of body. With my eyes closed, I listen as he makes his way into the washroom and the water starts running. The water turns off, and he returns to bedroom with a washcloth to clean me up.

He kisses my shoulder blade and whispers, "Are you okay."

I smile at him. "I'm beyond perfect."

He returns to the washroom, and a minute later I hear him ask, "Can I throw these out?"

Opening my eyes, I see him leaning against the door frame holding my birth control pills.

My eyes widen. "You want to throw out my birth control?" I ask, my voice scratchy.

"I'm all in this with you Bailey. I want to grow our family, but when you're ready. If you're not, we'll wait. I would love to give Charlie a sibling soon so she can enjoy it."

Where was this man seven years ago? I have no doubt in my mind that Caleb is who I will spend the rest of my life with, and that he'll make a great father to our future children because he already is with Charlie. Why wait when this is something we both want?

"Throw it out," I say.

The grin that spreads across his face just reinforces my decision. He turns and tosses the pills in the garbage before coming to bed. He kisses my stomach before looking up at me.

"I can't wait to see you pregnant with our babies," he says, his voice wistful.

I run my hand through his hair, scratching his scalp before he lies beside me, pulling me into his arms.

I lie there with my head on his chest, listening to his heartbeat with Charlie peacefully asleep down the hall. I know we've finally found that happily ever after I dreamed about as a kid, and I'm so excited for the future we're going to share together.

THE END

♡

Want more of Caleb and Bailey? You can now in this bonus epilogue
https://BookHip.com/PJNKDBG
Want to read Josh and Liv's story? You can now in Always Been You
http://mybook.to/dlalwaysbeenyou
Missed Josh and Liv's bonus epilogue? Check it out here: https://BookHip.com/VQARQQX
Can't wait for Grayson and Hannah's story? Pre-order Keeping You now: https://mybook.to/dlkeepingyou

Dicktionary

Acknowledgments

To my husband who has supported this journey that I randomly decided to go on. You've been in my corner every step of the way making sure I know you're proud of me. Thank you for all your love and support. I know that neither of us foresaw any of this, but you have supported me in the journey and are always there to help name a character.

The SMUTTERING, thank you for all being unapologetically yourselves and always being there for advice and when I needed to vent. You guys are amazing, and I'm not sure I could have managed the stress without you all. Bailey, thank you for letting me jump into your DM's when I read *Alive and Wells* and embracing me and bringing me into the fold. You are truly amazing, and I can't wait to meet you in person!

To the french fries in the LPP, it's been so amazing to be in such a great group. You guys are always there to provide a laugh or a video that helps during the stressful times. I can't wait until we do a little getaway!

Chelsey. It's hard to put into words how grateful I am for you. You agreed to ARC read *Always Been You* and from there we found our mutual love of Taylor Swift and realized that we are in fact the same person in different provinces. Thank you for beta reading *Saving You*, I lived for your comments every day. I am so unbelievably excited to meet you in person and fangirl at all the signings we have planned. Thank you for all your support.

Ellie, I went from being a major fan of your writing to not only being a fan, but to being able to call you a friend. Thank you for all the support and accepting the fact that as soon as I start *Bridgerton* you'll be getting all the unhinged messages.

My amazing beta readers, some of you have been here since *Always Been You* and the ones who I either messaged or offered, thank you. You were all wonderful, and I deeply appreciate the feedback and help with Caleb and Bailey's story.

To my amazing editor, Andrea, thank you for being understanding that when I first messaged you my life was all over the place, and helping get a timeline set. I was so excited to work with you and you have not disappointed. Thank you for being such an amazing hype woman!

Thank you to my cover designer, Kim and my character artist, Paige. You two are both amazing and I can't thank you enough for turning my vision into a realty. I can't wait to continue to work together.

Lastly, to my readers, I can't say thank you enough. I wouldn't be here without each and everyone of you. I can't wait to share more stories with you all. Thank you for loving these stories as much as I do.

About the Author

Living in the Vancouver area of British Columbia with her husband, Alex enjoys spending her free time reading, watching Hockey (go Canucks), watching Disney movies and crime TV shows, and spending time outdoors. She started writing in 2023 when her first story just wouldn't leave her mind. From there, the ideas of a series formed and she's never looked back.

She enjoys talking to other authors and romance lovers. Her TBR is never-ending, but that doesn't stop her from adding at least one new book every day. Alex looks forward to experiencing more in the indie author community and can't wait to share her books with the world.

Connect With Me:

https://www.instagram.com/authoralextaylor/
https://www.threads.net/@authoralextaylor
https://www.tiktok.com/@authoralextaylor
https://www.facebook.com/profile.php?id=61552508379128
www.authoralextaylor.com
alex@authoralextaylor.com

Also by Alex Taylor

DESTINED LOVE SERIES

Always Been You

Saving You

Keeping You - Coming November 14, 2024